INTENT
to
BETRAY

DAVE OLIVER

SilverWood

Published in 2018 by the author

Copyright © Dave Oliver 2018

The right of Dave Oliver to be identified as the author of this work has been asserted
in accordance with the Copyright, Designs and Patents Act 1988 Sections 77 and 78.

ISBN 978-0-9994718-2-1 (paperback)
ISBN 978-0-9994718-3-8 (ebook)

British Library Cataloguing in Publication Data
A CIP catalogue record for this book is available from the British Library

Page design and typesetting by SilverWood Books
Printed on responsibly sourced paper

DAVE OLIVER was born in Indiana and educated at the United States Naval Academy. In the Navy he served aboard several types of ships and commanded a nuclear submarine. Dave also worked in business at Airbus and as a political appointee in the Department of Defense.

Dave has consequently traveled six of the seven world continents as a naval officer, business leader and a political appointee. His novels use Dave's personal experiences to provide background to his stories.

Find out more about Dave and his work at www.daveoliverbooks.com

Also by Dave Oliver

Intent to Deceive

My sister, Leslie Ann Zimring,
has not only assisted me with every book I have written,
but is also the soul of our interconnected families.

CHAPTER ONE

The fog west of the city of San Diego had lifted and again revealed a seascape of undulating blue-green waves. The monochromatic scene was only occasionally relieved. Sometimes by a fleeing flying fish as it left his signature white dash across the surface. More frequently as the rising wind from the coming storm caught a wave crest just right. It was Friday mid-afternoon, the very shank of the San Diego workweek.

As soon as the fog had lifted, two multi-deck cruise ships, with well-established itineraries, had hurriedly exited the channel, their radars locked on the oncoming storm. They had each turned north-northwest as soon as they passed buoy 1SD, bound for the vistas of Alaska. Each was now west of Catalina Island, well clear of the oncoming blow.

1SD was the large bell buoy that marked the seaward-most approach to the San Diego channel. It was a common reference point for nearly every San Diego maritime visitor and had been a godsend to many a sailor. The San Diego fog was frequent and often thick. The buoy's bell could be heard for miles and the buoy structure made a distinctive spoke on radar screens from tens of miles away. The buoy even had angular steel reflectors welded on to augment the signature, a useful navigational feature from the home of the stealth industry. The exact location of the buoy was known to each local fisherman and shown on every international sailing chart. The label was always the same. The standard two initials for the port. In San Diego, this particular buoy was listed on the charts as "SD." Since it was the first in a chain, it was locally known as 1SD.

At this moment, the incoming storm was beginning to affect buoy 1SD. The slowly increasing ocean swells and the pitch black horizon to the South-southwest foretold a local nasty blow. The buoy was rolling and pulling against the links of twelve-inch chain that anchored it solidly to the rocky bottom. Nevertheless, two fat seals still slept soundly amidst in the angular frames, soaking up the last rays of the fading sun. The US destroyer *Omaha LCS 12* had passed 1SD an hour ago, inbound from a week of drills and evolutions in the local operating areas. Anyone listening to the Channel 12 discussion between the San Diego tug masters would know that *Omaha* was the last ship to complete her weekly tasks. Hurrying home to reach her berth before the forecasted torrential rains, she had slowed to twenty-two knots only after she was abreast 1SD. In three months, his continued use of excess speed inside the San Diego harbor would earn her skipper a written reprimand. Her bow line was just dropping over a cleat at the 32nd Street Naval Base.

A flurry of raindrops from the outer ring of an early squall suddenly dappled the sea surface all around 1SD with enormous drops and then just as quickly stopped. Several thousand yards to seaward a seal's head popped to the surface and rather awkwardly looked around. Suddenly the head extended nearly a half-meter above the water and spun in a quick circle as it magically transformed into a submarine periscope. Eight and a half meters below, in a polished chrome and steel chair, sat Captain 3rd Rank Hsu Wing-tsit, Commanding Officer of the Chinese Han Submarine 404, the *Western Wind*.

After a safety look around, he made his own lengthy appraisal of the approaching storm and nodded. It was going to be an early night. Just what the Chairman had ordered.

CHAPTER TWO

Two Years Earlier

Steve and Kristina stepped off the Singapore Mass Rapid Transit car at the Chinatown exit and joined the crowd strolling down Pagoda Street. Their destination was the food court at Maxwell Road. As they walked, Steve continued the conversation he had been single-mindedly pursuing on the train. "I can't believe you're even thinking about grad school. You don't need it. My dad is friends with the Harbor Master. The Master says you've more than tripled revenues! Why in the world would you even consider wasting two years at school?"

Steve was good-looking and hunky, which was certainly one of her soft spots. She had dated him for several months, but how the hell did someone who wrote software for a living think he could interject himself into making decisions about her management career! The reason was clear enough to her and she was definitely leaving.

Everyone in Manila would always believe any success rightfully belonged to Aunt and Uncle Toseña; no matter how often she doubled or tripled company revenues. She needed her own success!

Nevertheless, the facts evidently weren't obvious to everyone. Steve had started harping on the subject the moment he had walked in to her apartment tonight. Of course, it was her fault. She should have broken the news about her intentions to him before yesterday. She had known his feelings would be hurt. Feeling guilty made her distracted. And then she started doing dumb things. As one good example, she had grabbed the wrong purse when they left her apartment. Now, she was carrying around her Louis Vuitton purse from the Raffles charity ball last night instead of her normal cloth bag. Damn it.

They turned right at the South Bridge Road intersection. Even in ultra-disciplined Singapore, a $10,000 handbag on your arm was an open invitation to a mugging. She would have to insist they take a taxi back. Fortunately, the hawker centre was just up ahead. Eating might even finally persuade Steve to stop bitching. She enjoyed the informality of Maxwell Road with all the different foods. If they could only find someone trustworthy to share one of the communal tables.

Over to the left were four empty seats. Heck, two large men were already claiming them. She started to turn away, but stopped when she heard distinctly American accents – "Art, you lost today – get me anything Filipino except a balut and I'll hold two seats."

"Anything, Pete?"

"OK, maybe longganisa, adobe, rice and two San Miguels."

"How about a whole pig, too!"

"I'll run it all off early tomorrow morning before I catch my plane. This is my last chance for great food."

"There are lots of good ethnic restaurants in Wash…"

The two men's short haircuts, buzzed all around the ears and neck, broadcast they were military. Along with their interest in her hometown food, this was good enough for Kristina. She plopped her too-expensive bag and her butt that needed a few more klicks during each morning run down at the same bench and dispatched Steve for the food stalls. Personally, her mouth was set on Chinese from one of the sellers that ringed the tables.

It was not unusual to find military men wandering the streets of Singapore. Because of its strategic location alongside the Malayan Straits, most Far East governments had a mutual interest in keeping each other's fingers out of the Singapore pie. For those neighboring countries who might hold some dark thoughts, the tiny independent nation promised, like a porcupine armed with exploding quills, to be an indigestible stomach-ache. To assist this visualization, allies like the Aussies provided security for a portion of the wharfs. Their commander had been a frequent guest at her quarterly cocktail parties. Hopefully, this would be a good table for her purse's unexpected outing.

A rumored close relationship with America was also part… Whoops! She shifted her hips to one side of the bench. She hadn't intended to slide quite so close to the good-looking one.

"Sorry, Miss. It's a little crowded in here. Didn't intend to hip you off the end."

"Not a problem. I'll slip my bag between us."

When Steve returned with their two platters of food, he quickly became more interested in talking to the two men than in reopening the question of the direction of Kristina's career. She had been right about their table-mates – both were in the military, in this case, the American Navy. The one named Art Sullivan was assigned with the American nuclear submarines operating out of Yokosuka, Japan. The other, the one who had nearly pushed her off the bench, was Pete O'Brien, who had also been "stationed" in Yokosuka. Apparently, Pete had been there for the last two years. He had also certainly been traveling to lots of places during that period. (Had he been in charge and Art his number two? They never made it clear.)

Pete was headed back to some sort of assignment in Washington, DC. The two didn't volunteer exactly why they were currently in Singapore, but nevertheless, as expat conversations tended to do, over several rounds of beers, the four of them had a warm conversation that covered the waterfront of Malaysian, Thai and Singaporean notable places and politics. Kristina found herself truly enjoying herself. Despite the earlier storm warnings with Steve, it became a most pleasant evening.

The finished eating, made their farewells and she and Steve walked back down South Bridge Street. Suddenly a gang of three knife-wielding teens ran out of an alley! The group cut in front of Kristina, shoving Steve to the ground and snatched at Kristina's purse. She knew something like this would happen! With a knife literally inches from her eyes, she straightened her arm as fast as she could, and let her valuable Paris bag fly away.

She must have blinked, for she heard an "oomph" and the clatter of steel on cement. One of the teens was lying unconscious on the street with his right arm at an unnatural angle. The crowd had moved well back. Pete was standing astride the body, facing the other two teens, Art a pace behind him guarding his back. It was strangely quiet in the street around them. It was as if they were all in a bubble that deflected sound away. She only heard Pete. He was speaking in an unnaturally quiet voice. "Bring it on, men."

One of the teens was holding his hands at shoulder level. The blade on the razor knife in his right hand was beginning to tremble. Now it began swaying back and forth a few degrees. Kristina glanced at Pete. He was motionless. His arms were crooked, hanging loosely at his side, knees slightly bent. As she watched, he took a step toward the man with the knife. Pete had a slight smile on his face. Kristina found his expression slightly disturbing. He was speaking again.

"Don't do it, son. If you take one little step toward any one of my friends, I will be forced to make you hurt very badly." Pete looked around and motioned them back. He then took three short steps back from the body on the ground. "I will give you to the count of four to take your friend away. If you don't, I will hand him over to the police and you know he will lead the SPF to you. One, two..."

After a second's hesitation, knifes disappeared, the two young men picked up their accomplice and disappeared down the same alley from which they had arrived. Pete watched them out of sight. She saw his body gradually straighten and his face relax.

He picked up her purse, dusted it off with the palm of his hand and handed it to her. "Art and I will walk you and Steve to your train."

Two years and two days later

"Kristina Baclayon, you drive very carefully, and call us as soon as you get there. You know Czeriza and I will be worried sick until we hear from you."

"I will, Sophia."

Sophia reluctantly released her hug and stepped back from the side of the car, "I can't believe Francis wouldn't change his flight to fly into LA. It's a shame to make you drive all the way to San Diego on a Sunday afternoon."

Kristina snaked a hand out of her car window past her aunt's best friend to shake Czeriza's hand as she simultaneously started the quiet Accord engine. Sophia kept talking. "You'll have horrible traffic and if they have those torrential rains the TV is talking about, they always get mudslides down there…"

Czeriza interjected: "Mother, I'm sure her uncle has a good reason. It undoubtedly has to do with the upcoming campaign. He'll want to talk to her in private. No one trusts telephones anymore. Kristina, you be sure and tell Francis that if he decides to run, just like last time, Sophia and I will take responsibility for fundraising on the West Coast."

Damn it. She had wanted to get started. Kristina turned off the car, pushed open the driver's side door and stepped out, wrapping her arms around the smaller Sophia. She knew Czeriza loved Sophia, but sometimes he seemed like nothing more than the prototype for an insensitive Filipino male. After their only child, Analyn, Kristina's best friend, was killed in a car crash, the couple had sold their thriving business and left Luzon. Yet, after seventeen years, Czeriza still didn't understand how much it upset Sophia every time he called her Mother.

"'I' will be very careful, Auntie. Very careful." Kristina held Sophia tightly for nearly another full minute. She could feel the older woman's tears soaking the thin sweater she had selected this morning to counter the cooler San Diego weather. "And I'll call you when I arrive at the restaurant. If the storm is bad, I may stay at a hotel overnight. If not, I intend to drive back to the UCLA campus. She slowly pushed the woman away, looked at her bleary eyes and then kissed her tenderly on both wet cheeks. "I still plan to see you both the middle of next month if you will have me, OK?"

Sophia tearily nodded and Kristina got back in the car, backed up the driveway, waving to both of them and driving a couple of blocks before pulling over and setting her GPS. While she was parked, she cleaned her sunglasses and wiped the wetness from the corners of her eyes.

Kristina shook her head before pulling out into traffic. She tried to stay with Czeriza and Sophia whenever she got a weekend away from her MBA program. Normally, she could fit a weekend in every few months. Aunt Toseña had originally suggested it and Kristina had found she enjoyed it. She saw so much of Analyn in Sophia… She took a drink from the bottle of peach Tazo that Sophia had insisted she take along. One more series of turns before she was out of their little neighborhood. Finally: Interstate Highway 5! Now, to begin the grind south. Good thing she had left early, with all this Sunday traffic, she thought. Oh, great – here comes the rain they were talking about!

My Mother's tears are because you remind her of me.

This rain is making driving tough enough, Analyn, so don't start on me – I'll never get to San Diego.

I appreciate what you do for her. You are a mature woman.

Easy enough, Analyn, I have had the opportunities. I have an uncle and aunt who were born with engraved silver spoons in their brown Filipino mouths.

And you graduated from the London School of Economics and doubled the profits of their Singapore shipping company before you were thirty!

Kristina decided to drop back another couple of car lengths, behind a truck that was sending off double streams of water. A red Mazda promptly cut into the space she had opened up.

Inside her car, there was only the sound of the rain on the roof, the swish of the wipers, the occasional wave of water thrown against the side of the car by a passing truck and the steady hum of the defroster… along with Analyn…

It is not down to luck. You are only thirty-two, about to get your MBA, and more importantly, you have always been good to my mother.

I like her… I liked you.

We were good friends. But it's been a long time. That's a nice boy you are dating.

Aaron?

The sound of Bollywood came over the car's speakerphone and, after a surprised second's pause, Kristina thumb-swiped the steering-wheel key to answer. "Hello?"

"Kristina, this is your Uncle Francis. I'm going to be hung up in some meetings for a while, but wanted you to know the DC plane landed safely in San Diego. I'm very much looking forward to seeing you tonight."

"Likewise, Uncle. I'm still a couple of hours out and it's raining cats and dogs. Looks like Manila in summer."

"I won't distract you from your driving then, but we still need to discuss what your aunt and I have decided to do about the election and your role this time. Let's meet tonight at Mister A's on 5th Avenue. I've made reservations for the two of us at seven."

"Looking forward to seeing you, Uncle. *Te amo. Adios.*"

Interesting. Sounded like Uncle definitely planned to run. That meant their daughter/niece was certainly going to be involved. She wasn't sure she was looking forward to it. From everything she was reading in the Philippines press, despite the constitution, it certainly looked like President Legaspi had figured out a way to finagle another term. He was infamous for his negative campaigns. He had certainly steamrolled and made fools of everyone, including Uncle Francis, who unsuccessfully ran last time around. Well, whatever baked his and Aunt Feliciano's biscuits – it was their money that would fund the campaign and had paid for Kristina's schooling, after all. It would be ungracious if she didn't wait a year to spread her own wings.

She shifted her window wipers to the highest speed, tapped her brakes and gave the Mazda another twenty feet.

Maybe her Aunt and Uncle had a secret plan. They had been unusually secretive over Christmas. Archbishop Ver had been underfoot more than usual. Perhaps the three of them had figured out how to neutralize American support for Legaspi. Maybe that was the reason Uncle had been in Washington last week. Kristina looked around. The sky was getting even blacker. Do airplanes take off in driving rain like this? Perhaps Uncle would stay over in San Diego tonight. She could get a room and they would have time to talk about what he had accomplished. Did the United States bureaucracy inside the Beltway even recognize the importance of the Republic of the Philippines? How did America hope to control the South China Sea and the Chinese without them? It was certainly a hot topic on the Bruin campus. She wondered if the reverse question was commonly discussed on campuses in Beijing. Her brother would know. He had been surprised when Aunt Toseña had sent him to school there for his MBA. She was glad it hadn't been her!

The Philippines general elections were in May. Uncle would need to begin organizing very soon if he were indeed serious. Would they want her to help this time or shunt her off to run the family shipping business again? That Mazda was having difficulty staying in one lane.

Did you avoid my question about Aaron?

I think I'm ignoring my own questions about Aaron. I'm not sure he rocks my boat. By the way, did I tell you I got a tattoo on my right heel! I had this old man put a sampaguita blossom on the inside. I've always wanted our national flower somewhere on my body.

She suddenly bit her lip.

The same tattoo I got the week before Rodel Luzario raped me? It's been seventeen years, Kristina, so don't keep worrying about my feelings. Let's return to the subject of Aaron. I know I may be a few years out of date on these things, but if you say you are in the midst of deciding, haven't you already...

Her cell tone burbled over the car speaker.

"Hello, Aaron! And how are you this afternoon?"

"Sweetheart, when are you getting back? Want to do something tonight?"

"Not possible. I'm on my way to San Diego to see my uncle. Not sure I'll even be back by tomorrow, in fact."

"We have classes tomorrow. Mr Daro will notice if you're not there."

"Can't be helped. If I don't make it, take notes for me, please, and tell Staring Daro I'm still alive."

A nearby lightning flash illuminated the car.

"I will. I love you."

As the roll of thunder reached the car, Kristina took the opportunity to key the disconnect button on the steering wheel.

*

In principle, Kristina approved of the no-cell-phone rule in the restaurant. Mister A's was still relatively unspoiled. That this spot still existed, despite the ascendency of government agencies like the TSA and the Department of Homeland Security was a testimony to the strength of American capitalism. Here, patrons sat alongside the landing flight path like Roman consuls viewing some Coliseum event, watching aircraft descend into San Diego airport.

She only wished the Philippines had a location this grand. Too many of her fellow citizens thought the cigar bar in the Manila Hotel... She used the nail of her index finger to again check that the ringer on the cell phone under her napkin was set on silent.

She tasted the prosecco and nodded her approval to the steward to pour another flute. She was not surprised her uncle was not here when she arrived. But he was now more than a half-hour late, which *was* unusual. She shivered and realized she had been staring for some time at her reflection in the window glass alongside her table.

She repositioned the black hair that hung nearly to her waist so it was more across her chest – she should have worn a blouse rather than this sweater. She reflectively cocked her head and stared out into the gusting rain. It was not that often she had nearly an hour of downtime all to herself. With the exception of her chest, she was slight, just like her mother. Her father had always loved putting both their faces together and calling them his angels. The view from the panoramic window blurred. The lights of another plane were approaching. The whoosh from the aircraft's enormous engines wasn't loud enough to affect any of the dining-room conversations, however. As the latest aircraft dropped out of sight, she realized her wine glass was empty and Uncle was now a good forty-five minutes late.

Francis Toseña couldn't believe this rain. Normally, San Diego was as dry as a bone in the desert. He shook the water free from the fringe of hair around his scalp. This downpour would be merely irritating in the Philippines. But the man *Time Magazine* had listed last month as the fifth most influential man in Asia was thousands of miles from home. Furthermore, rather than rubber flip-flops, he was wearing expensive leather shoes that slipped on the San Diego cobblestones. The streets were running free with water and the mother-of-a-whore cab driver had dropped him ten meters short of where he was to meet his niece! Using a linen handkerchief to protect the silk tie he had purchased only yesterday in Georgetown, Francis lowered his shoulders and sprinted toward the restaurant's protective awning.

Then his chest suddenly exploded. He grunted. The pain! The wind whipped any sounds away. A second knife cut off his air before his lungs could grab another gulp.

CHAPTER THREE

"Master Chief Dawkins, excuse me, I'm Captain Pete O'Brien. I'm here to see Admiral Hallmark."

The Admiral's Writer looked up from her keyboard. She had been expecting him. Yesterday afternoon, in their routine process of going over the Admiral's next day's schedule, the staff had reviewed Captain O'Brien's biography. Last night, to fill in what was not in O'Brien's personnel records, she had taken advantage of her marital bed to ask some pertinent questions of her husband, Bob. "The Admiral will probably be another ten minutes. Would you like coffee, Captain?"

"Please – black."

His CV had recorded that O'Brien was a Naval Academy graduate, thirty-eight years old, six three, with a broad chest and an absurdly small waist. But her husband had filled in rather interesting information chinks. Bob had been a couple of classes behind O'Brien during SEAL training. Pete was well known in their small group and Bob had shared an account involving the extraction of a female Russian spy from Vladivostok.

The Master Chief drew two cups of coffee from the large urn in the former closet, putting a dollop of fresh cream in hers, the latter a shore-duty perk, piling both cups atop a ream of copy paper to save a trip. She mentally shook her head. Captain O'Brien's visit this morning reminded her of one of beloved husband's clearest flaws. Bob was like one of those expensive navy-ship radars that automatically target threatening missiles but permit life-saving helicopters to fly unchallenged. While he immediately registered and catalogued each and every female who entered a room, her husband's discriminator simply screened out male Y-chromosome carriers as uninteresting. In two hours of tales about missions last night, her husband hadn't thought to even mention that Captain O'Brien was strikingly handsome, even with his broken nose and the two-inch knife scar on his dimpled chin!

By the time she returned to her desk, Admiral Hallmark was opening his door. "Pete, I appreciate you flying all the way back to talk to me; Master Chief, I see you have his coffee – good."

The Admiral's Aide was moving through the office to join them and the Admiral held up his hand to forestall him. "Never mind, Sam – I won't need you for this conversation. I just intend to go over some administrative things with Pete." The Admiral turned and entered, with Pete on his heels. Hallmark didn't say anything more until the two were seated and Master Chief Dawkins had firmly shut the outer office door behind her.

Administrative things? Pete pulled out his notebook while the Admiral took a sip from a glass of water and straightened the one file on his otherwise immaculate desk. The Admiral had called his boss yesterday and requested Pete immediately get on an airplane and fly halfway around the world for...

"I didn't want to put anything about this conversation in a message, so I'll rely on you to pass my thoughts directly to Admiral Paul McDonald. Don't take any notes."

"Yes, sir." Pete restored the notebook in his inside coat pocket. Damn. No notes and you don't want your staff to know about this. This is probably going to be another one of those conversations I could never tell my wife about – if I had ever acquired one of those – and Ashley isn't the answer to that problem either, which is a different task for later.

Admiral Hallmark eased up from his chair and walked to a multi-colored chart tacked to an easel. "I know you're familiar with the South China Sea, Pete."

The Admiral's hand lay on the irregular body of water that was key to trade between Asia, India and Japan. Slightly larger than the

Mediterranean Sea and bordered by exotic lands, including Vietnam, China, the Philippines and Singapore, this particular ocean was historically an area of continuous political and military unrest. Generally unrecognized by most Americans, the South China Sea had increasingly become the focus of great power struggles.

"Japan gets more than sixty per cent of its energy from tankers carrying liquefied natural-gas from Brunei via this seaway. These shipments are particularly important to Japan after her nuclear problems at Fukushima Daiichi. That's just one example. More than half the Asia/India trade passes through the Malaccan straits."

Pete worked to keep his face expressionless. If by any chance he were ever selected for Admiral, he swore he was going to take extra care not to make speeches during what were supposed to be conversations with subordinates.

Admiral Hallmark was now running his finger along the seven to eight thousand islands that formed the Philippine archipelago. "As long as the Philippines were friendly, it didn't matter that the Chinese influenced a great deal of the north side of the sea." He paused. "But I don't have to tell you how the Chinese are growing their navy." Pete nodded. That was obvious.

"And we're very concerned that they intend to influence the Philippine elections scheduled for this May. I want the Seventh Fleet to establish a much higher American presence within these islands in the next sixty days. In the process, you should work with Ambassador Coyle in Manila to ensure the general elections there do not serve our enemies."

Now we were getting down to where the rubber met the road. When an admiral says the magic words "I want", he has cast his philosophical hat aside for the gold-braided one. And, as Pete noted, Hallmark had not even paused to pretend that he might care what Pete or his boss might suggest or recommend.

"Aye, aye, sir." Only sixty days! Pete's mind was churning through the logistic challenges. The Admiral wants a visible American imprint. OK. We will need an impressive headquarters – which means our flagship *Blue Ridge* will have to relocate from Yokosuka, Japan to Olongapo in the Philippines as soon as possible. That unplanned evolution will require at least two weeks, even if I make a couple of phone calls as soon as I leave the room. No, I'll have to speak to my boss face-to-face first. I can't give him the texture of this conversation over any electronic media – who might be listening?

At sunset, the panorama from Diamond Head was easily the best on Oahu. The sky held at least half of the color spectrum. Dark was closing in on Waikiki from the west while the light blues and gold were still visible in the west. Pete had purposefully selected this spot for tonight. The view always dazzled and he had not brought Ashley here before.

The server had just left their table with their meal orders.

"I gather this is our farewell dinner."

Pete eyes left the horizon and swung to Ashley.

She swung her hand around the restaurant. "You didn't fondle my ass when you helped me out of the car. You're looking at the ocean rather than at me. Before yesterday, you hadn't called or texted me in over a week. You have no idea whether or not I'm wearing a bra tonight." She paused. "The maître d' knows."

She retrieved her purse and pulled out her cell phone, quickly keying in the code. "Shall we exchange notes on how each of us should do this better next time? I have mine prepared."

Pete felt his ears getting red.

Ashley looked at her phone. Pete took a breath to speak and then realized she had only paused because the steward had arrived with their drinks.

As soon as the man stepped away from the table, Ashley resumed, looking him directly in the eyes and then back down to her phone, obviously reading from prepared notes. "In a couple more years, you'll be forty. If your life depended on it, you still couldn't commit to a serious relationship. You don't have a mother problem – you have a navy problem. It's not that you don't understand women, because, God knows, you've had more than enough practice."

She placed the phone aside and took a deep sip of wine, put down her glass and keyed her phone again. "Damn screen locks too quickly. I added some new notes yesterday." She paged through, found what she wanted, read it, nodded, and then obviously decided not to read what she had written, only looking at him and adding one final comment, "You don't have that many more chances."

Pete winced.

Ashley put her phone away in her purse and then drained her wine in one long swallow. She carefully balanced the empty goblet on the tablecloth and stood, shaking her head at his attempt to stand. He could see tears in her eyes that she seemed determined not to wipe away, "Pete, you're nice. You're honorable. You do good things. You're cute. I thought I loved you. But you can't commit. You cost me six months of my life."

Pete began to stand and she pushed down hard on his shoulder. "Don't get up. Let me walk away with some of my pride. Have another drink and enjoy that sunset you were so carefully watching while I looked at you one last time. I'll take a cab. Have fun out there in the wild west and don't ever, ever call."

He stared east until he was sure she was gone and he was no longer blushing. Might as well go directly to the airport and see if there are any seats left on late flights west. Without a lover, Honolulu wasn't worth a drink.

Three weeks later

Captain 3rd Rank Hsu Wing-tsit, Commanding Officer of Chinese Han Submarine 404, *Western Wind*, spun his hat around and leaned into the periscope faceplate. The neoprene adapter contoured exactly to his cheeks and blocked out all extraneous light. The computer was generating the torpedo-firing solution. The periscope assistant had aligned him exactly on the bearing currently being tracked. As the periscope broke water, the Republic of the Philippines ship *Gregorio del Pilar* filled three of the sixteen vertical marks in the periscope mirror. Since *Pilar* had been commissioned in 1965 as the US Coast Guard ship

Hamilton, Captain Hsu assumed it still had a masthead height of 67 feet. Three marks and 67 feet – he did the mental mathematics to check the computer – a target range of 4,800 meters.

He glanced away from the periscope. The generated computer solution was 4,760 meters. He had always been excellent at mathematics. In these waters, the torpedo would acquire while it still had 1,600 to 1,900 meters left to run. Perfect! Sinking the *Pilar* was not going to be a problem – using more than one torpedo would be a waste of good Communist China yuan.

The real challenge of this operation was how to guarantee survivors in these shark-infested waters. It was important that the message get back to the Philippines that the Scarborough Shoal was to be left to the Chinese. But it had been decided that problem was too difficult to plan... *Wei wu wei.*

And *Western Wind* had her own problems. This was the last week of their extended deployment away from the friendly home waters of Yulin. The crew had performed well, but extended voyages were particularly demanding on submarines. Already, two saltwater pumps needed to be rewound, and their absence limited the propulsion plant to 22 knots. In addition, there was a worrisome oil leak on the torpedo cross-aligning mechanism. None of these mechanical defects would affect the single torpedo needed to sink *Pilar*, but if they ran across a US submarine – at best a very uneven contest – he wanted to have his full weapons capability. Perhaps he could fire enough decoys to confuse the Americans and get away. Maybe not.

Furthermore, the rigging on the port motor generator, even after twice replacing the complete brush set, continued to excessively arc. This was a fire hazard and probably foretold a mica deterioration within the machine. This possibly promised a catastrophic turn-to-turn failure. If so, it meant the entire motor generator could blow at any time. Finally, they were no longer making fresh water for anything more than the reactor and the sailors were beginning to grumble about missing their tea! It was obviously well past time for Han Submarine 404 to set sail for home.

In another four minutes and twelve seconds, after a torpedo broke the back of the *Pilar/Hamilton*, Captain Hsu planned to do exactly that. He took a final look to check the bearing in the computer was still tracking. He then spoke the words that would commit eighty-two Filipinos to their death: "Fire tube four."

CHAPTER FOUR

Rachel Townsend, the American Embassy's Deputy Intelligence Officer in Manila, had completed her solitary lunch and was walking through the Manila Hotel's lobby on her way back to work. She smiled at several people she recognized as she mentally ran through her afternoon schedule. The only thing of importance was a meeting with the Ambassador and there was loads of time to prepare. With that item mentally checked, she returned to enjoying her stroll. One nice thing about The Manila Hotel was that she was never the only expat woman. The Hotel was also convenient. It was less than a block from the American Embassy. In addition, the normal clientele included the top strata of Manila society as well as the ambassadorial crowd. The Manila was one of the few establishments in which she could be thirty, blond, nearly 6ft in her three-inch heels and not have to use her elbows on each and every elevator to keep from having bruises on her breasts and ass each night.

As she headed for the heavy teak and copper doors that opened from the hotel out onto Rizal Park, she passed a row of indoor palms that informally delineated the cigar bar from the rest of the lounge. The strip of carpet that ran along the marble caught at her heels and her hips brushed against the slowly stirring green fronds. Both acted to slow her step. Against her better judgment, she paused. She would only watch for a moment. The Philippines was unlike anywhere Rachel had been posted.

Within the semi-circle of fronds that marked off the cigar bar, a lovely young Filipino woman sat on a low wooden stool. The woman's back was erect, as if perched on a queen's throne. Her eyes were fixed across the lobby, apparently on an oil painting of a carabao standing patiently in a rice paddy. The woman's ankle-high black skirt was carefully folded off to one side of her long slim legs. Her fingers were slowly rolling a cigar up the inside of her very naked left thigh – to the rapt attention of the man sitting in the leather chair inches away from her stool, as well as the half-dozen nearby observers, currently all men, who had lowered their own newspapers, magazines, iPads and cell phones. Despite this scrutiny, every fiber of the woman's being, from her bare shoulders to the pink bottom of one light brown sole, appeared singularly tuned to her task. She did not even flinch when a waiter with a silver tray brushed her hip as he passed, a single frosted gin and tonic centered atop the white doily.

With a graceful shrug, the cigar girl cast her long black hair back over her right shoulder, raised the tobacco to her ear and slowly rolled and teased the leaf with her thumb and forefinger. Her eyes rolled back as she appeared to listen for a particular crackle foretelling of an easy draw.

The Manila Hotel was world famous – General MacArthur had made his headquarters here between the World Wars – and it was just down the street from the American Embassy. Its accommodations were luxurious and the dining world class. It was thus the logical spot for official events hosted by the American Embassy as well as other representative organizations. Rachel's official duties brought her here several times a month.

After the event, there was often a need for a convivial area to follow up on conversations and partake of an after-dinner brandy. The usual solution was within the palms, where overstuffed chairs cocooned weary bodies and attentive wait staff stood respectfully back from low conversations but well within beckoning range. And the cigar girl's stool was always positioned in the center of that space.

Of course, sitting 'behind the palms' was also a rite of passage for visitors. Visiting diplomats often tried to remain aloof during the cigar ritual. Frequently, to show their worldliness, they sometimes attempted to engage Rachel in conversation. After a year in Manila, Rachel was very experienced at maintaining a straight face as men's eyes widened and their words stumbled. The cigar ritual was more sensual than any lap dance, and so far in her career, she had also seen more than a few of the latter.

The cigar girl had tucked her skirt even more impossibly higher and was making a second pass with the cigar. Just before the scene dipped into indecent, she apparently decided the texture was satisfactory. She sighed, stopped and wet an end of her seductive prop in a snifter of expensive cognac. After lifting the tobacco from the silver goblet, she ran the newly brandied end just beneath her nose for one soft inhale before extending her long tongue to enfold the tip.

Rachel reached out one hand to the closest palm tree, which remained firm in its bucket of soil, steadied herself and closed her eyes. Next lunch, it was strictly iced tea. By now, she should know better. In this heat, a Westerner would feel the effects of even one gin.

She heard the match strike. The faint whiff of sulfur wrinkled her nose. The woman had clipped both ends of the cigar and now held a flaming wooden match steady two inches below the largest end. As the leaf turned white, then red and slowly began to smolder; the Filipino took a short sip of smoke. The rich aroma snaked out across the lobby, wound up around the trunk of Rachel's palm tree, slipped between the leaves and teased her nostrils. The white-suited Chinese businessman who had selected the cigar shifted in his chair. It was difficult to tell if he was adjusting his trousers or reaching for a more significant tip.

Rachel had seen enough for any one day. She resumed her journey to the hotel entrance, stopping just short of the door. It was always necessary to prepare herself for her inevitable shock of the transition from the Manila's air-conditioned comfort into the heat of the noonday sun. She slipped on her Louis Vuitton frames, took two long ivory pins from her purse and held them between her teeth while she gathered her waist-length blond hair into a cooler chignon and secured it in place. She smiled at the doorman and stepped out onto the portico.

As she drew in her first breath of overheated Manila air, every man near the hotel entrance gave her at least one appraising gaze. Those few onlookers not interested in beautiful women focused on the sun-fed flashes from the weighty gold bracelet purchased on her last visit to Macao.

The heat waves were already bombarding the thin material of her dress. She didn't think any Westerner ever truly became accustomed to the Luzon heat and humidity, especially during the late summer. She was seriously considering carrying an umbrella. Nearly every Filipino woman did. The little spot of shade certainly wouldn't offer any protection from the torrential afternoon rains. Goodness knows, the daily downpour seemed to sweep in from nearly every direction, but a cute little umbrella – she had been thinking a yellow one – might deflect at least some of this nearly equatorial sun.

Rachel thanked the black-hatted porter who had opened the door and set out upon the four-block walk along Quirino Road. In Rizal Park, several teams of shirtless men were playing futbal. As she glanced their way, a scuffed leather ball came bounding toward her. She neatly trapped it with the side of her foot, waited until the short muscular man in pursuit was ten feet away and briskly snapped it back to him. Three years of Marymount varsity soccer had some uses.

The man's toe caressed the ball and it literally jumped up into his hands, "*Pasasalamat! Gracias!* Thank you," He strung together the three languages – Tagalog, Spanish and English – nearly every Filipino spoke. While his lips smiled, his eyes never rose past her chin, much less to the reflective surface of her sunglasses.

He turned to re-join his game, hopping slightly forward with his first step and casually let the ball drop, the arch of his powerful right foot catching it before it hit the turf. The leather rocketed forty meters away to a teammate's chest. Rachel's gaze lingered on the sweat that ran down his muscular back and converted into three rivulets. They disappeared into the stained narrow waistband of his once-white shorts. She awkwardly stumbled on a sidewalk crack. Catching her balance, she disgustedly blew some air between her pursed lips. It was time to forget about her lunchtime follies and focus on her afternoon's work.

She surely had enough tasks to occupy her time. More information was pouring into her cryptographic section than in any month for years. It seemed everyone was suddenly interested in the Philippines. Indonesia was supporting several clearly frivolous claims from Muslim separatists in Mindanao. The Chinese were pressing claims in the South China Sea. General violence in Luzon was on the rise that no one seemed able to explain, and suddenly, the United States State Department, National Security Agency and Central Intelligence Agency had simultaneously submitted separate requests for information. Something must have been said about the Philippines at a recent Washington Cabinet meeting. Don Collingsworth, her boss, had requested her own assessment. It was to be the subject of the meeting with the Ambassador this afternoon. She mentally counted: it would be only the third official meeting she had attended when the Ambassador had been present – maybe this time he would remember her name.

While her mind was wool-gathering, she was almost to the old Army-Navy Club, or rather, the *Museo ng Maynila*, with its beautiful swaying palms, or City Museum as it had been known for sixty years. Two workmen were trimming the hedges around the low building. She could see the long, sharp machete knives ubiquitous to Filipino manual laborers raise and fall in the sun.

As she stepped off the main road to take the shortcut through the hedges to the Embassy, the hairs on the back of her neck below her chignon stirred.

The feeling of disquiet stopped her. She had grown up in a small town in the west. Out there, people trusted their senses – or they did if they knew what was good for them. She stepped to one side of the sidewalk to let others pass and scanned the people in the square. There were the players in the soccer game. Nothing unusual there. They were preparing for a corner kick at the other end of the field. There were several dozen well-dressed people sitting on the wooden and stone benches under the trees in the park. Also, nothing usual. Brighter coloured clothing that you might see in the same crowd in an American park. And nearly all of the women were using umbrellas. She was going to have to get her own. Tonight. After work. Wonder how late the Adora stayed open?

The feeling was still present, but less intense. She took another slow look around. Actually, since leaving the men congregated near the front door of the Manila Hotel, no one seemed to have paid her any particular attention. Perhaps she was losing her touch! Shaking her head once, she increased her pace toward the Embassy and her afternoon responsibilities.

As she passed through the opening between the hedges, a brown arm slipped out and circled her neck, jerking her violently backward. Before she could scream, a second hand, wrapped in a rag, covered her mouth. In front of her appeared a half-naked Filipino, a red bandanna tied around his forehead. A wide white scar ran from his left cheek to his jaw – a razor-sharp machete gleaming in one raised hand.

The flagship of the United States Seventh Fleet, USS *Blue Ridge* (LCC-19), began a graceful left turn into the channel that led to Subic Bay. *Blue Ridge* was a amphibious landing ship, built to carry three thousand armed marines, as well as the several hundred officers who formed the staffs of the senior Navy Admiral and senior Marine General in the far Pacific. The ship and its staffs – currently, the navy one was the only one aboard; the marines would join after they completed disembarked training near Pohang, South Korea – had sailed a week ago from Yokosuka, Japan. In the center of the navigation bridge, the helmsman carefully waited for the precise moment to reverse the rudder and steady the ship to keep *Blue Ridge* steaming midway between the buoys.

A thousand-foot-long warship is not in its natural element close to shore, and this particular vessel, displaying a Vice Admiral's personal flag, not only needed to be physically safe, but also to appear both graceful and majestic. Hollywood movies, American music videos and this gray flagship were the only representations of America many Asians would ever see. The real one didn't get time to titivate and sweep up spilled popcorn between shows.

Accordingly, the *Blue Ridge* Commanding Officer, as well as two hundred of his best men and women, were currently working very hard to maintain the image of effortless power. This was an important occasion

– the second historic return of the United States to the Philippines, represented in this case not by an Army General and his corncob pipe, but by an actual warship. The ship's thousand sailors, less those working or on duty below in the engineering plant, were already standing at attention around the lifelines 'manning the rail' in gleaming white uniforms.

In the "Flag" spaces, empty at this moment, Navy Captain Pete O'Brien casually leaned against the gray steel bulkhead near the auxiliary magnetic compass. The thick steel that supported several tens of thousands of pounds of rotating radars didn't even notice his 190 pounds. It was quiet time for Pete. It had been a frantic two weeks since he returned from Honolulu, but the first step to rebalance the Chinese aggression in the region was nearly accomplished. In less than half an hour, Seventh Fleet headquarters would be relocated from Yokosuka to the Philippines.

He took a deep breath of the jungle air and removed his dark glasses, folding and slipping them into his shirt pocket. He listened to the quiet orders as they wafted up the ladder from the lower deck, reflecting on how many years had passed since an American warship sailed into Olongapo to establish a permanent presence.

A hundred years earlier, American Commodore George Dewey's order "You may fire when ready, Gridley" had signaled a furious bombardment that sank the entire Spanish squadron at Manila. The defeat presaged a nearly continuous United States presence in the Philippines. American troops had left when the Japanese overran the islands in 1942 – only to triumphantly return as the Allies pushed the Japanese back to their homeland.

We had also departed after the Cold War, when a new political calculus had combined with a natural disaster. Philippine hostility to the United States, fueled by our long political support of their very unpopular President Marcos, had peaked at the same approximate moment that Mount Pinatubo erupted to bury Clark Air Force Base and its new twenty-six-inch-thick concrete runway in tons of volcanic ash. Leaving had seemed propitious.

Thirty years later, the US Navy was back as a consequence of

Chinese saber-rattling. Had they really sunk the *Pilar* a couple of weeks ago? There were no eyewitnesses, but an abundance of rumors.

While Pete mused, *Blue Ridge* slipped into the inner basin between Maritan and Rivera Points. The blue water flowing past the ship's trim gray hull had changed to muddy brown from the clay a recent rain had scoured from the hills. The ship began a slow left-hand turn and three seamen on the starboard side cast their stiff nylon heaving lines out into the water to wet them. They quickly retrieved them hand-over-hand, neatly coiling them – now supple but no longer brilliantly white.

Lead weights had been tied in the ends of heaving lines. The arrangement was termed a monkey fist. A practiced sailor could throw such a line more than a hundred yards. As soon as the men on the pier chased down the monkey fists, the shipboard ends of the lines would be joined, or 'bent', as seamen say, to one of the half-dozen five-inch-thick nylon hawsers that were currently coiled in compartments below decks, and teams of men would begin heaving the heavy mooring lines across the water. On the wharf, the looped 'eye' in the end of each hawser would be draped around iron bollards or cleats. As the first eye dropped, the bosun would blow his whistle. That shrill trill would mark the moment *Blue Ridge* was officially deemed moored in the Philippines, and Pete could move to Phase II.

The bow of the ship was just passing the head of the mooring wharf. She was nearly abreast of their berth. Pete heard the Captain increase the backing bell to kill the 'way on'. The ship's engines' work was complete. Tugs and human muscle would suffice for the remaining fine adjustments involved in mating a huge steel ship to the wooden pier. At a chief's hand signal, three muddied nylon lines simultaneously rainbowed toward the pier.

Pete turned to descend the steel ladder to his stateroom. He had a meeting scheduled with the ten most senior individuals on his three hundred officer staff. It was time for him to share more from his discussion with Admiral Hallmark.

CHAPTER FIVE

The assailant in front ran the back edge of his machete slowly up between her breasts. Rachel felt the metal press against her breastbone and slide under the leather strap of her purse. She shrunk back and involuntarily pressed against the man behind her. The pressure against her chest eased and she heard her handbag sprawl near her feet. Rachel reflexively drew a deep breath and the second man slightly turned his blade so the razor edge indented the thin skin of her throat. She froze as the clasp on her bracelet was flicked open and the gold weight fell away from her wrist.

The man behind was now using only the sharp-edge blade at her neck to control her. He had dropped the rag away from her mouth and was slowly raising the back of her skirt. Even as one part of her recognized what was happening, another quadrant of her mind was gathering information. She was, after all, an intelligence officer. She had been groped before. Their little tableau couldn't be happening more than ten feet from a busy street. He would have to move the blade in order to…and she would scream…she had to think that way…

With her heels, the man behind her wasn't as tall as she. She knew because she could feel his erection pressing against the back of her right leg just below her butt cheek. She might not be able to identify that one but she would have no trouble pulling the man in front of her out of a line-up. When he smiled, his rippled scar tissue on his left cheek pulled his left upper lip up to expose two metal-covered molars in the back of his mouth. He smiled now as he seized her right breast through her bra. His right thumbnail was hooked and black. Looked like it had been sliced with an axe. She involuntarily winced as he twisted.

She forced herself to accept the pain as she compartmentalized. Had she seen red bandanna's face on any lists? He was squeezing even harder. Damn, that hurt! Were they the men who had been trimming the hedges…?

"*Pahintuin!*"

Rachel felt a swish in the air and, suddenly, the machete was no longer pressed against her throat. The man in front of her was backing away, holding his right arm. Her raised skirt dropped and she was shoved forward. She stumbled on a tree root. As she fell, a strong hand grasped her around the waist and pulled her back up. She had the fleeting thought that the new body was a firmer one than either of the bandits'. Behind her, she heard footsteps rapidly running away in the direction of the museum.

She took a relieved breath before turning to face her rescuer.

"Rodel Luzario at your service, Madam. I assume those two peasants are no friends of yours?"

The man pulled the coat of his white linen suit aside as he slid a small automatic weapon into a brown leather holster. As he did, Rachel glimpsed a slim waist covered by a tailored pinstriped cotton shirt. Rodel stooped to pick up a silver-tipped cane as well as her purse and then stood, running a manicured hand through the dark mustache that covered his upper lip.

This was a face Rachel would easily remember. He was as dark as the coffee beans she had ground that morning, with prematurely silvery, wavy hair and, very blue eyes. She was looking directly into those eyes, for this Rodel Luzario was much taller than the average Filipino. He was also very, very handsome. Suddenly, Rachel felt faint. The memory of the machetes and the smell of fresh-cut boxwood was making it difficult for her to breathe. She put a hand on her throat, where she could still feel the edge of the blade, and quickly examined her fingers – no blood.

Rodel was looking at her anxiously. "Are you all right?"

She nodded slowly, still trying to fill her lungs.

"Do you need a doctor?"

She closed her eyes for a few seconds, not knowing what she wanted. Perhaps he would just go away.

When she opened them, Rodel had put his cane under his arm and knotted the severed ends of her purse straps while she gathered herself.

"Would...would you walk me to our Embassy?" Her voice was hoarse.

"Certainly." Rodel handed Rachel her purse and then looked around the path. He moved away from her a few steps and she followed a half step after him as he bent down, reached under a hedge, picking up a dropped machete. It had a black taped handle. He then gracefully rose, tucking both the machete and his cane under his left arm. He extended the crook of his right elbow to the unsteady woman, "Ready?"

As a professional, Rachel knew the cold in her hands and legs meant she was probably in shock. She wasn't sure she could even make the remaining few hundred feet to the steps of the Embassy. She accepted the helping arm, focusing on breathing and keeping her feet under her. She clung hard to her new friend until they reached security. The marine sentry stepped forward, his hands tighter on his rifle than usual, his eyes pointedly fixed on the long knife peeking out from under Rodel's left arm.

"Excuse me, young man. I was just escorting this lady to your Embassy. I believe she would like this machete as a souvenir of Philippine culture." As Rachel balanced unsteadily, Rodel handed Rachel the sharp knife as well as a calling card. "I would very much like to buy you a drink sometime. Perhaps you can explain how you came to have such disreputable friends."

Rachel only nodded as she silently accepted both the machete and his card. As her fingers closed on both, Rodel bowed, turned and strode off down the walk, jauntily swinging his cane.

Aboard the USS *Blue Ridge*, Captain Pete O'Brien, the Seventh Fleet Chief of Staff, accepted a cup of black coffee from his yeoman and sat down at the head of a twenty-foot-long table. Pete was effectively the senior officer whenever the Admiral was not aboard the flagship. He was also in charge when the Admiral did not want to be bothered with the minutiae, processes and problems involved in moving ships, sailors and marines to solve the thousands of daily crises in the Pacific. Since this was nearly all the time, most meetings were held in Pete's stateroom. A large table was installed just for that purpose. The table, along with a stretched yellow couch, took up fully half of his stateroom. A large desk and a conversation area occupied the rest of the room.

When Pete sat, nine officers quit their animated discussions and took seats around the table while the Marine Liaison Officer and the Logistics Officer, as was their practice, sank into either end of the couch. The mess specialist began placing fresh steaming cups of coffee before each man and the one woman. These were the trusted ten officers Pete used to manage the other five hundred that made up the Admiral's staff.

Pete opened his MacBook and looked down the table at the staff's senior intelligence officer. Pete had fully briefed her on his San Diego call last week. The Admiral was in the process of making his own personal assessment by visiting the capitals of each country around the South China Sea. That would take three weeks. In the interim, he and Pete had decided on an approach that would get the entire staff immediately involved but would still keep as many options open for Admiral Hallmark for as long as possible. "Mary Ann, why don't we start with a review of the situation in the Philippines and follow it up with any particular twists you have on why we are here?"

Captain Mary Ann Saunders was a slight woman with unruly hair that was forever escaping from under her uniform cap. When she had been in college the Army and Air Force officers had religiously worn hats indoors and out, while the Navy seemed to consider a cap more as something reserved for special occasions, like when eating liver and onions. Mary Ann had thus decided to enroll in the Navy Reserve Officers Training Program at Indiana University. She had never regretted her choice. She hated hats! She pushed back both her hair and her wide oval glasses back on her nose before she began. "Ambassador Coyle, who reportedly is a very close friend of the Secretary of Defense, and is, of course, our Ambassador here in the Philippines" – she looked once around the room to ensure everyone was listening – "is concerned that the last hotbed of communism" – she paused, and quickly added for anyone interested in taking her literally – "outside of Cuba and China, lies in the forests of Mindanao, which you may remember is the southernmost Philippine island."

She held up her hand to forestall any raspberries, which she expected were probably forthcoming from the two teammates on the couch. "I know – who cares about communism any more, but the Defense Secretary gave a speech last month up at West Point where he spoke with concern that Al-Qaeda terrorism embedded itself by initially using communism as a cover." She turned to a map she had pinned with magnets to the bulkhead behind the couch. "As you can see, Mindanao is the closest land mass to Indonesia, the largest Muslim country in the world. We are here to nip any such movement in the bud."

She looked quickly at Pete. "Well, the Ambassador asked for us to be sent here for that reason, and the Philippine President, Emilio Legaspi, bypassed the Ambassador and paralleled that request with a note directly to State. Let me explain that first and then I will discuss an additional problem."

She rose from the table, pulling from her front pants pocket the old-fashioned telescoping pointer that none of them had ever seen her without, and moved around the table to stand next to the large map. The men on the couch stood so they could better see.

"Mindanao has always been a hotbed of revolution," Mary Ann began, "and Islam spread across from Borneo" – she tapped with her pointer a country coloured blue on the map a few sea miles southwest of the Philippines – "in the 12th century." Her pointer tapped each main island of the Philippines as she proceeded with a quick sketch of recent intelligence, all of which she brought forth as needed from her memory. Each of the officers in the room was a seasoned professional, but, as usual, all were still impressed with Mary Ann's command of the data. Even for someone who lived her craft, it was a remarkable tour de force.

As they looked at the map, everyone around the table could easily appreciate the strategic situation: just as Japan, sitting on the Pacific doorstep of Russia had been a key base for America during the Cold War, the Philippines archipelago was now critical to controlling terrorism in Asia and having a platform to push back against China.

Mary Ann's last words had been, "President Emilio Legaspi has informed the United States that the Mindanao Communist movement has merged with Al-Qaeda, and has asked the United States for assistance with the *Pula Alcorán*."

"The latter," Pete interrupted her brief to add to everyone, "translates from Tagalog as the Red Koran."

Mary Ann nodded her agreement and pushed her glasses back up her nose on the way to her seat.

Pete took a sip of his cooling coffee. In the euphoria of her performance, it looked as if she were forgetting their script. "Mary Ann, you said there was a possible second problem?"

A guilty look crossed her face and she nearly skidded on the painted steel deck as she reversed direction while again yanking out her pointer. "Right. Let's go back to the chart of the South China Sea and look at it from a great power perspective. In addition to all the Chinese work on the various island complexes, there is some message traffic and other NSA intercepts that indicates the neighbors to the north are interested in turning this into a Chinese lake. If this is true, the optimum time for China to make a move could be during the next Philippine general-election period."

"Less than four months from now." The interruption was from the staff's senior marine, Colonel Tom Cooper, a taciturn, buzz-cut, prematurely gray-haired man. He and his wife had no children. They had been stationed in the Far East for the past twelve years. Personnel policy was very strict that no one was to serve in continuous overseas assignments for longer than five. Tom was considered invaluable by everyone who knew him and few truly insightful individuals wanted to serve on this particular frontline. The orders for Colonel Cooper to be transferred home had been getting lost for seven years.

Mary Ann nodded her agreement, sat down and Pete took over.

"All right. Two possible scenarios and if either one becomes a fact, it is going to require us to put on our big-boy boots and wade into deep water. In the meantime, we also need to worry about everything that normally keeps us busy twenty-four hours each day.

"One of our goals that caused us to move *Blue Ridge* to Subic is we want everyone to recognize that America is committed to the Philippines. They must realize we are here to stay. To make that point, instead of immediately visiting somewhere else, as we normally do, the flagship will remain here for at least a month. Then we may make a quick jaunt over to Hong Kong to host a reception for the Admiral, but for the foreseeable future, we will center our operations around Subic even more than we did from Yokosuka." There were several frowns around the table, as those with families or 'arrangements' generally housed dependents or mistresses in the villages near Yokosuka, Japan. Pete ignored those reactions. Unexpected separations were part and parcel of military life.

"We will focus operations around the Philippines until something happens," he repeated, expressively opening his large hands. "Or doesn't." He placed them flat on the table.

"I know many of our staff were planning to do Christmas shopping in Korea, but that trip has been cancelled for the moment." Several officers made notes and Pete watched Mary Ann electronically forward everyone the new schedule file. This would not be popular. The crew had been anticipating visiting the Itaewon district of Seoul. An American could still find bargains there, especially in athletic and electronic gear.

"The Admiral won't have much time aboard. Since his travel schedule is a bitch, we will need to provide him an electronic status report at least twice daily. In addition to fleet activities, I especially want to pass upward everything we have on the Philippines, so have your staffs get their paragraphs to Mary Ann on whatever routine she establishes."

"Mark" – Pete shifted slightly in his chair and focused on the slightly overweight logistics specialist sitting on the couch – "have your people compile a report on what is left from when we were last here, specifically including whether the old ammunition storage bunkers are still usable. I know that FedEx has moved into the Cubi airfield, so the question is, how many airplanes could we station there in a pinch and what would we need to do to augment the facilities so we could service Air Force planes along with our own?" Mark was taking notes and nodded without looking up from his pad.

Pete continued, "Many of their planes have different refueling requirements than ours, so make sure someone considers those physical differences. Before we leave for Hong Kong, I want a thick logistics report to send up the line. Ask anyone on the staff for whatever help you need."

"A couple of us have been out here before," Pete glanced at the other end of the couch, where Tom Cooper was sitting – and then down to the end of the table to his Sea, Air and Land Specialist, Bruce Parks, who, while Mary Ann was briefing, had begun idly cleaning his nails with a long thin-bladed knife. Pete had never examined that weapon closely, but he was fairly certain it was an old-fashioned switchblade illegal in nearly every state north of the Mason-Dixon Line. Of course, *Blue Ridge* was definitely not in the USA and Bruce was another of those officers who assiduously avoided the subject of visiting 'home'. It was not unusual for an officer assigned to the Pacific to have a 'story' in his or her past. Naval officers with nary a blot on their record were assigned duty in the Mediterranean and Europe. They attended teas in their dress white uniforms. Officers stationed in the Far East were a different breed. Some carried thin knives with ivory or onyx handles in special pockets sewn inside their uniforms, had tattoos that no flag officer even saw, and on liberty, could be found in sleeveless sweatshirts hanging around the equivalent of Asian biker bars.

"Tom, you and Bruce go see what old relationships you can re-establish. We need to find the ground truth on what is happening here."

Pete anticipated Mary Ann's reproachful look before it had even fully formed on her face, "Mary Ann, don't even start. I know the Embassy thinks they know every little thing about their country, but they get captured by the people they are dealing with each day and lose their objectivity. We do this in every country where we drop anchor. We bring a different perspective. Embassies view things and report to the Secretary of State. We listen from an action point of view and our chain-of-command leads to the Secretary of Defense. I always feel better when people I personally know are telling me the same things I'm reading in our cable traffic. OK?"

Mary Ann pushed her glasses back. She didn't argue, but her body language shouted that she didn't agree.

He had completed his list. He closed his Mac. "The rest of you, tell your people the buddy system is in force. Olongapo used to be a high-crime area and, until we know it better, I do not want any of our sailors found in an alley with their throats cut. No one walks around by himself or herself outside the immediate vicinity of the ship. If anyone goes into the city on liberty, I want them to be in a group of four minimum, understand?" Pete looked around the table, making sure he heard a verbal acknowledgment or received a nod from each officer.

He then deliberately changed the tenor of the meeting by reaching in his pocket and pulling out a twenty-dollar bill. "Now, let's discuss something truly important. I have to go see the Ambassador in Manila tomorrow morning, but this twenty says that when I get back in the afternoon I will kick all of your asses in Hares and Hounds." He carelessly threw the twenty on the table. "Loser covers the beer. Which one of you wimps is afraid to bet?"

A chorus of insults about Pete's parenthood and virility accompanied a flurry of small bills thrown on the table. Pete noticed that Mary Ann had a quizzical look on her face. He knew it was her first tour in the Far East. He mouthed the words, "I'll tell you later."

CHAPTER SIX

Rachel spent most of her afternoon filling out reports. The Manila Metropolitan Police required robbery and assault to be reported as separate crimes and the Embassy security functionaries mirrored that inefficiency. She nearly felt like she were being assaulted anew! Both sets of bureaucrats seemed much more interested in how she justified believing her attackers to have been Filipinos rather than in getting information that might be helpful in identifying the assailants. After an hour, Rachel fled to the ladies' restroom.

Fortunately, no one followed her. After a few minutes, she put a cold washcloth over her eyes, sat down and leaned back in one of the chairs by the vanity unit. Quiet time would do wonders for her soul. As the minutes passed, she could literally feel her blood pressure slowly cease ticking in her ears. The slight tremor in her fingers subsided. Finally, she pulled the washcloth away and looked in the mirror. Color was returning to her cheeks and the thin red line across her throat was well on the way to fading. She let the cloth drop back – another five minutes. She deliberately let her mind drift off to better subjects – to the yellow sun umbrella she was going to buy; perhaps it should be black, with a silver tip, like the cane Señor Luzario had been carrying…

Oh, shit! She abruptly sat up, the washcloth felling to the floor, as she looked at her watch. She had fallen asleep! In three minutes, she and Don were scheduled to meet with the Ambassador! She took a pass at her hair, pushed at her cheeks and hurried to her office, quickly spun the safe dial back and forth three times, stopped only momentarily on the familiar numbers, retrieved a steel briefcase, and ran as fast as her skirt would permit down the hall.

"Rachel! Don was just telling me about the terrible attack! How are you?" The Ambassador stepped from behind his large desk to take her free hand in his. She felt slightly silly, holding the heavy briefcase suspended in the air between them and looking down on the short Ambassador's thinning hair – she really needed to bring in a pair of flats for the office – and at the same time more pleased than she wished she were that the Ambassador had recalled her name.

"I'm fine, Ambassador Coyle. Truly, I'm fine."

He was still holding her hand. Did he have any idea how much this briefcase weighed? She lowered it as unobtrusively as possible.

"Was it one of those *Pula Alcorán* fellows?"

"I couldn't tell, sir. The police are going to have me look at several six-packs of photos tomorrow. The only one I saw was wearing a red bandanna around his head."

At the word 'red', the Ambassador's face took on an 'Aha!' look, and he turned to Don.

"Actually, sir..." Rachel flushed as she remembered the insensitivity of the metropolitan police and the Embassy security personnel, and she pulled her hand back from the Ambassador's grip and ran her fingertips over her throat, feeling for the thin mark her skin still remembered... "They seemed more interested in my gold than in the fact I was an American, and my breasts."

The Ambassador's face flushed, which turned it even pinker than Rachel would have believed possible. He turned and headed for his desk. Rachel had heard more than one women remark that the Ambassador was surprisingly shy for a man who had made his fortune in waste management.

His blush had disappeared by the time he circled his desk and lowered himself into his large black chair. "Don, I want a cable back to State identifying this as another *Pula Alcorán* incident. I believe those fellows must have known who Rachel is and the key position she holds here."

He shifted his gaze back to her, his forehead furrowing. "You didn't have any classified papers with you, did you, dear?"

The "dear" she might forgive, but his suggestion that she might take secret documents with her to lunch implied unprofessional behavior on her part. She didn't even try to keep the indignation from her voice. "Certainly not!"

The Ambassador ignored her voice as he had ignored her professional opinion. Rachel mentally sighed. Evidently, the rumors were true: the Ambassador was a 'good-ol' boy's good-ol' boy'. Nevertheless, he was also her bosses' boss.

"Good." Ambassador Coyle was dismissively rubbing his palms together as he turned back to the resident CIA agent. "Now, Don, what else do you two have for me?"

She and Don sat down across the desk from the Ambassador, Rachel lifting the case atop her knees, where she unlocked it and handed Don two copies of her memo. He and she had discussed her conclusions at length yesterday afternoon. Rachel opened her notebook in preparation for taking notes. Electronic devices were verboten in the Ambassador's offices as well as other key Embassy areas. It was a minimum precaution to take – geeks were always finding new ways to manipulate and intercept anything that used electrons. Cell phones were particularly targeted.

Don casually held her memo in one hand as he briefed the Ambassador, only occasionally referring to it to quote specific numbers relative to the rising violence being reported in the island of Mindanao as well as some sporadic incidents in northern Luzon. Despite the fact they had spent several hours discussing the memo, Rachel was impressed. Don was displaying nearly verbatim recall.

"…as you had requested of the President and the Secretary of State, the Seventh Fleet finally showed up in Subic Bay yesterday…"

"About time. President Legaspi is under a great deal of pressure from the Chinese and those damn *Pula Alcorán*."

"Yes, sir. But the Navy now gives us the very visible and powerful US military presence in the Philippines that you envisioned."

The Ambassador was looking distractedly out of the window. "Now Emilio says he can put all local terrorism stuff back in the box so he can focus on the Chinese threat if we can only provide him a few surplus army trucks." He wheeled his chair around to face Don. "Just how do we go about getting them for him?"

Rachel knew the Ambassador was now speaking about Emilio Legaspi, the Philippine President, who seven years earlier had used his social status as a major landowner, always a plus in Philippines politics, along with his personal fortune from his family's beer company, to gain the Presidential Palace. He had then revised the succession law to enable another term. In fact, the hot rumor around Manila was he was about to go for a third…

Don was nodding and smiling. "That's easy, Mr Ambassador. We file a request through State and simultaneously ask our new Seventh Fleet friends to recommend parallel approval to Defense. I can't imagine anyone is going to do anything other than rubber-stamp a request from you."

Rachel caught Don's eye and tapped the page in her briefcase that held both his and her daily schedules. Don turned back to the Ambassador. "In fact, the Seventh Fleet Chief of Staff and their Intelligence Officer are both helicoptering over from Subic this afternoon to talk to Rachel and me. I want to ensure they begin with the right slant on what's happening 'In Country.' I'll bring them by for a quick meet-and-greet and you will have the opportunity to impress them with the importance of the trucks." Don paused and thought. "Then we can follow up with a personal memo from you to their three-star discussing the nexus of local terrorism and the campaign against Chinese encroachment."

"Good, Don. Interrupt me whenever you are ready."

Don and Rachel returned to their offices in silence. As they reached her door, Don placed a friendly hand on her shoulder. "That was quick thinking about those Seventh Fleet people." His voice dropped a quarter-register. "Why don't we kill two birds with one stone? We can erase your bad memories from today and I can also recognize and reward a bright young woman with a dinner at the Manila Hotel this evening. What do you say?"

She turned so his hand slid off her shoulder and ignored how his falling fingers lightly caressed her hip. "I would love to, Don, but I have a date with Jamie Bautista this evening."

"Jamie? The same Jamie who is the Executive Secretary to Emilio?" Don was obviously surprised. "Is he picking you up in that Rolls of his?" Rachel detected a twinge of envy.

"I don't know. He just asked me out to dinner."

Don continued down the hall to his own office and Rachel resisted adding "perhaps another time." He was attractive and they enjoyed the same things but, while he never wore a ring, she had met his wife at an Embassy social. Even if he weren't married, she was determined not to get involved in an office romance. Relationships in the small community of an Embassy always bordered on incestuousness. She had never heard of one of the romances turning out well for the woman involved.

She deposited the briefcase on top of the safe and sat down at her desk. She wanted to gather her thoughts before she briefed those two officers from the Seventh Fleet. As she squared the loose papers before her, her eye was caught by the cream-colored calling card she had earlier dropped on her desk. The police had taken the machete for their evidence locker.

She ran her fingertips across the embossed letters – Rodel Luzario, Teak World, Vice President of Exports. She closed her eyes for a moment, remembering Rodel's strong hands and how he had taken on her assailants today. She flicked the calling card so it slid across her blotter and sat at an angle, tucked partially under the border.

She needed to open the safe and stow the briefcase before her next guests arrived. She would think more about Rodel later.

"Hares and Hounds was originally a way for the Brits stationed in the Far East to encourage exercise." Pete and Mary Ann were in the helicopter on the way back Subic. Even with the intercom headsets built into the crash helmets everyone wore, it was still crazy noisy in the cabin. As passengers, Pete and Mary Ann were seated in the helicopter facing each other, so, despite the uproar from the huge rotating blades a few feet above them, he could watch her eyes to ensure she understood what he was trying to explain. Of course, since the game had originated in England, it never would fully make sense.

"It's a race, but not exactly. And drinking beer is key. Several fast runners, like Bruce, are designated as Hares. They go out into the jungle a half-hour ahead of everybody to leave clues. The Hares also lay dead ends and false trails to slow the faster runners. Behind them, in the main group, the speedier Hounds try to sprint and catch the Hares, even if they have to run down all the wrong leads while the rest of us in the pack plod along just following the shortest path. If properly done, even the slower members in the main body of Hounds will stay roughly together, which is good since there are a large number of poisonous snakes and even some boa constrictors in the jungle around Olongapo."

Mary Ann grimaced and Pete smiled, "I feel exactly the same way about snakes. In fact, if you want to really overload your sense of danger, some afternoon when you have caught up with your work, there is an area over by Cubi where they used to teach jungle-survival techniques. Take a walk over there and you will find every one of the nasty poisonous snakes, spiders and centipedes that are native to Southeast Asia.

"But, given all the noise the Hounds will be making this afternoon, our vertebrate brothers won't be a problem if you just stay with the pack. We'll cover about eight to ten miles to ensure everyone gets up a good sweat, and then, since it's originally a Brit tradition, we'll end up at a bar and rehydrate with beer.

"Finish the run, Mary Ann, and you will be considered a soul sister in a genuine Far East tradition. We only insist on one change to the original format – our beer will be ice cold! Running ten miles through a jungle for the reward of a warm tepid beer is completely un-American."

Mary Ann still had a question in her eyes, but Pete couldn't think of any aspect he had omitted. She pushed her glasses back up her nose and pressed her mic button, "Trucks?"

Trucks. Smart girl. She was correct to be concerned. Filipino truck drivers routinely sped around blind turns at excessive speed. "We won't be near any roads – we will actually be following game and carabao trails during our run."

Mary Ann closed her eyes for a moment, then mashed her voice button hard enough that Pete could see her thumb whiten, "I mean the trucks the Ambassador wants."

Pete shifted mental gears, "Right. Those trucks." He was silent for a while and Mary Ann could see him compose his thoughts before he answered. "We've been in country less than twenty-four hours. I don't want to take an official position on this until we have time to gather a few more facts. Bring this up at our next staff meeting and we'll kick the issue around."

Mary Ann's helmet nodded, but she looked as if she had another question. Pete held a hand out and motioned with his fingers for her to bring it on, "Yes?"

"What about the woman?"

This time, Pete knew exactly what she was thinking. He wrinkled his nose, "Are all intelligence officers this nosy?"

"Just the ones who care about their Chief of Staff. You are a handsome, successful man and very unmarried. You must know there is a staff pool on when you will finally succumb. In fact, I am the official holder of the bank, which totaled fourteen hundred and eighty dollars as of last Friday."

"What date do you own?"

A grin crept over Mary Ann's face, "First, there were only a couple left to pick from when I reported aboard, and second, it is none of your business. If you knew, you'd pick a different one just for spite, and I wouldn't be able to buy my husband that new set of Ping irons he lusts after." She paused for Pete to comment and when he didn't, she renewed her quest for scuttlebutt, "So, did you ask that blonde bombshell out?"

Pete simply relaxed his body back in his harness and closed his eyes. "None of your business."

As the helicopter winged its way back to the ship, Pete reviewed the meeting. The whole event had been embarrassing, from the moment he and Mary Ann had walked up to the Ambassador's office.

"Captain, I have looked forward to meeting you."

"Mr Ambassador, this is my Intelligence Officer, Captain Mary Ann…"

The Ambassador interrupted Pete's attempted introduction by pulling a tall blonde woman forward by her upper arm, "And this is our Intelligence Officer, Rachel Townsend, who will be working directly with you, Captain O' Brien. She is going to ensure you get everything you want."

Pete had taken a step back. "In the other twenty or thirty countries we routinely visit, we find our relationship works best if the liaison is normally conducted through the intelligence officers. They speak the same language and are frequently conferring with the same offices back Stateside."

Ambassador Coyle's eyes narrowed and Pete saw his fingers tighten around Rachel's upper arm. "Young man, are you trying to tell me how to run things in my country?"

"Certainly not, sir." Pete tried to keep his face placid. The Ambassador had walked in the room, immediately dissed one of Pete's key officers and was now jigging this Rachel woman past him like a fisherman trolling for haddock.

Ambassador Coyle didn't notice Pete's reaction, "Fine. then. Rachel is perfect for this role. She knows all about the *Pula Alcorán* and why we need army trucks out here as soon as possible. In the meantime, she is our high-society gal in Manila and can make sure you are entertained."

Jig…jig…jig…is the haddock going to strike? Pete didn't know whether to feel embarrassed for Rachel or to take advantage of this opportunity and use the Embassy blond to accomplish Admiral Hallmark's tasking. With only ninety days to go until the general election, some shortcut to understanding the current Chinese influence in Philippines high society would be greatly advantageous. Of course, Rachel might be a co-conspirator, but, from the tightness around her mouth, Pete suspected that Ambassador Coyle had just surprised her as much as he had Pete and Mary Ann.

After Don made the case for why the Philippine military needed

US Army surplus trucks, and the Ambassador added his forceful support, Don and Mary Ann withdrew to the SCIF to discuss specific 'black' intelligence matters, and the Ambassador returned to his office, leaving Rachel and Pete alone in Rachel's office.

"Rachel, I guess we're now soulmates."

"Certainly looks like the Ambassador has made that assignment, Captain."

"Please, call me Pete." He looked around her room. "May I sit?"

She indicated the chair in front of her desk and he fell into it.

"Rachel, since we're new friends, how about if I take you out so we can get to know each other better?"

"I'd rather not. I'm seeing someone else."

"Engaged?"

"No."

"Exclusive?"

"Not exactly."

Pete had raised his right eyebrow quizzically.

"I'm dating a couple of guys." She said weakly. "I have a pretty full calendar."

"Rachel, let's make this painless for both of us and get it over. You must have two or three official functions a week you have to attend. I want to meet the people in the Palace. I can clean up nicely. For the next official function at the Palace that you don't already have a date, how about I become your plus-one and I let you talk about trucks to your heart's content?"

"Nothing more?"

Pete had raised his right hand with three fingers pressed together – a memento of his Boy Scout days. Already dating a couple of guys – another one of those women with an inability to commit. He jounced awake as the helicopter landed atop the Subic Bay concrete pad.

CHAPTER SEVEN

The lead Hounds, three whip-thin officers who lived to run, bayed once and sprinted off into the jungle as if they had the scent of blood in their noses. The pack of other officers followed at a slower pace but were soon out of the town of Olongapo, off the dirt road, into the jungle and onto a trail of grass and trampled underbrush. The temperature immediately dropped ten degrees. Under the triple canopy, the air seemed easier to breathe. The lavers of leaves also softened and filtered the light – it was now a deep green, which was gentler on the eyes. The downside to the shadows was the footing became more difficult to judge. Since they were on a carabao path, there was also mud and dung.

Pete fell back a bit behind the pack as he talked with the Fleet Surgeon, Doctor Bill Rogers. A former All American college athlete himself, Doc purposely lagged behind on these runs, so he was positioned to care for the occasional injury. Pain and no gain was a real possibility in the jungle. On the upside, making your own trail through a jungle made for a very stimulating run, even if all you experienced were monkeys and parrots.

As they jogged, Bill was doing a bit of business, explaining what he intended to do about an outbreak of malaria that had recently been reported in Mindanao. "…prophylactic medication, Chief of Staff. We need to get everyone accustomed to taking a daily pill."

"I thought malaria was a disease of the past?"

"Maybe in Europe and North America, but certainly not here in the tropics. In Africa, a kid still dies from malaria every thirty seconds."

Doctor Bill paused as they both adjusted their strides to leap a small stream. The far bank was slippery with mud deposited by several previous Hounds who, rather than then jumping over, had decided to run through the shallow water. As they landed, Bill's foot stubbed against a root or limb semi-hidden in the wet grass, and he took a stride or two to regain his balance before he continued, "Millions suffer damage from high fevers that literally cook their brains."

"I thought there were effective drugs for it?"

They had covered about two miles and some of the slower runners were beginning to lose contact with the main group. Suddenly, a Hound running in the very front of the pack bayed as he spied the three speedsters reverse direction and race back toward the pack – indicating they had been led astray by a Hare's false lead. The pack stopped in place, some helping the Hounds sprint in different directions in search of a new clue while others jogged in place to prevent cramps. The weariest simply leaned over, grabbed the hem of their shorts, and took a fifteen-second breather. A chalk mark was soon discovered on the weather side of a tree alongside a narrow winding path that led up over a rise. Although the path looked faint enough to have served no more than a pair of brown deer, someone spied a partial heel mark and the pack was committed, some using small bushes to pull themselves up the hill.

Doctor Bill resumed their conversation, "As long as everyone in the fleet faithfully takes their pills, the great majority will be protected."

Bill and Pete jogged the next half-mile in silence. It wasn't hard to follow the pack. After nearly a hundred feet had trod through one concentrated area, the trail looked more like a carabao wallow than a jungle floor, but Pete knew from past runs that after three or four days of the normal drenching daily rains, the bruised carpet would fully recover. Doctor Bill continued his explanation, "We need to make sure everyone understands they are only protected against three of the four possible kinds of malaria. I'm not giving them anything to protect against the most virulent type – the one that kills within twenty-four hours."

"Why not?"

Bill gave him a wry grin; "Medicine is often a tough mistress. This is one of those cases. The protective pill saves most from dying but it is also so strong it kills five per cent of healthy adults."

"Damn!"

"Right. The drugs provide a high level of defense against the three less deadly forms of malaria. Then, if someone still suddenly comes down with a high fever, we know they must have the really bad type, and we hit them with the hard stuff."

"And there is a five per cent chance they will die?"

They were at another shallow stream. This one was wider. The faster runners had run directly through it. Some of the slower ones were attempting to cross by hopping from rock to rock. It had been a while since a false trail had caused the leaders to backtrack. As a consequence, the pack was beginning to string out. Already the first twenty or thirty runners were out of sight.

"You are looking at the problem wrong, Chief of Staff. Data proves that if they don't get the hard stuff, everyone with the wrong kind of malaria dies. With the medicine, ninety-five per cent live."

Pete glanced at Doctor Bill. He was not kidding.

Ahead of them, as if in slow motion, Pete saw Mark, their logistics ace, who was attempting to cross the stream by hopping from rock to rock, lose his balance. Bill and Pete sprinted forward as their friend teetered, waved his arms wildly, and fell heavily into the water

By the time they reached him, Mark was already sitting up, a rueful expression on his face. The stream was swirling past him, chest-high. Two other runners had seen or heard him fall, doubled back and were gathered around. The other Hounds were out of sight. Bill and Pete waded into the stream to lift and carry Mark to shore while Pete ran after the Hounds to get four more volunteers.

After probing the suspect ankle, Doctor Bill pronounced it a severe strain. He prescribed bed rest and a walking cast. He took charge of the runners who would assist in getting Mark back to the ship.

Pete contributed his shirt to jumpstart a litter frame and assumed safety-sweeper duties for the rest of the run. He estimated that by now he was at least ten minutes behind the slowest runner, so he picked up his tempo to the pace he used during his daily runs. It wasn't necessary any longer to watch for chalk marks; he only had to follow the bent and bruised vegetation while watching to ensure he didn't step in a hole and break his own leg.

Now that the pack had passed, the jungle was quickly coming back alive. The noisy "aawk-aawk" of numerous parrots flitting in the trees above was picking up. Ahead of him, roughly following the ground trail, Pete saw three monkeys swinging along their own vine highway. They veered left as he broke out into sunlight and found himself on an asphalt road. The grasses on either side of the road were undisturbed, and a smudged and now largely indistinct chalk arrow near the center of the road indicated the path was to follow the road as it bent around to the right.

The macadam was bordered by a very serious fence. The latter was ten-foot high and made of steel. The vertical ribs were four inches apart, painted solid black, each rib topped by a nasty-looking spike that curved outward toward the road. And like a blue ribbon on a package, at the very top, a roll of barbed concertina wire was held in a Y behind the spike. On either side of the fence, the underbrush was carefully cut back several meters. On the inside, Pete could see a line of cameras about every forty feet. Whatever the fence was protecting, someone was serious – a suspicion confirmed several seconds later, when he passed two locked gates and saw a bare-chested guard, smoking a long black cigar, sitting underneath a tree, a shotgun across his lap. Beyond the guard, a branch of the asphalt road led to a mansion.

Pete was so interested in the large house with its two sweeping wings that he nearly missed where the Hounds had abandoned the road and plunged back into the jungle.

As his feet led him back into the underbrush, he returned in his mind to the malaria issue. He would have Doc Bill draft an appropriate warning for the Admiral to send out to the fleet's hundred

Commanding Officers. Maybe it should be a 'Personal for' message to ensure it connoted the gravity of the issue and…

He heard the snort before he realized he was in danger. A water buffalo was rapidly moving toward him, head lowered. It was already only ten feet away, moving fast, the long green shoots of undergrowth disappearing beneath the broad chest like foam under a cruiser's bow. Its curved threatening tusks were widely waving back and forth. They broadcast their intent to hook and throw his body into the middle of the South China Sea. Pete leapt for a branch of the nearest tree and swung his body up as high as he could, grabbing yet another higher branch over which he threw a leg and pulled himself even higher. The closest tusk missed, stripping a chunk from the tree and flinging a long strip of bark across the clearing.

Pete checked he was out of range, and then, remembering his recent conversation with Mary Ann, looked for any little pit vipers he might be curled up with – thank goodness, no!

Several feet below his dangling legs, the carabao loudly snorted before backing up and ramming the tree trunk again, causing Pete to grab the limb with both hands. The animal stepped back, grunted and fixed Pete with two red baleful eyes. More than a ton of meat and two curved brown tusks of serious business. Out of the corner of his eye, Pete saw a small calf splay-legged in the soft ground, looking back and forth between what must be his mother and the intruder in the tree.

He softly banged his head back against the trunk. He couldn't believe he had gotten between a mother and her calf. He was going to take some severe razzing when he finally joined the beer party.

The calf slowly made its way through the bamboo shoots to join her mother, butting her head under the water buffalo's ponderous side as she sought to nurse. Apparently satisfied with the world, the mother carabao began to graze. Pete waited a minute and then tentatively moved a leg. The carabao's head snapped up and her legs shifted as she rebalanced herself in the long grass for another charge. The calf bleated as it lost her teat and nosed insistently at her mother's belly. Pete sighed. Now he was stuck until the carabao lost interest.

Fifteen or twenty minutes later, while he was busy flicking off the large red ants determined to climb over his legs, he heard a soft whistle. When he saw a young girl start down from the road, he yelled a warning, "Careful, there's a big mean water buffalo over here and she's got a calf!"

The girl looked up at him with some curiosity but continued on, ignoring his warning. As she got closer, the carabao began switching her tail menacingly. Pete didn't know whether to yell again or whether it might anger the carabao. He knew the girl had heard him.

The girl murmured something in Tagalog as she walked directly up to the beast. The carabao raised her head ever higher as the girl neared but the girl didn't stop until she was squarely between the two large horns. She reached up and scratched the water buffalo's long nose. The carabao closed its eyes and began switching her tail in a different rhythm as the girl slipped a rope halter on its muzzle. Keeping one hand on the animal's mane, the girl walked to the side, away from where the calf still nursed, and vaulted onto the beast's back. It was only then that she looked up into the tree.

"I don't think Gloria likes you. I recommend you don't come down until I ride her away." For a moment, Pete could swear her eyes focused on his bare chest. Of course, now that he could see the girl more clearly, he was also unabashedly staring. She was simply stunning. And she was no girl. Although many Filipino women looked young, given how this one's T-shirt fit where she had tied it off high on her waist, she was probably at least in her early twenties. Even astride a water buffalo she was startlingly beautiful, all the way from where her black, black hair fell below her shoulders, to where her long, long legs grew out of her faded cut-off denim shorts.

When he realized he was staring, Pete was embarrassed. He was thirty-five years old. She could be his daughter. He looked away and was instantly drawn back by her dark eyes, which were still fixed upon his. "My name's Pete, by the way."

The girl's bare heels kicked the carabao in the ribs, and the beast slowly turned toward the road. The calf kept pace as her food source moved, bumping her mother's udder with her head. Finally, the water buffalo settled into a lumbering, rolling walk through the tall grass as she headed back toward the road.

It was another thirty minutes before Pete finally reached the waterfront. The Hares and Hounds were enjoying their beer on a bar built out over the water. Pete grabbed a bottle of water to rehydrate as well as a beer to nurse and joined the group to take his medicine. Mary Ann and the other staff members devoted five focused minutes to giving him grief. As he moved between the various conversations, he heard "wild carabao!?" more than once. There was nothing to do but smile.

The Pete-baiting ceased when the food was served and everyone descended on the laing fish, pork adobo and crisp lumpia rolls. At the same time, Filipinos finishing work began filling the bar. They were dropping by for their customary end-of-the-day beer. It was peak hour for the bar staff. It was the same for the Americans, as they were bent on gathering intelligence a few beers might jar loose – or at least demonstrating by their presence that the US was truly in the Philippines.

From the looks of the crowd that was gathering, the bar they had chosen was apparently a popular one. The tables in front partially impeded the traffic on the board sidewalk. Further back from the road, behind a long L-shaped polished and gleaming solid-mahogany bar and protected from rain by the thatched roof, an extensive array of bottles sat on mirrored shelves, Two attractive women in white cotton peasant blouses tended the latter, dispensing beer, peanuts and hard-boiled eggs, as well as cold cokes.

The workers flowed in and the *Blue Ridge* runners offered to share their food and kegs. Soon, there were nearly a hundred Filipinos standing with the Americans, all enjoying a cold San Miguel. The two-lane blacktop in front of the hut was now crowded with people hurrying home – most walking, several women balancing a cloth bundle or wicker basket on their heads, some men and a few women on bicycles chinging the small bells on their handlebars to try to gain a couple of feet while a half-dozen noisy motorbikes darted around the walkers as if they were using HOV-1 lanes.

Other commuters passed by in slowly moving overcrowded Jeepneys, the latter a traditional Philippine method of travel that began when resourceful natives converted and lengthened the frames of discarded World War II Willys jeeps. The open-air taxis – two opposing benches, entry and exit via steps hung over the rear bumper, or, for the more adventurous, simply by stepping on the runners that ran on either side and hanging on – were immensely popular everywhere in the Philippines. Thinking about the paperwork piling up on his desk, Pete drained his beer and decided to catch an approaching Jeepney back to *Blue Ridge*. He had placed his empty on the bar wing and turned to leave when the shots rang out.

CHAPTER EIGHT

The young female Palace staffer was wearing a full skirt and a loose yellow blouse that showed off her trim brown shoulders. She poured two cups of coffee for the men before she retreated from the garden, leaving behind the carafe, a silver bowl topped with brown sugar lumps and a plate of sliced mangoes. Jamie Bautista waited until she was completely out of earshot, before he raised his cup in a mock salute to his companion, "We should give thanks. Our Seventh Fleet is here. We are finally saved."

Rodel Luzario tipped his own cup from its saucer, "Congratulations, Jamie. You have worked long and hard for this." Rodel was actually truly impressed. Although the man often took unnecessary chances, Jamie was only in his mid-thirties and he was already one of the half-dozen most powerful men in the Philippines. In addition, he was certainly dating the most stunning woman in Luzon – and this was despite the fact the man had the looks and manners of a toad. Rodel used his right index finger to smooth the silver mustache on his own upper lip. He frequently wondered what Rachel saw in this man. Or was she acting at the direction of the Ambassador?

Rodel leaned forward, used one of the ivory toothpicks in a crystal holder to spear a sliver of mango and winced at the saccharin sweetness. He took a quick sip of his coffee to ameliorate the taste. The Ambassador must be the reason, he thought. Jamie was an inch or two shorter than Judith and weighed at least two hundred and fifty pounds. The man's *barong* is already stained under his arms and it isn't yet noon. I wonder how many shirts he sweats through every single day? Of course, I'm not much better than the American Ambassador. The *barong* he's wearing was a six-hundred-dollar gift from me because my entire teak business is dependent on obtaining logging permits from government forests.

Jamie also speared a mango slice and responded to Rodel's original praise, "Yes, I have – ever since Emilio was first elected. But it was worth every laborious dispatch we sent and every dinner we held. The Americans always love the international status quo, and in the Philippines that is us."

Rodel pulled his hand away from his mustache, "Since Francis died so tragically last week in San Diego, I don't see a credible opposition to Emilio."

"A terrible accident," Jamie agreed, spearing another mango slice. They both paused for a moment as a breeze sifted through the garden, swaying the palms, rearranging the shadows and inducing a raucous squawking from the parrots that were permanently on display inside a large iron cage in the center of the courtyard.

"I understand his widow is furious with the Americans," Jamie continued. "She's convinced they should have better protected him. I hear she's nearly irrational on the subject." He held the toothpick up against the sun as if searching for a flaw in the ivory. "She's the one who didn't support Emilio on his approach to fighting terrorism and she's never been overly fond of the United States. She was always against our alliance." He mimicked a sober tone Rodel had heard President Legaspi use to good effect: "I fear the Honorable Feliciano Segura Toseña failed to appreciate the danger each of us faces from the *Pula Alcorán!*" He snapped the thin ivory in two and disdainfully flicked the pieces onto the bricks of the courtyard. "Perhaps now she understands."

Rodel felt a sudden chill. He glanced off in the distance, as if the parrot cage had attracted his attention. I cannot underestimate this toad, he thought. I need to always remember that it wasn't his connections that got him his position with Legaspi and it certainly was not because of his good looks. Is he implying that Emilio had something to do with Francis's death? That's a new consideration. The Seventh Fleet presence is all well and good – in fact, it could well make things easier. Once a government becomes dependent upon the military, it isn't really a question of principle any longer – it's only a matter of price. A junta was no different than a prostitute in that respect.

Rodel Luzario leaned back in his chair as he watched Jamie. It was an opportunity for a classic bait and switch. Of course, there was always the question of which Filipinos were destined to serve in the roles, but those were details to be sorted out on wash day, as his sainted mother used to say…

Rodel stilled the fingers that had begun absentmindedly drumming on his cane. If Jamie were completely happy with the Seventh Fleet arrival, then was the American presence in Rodel's best interests? He had not given that sufficient consideration. Should he insert some uncertainty? What would be the best way of doing so without exposing the limited assets his Oriental friends had so recently coughed up?

What was his friend whining about now?

"…we are incurring many new expenses. We have borne this as long as we can from the fund, but as you well realize, there is also an election on the near horizon and, while Emilio is currently unchallenged, there are still extraordinary expenses. There's always the possibility of a late challenger, for which we need to be prepared. To be prudent, the President has decided to increase the Teak World contribution to 3 per cent, effective the first of last month. He asked me to check with you to make sure that was not too inconvenient?"

"Certainly not." The son-of-a-whore was doubling their rip-off! Rodel was surprised he could keep his voice steady. "Same Zurich account?"

Jamie didn't even bother to look up and meet his eyes as he selected a new piece of ivory and speared another slice of mango. "Yes."

"Are there additional logging permits I might be issued to help allay the added expenses? We are currently working in Virac and it would be the optimum location for such expansion."

Jamie held one hand in front of his face as he used the ivory pick to poke at something in his mouth before pitching the ivory on the table.

"I don't think that is the best approach. We already have some unrest in that location and the President does not believe that the few months between now and the election are the optimal period for visible increases in production."

But it was a perfect time for him to require more *mordida*! How do I pay for it? A parrot in the courtyard cage indignantly squawked and Rodel's index finger and thumb returned to thoughtfully stroking his mustache. Interesting. So, an increase in bribes was the toad's first step now that he and Emilio had the Seventh Fleet safely in their pockets?

CHAPTER NINE

While everyone else flattened themselves on the hut floor, Pete and Bruce leapt over the bar, coming up crouching behind the mahogany barrier on the wooden slats wet from an evening of spilled beer and slopped ice. The previously crowded street was now completely empty. An empty wicker basket still rocking in a tight circle was the only item remaining in the road. Pete had heard the pops of a handgun, not the distinctive longer echoes of cartridges from a rifle, but the shots had originated from somewhere close. The echoes still rang in his ears while he scanned the street for any indication of a gunman. He saw nothing unusual. The men and women on the floor were already beginning to cautiously raise their heads. Pete sent a quiet query to the SEAL twenty feet away: "Anything on your side?"

"No, boss." Pete shouldn't have been surprised, but was, to see Bruce had a knife in his hand. Where had he carried it while he was running? "Nothing."

"*Nada* here either," Pete concurred. "Watch while I canvass for anyone injured."

As he vaulted back over the bar, Pete saw a young man across the road with a distinctive scar on his left cheek stare at him for a second before turning and vanishing down an alley. The movement was noticeable because most the rest of the throng was curiously moving back toward the street from where the shots had been fired. The youth's dark red shirt had been momentarily visible before Pete lost sight of him behind the dozens of advancing lookie-loos.

As the people in the bar gathered themselves and begin to complain about dropping onto the peanut shells on the bar floor, Pete was surprised to find there were no casualties, native or American. However, the party had definitely seen its peak hour. While Pete and Bruce waited to see if the police would ever show and watched for any unusual post-event interest, the remainder of the Seventh Fleet and *Blue Ridge* officers caught Jeepneys headed toward the ship. While the two waited, they searched the vicinity for evidence. There had been three shots. The only new damage in the bar was a broken hanging light on the edge of the pavilion. Bruce swore that it had been burning before the shooting, but Pete's memory couldn't confirm that observation. There was no glass on the wooden deck, but any shards could easily have fallen into the dark water alongside the hut.

An hour after the incident, activity at the bar had returned to normal, and the local police had yet to show – which were two bits of local intelligence in themselves. Pete decided the evening had been reasonably valuable, even if they had no idea who had fired the shots – or their target.

He left the bartender his name, along with the number where he could be reached at the ship, before he and Bruce swung aboard a purple and orange Jeepney. Sitting across from each other, each one could visually cover the opposite side of the street.

"Boss, did you notice the young man with a scar?"

"Dark red shirt?"

"Yeah." The Jeepney chugged to a stop and a couple of *Blue Ridge* sailors boarded. Not surprisingly, neither chose to sit next to the two senior staff officers. "What do you think? *Pula Alcorán*, anti-American, or just some guy mad at his wife's lover who had stopped to have a beer with us?"

Pete shrugged. There was no good answer. He realized that a separate issue had been gnawing at him all evening. "How many Chinese did you see in the street crowd?"

Bruce flicked away a mosquito that had landed near a scar on his forearm, "None. In fact, I'm not sure I saw any the entire time we were at the bar."

That same observation had been bothering Pete. If the Chinese were coming to Subic, they were certainly taking their time!

*

The next day, except for a lunchtime run, Pete was bogged down with all the minutiae involved in operating the largest fleet in the world. The challenges on the Pacific Rim weren't only military – distances made everything harder. Events often occurred five to fifteen thousand miles apart. There were never enough ships to cover where trouble might break out, so making a judgment about the lesser threats was a daily trial. The goal was to keep ahead or at least abreast of what might become a headline event while leaving those things destined for page 28 to the local commanders.

Since every day was impossible, the staff worked seven days a week frantically sorting wheat from chaff. Success or failure often depended on finding – and identifying – one particular intelligence fragment. And, of course, most of the pieces did not fit neatly into any mosaic and some were outright conflicting. Local knowledge and a special instinct were invaluable in this uncertain world. As the saying goes, a few days ended in chicken dinners with all the fixins, but there were others when supper consisted of chicken feathers.

The Pacific was by far the most challenging environment for the Navy. Pete's Atlantic counterpart was stationed in the Mediterranean, and the Mediterranean was relatively minuscule – even smaller than the South China Sea that Admiral Hallmark was currently worried about. In addition, the number of friendly airfields in Europe meant that United States military forces could be available nearly overnight at potential trouble spots. In the Mediterranean arena, the United States had sufficient resources to always regain the offensive. Consequently, military commanders there could react measurably and gradually to indications of danger. In the Pacific, if a situation found you playing catch-up, you were not only not in control, you were soon likely to be the last man on a crack-the-whip chain.

The Hares and Hounds outing yesterday had been disruptive. *Blue Ridge* in-boxes were overflowing. In addition, it was Saturday, the weekly day of disconnect between sea-going and shore staffs separated by the International Date Line. That imaginary line snaking down the center of the Pacific Ocean was a certified troublemaker. At this very moment, voluminous message traffic from Washington and Honolulu was clogging computer terminals all over the Far East, including many aboard *Blue Ridge*. Those back-ups were the natural result of thousands of desk-jockey staffers Stateside and in Hawaii meeting their own end-of-week deadlines by hitting 'send' to clear their own outboxes for their weekend.

Nevertheless, even though the avalanche hit the Seventh Fleet on Saturday afternoon, some habits are hard to break and Saturdays remained the main night for relaxation on the flagship side of the dateline. With the ship in port, the opportunity to dine someplace other than the flagship mess was not lightly missed. Most Seventh Fleet staffers who planned to eat elsewhere had begun departing all afternoon. Several groups asked Pete along, but he was still immersed in sifting through the blizzard of weekend paperwork to see if anything required immediate action. By the time he had dealt with every electronic message that looked urgent and finally realized he was starving, his stateroom's portholes were dark, the shipboard mess was long closed and it was nearly 10pm.

A walk would do him good. He took a shower, changed into slacks and a collared shirt, and meandered down the wharf past the Norwegian tour ship that had moored in front of *Blue Ridge*. Pete had decided to see if Subic's old Officer's Club was still in operation. He soon heard music. From the outside, it looked as if very little had changed.

When he entered, he was surprised to see the slot machines were still just inside the entrance to the left, and, from the electronic whirls and dings, appeared to be doing their best to churn out a steady cash flow. Those babies had once had the reputation – how well deserved Pete had never known – as the "loosest" in the Pacific. They had nevertheless swallowed many a sailor's pay check, a quarter at a gulp.

Some senior officers frowned upon them, but frankly, dumping your money into a slot machine was much safer than going out into Olongapo, and the end result was the same, except you didn't wake up the next day with a headache. Pete walked into the dining room that looked over the bay. It was packed with older people who, from their white skin, high cheekbones, and the cruise-ship lanyards around their necks, Pete made the wild assumption were possibly Scandinavian. A Filipino band was playing American favorites and the petite and gorgeous female singer had a soft, sultry voice. After a harried passing waiter assured him he could be served at the main bar, Peter retreated there.

It was nearly exactly as he remembered. An oversized room with the bar stools running twenty feet across the front of a polished mahogany counter and a bar back nearly that high. There were three shelves for an expansive line of expensive liquors and room for three or four bartenders to work. Pete thought he could once remember an evening in which there had been five men serving drinks, but now there was only one – a trim Pilipino in his late fifties, white linen towel neatly wrapped around his waist, a comb-over of gray hair where he was beginning to bald on the front half of his head.

Pete nodded at two officers seated on stools whom he vaguely recognized as members of the *Blue Ridge* wardroom. From the looks of the cigar box in their hands, he assumed they were amusing themselves playing liar's dice.

Pete took a menu from the bar and ordered from the bartender, receiving an iced tea, and looked around for a comfortable place to read. The bar area was about forty by forty feet, with several booths and twenty or thirty tables. There were only a half-dozen scattered men and three single women in the spacious table area. The women sat by themselves – obviously professionals waiting to be approached by potential customers from the two large ships in port. Pete selected a table against the wall in a deserted section directly under a dim wall light. He let his eyes drift closed while he waited for his steak and salad to arrive. His workday this morning had begun before five. It had been stressful to speed-read through all the traffic and he still had no idea why anyone might want to shoot at them yesterday.

He was startled awake when the bartender delivered his steaming thick steak along with a heavy cotton napkin and real silverware. The nearest whore had moved. She now sat only two tables away, smoke curling upward from the cigarette that lay in her ashtray.

"Will you be wanting anything else, sir?"

"No, thank you."

Although long black hair hid the woman's face, it wasn't hard to notice that her dark blue dress hugged generous breasts. The slit on the side of her skirt exposed…

The bartender had moved between the two of them with a pitcher. "More iced tea, sir?"

Pete drank a third of his glass and let the man refill it.

"Thank you."

The bartender left.

There was a hint of jasmine in the air. It hadn't been there when he sat down. He would have noticed it. The scent was…was…decadent. He stared at the closest woman, trying to will her to turn his way, but she did not, seeming lost in thought as she slipped her thin fingers under the links of a gold bracket on her wrist and stared toward the bar. Finally, Pete shifted his attention to his salad, the steak and a novel he had brought along to read.

The novel's protagonist was in serious trouble when the two *Blue Ridge* officers noisily abandoned their game. Looking around the room, they scraped back their stools and made their way across the room toward Pete. He looked up to greet them, but they stopped two tables short to speak to the woman in blue. The taller one's voice was gratingly loud. "The other girls said they would do both of us for US$50. What's your rate?"

As usual with men who have drunk too much, not only were their voices too loud for the room, they had also gotten careless. One hadn't bothered to remove his wedding ring, while the other's left hand's third finger was marked with a conspicuous band of white. Nevertheless, Pete was not a morality monitor. He returned to his book. He had recovered his spot and was halfway down page nineteen when he thought he heard a soft "no" from the woman.

He looked up. One of the men had sat down at her table and was leaning into the woman's personal space, pursing his lips toward her turned-away head. The other had his hips against her chair so she couldn't push back from the table. One of his hands was on her shoulder while his other was on the table, bracketing her in place. The fingers on her shoulder were deliberately walking their way down toward her left breast. Pete glanced around the room. The only person paying any attention was the barman leisurely polishing a glass with a thin white towel. His face was blank. This scene had to be a nightly occurrence for him.

"Get away, you pig!" The woman's voice was low, but intense. She had grasped the fingers on the hand moving down her front, but the man was much stronger. As her arm muscles clenched in effort, his loose index finger slowly began circularly stroking the silk on her left breast. "You will love it, sweetie."

"That's enough, men. Leave her alone."

The two officers looked over at Pete, alcoholic belligerence and surprise fighting for supremacy in their faces. He remained seated at his table, and as he spoke, he cut another small piece of steak.

"She told you 'no'. That specific word from a woman should be enough. Take your hands off her and go find someone who wants your attention." Pete started to put the piece of steak in his mouth, but stopped when he heard a soft cry from the woman. The man who was hipping her tight to her table now had his index finger and thumb pinching her nipple.

Pete pushed back his chair and stood up. It was time to underline the facts of life for the two men. "Are you both too drunk to recognize me? For the next few seconds, you have a choice. The one I prefer is we go outside and I kick your asses. Second choice is I bring you up on charges for disobedience of a lawful order. Either that, or you get the hell back to the bar. Take your hands off her and choose your door."

The one who had been sitting suddenly apparently recognized Pete and stood up, noisily knocking his chair over. He whispered loudly to his compatriot. "It's the Chief of Staff!"

His partner released the woman's nipple and she immediately flung his hand aside. He aggressively turned toward Pete. "She's just a whore!"

Behind him, the woman cupped her breast in pain. As she leaned over the table, Pete saw a tear mar the table's polished surface.

He lost interest in a face-saving settlement for the men and shoved his chair back against the wall, taking two steps until his hip was against her side. "It's very simple, men. She said, 'no'. Don't you recognize the word when someone other than your wife uses it?" Behind him, he heard his silverware clatter to the floor. The navy frowned on fighting. Especially by senior officers. Oh, well. He felt the woman shift her weight in her chair and lean against him. It was going to make it awkward if he had to shift his feet to hit someone.

Each man gave Pete his best evil stare before turning to saunter back to the bar. Halfway there, one of them tripped over his own feet and nearly fell, before sliding onto a stool and ordering, "Manuel, another couple of beers."

The bartender nodded and began running beer into the glass he had been polishing.

Pete slowly let his breath escape. His fists uncurled. It would have been majorly stupid to hit either one of those two clowns. He had been fortunate they backed down. But what jerks! He pulled out his money clip, found the US$100 bill he kept hidden in the center, and sat down in the chair opposite the woman, pushing the bill across the table so it was between her elbows and her downcast head could see it. "Why don't you take the night off? I will walk you home if you like."

She didn't raise her head and Pete kept his voice low and as soothing as he could make it. "I don't want anything. I have a book to read. The hero is in a terrible jam. Take the money and spend the rest of the evening with your family."

Her fingers closed over the bill and tucked it back in her palm. Then she raised her head. She was smiling, even though her cheeks were streaked with two shiny wet tracks, "Ple…please walk me home, Pete."

He immediately recognized her. Christ! She was the carabao girl from yesterday! He looked again. "Kristina?!" She nodded.

What the hell? How had the woman from Singapore fallen so far in two years?

Pete picked up his novel, shoved it in his hip pocket, threw down two twenties and offered her his arm. As they walked to the door, he heard, "Holier-than-thou asshole" behind him, but didn't turn around.

Pete couldn't think of anything to say as they walked across the base toward Olongapo. Kristina only let go of his arm once to wipe her face with a Kleenex from her purse before again linking them. When they reached the Jeepney stand, she spoke in Tagalog to the driver and sat close beside Pete on one of the benches, still holding his arm, "He will want a dollar when we get there."

Pete nodded, memorizing the route. He should probably have been making small talk, but he was silently steeling himself to meet her parents, aunts and uncles, her children and possibly a husband. Olongapo was traditionally a poor area, even by Philippines standards. He was so not going to enjoy this. Frequently, the only person in the family who could get a job was the youngest woman and the only work in this area involved servicing the tourist trade. A young girl as pretty as Kristina would be able to support an extended family. Sometimes, a dozen people lived in a single room in some tin-sheet metal-roofed house alongside a dirt road. For a working girl like Kristina, they would curtain off a corner of the room. If it weren't raining, after serving tea to their daughter's evening guest, the adult family members would leave the house.

What had happened to her plans for grad school?

When the Jeepney stopped, it was near the large house Pete had noticed during the run yesterday. Kristina took his hand and walked them up to the gate. A different man, carrying what looked very much like the same shotgun, nodded to her and opened it. As they continued up the walk to the porch, Kristina had slipped her fingers down until she was holding Pete's hand, swinging their arms and humming a tune he didn't recognize.

As they began to climb the stairs to the wide veranda that held several large wicker chairs and a cushioned two-person swing, the screen door was forcefully flung open.

"Don't even think about bringing that *kano* in here!"

"Auntie!"

CHAPTER TEN

The woman standing in the mansion doorway was a trim female in her early sixties. She filled nearly three-quarters of the doorway, but her high heels and the gray bun on the top of her head were much of that. She was possibly attractive, but at that moment, her lips were compressed into two fine white lines with anger. Fortunately, he was not in her direct line of ire, but Pete still thought he knew how Hansel and Gretel must have felt upon meeting the Wicked Witch. Currently, she was literally spitting her words out at Kristina. "You disgrace our family!"

Kristina didn't even blink. Instead, she assumed a defiant position, hands on her hips, legs spread apart. "I told you I wanted to meet him again."

"And I told you I disapproved! Now he thinks you are nothing but a whore!"

"No, Auntie, he doesn't. Call Uncle Manuel. He watched us. He will tell you that Pete was a perfect gentleman. Which is why I have invited him home for tea." Kristina's composed voice dared her aunt to doubt her.

She was so positive, Pete nearly crossed himself. Was that really how things had gone?

Obviously not content with only defending her ground, Kristina drew her shoulders back another notch, lowering her voice a quarter octave and adopted a surprisingly imperious tone, "Aunt Feliciaño, you will not keep me out of my own mother's house. You will welcome my guest!"

The old lady didn't yield an inch. "You two sit on the porch while I ring my cousin."

Apparently unworried her bluff was being called, Kristina dropped bonelessly into one of the two high-backed rattan chairs on the porch. She began humming as she fished a nearly new pack of Winston's and a lighter from her purse. Pete also sat. As he did, he heard a crinkle in the breast pocket of his shirt. His hundred-dollar bill was back. Pete replaced it in his money clip while looking questioningly at Kristina.

She met his quizzical look with a frank one of her own. "You made a handsome coconut sitting in our tree." She lit a cigarette, pursed her lips and blew a perfect smoke ring in the direction of his chair. "I decided I wanted to taste the milk." She kicked off her shoes, shimmied up her tight skirt to give her some flexibility, drew up her legs into the chair and limberly crossed them, then leaned accusedly forward to place an elbow on each knee. "You didn't even remember me." He had thought of her often, but believed her long married to that software guy. Now all he could see were her long legs, the small blue tattoo on the inside of her right heel, the long black hair that fell past her waist and everywhere fringes of her red, red underwear.

Suddenly she unwound. A bare long right leg extended across the gap between the chairs and came to rest across his thighs. "Here, Peter; look at this tattoo. For first prize in this week's Baclayon sweepstakes, tell me the significance of this flower."

The front screen flung open and Kristina unhurriedly swung her leg down and stood up. Had she seen or heard her aunt approaching? Feliciaño didn't waste a glance on Pete. Her gaze was focused on Kristina, frustration filling her voice, "Manuel said the bar was too busy. He didn't see what happened."

The older woman took a deep breath. Pete prepared for her to stamp her foot and shoo him off the porch or maybe change straw to gold. Instead, she slightly inclined her head and, obviously swallowing her emotion, forced polite stillness into her voice and held the screen aside with one hand. "Please come in. You are most welcome in our home."

Pete rose and the woman turned to Kristina, her waspishness immediately returning – "Don't even think about bringing one of your cigarettes in here!" – and turned away, swinging the screen door wide open behind her, an opportunity a large white moth promptly seized to flutter its way inside.

Pete stepped aside for Kristina to enter first. She stood up, slipped into her shoes and flicked her cigarette in a high arc out into the grass before tucking her arm in his, "Come. The tea is probably some of the crap we import from China, but Maria's cookies are exceptional."

The living room was as grand as the exterior of the house had promised. To the right, a twelve-foot-wide staircase curved up to a second floor. The banisters and spokes were ebony, the steps highly polished mahogany. The floor planking was twelve-inch-wide boards cut from a lustrous red finely grained hardwood Pete didn't recognize. A narra-wood baseboard edged where the gleaming walls met the floor. Dark red and blue woven rugs marked four conversational areas, each built around heavily cushioned bamboo love seats and high-backed ornate rattan chairs.

In the conversation area furthest from the front door, partially blocked off by a series of wooden screens featuring carvings of various carabao work scenes, stood a tall male Filipino. He was wearing a priest's white collar. Feliciaño walked toward him, turning to make introductions, "Archbishop, you know my niece."

"I do. *Mabuhay*, Kristina."

"Good evening, Father."

Pete extended his hand, "Captain Pete O'Brien of the United States Navy."

"And I am Archbishop Ver."

Mary Ann's intelligence briefings had specifically covered the Archbishop, who was believed to have unusual clout in this predominantly Catholic country. Her description had failed to convey the keen intelligence that emanated from his soft gray eyes. Pete couldn't have explained it, but he immediately liked this man. Of course, he might well be in need of an adjustment to the vernier on his people-evaluator…he had also initially believed Kristina to be shy.

Before they were all seated, a uniformed maid, complete with an embroidered white apron and a lace-trimmed cap, appeared from behind the wooden screen and looked to Aunt Feliciaño for guidance.

"Maria – Kristina and Captain O'Brien will be joining us for tea."

No one spoke until they all were served. Toseña sipped her tea and intermittently frowned at her niece. The Archbishop held his cup and saucer still and let his eyes drift shut. While Maria was making trips into the room, Kristina twisted her body away from the Priest, again kicking off her shoes and crossing her legs, an action that hiked up her skirt an inch or two. Pete realized she was doing this more for her aunt's benefit than for Pete's.

When her tea was poured, Kristina used small silver tongs to sweeten a cup with a lump of brown sugar before offered it to Pete. He accepted. He hated the taste of sugar but he was bright enough not to want to draw attention to himself in this ongoing drama between aunt and niece. He had already decided on the best course of action. Kristina was very, very attractive, but she was a distraction from Admiral Hallmark's tasking. And, honestly, where women were concerned, Pete was much more comfortable with someone who let him be in charge. He risked a surreptitious look at his watch. Fifteen more minutes and he could gracefully depart.

When Maria retreated, having delivered her famous cookies, Aunt Feliciaño placed her own cup and saucer in her lap. She looked down at the several rings on her fingers for a moment before she began to speak. Her voice was not nearly as shrill as before, "I apologize, Captain, for my niece's" – he saw Kristina stiffen in her chair – "as well as for my own behavior." Her tone gained strength. "Let me properly introduce myself. I am the Honorable Feliciaño Segura Toseña. I am the Secretary of the Philippines Department of Social Welfare and Development."

"And," Kristina inserted, mimicking her aunt's formal tone, "formerly the Vice Governor of our Tarlac Province."

Feliciaño frowned. "Yes." Her lips pursed for a second and then words that she could no longer hold back hissed between her lips. "And

I have always completely opposed the Americans returning to Subic Bay!"

The small woman rocked forward in her chair, nearly spilling her tea, to ensure she had a direct line of vision around her niece to Pete. Her words rushed forth, "You supported Marcos far too long and were no help to Ramos, even though he had gone to your West Point. Your newspapers laughed at Estrada. Your diseased sailors introduced AIDS into Olongapo, resulting in many unnecessary deaths. And American money has seduced generations of our young girls into living disrespectfully. In addition, your presence in the Philippines now will only attract unwanted attention from the Chinese." Pete was impressed. She managed to say all of this in one breath and was still going strong!

"You Americans are simpletons who have never understood the Philippine people, and your Ambassador lets President Legaspi lead him around as if he were a pig with a silver ring in his nose!"

Finally she took a shallow breath. "Over the centuries, we Filipinos have been controlled by the Spanish, the Japanese and the Americans. *Sobra na, tama na!*" She took a deep breath before she translated to ensure he understood. "Enough is enough! Only Filipinos should control the Philippines!"

Her voice had risen almost to a shout. The maid and a young man peered around the wooden screens that apparently led back to the kitchen. When Feliciaño glared their way, they quickly drew back.

She put her teacup carefully down as she visibly gathered herself. She lowered her voice, keeping her eyes firmly focused on Pete. "When her parents died, I sent Kristina to Cambridge and her brother to Beijing. I did so to keep both of them away from America." Her voice was slowly creeping up the register. "However, two years ago, my niece applied to the business school at UCLA without my knowledge." She thrust her chin out, recast her voice down an octave and began the next sentence very slowly and deliberately. "In the United States, where my beloved husband was murdered."

She visibly swallowed. "I do not want Kristina to be around Americans! I do not know why she fights me so hard on this." Pete thought for a second that the aunt was going to cry, but he could see her swallow and harden her face. "In fact, I want all Americans out of the Philippines." She paused and then practically whispered, "Just as I ask you to now leave our house."

He rose and Kristina stood with him, smoothing her shirt as she did, not bothering with her shoes. Pete was saved from saying anything stupid by Kristina, who gently spoke up: "Pete thanks you for your tea and your hospitality, dear aunt. While you know I do not agree with you about America, I did not mean tonight to dishonor Uncle Francis. You know I loved him too. I will walk Pete to catch a Jeepney."

When they were on the porch, she took Pete's hand in hers. While the security guard opened the gate, she whispered, "I'm sorry, Pete. It was a weak moment. I have been lonely lately. I let your pretty face and big muscles affect me. But Uncle Francis' funeral was only three months ago. They were married for twenty-eight years. Sometimes I forget how much she lived for him. I dismiss her irrational blame of America. Today, I was playing when I should have been focused on being a better niece. I apologize for putting you in an uncomfortable position."

They were fifty feet further down the road before Pete replied, "So, the barefoot girl who saved me from the vicious carabao is really a rich graduate from Cambridge with an MBA from UCLA?"

"This woman," Kristina corrected, "is older and worldlier than you think. Before UCLA, I spent five years in Singapore trading with the Chinese up close, thank you very much. While they will always be our neighbors, I happen to agree with my late uncle that the future of the Philippines is inexorably linked with the United States. My aunt is letting her loving memories and the stresses of the upcoming election affect her judgment."

"So, why are you here rather than in America?"

"Auntie wants me to learn to run our shipping company. We have eighteen freighters that haul rice from the Philippines and Vietnam to Japan. On the return voyages, we bring back electronics destined for Singapore as well as Manila. As the Japanese open their inefficient agriculture markets to the outside, our business is rapidly growing.

With my uncle's passing, I am the best person in our family to manage this business."

"That may be what she wants you to do, but what do you want to do with your life?"

Kristina tossed her long black hair. "I don't know. For the past two days, I have been focused on meeting you. Do you know how many men approached me this evening before you finally walked in that bar? I thought uncle was going to have a heart attack!"

Ahead of them, a Jeepney idled at the intersection.

Peter stopped in the roadway and used a hand on her waist to bring Kristina around to face him. "Thank you for a very interesting evening, Kristina. You are a beautiful and bright girl. I wish you the very best of luck."

Her eyes flashed in the moonlight. She reached up and encircled Pete's neck, drawing her lips up to his, her breasts and pelvis pushed hard against him. "I am a woman, Pete, and some Filipinos like Americans." She kissed him hard, running the tip of her tongue against his clenched lips.

Slowly, she relaxed her arms and deliberately slid down his chest. As she did, she watched his eyes as her erect nipples massaged each of his ribs. Finally she stood flatfooted between his legs, both of her hands clenching his biceps. In spite of his best intentions, he knew she could feel his heart rapidly pumping. She could also feel his worst intentions. "You will see me again, Peter," she promised.

Pete turned and began quickly walking toward the Jeepney. He didn't look back. Christ, what a wilful woman! As the Jeepney pulled away, he ventured a glance toward the house, but the road was now dark and empty.

As he walked up the gangway and came to attention to salute the *Blue Ridge* Quarterdeck Watch, he was thinking about the man who had peered around Kristina's aunt's sala screen. He was reasonably sure he was the individual he and Bruce had noticed yesterday in the alley across from the bar. The one in the red shirt.

He was also aware he was walking in a sweet cloud of Kristina's jasmine.

CHAPTER ELEVEN

When Rachel Townsend opened her door to Pete, the corners of her mouth momentarily quivered with suppressed amusement. He had already removed his uniform cap. At her look, he ran his right hand self-consciously through his hair. "That's no way to greet any man, much less one serving our country in uniform. What's so funny?"

She smiled and leaned forward. "It's nothing," she said, as she leaned forward and smoothed down his cowlick, her right breast lightly pushing against his chest. "But this high-collar starched thing you're wearing, with its bright brass buttons and dangling little medals, reminds me of nothing less than a grand costume for a Broadway musical." She stepped back, brushing away a bit of her face power that had drifted down onto the black of his right shoulder mark. "At any moment, I expect to hear the music from *Brigadoon* begin to swell from a flash mob secreted somewhere down my alley."

Pete matched her amused grin. "We stole these uniforms from the Brits when we absconded with our own country several centuries ago. I suspect the braid and buttons were intended to impress the natives of the countries the Brits were always invading. On the other hand, it simply could be that military men enjoy wearing gold."

His face took on a look of resignation and he ran a finger between his neck and the high stiff collar of his uniform. "Now we're stuck with them. They've become tradition. You have no idea how uncomfortable this high choker can be." He extended his elbow to assist her down the stairs. "And woe betide anyone who has the chutzpah to think they can successfully change a military uniform. Congress loves tradition. If it were completely up to them, we would all be wearing polished chainmail! But enough of my complaining. Is the lady ready to be escorted to the ball?"

Rachel handed Pete her light blue shawl and held her long hair aside to permit him to drape the shawl over her bare shoulders. Picking up her *capiz*-shell clutch purse, she took his arm, her fingers crinkling the heavily starched sleeves of his white jacket. "I am, kind sir." She was wearing a strapless white silk sheath that left her uncovered until halfway down her breasts (and her earlier lean forward had confirmed to Pete that the bodice contained no under-wiring). The sheath hugged her body until just below her knees, where it flared out into a soft wave over blue peep-toe high heels with crossed ankle straps. The cashmere shawl highlighted her golden hair and drew attention to her tanned shoulders and arms. As they walked to his sedan, Pete was mentally shaking his head. Since he had arrived in the Philippines, every time he turned around, he ran into another self-assured woman. This was the second one this week who seemed completely comfortable with using all the weapons in her personal toolbox. There must be something in the hot, humid Philippine air. Apparently, after the sun disappeared below the treetops, the scent of the Philippine flowers had a carnal impact.

He had looked up Kristina's heel tattoo on his computer. It was a single bloom of sampaguita, also known as the white jasmine flower. What other tattoos were on her body? And why was he even thinking about Kristina while he was out with the lovely Rachel Townsend?

The guards at the Palace gates passed the official Seventh Fleet car through the barred entrance. A hundred yards later their driver eased to a stop in front of three stories of white columns and wide arches. Tuxedoed staff assisted them from the car and a trio of lovely young women in long blue gowns funneled everyone up the steps to a short receiving line. The President's wife was a tiny woman, barely as tall as Pete's waist. She was wearing an exquisitely black embroidered, long-skirted, butterfly-sleeved *terno* that drew attention to her waspish waist. President Legaspi's cream *barong tagalog* was equally showy. While the

President held both of Rachel's hands and made small talk about the Embassy, he rose on his tiptoes and tried to surreptitiously look down the front of her dress. During this charade, Pete contented himself with counting the number of black hairs longer than eight inches in the elaborate comb-over circling Legaspi's balding crown.

Accepting a wine glass from the tray presented at the end of the line, Rachel and Pete stepped to the side to assess the gathering. The guests were nearly evenly divided between Filipinos, foreign country diplomats and businessmen. Rachel was there to work the crowd for new information and contacts. Pete intended to begin making his own contacts and do his best to gauge the influence of the Chinese businessmen.

He would have to take care. This was a gathering awash with the human equivalents of information dung beetles – men and women selected for their language proficiency, liquor tolerance and near-perfect recall. A gathering such as this was not the place for conversations one did not wish, as the British phrased it, "reported in dispatches" to many different capitols the next day. A Trojan horse would be present, champagne glass in hand, in nearly each small group, bent on parsing every off-hand comment. The shrewder ones would be simultaneously sowing false information. The man or woman who drank excessively or tried too hard to impress a pretty face was not destined for a lengthy diplomatic career.

At the moment, the game was not yet fully on. Rachel was iden-tifying the personages for Pete's benefit and Pete was trying to pick out characteristics to help him discriminate between the different Asian faces. Rachel interrupted his concentration, "Did you notice the President's lovely pina *barong*?"

"I had ample time while he was examining your own personal assets."

She chuckled and had a passing waiter recharge her glass. "All part of the play, Pete." She used her unoccupied hand to hitch her dress up a bit. "I gave him another half-inch, just because he's President. Seriously, do you know what is special about his *barong*?"

"Other than it looks much cooler than my high-collared whites?"

She laughed into her tall goblet. "I am sure it's also more comfortable. That particular formal shirt is made from fibers extracted from pineapple leaves. The industry was nearly wrecked during all the years Marcos was in power because almost all the Filipino officials wore American suits. Now the pina business is making a comeback. Those *barongs* are incredibly dear. It takes almost two weeks for a weaver to assemble enough cloth for just one shirt!"

While Rachel was talking, Pete had been trying to count the number of Chinese businessmen and also compare Filipino faces in the room with what he recalled from the mugshots in the fat notebook Mary Ann had gone through with him before he departed the ship. Two men across the room looked very familiar, and were, from the intense looks they were telegraphing, clearly discussing the American couple. "Rachel, who are those hombres over by the ice sculpture?"

She turned, looked and smilingly raised her glass to them. "Merely two of the most important people in the Philippines." She placed her empty glass on a passing waiter's tray. "Come, I will introduce you."

She lightly rested her hand on his forearm as they weaved across the ballroom between guests. "Pete, I would like you to meet Rodel Luzario, who is Vice President of Teak World. And this gentleman is Jamie Bautista, the Executive Secretary to the President." Still resting her hand on Pete's arm, she smiled warmly at each of the men in turn, adding, "In our small Manila social world, Jamie and I have been dating, and I owe Rodel a drink for saving my virtue from a dreadful duo of muggers this week past."

She extended her hand to Jamie, who bowed slightly and kissed the back of her fingers, and then to Rodel, who took her hand in both of his, holding her little finger and her thumb slightly apart while brushing his mustache across the back of her wrist. As the latter man did so, Rachel's hip was touching Pete's and he thought he felt her tremble.

Another American walked up just then and Rachel turned to include him in her smile. "And you all know my boss, Don Collingsworth." Pete did not know Don well, but he was willing to wager that Don's smoldering look at Rachel implied an interest not covered in the State Department boss/subordinate handbook – or at least not favorably covered. She attracted men like sugar drew flies.

Each of the men exchanged handshakes. A servant joined their group with a drink tray and Jamie took a scotch. Rodel looked at Rachel enquiringly and she said, "I think I'll change to champagne, please." Rodel passed her a flute while Jamie addressed Don: "Did you hear that the *Pula Alcorán* beheaded three peasants in Catanduanes yesterday?"

Don shook his head.

"Well, they did. Apparently, the village wasn't forthcoming with sufficient food and the men were executed as a warning." He drained his glass and waved at a waiter near the wall for a replacement. "You need to make sure Ambassador Coyle knows we need those trucks pronto!"

"What village was it?" Rachel asked. She handed her flute to Rodel and turned to Pete for a pen. Pete also provided his cocktail napkin.

"Virac, on the edge of our largest mahogany forest."

Rachel wrote down these details and tucked the cocktail napkin in her purse.

She turned to Rodel for her flute and they all watched him carefully place his own lips over the slight red smear on the rim and sip before he returned her glass. Rachel flirtatiously lowered her eyes for a second before raising them to smile at the men who encircled her. "I think I need to circulate. I already know all of you. Perhaps you can entertain Pete while I see if anyone is sufficiently drunk to wish to share his secrets with an old woman."

Don nodded approvingly as Rachel patted Pete's shoulder lightly and moved off. Each of the four men watched her float across the floor. No one spoke until she stopped at a group and placed her hand lightly on the shoulder of a florid-faced European. Jamie motioned for another drink and, ignoring Pete, lightly pushed a manicured finger against the third stud on Don's dress shirt. "I assume escorting senior naval officers is one of Rachel's official duties?"

Pete noticed Jamie's enunciation was already suffering. He wondered how many scotches Jamie had consumed before the reception had begun.

Don stuttered, "We...ll no..." He spoke quickly before fully engaging his brain. "As you know perfectly well, Rachel's private life is her own."

Jamie quickly swung his finger toward Pete, but Pete's large right hand encased the brown digit before it came to rest against his uniform. Nevertheless, Jamie leaned forward, as if to drive the finger into Pete's chest, his alcohol-fogged mind apparently unable to process that he was physically losing control of himself and the situation. "And you, Amerishan Capshain, are you part of my Rae's private life?"

"From what I've seen, I think you should worry more about your friend Rodel."

Out of the corner of his eye, Pete saw Rodel's even white teeth form a small smile that the executive quickly swallowed.

Jamie was not to be deterred, and leaned closer to Pete's chest, drops of spittle spraying from his mouth. "I'm talking to you, Amerishan!"

Pete effortlessly used his grip on Jamie's hand to hold him steady, twelve inches from his chest, until the Filipino realized he could not physically force himself closer. Once Pete saw Jamie's eyes widen, Pete vigorously pumped Jamie's arm up and down for anyone in the crowd who might be watching, "Nice to meet you too, Mr Secretary. I've enjoyed our conversation." He pushed Jamie's hand sharply backwards as he turned away, and saw Don and Rodel quickly move to Jamie's side to keep the latter from staggering.

For the next hour and a half, Pete circled the room, sampling the hors d'oeuvres and exchanging pleasantries with the many Filipinos attracted by his uniform. He was the only uniformed American in attendance and a good number of those present wanted him to know how pleased they were the Americans had returned to Subic Bay. Other country representatives were more cautious. Pete politely parried several pointed questions from various foreign diplomats on the subject of American goals in the Philippines, pointing out that he was merely a warrior, and neither the American President nor the Secretaries of Defense or State had yet seen fit to discuss with a lowly naval captain what plans they might or might not have. None of the four Chinese in the room approached him, and when he tried to engage them, each pleaded he didn't understand English. Fair enough – he only knew a few phases in Mandarin – but if they were really businessmen, they were lying. English was the worldwide language of commerce.

He had stopped to do some crowd-watching and was coming to the conclusion that Rachel's white uniform seemed to be attracting even more attention than his own, when he saw Jamie weaving across the room in his direction, drink firmly in hand, apparently intent on a reengagement. Since their earlier 'conversation', Pete had carefully kept the center of the room between him and Jamie, and, following that pattern, he turned to begin another circuit around the perimeter.

"Amerishan Capshain, I want speak to you!"

Jamie's voice was both imperious and loud. It halted other conversation in their locale. The guests near Pete stepped away and looked back and forth between the two. Pete pretended he didn't hear and reached down and picked up a lumpia from the food table centered in the room. In whatever capacity he was here, it was always a mistake to insult high-ranking nationals. Pete was going to have to forego his original intentions of a quiet drink with Rachel after the reception. Her nectar had too many bees buzzing round. He would plead an early day tomorrow.

"Capshain!" Pete felt Jamie's hand on his arm. He turned slowly so the onlookers would not think him offended.

Jamie held up his glass of scotch. "I brought you drink!" His eyes were focused and Pete had only an instant to realize that Jamie was not nearly as drunk as he had wanted others to think before the chubby man's hand deliberately sloshed the glass's contents into the center of Pete's chest.

He reflexively grabbed Jamie by both biceps and pulled him close, the empty glass shattering between them on the wooden floor. The slight smile on Jamie's face kicked Pete's brain into gear, and Pete loudly announced for the other guests, "Thank you for your gracious thoughtfulness, Mr Secretary. Unfortunately, the drink ruined my uniform. I will need to leave and change my clothes. But first I must thank your President for the lovely event."

As Pete continued to hold Jamie motionless, he could sense the other guests in the vicinity collectively release held breaths. Still controlling him with his left hand, Pete took Jamie's right hand in his own and shook it, childishly crushing the other man's fingers for a moment as he leaned in close to whisper, "But first I must collect my date."

When Pete turned, Rachel was standing not more than eight feet away. She wordlessly took Pete's arm as they moved toward the President to offer departing respects. Pete apologizeed to Legaspi and his wife for his clumsiness, and profusely noted how much he had enjoyed the reception.

As they stood at the top of the Palace steps and waited for the attendant to call their car, Rachel apologized for Jamie, a worried expression on her face. "I have never seen him behave like that. I wonder if he is ill?"

Pete waited until he was assisting Rachel into the backseat to reply, "It's a simple chemical reaction. In the future, remember you can't have four testosterone generators in the same space, no matter how large the room. Your personal limit appears to be three."

She turned red, coughed, got her breath and then laughed out loud as he closed her car door.

As Pete got in the other side, she scooted over until their hips touched and placed her right hand on his knee, "We can't have you walking around in wet clothing. I know your uniform will dry soon, but would you like to have a drink in my apartment while it does?"

Pete gave the driver her address. Seemed like just compensation for the superhuman restraint he had just exercised!

CHAPTER TWELVE

The car had not rolled completely out of the Palace grounds before Rachel asked, "You seemed inordinately pleased at yourself. Why?"

"I didn't hit him."

She shuddered. "Of course you didn't hit him. You're a grown-up, not a teenager."

Pete shrugged and looked out of the window. He had once had a similar conversation with the Congressman representing Darien, Connecticut. The Congressman was 'enquiring' why the Naval Academy required everyone to learn stick-fighting and boxing. It turned out someone had slipped the Congressman a Naval Academy record search. It documented that the average Midshipman suffered more injuries and concussions from the martial-arts portion of the Academy's physical education programs than players suffered on the navy's famous football team.

The Congressman had been appalled. Even more so when he learned Pete had read the report with obvious approval. Pete had pointed out the instructors were trying to teach each of the Midshipmen to become warriors. Not all of them had been wrestlers, boxers or football players in high school. But they had all enrolled at the Naval Academy. They had signed up to be professional warriors. Now, no matter what their past or gender, if they were knocked down, their unthinking and immediate action had to be to get back up and hit back. Not after a while. Not eventually. Immediately – as a pure reaction.

Get hit. Snap back up. Hit back. Without even thinking. Someday it would save your life. But you had to do it by reflex. And you taught it by hitting the Midshipman in the face. More than once. Until each person not only understood but acted. You could never teach the right response through reading a book. And sometimes lessons brought lesions.

He felt a hand tuck under his arm. "Pete, what are you mumbling."

"I was thinking that the best seminar I ever received in college was when I was disoriented from being knocked on my ass."

She wrinkled nearly her entire face in disgust. "As a future mother, I want you to know I think any concussion is absolutely horrible, dangerous and completely unnecessary. You are a smart person. You were a Naval Academy graduate! You should know better. You have women attending the Academy!"

"But women don't go to there to learn how to design or sell software; they go to grow up into someone like you or me. One who is going to be out and about in the world, scuffing around, trying to make it a better place for America. Before they get here, they damn well better learn what to do when they get knocked on their ass, because it is going to happen."

Rachel used her finger to push the tip of her nose to one side, "And just what would I have learned if I looked like this?"

Pete couldn't help smiling. "I'm not sure that would have been the best course of instruction for you – you may have required some very special instruction. But for me – I learned two things when I got knocked down – it hadn't killed me and, even though it hurt like hell, I had the guts to get back up."

"Even if you were only going to get knocked back down?"

"Yeah. Even then."

"Are all naval officers this slow or just you?"

Pete remembered that the Congressman had begun studying his face, probably wondering if he could ask just how many times his nose had been broken (six was about correct, but Pete was no longer sure – a non-answer he knew the Congressman would find unacceptable). The Congressman was ready to move on and talk to someone else, so Pete had not bothered to explain that when the person who is knocked on their butt stays down, you can then easily step on their throat – or worse.

He had decided the Congressman wasn't really ready to learn how life was lived out in the real world. But Rachel was out here on the frontline, "The most important lesson is that if you don't want to be getting up off the ground, you should work harder so you're always on the delivering end." From her moue of distaste, he wasn't sure Rachel appreciated this observation any better than she had the first two. Fortunately, the car was pulling up to her street. Military Philosophy 101 was over for tonight.

Rachel's apartment was accessed by a small bicycle lane that led over an open sewer. Three thick planks bridged the trickling water. The path beyond followed an unlighted trail past a partially completed bricks-and-mortar two-story apartment building. He was going to at least walk her home. Pete used the car's short-wave telephone to check in with the Staff Duty Officer. Back on the flagship, Commander Rodriquez reported no unusual intelligence message traffic received during the last several hours. Neither had there been any unexpected spike in liberty incidents in any of the eight different ports Seventh Fleet ships were currently visiting.

In turn, Pete provided Rachel's landline number in the event her apartment was out of cell-phone coverage. He directed the driver to wait for his call in one of the better-lit areas they had passed.

As the car's tail-lights disappeared around the corner, the black of the city closed in. Down her lane, only the glow from an occasional lit window inched the shadows back. As soon as they crossed the planks, Pete tripped over a loose brick. "Doesn't this bother you, coming home in the dark? I don't think you have a working streetlight within four or five blocks."

"It was better when I moved here," Rachel admitted. "Don says you can measure the strength of the Philippines financial system by counting the number of operating lights in the typical block. Our economic team estimates this will be a tough year for Filipinos of marginal wealth."

"The men I've sent out into the barrios are coming back with a simpler explanation. Their intel is that Emilio is a terrible President and his administration is screwing the poor. Does the Embassy hear much the same thing?"

They were starting past the construction area and he banged his shin hard. He reached down and found he had walked into a loose pile of rebar. A six-foot segment had tangled on his pant leg. He pulled it free and used it to feel ahead of them. It was like using a cane, a very heavy one, but it was a better guide than nothing. With it, he felt out the path ahead. He clinked the bar against something that sounded like broken glass and pulled Rachel left a bit to avoid it. Previously he had simply been following her, but Pete wasn't sure she could see any better than him. It was nearly pitch black where they were.

Two blocks ahead, he could see the apartment she had pointed out as hers. It was easy to recognize – the only lighted one on the block. It was surrounded by giant moths that were flying large, erratic circles around the unglobed bulb above the door.

He forced himself to look away from the light and back down at the black ground in front of them, where he was poking with the rebar rod. After a few seconds, his eyes adjusted and he realized he could see a few short end pieces of discarded one by threes, along with a few galvanized nails ground into the mud…and four feet in tennis shoes!

He shoved Rachel behind him.

There were two Filipino men in front of him. Both were shirtless and wore ragtag shorts, one with a scraggly beard, the other a blue kerchief wound around his head. Neither was old enough to shave. However, each had razor-sharp deadly butterfly knives hanging like talons from their right fists. The men had already begun to circle apart, Scraggly going left and Blue right, maneuvering to get on opposite sides of him.

Now here was where that sweet little fighting analogy he had been wasting his breath explaining broke down. If someone stuck a knife in you, you didn't just shake the cobwebs away. As he shifted his feet to ensure he was on level ground, Pete could hear Bruce's voice "…against a knife, the best defense is always offense."

If you want advice on interest rates, you listen to the Federal Reserve, but if you want advice on knife-fighting, you ask a SEAL. Pete gripped the rebar in both hands and swung it as hard as he could into Scraggly's chest, trying his best to crush a set of ribs. As the man went to his knees, Pete urged, "Rachel, run for home. Lock the doors. Call the police."

Pete shoved her forward with his shoulder while he shifted the rebar so it was vertical and closed with the second attacker to push him back and give Rachel room to get by. He needed to get his body between her apartment and the two men. Then he would slowly fight his way back to join her.

Damn! He felt a sharp burn in his chest and Blue sprang back, his razor dripping. Pete leapt toward him, raising the rebar like a spear, as if he intended to drive it through the man's nose, and then stopped and stepped back so quickly the miniature medals on his chest jangled as the man's knife blurred by his stomach. As Blue leaned forward to get another two inches of reach, Pete kicked him as hard as he could in the groin.

He didn't bother to even look back for Scraggly. As his right shoe lifted Blue slightly off his feet, Pete shoved him in the gut with the rebar and dropped to his knees to use both hands to sweep the rebar in a circle behind him. He had expected Scraggly to rush him from behind when he focused his attack on Blue. He hoped the man had.

Pete was lucky, but by only a few inches. The bar caught Scraggy's foremost leg and spun the assassin around. Pete saw him stagger to catch his balance as his knife flew from his hand and clattered against the bricks. He didn't even look back in Pete's direction. He just ran. Limping, by God!

Pete wheeled to where he had left Blue. He was also gone.

As the thump of running feet quickly died away, the only sound in the alley was his own heavy breathing accompanied by a buzzing in his ears. He stood for a moment catching his breath and then realized his chest hurt. He looked down. The bottom half of the front of his dress whites was already drenched with blood. A thin line of red was bubbling out with each breath from where his jacket stretched tightly across his chest.

Pete dropped the rebar. He tried to press the sides of the cut together as he began walking toward Rachel's door. Now here was where you got to the next level of that lecture he had been trying to give. Life 201 so to speak. He had not even considered discussing this with the Connecticut Congressman that day. You didn't learn this from just one boxing lesson or only one bloodied nose. Whoops. He had almost tripped on another one of those damn loose bricks. Life 201 was when you were badly hurt, but you knew what was necessary to live. You and your body had reached an accommodation, so to speak. You both understood pain was really shitty but the likely downside consequences were much much worse.

Your body would go a good distance for you when asked. It would sort of ease into shock. It would let your will take over... He tripped and went to one knee. Damn, that one hurt. He let go of his chest with his left hand and helped push himself up to his feet. Double-damn. Some of those muscles on that side had also been cut. Up now. Keep on rising. Steady. Start moving. Ignore that slippery stuff on your fingers. Now use those same digits to push the edges back together. Keep yourself going. You're doing great, man. No weaving now. You can do it. Just a few...

Rachel was out onto the stoop.

Pete mustered a last breath: "Call 2-9538. Tell *Blue Ridge* I need a doctor." His body was shutting down. Weak bastard! "Press over the..."

Pete regained consciousness to the sound of a helicopter sweeping over the apartment. A few seconds later, Doc Rogers burst through Rachel's front door, followed by two corpsmen and Pete's personal knife-fight advisor, Bruce Parks. He needed to talk to Bruce about re-emphasizing the importance of extending his arms to keep those goddamn razors a little further away. Doctor Bill didn't even appear to notice the pool of blood on the floor, turning immediately to his cohort, "We need to cut this off him."

Pete had been doing his best to stay conscious until the problem was no longer Rachel's. Now he could feel himself sliding away. His last image was of her beautiful while silk sheath dress streaked with his blood. He felt a hand breaking his dog-tag chain and Bill's voice: "He's A-positive. Hold his arms down and start running that shit in him while I get this stabilized."

As he felt a dull pulling sensation near his pectoral muscle, Pete could hear someone commenting, "Lucky, lucky man! If the knife hadn't hit that brass button, it would have carved his whole fuckin' chest away."

CHAPTER THIRTEEN

A quick knock and the watertight door to Pete's office clanged open. The heavy steel spring behind the hook at the top of the door wasn't nearly strong enough to prevent the door from rebounding off the metal frame and smacking into the palm of a very excited Charlie Harper and his announcement, "Boss, CTF-70 wants you on the horn!"

Before Pete had completely disengaged his mind from the data on the screen in front of him, Charlie had cast the rest of his message into the air and was pivoting to leave. "The Chinese carrier is south of Scarborough and -70 suspects it's escorting at least two of their new Shrang submarines!"

He was already out the door, throwing "The best picture is being projected in the Command Center" over his shoulder, clearly expecting the Chief of Staff to be right on his heels. As his door banged shut, Pete pushed himself slowly to his feet. He paused for a second while the stitches in his chest adjusted to the new position. Good thing the blade had not carved any deeper. The challenges in the Far East didn't slow for anyone and he had lost two days as it was.

USS *Blue Ridge*'s firepower was human and artificial intelligence, not the number of missiles or diameter of the bore of the guns. The ship was essentially a troop carrier chock-full of the latest in computers and communications.

As a consequence, the large, high-ceiling room Charlie and Pete entered wasn't packed stem to stern with terminals controlling dozens of sensors, guns and launchers, as would be the case aboard ships such as

USS *Chancellorsville*, USS *Cowpens* or USS *McCain* – all three of whom happened to be out and about in the South China Sea today. Instead, the computer processors, officers and sailors packing this huge room were busy gathering intelligence and teasing secrets from more than two hundred different Pacific sources, comparing the information with South China Sea history and the proclivities of the region's politicians and military leaders, linking the data to recent and related events at the same time they rubbed discontinuities against each watchstander's own personal knowledge base.

The result of that factual and intuitive process was being displayed in front of each individual on his own personal screen as well as on a forty-six-inch screen hung immediately above each station so that any supervisory might view it. Depending on the situation, a particular set of data might be enhanced by mathematical algorithms that had taken decades to develop and thrown up on the much larger screens hanging high up in the overhead of the Command Center.

In the adjacent room, two men (the previous team had been a man and his wife) with mathematic doctorates from John Hopkins University labored day and night to develop even more powerful replacement algorithms for the machines in the room. Every three months, or whenever possible during port visits, technicians from three different contractors installed improved new and improved software for a quarter of the equipment on a rotating basis. *Blue Ridge* was truly locked into the information age.

From the moment he stepped over the doorframe knee-knocker and entered the compartment, Pete was focused on the three terminals assigned to anti-submarine warfare (known to sailors in Seventh Fleet by the acronym ASW). He was halfway across the room before he realized Mary Ann was standing in his path, her right hand raised, index finger pointed toward the overhead, her left hand holding out toward him the red telephone that would carry his encrypted communications to CTF-70, the Admiral running the American carrier task force. Pete came to a halt in front of her.

She waited until she was sure she had his full attention before she spoke. "I stationed a Global Hawk in a race-track pattern at 100,000 feet. It's a clear day. His visual image of the Scarborough Shoal area is shown on the center screen."

Pete looked up.

She used her powerful laser pointer to sweep a circle on the middle one of the overhead screens, "The white specks in the lower-left corner are the USS *Eisenhower* and the screening ships *Cowpens* and *McCain*. They are about 400 miles west-southwest of the Shoal. Admiral Danway is aboard the *Ike*. He detached the *Chancellorsville* for the Straits earlier this morning, but thirty minutes ago issued a recall order. *Chancellorsville's* now making best speed toward getting his ass back in the game."

She was speaking in a nice, even conversational tone, but Pete wasn't sure he had ever heard Mary Ann say "ass" before.

She shifted her pointer across the screen to the top-right corner. "Those blobs up near the northeast just starting to come into the picture are the Chinese ships. The largest one is the aircraft carrier *Liáoníng Jiàn*. From communication intercepts we know that the others are three of their brand-new Kunming DDGs, along with three older Lanzhous."

Pete could hear her voice begin to shift to the lecture mode. He had never met an intel officer who could resist providing too much information. "The *Liáoníng Jiàn* is the former Russian Kuznetsov-class Riga carrier and was originally built to support their submarine operations. We've not seen this many Kunming and Lanzhous operating…"

"And you were doing so well, Mary Ann."

Her lips tightened. He could see her momentary urge to hit him between the eyes flash across her face right before she thrust the phone handset square into his chest. He chuckled to himself. She was coming right along.

Pete keyed the phone, waited for a few seconds for the electronics to align the crypto between him and the carrier before speaking. "Red Rider, this is Tomahawk, I have a picture of the Shoal up on one of our screens. I assume you are looking at the same. Let's go to a private circuit: channel 21." There was no sense in everyone in the fleet listening to their conversation.

He watched Mary Ann hit two buttons on the red system-control box before he keyed his transmitter again. "Let me know when you are in sync. OK. What are you thinking, Admiral?" These were always delicate discussions. While Pete was junior to Admiral Danway, he not only carried the authority of his boss, it was an open secret in the fleet that admirals senior to Danway assigned value to Pete's advice. Danway could challenge him, but it would be at his bureaucratic peril. Nevertheless, Pete was careful never to draw attention to this unique inversion in navy rank structure.

The Admiral's Alabama drawl filled the space: "I'm not sure. That Chinese carrier has been operating in its normal area for the past week. We always pay attention whenever it's at sea. There was nothing unusual this week, then, all of a sudden, the surface task force sails out of the Bay, and off they all go, apparently right after sundown, straight for the most sensitive place in the entire South China Sea!"

The transmission dropped synchronization for a few seconds, the usual problem with encrypted discussions, as one of the ships turned or a sunspot pulsed. Then he was back: "The first P-3 patrol actually missed the carrier, but instead misidentified the infrared signature of a big merchant and went home to Atsugi fat, dumb and happy, so they didn't scramble a new flight. This gave the Chinese an eight-hour head start. Then the next flight had mechanical problems and the third flight didn't locate them and thought they had returned to port. I understand Dick Covell is so mad he has cancelled all liberty in Atsugi."

"Some days chicken…" Pete said, scanning the second overhead screen that Mary Ann had also directed be put up, which showed the readings from the last three sonobuoy patterns the first ASW commander on scene had dropped. Whenever something heads south, there was always enough blame to go around.

"Yeah, and some days chicken shit," Admiral Mike Danway replied. "Covell tells me his P-3's are receiving indications there are two Shrang-class submarines traveling with the Chinese carrier. You know the Philippines have nothing in their navy that can stand up to even one of the Lanzhous, much less this armada, and I'm not sure how close I want *Ike* to get to those Shrangs."

"OK, got it. I think you are doing the right thing in getting *Chancellorsville* back. Anything else you want me to include in my briefing to our boss?"

"No. Tell him I know we dicked this up but I still don't like taking the *Ike* in there."

"Let me brief Admiral McDonald, give our Philippine friends the news that their island is about to have visitors and get back to you."

Pete looked at Mary Ann and she pointed at the Command Watch Officer, who pushed a button on his console. The third overhead screen bloomed into life with the current location of every Seventh Fleet unit. Other ships meant other options.

Pete ran his thumb over the chin bristle that appeared whenever he didn't shave again in the afternoon. He was going to need an alternative for his boss. It was fairly evident that Admiral Danway was not terribly eager to close the Chinese, and it was not a great idea to put a military commander in a situation that made them uncomfortable. It so seldom worked out well. Using CTF-70 was a non-starter in Pete's mind.

The problem was that, just as submarines made carriers nervous, and might induce aggressive behavior as a result, airplanes did the same thing to surface ships. If they were today going to increase the changes of inadvertently sliding into a shooting war over some Philippine islands with the Chinese, both of those were a damn good way to start. It's hard not to have a hair-trigger firing finger if you feel threatened – as when standing on a surface ship bridge – and all navies are made up of mostly very young men and women. Young people are often very brave, which is obviously a desirable military characteristic, but the reverse of that coin is that the young are often easily excitable, often a deadly flaw.

Of course, Admiral Hallmark in Hawaii had been rather adamant about what he wanted. Pete turned to the Command Watch Officer. "Kill everything except for the submarines."

A young enlisted against the bulkhead by the door they had entered made some strokes on his glass and sixty indicators on the screen above them winked out.

Pete looked at the display of the entire Pacific Fleet area, from Africa to nearly Hawaii, for a second before he spoke to his Operations Officer loudly enough so everyone would have some understanding of the general plan, "Captain Harper, have CTF-74 put the submarines *Buffalo* and *Chicago* on a tight leash. Then call Don Collingsworth and fill him in on what we know about this Chinese task force."

Pete reached out and put a hand on Charlie's shoulder as he turned to leave, pulling his ear close to his mouth so no one else could hear. "But don't use the word 'armada' and don't share with him that CTF-70 and 72 may have been a bit late in reporting about the Chinese move toward the islands. Just tell him what is going on and ask him to inform the Philippines government. You might have Mary Ann do much the same with Rachel to build their relationship. I will talk to Admiral McDonald. I want you two to circle back with me in an hour so we can check signals."

CHAPTER FOURTEEN

"All ahead two-thirds. Right ten degrees rudder." USS *Chicago*, a nuclear-attack submarine, slowed and the block-long black steel hull began a slow sweep to the right. Commander Mike Pearson, who had assumed the conn after he established battle stations, sat back to watch the magic of American technology perform. Around him, as the ship slowed, sonar-repeater displays literally blossomed with information as the distracting dribbles, drips and ticks of turbulent noise died away and sensor data from the sea around them arose and began to stream through the powerful processors preloaded with enchanted algorithms.

"Ease your rudder. Steady 340." He turned away from the ship's control party and keyed a circuit that went only to the area where half a dozen sailors were manning the sonar sensors and processors, "This is the Captain, let me know when you begin picking up the Shrangs. As a second priority, designate someone to provide a continuous feed of bearings out here on the surface bogeys. I don't want to lose track or end up blundering into them. I intend to sit out here on the fence until we have assembled the entire picture."

"Recommend launching the buoy now and establishing the satellite link with *Buffalo*."

His executive officer, Bob Shu, was standing right at his elbow, literally whispering in his ear. This was their normal practice during battle stations. It was the only way to communicate without distracting the other three dozen men in the immediate vicinity. Mike kept his disagreement just as quiet as the recommendation had been. "Once we launch, Exec, we are limited by the buoy's length of optical fiber. Each one is good for only about six hours and we only have three buoys. I was planning to wait to launch the first one after we know something more about the Shrangs."

Mike could feel Bob shaking his head before the objections burbled forth. "You know communications are always a goat rope – and satellite coverage here in the South China Sea is iffy at best. We will undoubtedly have problems getting a good link. You are the only one who spoke with Captain O'Brien. I bet Captain Irwin on *Buffalo* is eager to know what was said. He is flying pretty blind."

Without comment, Mike adjusted two of the verniers on the screen over his head as he looked at three white lines nearly a quarter of an inch long just west of the broad noise sector one of the Chinese destroyer screws was making. Looked like a small ding in an otherwise carefully polished screw. He made a bet with himself that it wouldn't be more than two minutes before sonar would lock on to that particular set of white lines – and, furthermore, it would turn out to be one of the Shrangs. His Exec always pushed his positions too hard. The Commanding Officer on *Buffalo* was one of the sourest sons of bitches Mike had ever met. He was irascible and he was surely going to spin up into the overhead as soon as he found out 7th Fleet had personally contacted *Chicago* instead of him. Mike was not looking forward to that call. Was that the real reason he was holding off on launching the buoy?

The Exec was now running his fingernails across the velcroed area on his chest that held his name badge, his personal sure sign of stress. "In addition, dollars to doughnuts both submarines are going to have to execute some precise timing, especially with all those ChiCom helicopters in the air up there. I would much rather we figured out earlier rather than later how to enable the two of you to talk to each other." Mike turned away from the screen, so he and Bob were face to face. He raised one eyebrow but the Exec kept pressing, "This whole thing is a crap shoot anyway, but if we don't have good communications with *Buffalo* when…"

Bob was right and Mike knew it.

"OK. Go for it. Set up so that, in addition to comms, we automatically dump our tactical picture to them, and vice versa. After that, get Steve Irwin on the line, give him the general picture as you understand it, and when he finishes cussing, put the bastard though to me out here on the conn."

CHAPTER FIFTEEN

The normal early-morning Manila downpour had been particularly heavy last night. A good rain freshened the city air and was always of welcome assistance to the six men charged with the daily titivation responsibility for the Presidential Palace grounds. Several of the trees in the courtyard were blooming, which gave a distinct perfume to the air and made these particularly pleasant mornings. Often, the long rattan blades of the ceiling fans swept this sweet scent-laden air around for hours before rooms had to be closed against the brutal sun.

A pair of white-clad servants were serving President Emilio Legaspi and Jamie Bautista their breakfast in the Palace library. "Jamie, do you believe the report?"

"I see no reason not to. I'm not sure where we stand with the new Seventh Fleet people yet – in fact, I think Captain O'Brien is basically a prick – but even he is not stupid enough to lie about the Chinese steaming into Scarborough. Tomorrow, our people will be able to see with their own eyes! And Ambassador Coyle is more than eager to stay on our good side – he sounded like he was about to have a heart attack."

Jamie stirred a brown sugar cube into his coffee and took a sip while he mentally played back the frantic American Ambassador's call. Bautista had spent the past ten years trying to learn 'proper manners' – specifically how to drink without having a sugar cube between his teeth, the way he had taken coffee every day of his life since he was thirteen. No, Coyle had sounded completely genuine. "I have placed a call to the Chinese Ambassador. He has not responded. Which may be an answer in itself."

Bautista did not share with his Deputy that Chinese Ambassador Lu had not been with his Filipina mistress, which was his normal practice on Sunday evenings. As the woman was a secret member of Jamie's personal counter-intelligence unit, she was the first call he had made after hearing from Coyle. Her input was his best confirmation that today was not going to be a good day for a Capricorn. He had quickly checked the *Star's* zodiac page as soon as the newspaper had arrived – "A new adventure is coming your way today!" For Christ's sake, that couldn't be good news!

"Jamie, why are the Chinese doing this? I thought we had an accommodation? Don't they understand they can't be seen screwing around the Shoal? Doesn't someone over there in chopstick land remember we have an election coming up?" Some coffee slopped into the President's saucer and he carelessly threw his napkin across the whole mess and raised a finger to the older servant who was standing outside the room. "Shouldn't we get those two ships the Americans gave us out there and warn the Chinese off?"

Jamie didn't even look at the President as he put a sugar cube between his teeth and poured another cup of coffee he intended to truly enjoy, "Remember, we only have one left after the Chinese sunk the *Pilar.*"

"Oh, right."

"And those ships were really old American Coastguard cutters. As the Chinese already demonstrated with the *Pilar*, they are no match for real warships or airplanes."

The President watched the cube dissolve in the flow of hot liquid and heard his Deputy's teeth click shut. There were other military options, weren't there?

"The only worse possible move would be to send out our helicopters against their jets."

Sometimes it was scary how well his Deputy knew what he was thinking. The President kept his face expressionless as Jamie placed his cup back in the saucer and clenched his jaw before he spoke. "The situation hasn't changed from what we discussed three years ago. We need to roll over and give up, find a way to pay the Chinese off or suck in the Americans. At the moment, the Americans are here and everything you're touching is turning up roses."

Jamie filled the President's cup. "Your plan is working! Request they protect our sacred islands – the lands where something important happened some time ago, la de da. If it works out, you get the credit, if they fail, pile the blame on them."

Their conversation paused while the liveried man and woman entered and removed the fruit and coffee service by means of a wheeled wooden cart. The female had also cut a corona cigar for the President. She was now slowly rotating it as her sulfur match warmed the end like a marshmallow over coals. After a few seconds, she exhaled and used both hands to tender the cigar. After he made a slow draw and nodded his approval, the duo noiselessly steered their cart from the library.

The President watched the door shut and listened for a click, before he turned back to his Chief of Staff and reflectively blew out a smoke ring, which slowly rose until the overhead fan momentarily twisted it into a spidery figure eight before whisking it away. He nodded. For the moment, they were committed to playing the game Jamie had just outlined. However, there was an Irish pennant that had been bothering him. "Before you go demand the Americans save our poor Philippine butts, and send a rocket up the ass of the Chinese Ambassador, why don't you take a second to refresh my memory on any deal Rodel might think we possibly asked him to make with our pig-tailed friends."

CHAPTER SIXTEEN

"NSA confirms they have received our Notice to Mariners. Sunset officially occurred fifteen minutes ago. It will be seventy per cent overcast tonight, so it would be best if this happened during twilight."

"Very well, Charlie. Shall we see if Admiral Han speaks English?" Pete looked around the little group in the Command Center. He didn't recognize anyone other than the watchstanders and his immediate staff. "Who is going to be our interpreter?"

"Mary Ann."

"Another unrecognized talent," Pete murmured to himself. "OK, someone call him up and shift our conversation to a private circuit."

The background level in the Command Center suddenly became alive with the static and feedback squeals from the different hops and skips that high-frequency radio waves take in the at sea environment. Pete ignored the babble and used the opportunity to make some last-minute checks with Charlie. "How far back did you date the notice?"

"Ten days. That's normal when we close a large ocean area off for an exercise."

"What number did you dupe?"

"A buoy relocation in Boston Harbor. There was a garble on this one in the electronic file. It was corrected in an erratum, but someone sailing Chinese waters would have to be pretty disciplined to have followed it up."

Mary Ann interrupted by handing him a telephone handset, "Vice Admiral Wei Han is on channel sixteen, Chief of Staff." She had donned a headset to keep her hands free. She showed him her iPad screen with the CIA summary information about Admiral Han at the top, along with the one new entry. "Greetings. This is Admiral Han, who is this?"

"Admiral, this is Captain Pete O'Brien, the Chief of Staff of the United States Seventh Fleet. I decided to call you because I was afraid your staff might have made a mistake."

"I do not understand."

"Admiral, I am watching you and your task group steering south toward the Scarborough Shoal."

"Yes, Captain, and just as China may operate anywhere within the South China Sea, we are exercising our freedom to operate near Scarborough. I believe when you do these same operations you call them your 'Freedom of the Seas'."

The Admiral was well prepared. Sounded as if he knew who Pete was and had his cover story down pat. Goodness knows, all US Navy freedom-of-the-sea operations around Taiwan had stuck in the Chinese craw for decades.

"Well, yes, but I am afraid we currently have a major submarine operation ongoing north of Scarborough, accompanied by torpedo firings. As you know, it is very difficult to talk to submarines. It is therefore impossible for me to stop the exercise. I must request you have your ships remain clear of the area."

"I have seen no such notice!"

Pete lowered his voice a touch. He needed to get this just right. For a split second, he wondered if tones sounded the same in Chinese. "Admiral, I was afraid of that. I had the message re-sent as soon as I heard your ships were steaming into the operating area and then I took this unusual step of personally calling you. Let me have my Deputy Operations Officer give you the message identifier so your staff can search for it." He handed the handset to Mary Ann and while she was providing date-time groups to the Admiral, Pete typed a short message to the Commanding Officers of the USS *Chicago* and USS *Buffalo*, "Go get him, //s//Pete" copied their submarine boss ashore in Yokosuka, and pressed 'send'.

One of the messengers handed Charlie a two-page pink – that is, top-secret – message. He scanned it and started to pass it on to Pete, who only shook his head dismissively, "Ambassador Coyle?"

"Yes."

"Anything new?"

Charlie read it more slowly, "No, a repeat of the same points he made earlier today. It is important China does not get a foothold in the Shoal. The Philippines does not have the assets to resist militarily. It is all up to us, etc."

"He's writing for his memoirs in the event this goes south."

There was a squeal over the compartment loudspeakers as the high-frequency circuit once again came alive: "Captain O'Brien?"

"Yes, Admiral Han."

"I must insist that you call off this exercise and reschedule it in the future at a time that gives us the proper notice."

Mary Ann typed on her iPad. "We are in luck! They can't find the old message!"

Pete gave her a thumbs-up before keying the phone. "Admiral, you operate with submarines. You know any communication with them is difficult and nothing is possible at this late hour."

Pete paused and then rekeyed his transmitter, "Admiral, my sources indicate you are already in our exercise area. I respectfully request you turn north immediately."

Pete tried to picture what must be happening aboard the submarines. He knew they had been in position and waiting for his message. It was all in the hands of the two submarine commanding officers now.

The message from Seventh Fleet flashed on to the screen and Captain Mike Pearson could not prevent a "Yes-s-s-s!" from slipping by his lips. The only thing more dangerous than what *Chicago* was going to try would be if *Buffalo* and *Chicago* attempted it concurrently – so only one would get the chance. It depended on the relative position of the Chinese carrier. Well, now was go time, and USS *Buffalo* was out of position.

Mike picked up the phone that linked him directly to the *Buffalo*'s Commanding Officer, "Sorry, Steve. Looks like this is going to require a real professional."

"You're an ass, Michael, but a lucky one. Too bad it wasn't five minutes ago, when you were in left field and Liáoníng Jiàn was in my sector." His voice changed and Mike could picture him looking at the tactical display. "Just make sure one of those six escorts doesn't get even a sniff. They will be firing real bullets, and you are going to establish one hell of a datum."

The datum part was a drawback. It was much more daunting than the requirement to pierce the protective screen of all the Chinese ships. Mike was comfortable his crew and their equipment could accomplish the stealth portion of the mission. But no one wanted to voluntarily establish a signboard pointing to a submarine's exact position. In this case, it was part of his tasking. They would have to leave subterfuge and excitement behind as a distraction.

"Understand and agree. Why don't you operate near X-ray Mike at 600 feet for a while? If I get in a situation where I need to scrape off any troublesome barnacles, I will know where there is a piling to rub up against."

"Will do. See you on the other side. Out."

Pete hung up the phone. "Cut the buoy. Lower all masts. Let's go down to 300 feet. Standard speed. Set an intercept course for a position a thousand yards aft of the *Liáoníng Jiàn*."

Mike looked over the plots for a minute, while *Chicago* silently slipped deeper and began to build up speed. Above them, the surface ships had established a standard anti-submarine warfare pattern around the carrier. Sonar believed the two Chieses subs were about five miles in the rear of the carrier, one off either flank. Good. The carrier helicopters were working the waters off the carrier bows. No sensor made in China would ever detect the ultra-quiet nuclear machinery that pushed *Chicago* along. Ten miles to where he wanted to be.

As Captain O'Brien had explained, the goal was to make the Chinese believe they were operating in the middle of a submarine torpedo-firing area, and thus to cause them to then back off from the Shoal, since even an exercise torpedo had enough energy to put a large hole in any surface ship.

They just had to make a case believable to Admiral Han – and that is where *Chicago* came in. While surfacing would, in principle, definitely prove the submarine was there, many surface ships never saw submarines, especially in low visibility or after dark, which might easily lead to an inadvertent collision. In addition, who know when a nervous nelly might decide to pump off a round? No, they would need to demonstrate a submarine's presence without making her vulnerable. Fortunately, international practice was that, even in the era of GPS, a submarine would customarily release a green smoke when it fired an exercise torpedo, thus establishing a datum for all parties to center and zero their relative plots.

Not surprisingly, most surface ships being fired on in exercises managed to never 'see' the green smoke, and subsequently argued they had never been successfully attacked – which had led to some souls in the submarine into developing a tactic that was absolutely forbidden and totally irresponsible. Pete had discussed it with Mike for several minutes. It was an experience the Chinese carrier was about to undergo.

Mike turned to his Executive Officer, Bob Shu. "Rise time for the smoke?"

"Actually, a prosperous flare, sir. It goes nearly 500 feet in the air."

"Right." Mike kept his voice patient. "Rise time through the water after release from the signal ejector?"

"Eight seconds. And given the carrier dimensions, we are good for up to a 15-knot crosswind and a 38-knot headwind. Last time we were at periscope depth, it looked like sea state four, so I estimate wind speeds between 11 and 16."

One of the watchstanders at the exec's elbow made some entries and the exec read out the results: "At six knots, we need to be 780 to 810 yards ahead of him at this depth."

"Very well."

"Sir, remember the forward signal ejector won't work at speeds greater than ten knots."

Mike announced clearly to everyone in Control: "I have the conn. Make your depth six hundred feet. Come left to 352." He changed his tone to an informational one for everyone in the compartment to hear. "We're going to steer directly under the *Liáoníng Jiàn*, then pull out slightly ahead of it, release two flares that I expect to land on its flight deck, use our rudder to leave a big knuckle in the water for them to attack while we disappear like a gray ghost in the mist. Anyone have any questions?"

Mike saw several grins and no grimaces. Good. "Bob, you take a team and man the signal ejector. On my signal, I expect you to get two of them off in thirty seconds. We will be below ten knots for about thirty seconds. I'll handle things here. We are going to first drive under the closest Kunming DDG. No one in that class can hear a train in a tunnel. All ahead full."

Mike adjusted *Chicago*'s course slightly to avoid anything the Kunming might be towing, while Bob put aside his headset and raced toward the forward signal ejector.

Petty Officer Harry Richards had the sound-powered headset on and two green flares broken out of the pyrotechnics locker when the Exec arrived. Petty Officer White had a bale of rags standing by, because, no matter how careful you drained the barrel, seawater inevitably ran over the deck and threatened something electrical. "OK, men. We're going to have lots of time to drain the barrels, so just make it routine. Does someone have the check sheet?"

Richards raised the white plastisoled sheet and Bob took it to read. He had reviewed it last night. They were actually going to have only seconds. If one of those phosphorus flares activated inside the submarine, there was no way to put it out, and this compartment was chock-a-block with high-explosive and nuclear weapons. Alongside the signal ejector, the speed indicator showed that *Chicago* was still well in excess of twenty knots and at nearly 800 feet.

The deck angled sharply up. Richards repeated what he was hearing on the 'phones. On our way to 250 feet. "Ready at the signal ejector, aye."

Suddenly, the submarine heeled over twenty degrees to the left and then began whipping around to the right. "They've gone to all back full and full rudder, Mr Shu, and speed is dropping off fast."

"Sir, we're passing 400 feet, going up. Request to drain the signal ejector. The Captain says release the flares at our direction!"

With a roar, the pressure was released from the vent and water overflowed the funnel. As soon as the flow stopped, the signal-ejector breech door was opened, emptying the rest of the water on the deck. Petty Officer White attacked the latter with a handful of rags.

Richards inserted the flare and the breech door was carefully rotated shut. Bob took the checklist out of Richards' hand and reviewed it again. Fuck! They had forgotten to pull off the safety lanyard. The flare would never fire! Now he remembered seeing the flash of the red ribbon as the door had been locked shut!

"We are at 250 feet, sir. Twelve knots, coming down. Eleven."

"Ten and a half."

"Richards, tell the Captain what is going on. Then we'll pull it back in the room, remove the lanyard and reload."

Several men ran into the torpedo room and began to help White finish mopping up the water on the deck. Petty Officer Richards was holding both hands over his earphones to grasp them tightly to his head.

"Captain says it is too dangerous to bring the flare back in the room. He says fire it and assume it duds, then fire another."

Damn it. The Exec knew Mike was right. If they pulled it back in the room, the phosphorus in the flare might activate, even if the firing sequence wasn't completed. "Richards, open the muzzle door to sea. Tell the conn what is going on and request permission to pull another flare out of the locker."

Petty Officer White reached up and tapped the repeater. The indicator needle dropped to ten.

Bob ordered, "Fire."

There was a satisfying whoosh from the ejector. OK, that was the sound of a flare away. A mistake disposed of. Twenty seconds to get it right. "Vent and drain the ejector. This time we do it step by step."

Pressurized water shot out of the drain and sprayed over the men and the adjacent equipment. "Shut the valve!" Bob yelled. "The muzzle door is fouled." He looked at Richards. Both of them were thinking the same thing. The ball valve was probably hung up on the red silk ribbon attached to the pin they should have removed.

"Let's cycle the valve, sir. Maybe it will unfoul."

"I agree." He recalled how he had almost made a mistake with the flare. "Tell the Captain first."

Ten seconds later, "The Captain agrees. He says fire again, then recycle the valve twice to cut the silk."

Neither one of them breathed until they had hydraulically rotated the muzzle door and it was shut again. Bob turned again to Petty Officer White: "Vent and drain the ejector."

When the water drained normally, everyone in the room knew they had dodged a bullet.

"Captain O'Brien!"

"Yes, Admiral Han."

"A green flare has just landed on the flight deck of the *Liáoníng Jiàn*! This is a fire risk! It endangers my pilots. I must formally protest."

Someone in the *Blue Ridge* Command Center quietly interjected, "And it scared the shit out of all of us!" and Pete shook his head warningly at the speaker before he keyed his handset to reply.

"Submarines routinely fire green flares during exercises. It is a good thing I called and warned you, Admiral. I respectfully request you reverse course and turn north."

CHAPTER SEVENTEEN

The Honorable Feliciano Segura Toseña and Archbishop Antonio Luis Ver sat without speaking at the large table adjacent to the carved wooden screen dividers that separated the dining area from the kitchen in the Toseña home. The five-bladed fan above them slowly stirred the air. It also undulated the newspapers on the table – *The Inquirer* and *The Times* from Manila – and *The Star* that had been flown in this morning from Cebu. All the newspapers had headlines speaking to the recent Chinese incursion into Philippine waters and hinting at a US Navy proactive response. Toseña and Ver were ignoring the papers and listening to a television normally hidden behind a decorative wooden wall panel. It was tuned to the most popular Manila station, GMA-7. On the screen, a breathless announcer was showing satellite photos of the South China Sea and drawing arrows on the satellite photos to discriminate between the Shoal and the Chinese ships.

The Archbishop was holding his reading glasses by their stems, This particular act was harmless, but unless he was very careful to avoid twirling them when he was stressed, he found he needed to replace a pair nearly every other month, which was a needless expense for the diocese. "I wonder where they got these pictures?" he asked.

"You can buy them commercially." Toseña's tone was dismissive. "Someone just had to tell them where and when."

"And the real question is do we Filipinos want the Chinese owning our Shoal and our sea?"

She looked at her closest friend for a few seconds. "Is that the real question, or is it whether or not we want to spend another fifty years dependent on the United States? Why was Emilio so eager to give the US Navy credit for the Chinese backing off?"

"I understand rumor has it the Americans actually did a good job in preventing the Philippines Government from being embarrassed. I've heard from several people that Kristina's new friend, Captain O'Brien, was particularly decisive." The Archbishop observed his compatriot while he spoke, but his words garnered no visible reaction. He folded his glasses, tucking them away in an inner pocket (a pair saved!) and returned his gaze to the television.

"No matter what you say, Antonio. I will never forgive the Americans for not better protecting Francis." Toseña took a strand of hair that had fallen down out of her bun and secured it. "But that is not the real issue. We need to be able to make our own decisions. We are not a small country. If we can't afford to fight the Chinese, we at least need to have our own sting, not one begged or borrowed from someone we will then owe. With all our islands and all of our smuggling and trade, we need and should be able to afford a coast guard and navy larger than one second-hand ship that only gets underway sometimes and another that disappeared at sea with all hands." She paused and flicked her hand at the newspapers covering the table, "If nothing else, we should develop a Philippine answer to our Chinese problem – not one controlled by someone halfway around the world who has never even eaten *longganisa*."

She grabbed the clicker and turned the television off. "We also need a better leader than that worthless Legaspi and his fat sidekick." She was speaking more to herself than her companion. "We need someone that spends more time taking care of our people than trying on new clothes, flying off to expensive meetings about matters that don't affect the Phillipines, or figuring out how to extort his next bribe."

She stopped and neither of them spoke for several minutes. Maria poked her head in the room, noted the silence, entered and provided them with coffee. As she left the room, the flounce of her skirt reinforced the flow from one of the blades of the overhead fan and the front page of *The Inquirer* rippled. The headline "US Navy saves Shoal" slid two inches nearer the edge of the table.

Finally, Toseña audibly sighed. "Will you support me, and is it even possible?"

Archbishop Ver's glasses were back in his hand and twirling. "You do realize that Holy Week is in a fortnight, the election is in May and Emilio has a machine at his disposal that, last time, delivered 86 per cent of the vote?"

"Most bought or miscounted!"

In the Archbishop's humble opinion, precisely the kind of votes that tended to stick. But his friend was interested in a personal answer. One of the eyeglass stems snapped in his fingers. "Well, then – as long as I live and probably not."

CHAPTER EIGHTEEN

Despite the several television vans haphazardly parked near the cemetery's main entrance, the Seventh Fleet driver was able to locate a parking place less than two blocks away. Even better, a large tree shaded much of the car so Pete didn't feel guilty leaving the driver and joining the crowd walking up the gentle hill. Rachel carried a new parasol and Pete the heavy wicker picnic basket she had brought from the Embassy.

He was still not quite sure of the purpose of this excursion Rachel had invited him on. "Explain this to me again."

"According to the Manila grapevine, Feliciaño Toseña has decided to challenge Emilio for the Philippine presidency. She's never been in politics before and the election is only seven weeks away, so her run seems quixotic,at best. On the other hand, she has some name recognition. Her family is one of the best known in the Philippines." Rachel twirled her bright yellow umbrella and the silver-tipped handle gave off flashes in the sun. "Reportedly, she intends to announce her candidacy today at the family gravesite." She waved her arm around at the people headed up to toward the resting place of many of Manila's finest. "If true, my guess is these are her core supporters – or maybe Emilio Legaspi's spies."

"And you are?"

"Following the Ambassador's orders to extend his best regards before she announces. I was also looking for an occasion to invite you somewhere where men don't have long knives." She ran her hand along his forearm for a second, brushing the blond hair growing there back and forth a couple of times. "I thought you might like to share with me some detail about what happened with the Chinese and the Shoal. There wasn't that much in your official report. The Ambassador was very pleased and your Admiral told him it was all your doing." She brushed at something, real or imaginary, on his shoulder. "You know we girls get all weak in the knees when we talk to men in uniform about warfare."

Pete chuckled. "Rachel, you forget that I've seen you in action. When I was with you, the only men I saw wobbling were those you shoved."

They walked another several feet before Pete asked again, "I certainly know from experience that Madame Feliciaño is an odd bird, but why in the world would she announce her candidacy in a graveyard?"

They were passing a couple of tin sheets newly stenciled 'Property of the US Navy' alongside an open cooking pit. Apparently, the navy presence was already contributing to the local economy.

"Her husband, Francis, was one of the also-rans in the last election, losing to Emilio. It was before I reported to the Philippines for duty, but our files hint that there were allegations of rampant voter fraud. Whatever might actually have happened, complaints didn't have any real effect, because Emilio controlled the Philippine Army. The army's always been the final court of appeals in the Far East, and that was true during the last election in the Philippines. Francis was probably going to challenge Emilio again this time, but he had a fatal accident in the States."

There was something floating in the back of Pete's mind about a murder in San Diego, but he couldn't get it to come clear. In the meantime, walking with Rachel was always a pleasant experience. She was a tactile person and her fingers were always busy. They were constantly bridging the distance between their two bodies, smoothing and ruffling the hair on his forearm, touching the texture of his shirt, hooking into the belt loop on his pants. This was a woman who knew her way around the block. It might be routine for her, but Pete could not deny it was pleasant.

"But the cemetery? Isn't that a bit beyond the pale?"

"We don't have many sources that have insight into her inner circle, but one just outside says she is convinced Emilio paid to have her husband killed. Consequently, she intends today to symbolically announce her candidacy from alongside Francis's vault. Goodness knows what she will say."

"Tough lady."

"That isn't the only message she is sending to Legaspi and his friends. The Toseña family is one of the original Philippines families. On the other hand, there is a persistent rumor in Manila that Emilio's father was a bastard child from a Japanese World War II rape." Rachel turned to Pete and lifted her eyebrows. "The Japanese are not well liked here." Rachel continued, "This is a Catholic country. The crypts in this particular graveyard are reserved for family members born within the sanctity of marriage. We heard another report she is doing this to spit in Emilio's face while providing the Philippine rag press with another set of headlines. If all this is true, today's announcement may infuriate him. I must admit, we in the Embassy had underestimated how much she must hate him."

About a thousand yards ahead, alongside the path to a group of larger crypts, Pete could see servants laying out food on long tables. There were nearly a hundred people already drinking wine and beer and at least five television stations conducting interviews. Dozens of children were playing in the grass.

When they got within fifty feet of the group, Rachel halted to check her hair and reapply a quick coat of lipstick. She extracted one of the four wine bottles from the picnic basket and handed her purse to Pete. "These are from a case the Australian Ambassador gave the Embassy. I would imagine they were quite dear." She focused on the small group of people around Toseña. "She says the meanest things about America and absolutely hates Ambassador Coyle. I need to quickly offer her some of this magnificent wine before she announces." Pete was beginning to understand his role with Rachel. He was the designated basket-toter and eye-candy escort. As she put her hand on his arm and steered him toward the vortex of activity, he wondered if Kristina was accompanying her aunt today.

Half an hour later, Pete and Rachel had been introduced to a large number of the Toseña family, including Enrique Baclayon, Kristina's brother. Enrique had a distinctive scar on his left cheek and, when he was introduced to Rachel, she hesitated in extending her right hand in greeting. The scar disfigured Enrique's face and Pete wondered if he had ever considered cosmetic surgery.

Feliciaño was polite enough to Rachel, with whom she engaged in a cordial fifteen-second conversation, but she ignored Pete, and although he was at her side, Rachel didn't introduce him. Pete was impressed with Rachel's timing. She had gotten in, presented the Ambassador's respects and done so before Toseña made her announcement. The crowd was quickly growing and now numbered many thousands, with a corresponding long line of people interested in personally pledging their support to the Toseña candidacy.

Rachel introduced Pete to several of the waiting individuals as she worked the crowd. After satisfying himself there were absolutely no Chinese in the crowd, Pete amused himself by trying to track Kristina. She stayed well separated from him and Rachel. Not only that, he suspected Uncle Manuel had assigned himself the responsibility to keep Pete and Kristina separated. He was nearly always between them. Only once did Pete get close. In the circular flow of the event Pete passed within a few inches of Kristina, who was conversing in Tagalog with her brother, and Pete stumbled, as if a hot wind had shoving him off balance. He paused for a second, but she continued speaking as if he did not exist. Thereafter, he kept his distance and focused on working the crowd. He and Rachel were speaking with the Adivongs, a prominent rancher couple from Batangas, when Rachel's cell phone rang and she stepped away to talk.

A minute later, she returned, making her excuses with the ranchers, before turning to him. "Pete, I'm sorry. I hate to ruin our day, but that was Ambassador Coyle. There has been another *Pula Alcorán* incident, this time on Leyte. He needs me to do an assessment." Her words of regret didn't hide the gleam of excitement in her eyes, "He is sending a helicopter. It can't land here. We need to move outside the cemetery as soon as possible."

Thirty minutes later, a helicopter had landed in the middle of the street and Rachel had boarded, taking her picnic basket. She waved as the helicopter rose. Pete watched it climb.

He looked at the car and then walked over to a street beer vendor. He bought two San Miguels and retraced his steps back into the cemetery. Halfway up, he met the first set of television-station people humping their heavy equipment down the hill. It looked like he had missed the big announcement.

As Pete walked, he wondered why the American Intelligence Chief in the Philippines had been picked up in a helicopter clearly marked 'Teak World'.

At the crypt, although there were still several hundred people left, Pete easily spied Kristina. Uncle Manuel was falling down on his job. He probably hadn't expected a feint withdrawal from the field of fire. Moving close to her, Pete held one of his purchases up near the center of her white peasant blouse. "Cold beer?"

"My aunt doesn't want you here," she whispered, the strain immediately clouding in her face.

"I sensed that, so I went out to a street vendor and bought my own beer. I didn't want her to think I was stealing hers." He took another swallow. "Mine is probably colder, too. To be completely honest, I am a little tired of your aunt. The better question is, what do you want? I thought we might begin with a beer."

"You came with Señorita Townsend."

"I did, and she abandoned me. That woman is one hard-hearted Americana. You may have heard of those sorts of women. I have given this some thought today and decided I need someone more sensitive. I think I should consider a Filipino." He moved closer to her. Yes. He had not been mistaken earlier. He could actually feel the heat from her body.

Kristina accepted the cold bottle and took a long swallow before she replied, looking past him. "If you should be successful in your search, do you also plan to abandon her?" She was still whispering and Pete glanced over at Feliciaño to judge whether she could hear. Beyond the matron, at one of the adjacent crypts, he thought he recognized someone who looked a lot like Rodel. Maybe it was another trim man with an equally flashy cane.

He looked down at the woman who was patiently waiting for an answer. Her face was now turned up toward him. Her lips were pressed firmly together, cheeks flushed, two wide brown eyes glistening. She was holding her beer in both hands as if it were the hilt of a heavy broadsword.

CHAPTER NINETEEN

As prearranged, six of the senior staff remained in their seats after the morning briefing concluded. When the door to the passageway swung shut, Mary Ann reflexively pushed her glasses back up her nose before again standing and addressing Pete. "That was a sanitized intelligence summary I just provided of the Philippines situation. Actually, nearly everyone in Manila, including our own Ambassador, is pretty upset at us."

"You can use the word 'pissed'. I think it might be more accurate," Pete suggested.

Mary Ann ignored him, "Each has a different reason. The Chinese diplomatic delegation is completely at sixes and sevens. They are distraught they didn't get to emphasize their military control of the Scarborough Shoal. And even more irritated because the clock is now working against them. From communication intercepts, we know their maintenance people are telling them it will be another two months, or after the Philippine elections, before they can get all those assets assembled at sea again." She pushed her glasses up as she looked over the top of them at the Chief of Staff. "We've also intercepted some message traffic in which Admiral Wen thinks you deliberately trapped him into looking foolish."

"I should be so smart."

Mark stopped midway in the act of pouring a new cup of coffee, "Whatever happens, we don't want Wen to know the truth. We might want to use that Notice to Mariners thing again."

Several people around the room nodded agreement.

Mark leaned forward in his chair. "What if someone in the *Chicago* crew gets drunk in an Olongapo bar and shoots his mouth off?"

Pete wordlessly pointed at Charlie, who raised a piece of the rose-colored paper that was commonly used for top-secret messages. "USS *Chicago* has been ordered to proceed under the North Pole ice for extended operations. She is currently on her way to Yokosuka for provisioning."

Mary Ann interjected: "The logistics stop in Japan will be a limited six-hour stay with no crew liberty." She continued, raising two fingers, "Meanwhile, the request from the Ambassador to supply the Philippine Army with American trucks is still held up in our offices. Our inaction is irritating both the Embassy and the Palace. In my personal opinion, this is an unnecessary flashpoint. Jamie Bautista says the army needs them to fight the *Pula Alcorán* and the Ambassador agrees. But if the Ambassador is mistaken and the Filipinos are lying through their teeth about the *Pula Alcorán* to manipulate us, we still have an issue. We may be between the devil and the deep blue sea. We know the Filipinos have a potential Muslim threat in the southern provinces. We don't want to turn them down because they are lying about the *Pula Alcorán* and then suddenly find out they have a budding terrorist problem they didn't know about." She paused and looked meaningfully at Pete, "It might be politically safer just to support them by giving them the trucks and permitting the graft to continue."

Pete looked around the room. "Anyone have any idea as to how to get an independent insight into the truth? We've gotten underground intelligence the Philippine Army is using the trucks they have to subvert the police. I am really reluctant to have the US seen as compromising civilian control. We've been trapped in that position in other countries before."

Pete stood and walked halfway around the table. "At the same time, I don't want us to be right for the wrong reason. I don't want to find out later on that they needed the trucks to solve a rising terrorist situation, even if they are currently lying to us and only discover the problem sometime in the future. If that happens, the Admiral is going to be testifying in Congress on the wrong side of the table."

Charlie gestured around the table. "We did some planning yester-day, while you were getting your picture on television with Ms Toseña."

Pete sat back down at the table. It had not been the most pleasant situation when Aunt Feliciaño had seen Kristina standing close to him. Especially when Kristina had heard her aunt's muffled cry and, instead of moving away from him, had gathered herself up on her tiptoes and kissed him on his cheek. He had heard nicer language from fishwives on the Newfoundland waterfront. Some of that one-way exchange had apparently been captured on television. Nice of his Operations Officer to bring it up. The man had the finesse of a Boston drunk. "Lay it out."

"Well Sir, I have my staff drafting a letter to our counterparts in the Philippine Army, asking for their numbers on truck-use activity. I was at the Naval Academy at the same time as their Operations Officer. I trust him to ensure we get a straight answer."

At Pete's own last Naval Academy reunion, his Bancroft Hall roommate had wanted Pete to invest in what looked a lot like a Ponzi scheme. He was beginning to believe Charlie didn't understand how much people changed over time. "Do you expect to receive any facts we can use?"

"Surely they wouldn't lie to us. They realize we're here to help them."

Ugh. Pete tried not to let his alarm show on his face. At the very best, a written request from the US Navy would be viewed as interfering in Philippine internal affairs. More likely – Pete mentally shook his head – more likely he couldn't even imagine all the downsides. But since many Filipino officers resented the very presence of Americans and others believed the US Army had nearly as many vehicles as soldiers, it would be very difficult for the Filipino military to not consider any inquiry as patronizing. An official letter on this subject might well be within the top ten of the dumbest things Pete had heard this year – maybe in his lifetime. "Anyone have any other ideas?"

Charlie hesitantly spoke up again, "Our first thought was to mon-itor communications in the country with a satellite to see how many *Pula Alcorán* transmissions we can intercept each week. If we're seeing hundreds a week, then it tells us something about the underlying activity of that group in the Philippines. If we collect thousands a day, it leads to different conclusions. However, since this is not an area of the world the US normally targets, it would require a lot of irreplaceable fuel for the National Security Agency to reposition a synchronous satellite over the Philippines. Our queries have determined they are not interested in moving that resource based only on a hunch."

Pete nodded encouragingly. At least the discussion was now moving in the right direction. Any action beat the hell out of a letter! The silence in the room was broken by the Fleet Marine's Texas drawl: "What about those little ships chock-full of electronics? The ones we sometimes use to do monkey business? Do we have one that is available?"

Charlie was electronically paging through the special classified iPad he carried to every shipboard meeting. Among other data, it held the current location and planned schedule of each of the ships in their area of responsibility. "One of them is busy with a National Security Agency tasking. A second is anchored in Hong Kong harbor on a week-long rest-and-relaxation visit and the third completes its Guam upkeep in four days."

Bruce slowly unfolded his knife, polishing the blade carefully with his handkerchief before refolding both and stowing them away. "You know, looking at something from 64,000 miles up in the sky always strains my eyes. I have never believed something that far away can tell shit from Shinola. So to speak, Mary Ann." He leaned back in his chair and cracked his neck, "I always get more from a walk in the woods. I think I'll take some guys and start my stroll in that particular stand of timber where Teak World currently has all their big logging trucks."

Pete finished his coffee and passed his cup down the table to the carafe to be refilled. "OK. Charlie, I like the intel ship idea. I want one – make it two, if possible – of those spy ships circling the Philippines continuously for the next few months. Get the first one on station as soon as possible. Arrange to replenish them at sea, because I don't want any crew members sharing what they are doing with some new friend in a Philippines bar. Have them circle the islands far enough away so they aren't seen from shore. Also make sure they meet the Law of the Sea requirements by staying outside twelve miles."

"Got it."

"Tell them to focus on the cell-phone spectrum as well as any other communication channels the *Pula Alcorán* might be using. Let's have a weekly report."

Pete buried his face in the steam from his coffee for a second. "Now, with respect to what Bruce is going to do, I also agree that we need boots, or, in this case, ears on the ground. We have four issues in the Philippines: the Chinese, *Pula Alcorán*, terrorists and any remaining old-fashioned communists. I don't know if any of them are valid or if they are related. What I do know is that we need to have a handle on each well before the Philippines election so the United States doesn't get blindsided."

Charlie straightened in his seat. "We can't just spy on our friends! That's illegal and not our role!"

Pete sat up straight. Where the hell did that come from? He didn't have time for drama. He rubbed his forehead for a moment, before raising his hand in a mollifying manner toward Charlie. "Whoops, I think you missed part of an earlier discussion. I'm worried about an outbreak of the malaria in the low-lying areas where we might send our ships. As a reasonable commander, I am going to send a group, under the guidance of our Fleet Surgeon, to investigate the spread of this dread disease. However, if anyone uncovers footprints of our Chinese friends, or terrorism, or the *Pula Alcorán*, I need to be immediately informed. Does that make sense?"

"Yes, sir."

Pete picked up one of the yellow pencils Mary Ann distributed and tapped the eraser against the table. "Doc, no telling what problems you might encounter, so take the Fleet Marine and a half-dozen other marines. I'll ask Bruce to delay his walk until he and I can take a doctor from the ship and canvas the low-lying areas around Olongapo and Subic City."

Charlie was again obviously not listening, instead concentrating on using his iPad to compute the distance the intelligence ships would have to travel and typing notes to himself. He looked up from his notebook. "I must have missed the message about malaria, Chief of Staff. Do you need me to write something for the Admiral to put out about ships avoiding the Philippines?"

"No, Charlie. The information I heard was not terribly definite. I think we should wait to take any action until our compatriots return." Pete looked at Mary Ann. She recognized Charlie had just given up his seat on the team bus. She was shifting in her seat, her eyes focusing on the papers in her hand. Pete watched her as he continued his answer to Charlie. "OK if I take Mary Ann with me to translate?"

"Of course."

Pete nodded. "I think we are done here. Bruce. Get the *Blue Ridge* doctor up to speed, find us a half-dozen marine volunteers and make sure there is a definite Plan B for our meeting."

Bruce gave him a thumbs-up and noiselessly left the room, holding the door open for Charlie.

Mary Ann kept busy rearranging her charts and papers until everyone except for Pete had left. They she stepped up next to him. "I'll keep this private as long as I can, but there's lots of little drips out on the intelligence wires and even in the Philippines newspapers, so it isn't going to stay quiet forever. In addition to the Chinese, the Philippines government and our Ambassador, all of whom are angry at the Seventh Fleet in general, Madame Toseña is really, really personally mad at you."

"Don't waste work time on my private life. I've heard the rumors. The aunt thinks I'm hitting on her helpless niece, but that young woman is well capable of taking care of herself."

Pete stood up and moved away from her towards the door to his stateroom, speaking over his shoulder as he did: "I also want you to know that the entire staff appreciates the good work you do. Consequently, Bruce and I are going to buy you dinner tonight. Be ready to go at seven. This may prove to be interesting, so be sure you bring your nine-millimeter along."

CHAPTER TWENTY

"You sons of bitches!" Mary Ann's voice was low, but Pete had never heard her sound more sincere. "You both are lower than the scum... m...m..." she stuttered for a second, "...than whale shit on the very b-b-b-ottom of the ocean."

"Now, Mary Ann," Bruce appeared so contrite he almost forgot to close his knife's razor-sharp blade before shoving it nervously back into one of his khaki pants pockets. "We weren't entirely sure balut would be one of the courses."

She was looking down at the nineteen-day-old egg on her wooden plate. The outline of the duck embryo was clear. The reek of the rubbery white albumen wafted up to her nostrils, mixing with the faint smell of human urine that had been in the air ever since they arrived in the clearing. She was not going to throw up! Pete and Bruce would see. The marine-guard contingent would all notice her retching. The Filipinos across the table would...

A set of chopsticks reached in from her left and removed the Philippine delicacy. "Look away," Pete whispered, and the over-aged duck egg disappeared from her plate. Out of the corner of her eye she saw one last limp leg sucked into Pete's mouth. Her stomach roiled. She belatedly screwed both eyes shut and tightly ground her jaws. Her stomach was about to empty through her nose. Oh God, if it did she would never be able to leave the ship again...

Pete carefully placed his chopsticks across the corner of his wooden monkey-pod plate. "I warned you not to look. Let's get started."

Rotting duck eggs aside, she would not soon forget this night. They were sitting at what was not much more than a picnic table covered with a white cloth. The table was positioned squarely in the center of an oblong clearing roughly eighty to a hundred feet in diameter. Torches lashed to a half-dozen trees around the perimeter gave off a flickering orange light, along with the pungent odor of kerosene. The overhead tree canopy was so thick it blocked out the stars as well as the occasional sweep of rain, although she could hear the rat-a-tap of the heavy drops. One stray large limb bent down and nearly brushed the seated diners.

"Gentlemen," Pete was addressing the five Filipinos seated across the table, four of whom were wearing polo or short-sleeved shirts and jeans, while the one at the end of the table sitting across from Bruce had shown up in a stained wife-beater and ragged shorts. "This is great food and we always enjoy Filipino beer." He paused for a few seconds, permitting Mary Ann to establish a Tagalog translating rhythm.

"Many of my colleagues are new to the Philippines. But, in the future, we expect to have several thousand sailors and soldiers here for most months of the year, which we know will be good for your economy." None of the Filipinos nodded or gave any expression of agreement, which Mary Ann thought was an odd reaction.

"But our experience in other countries is that there will always be problems. We want to assure you we know we need to be open to frank discussions. We are also very interested in what you think we should realize that we might not. There may be places you believe our sailors and marines should avoid. You may have other issues in the Philippines we should better understand. As only one example, since the day our flagship sailed into the Olongapo, we have been hearing a lot about the *Pula Alcorán*. Is this a danger we should have our people prepare for?"

Pete had been speaking faster than usual and Mary Ann caught up while he paused and took a sip of beer. "I would also like your advice on another important matter. Your government has asked us to help them maintain the territorial sanctity of Philippine lands from Chinese challenges. You can help by alerting us to any uptick in Chinese investments or agents in Subic City or Olongapo."

None of the Filipinos spoke for a long time. Finally, the forty-year-old man directly across from Pete drained his beer, sat the bottle forcefully down on the table and stood up. Although he was well under six feet tall and partially crippled, his overall appearance was striking. He wore his hair long and straight so it fell halfway down his back. His left arm was slightly twisted at his shoulder and extended back at an angle from his body. Mary Ann could see one of the thin leather straps beneath his shirt. She assumed the harness helped him with the struggle of keeping his arm in position. The brown skin of his forehead and cheeks held the deep creases of someone who had dealt with lifelong pain.

The man was now speaking in Tagalog. "We pushed the jungle back many hectares last winter. President Legaspi sent his people with trucks of golden rice seed. None of our carabao died. We had the largest rice harvests any of our families has seen. Some of us got as much as sixty or seventy sacks per hectare!" He looked in turn to the men on his side of the table and they each nodded agreement.

"USA may come to Philippines to worry about other things, but we Subic Filipinos only care about rice. Life here is good. Our beer…"

Mary Ann stole a sideways glance at Pete. Granted, she was relatively new to the staff and this was the first one of these informal meetings she had participated in, but this was not how she had expected it to go. Her mind was in neutral, while her lips continued the translation. It was all about rice, rice, rice. No politics. They apparently loved Legaspi. And what on earth had caused the Chief of Staff's eyes to flicker like that?

"Bruce. The bowl." Pete had spoken quietly while she translated even more information about hectares and sacks and rice.

"I see it, boss. Already called. Three minutes."

"On me."

Mary Ann was now trying to surreptitiously examine the rice bowls. There were four she could see. Three were, like the plates in front of everyone, made from monkey-pod wood. The fourth bowl was a bit larger than the other three and ceramic. It was decorated with a blue lace design. The rice was heaped high in the wooden bowls but depressed in the fourth. A breath of wind made it through the trees; the light from one of the flickering torches shifted and Mary Ann saw what Pete and Bruce had already noticed. A gold navy dress-uniform button, still attached to a brown-stained piece of fabric, lay tucked into the inverted mound of the ceramic bowl. Where in the world had they gotten that? Oh, goodness! Did it have anything to do with that attack on Pete in Manila? She resisted the temptation to look around the clearing into the darkness.

At her elbow, Pete was standing, pulling her up with him, holding his monkey-pod plate in his left hand. "I'm sorry to interrupt, but I can see this is going nowhere."

The Filipinos at the table started to stand, but their speaker held up his hand and they remained seated. The leader looked balefully at Pete for a second, closed his eyes, leaned his head back and rotated his neck until his long hair swayed back and forth on his back before settling. The creases in his face stretched longer. His right arm went down to his side and Mary Ann could see the tension grow in his left shoulder where the old strictures must be.

Pete spoke softly across the table, "I had a bodyguard who wore her hair the same way. Don't do it!"

The supposedly crippled arm unexpectedly dipped behind the long locks and, in the same motion, came out flinging a knife through the wildly flailing hair.

Pete shoved the plate in front of him like a shield and the knife thapped into the wood directly in front of his chest. He jerked the knife free while simultaneously reaching across the table and pulling the Filipino to him. He ripped open the man's shirt and used the knife to slice through the exposed leather harness. A board holding several more throwing knives fell into the grass behind the table.

Pete was holding the man tightly and speaking almost conversationally. "I told you I had a bodyguard who wore the same setup. I recognized yours the minute you walked in." He shoved the man back in his seat and picked up the button from the rice bowl, thrusting it deep in his pocket. "Keep your gun on all of them, Mary Ann. Bruce and I will do the ties."

The two Americans quickly moved around opposite ends of the table. As Bruce rounded the table, the wife beater's right arm swung out from under the table. He was holding a curved blade and drove directly at Bruce's gut. As the knife caught and tugged the shirt slightly outward, Bruce pivoted to his right, rose up on his toes and drove the barrel of his nine across the man's temple. The wife beater fell backward, blood gushing from his face onto the grass.

None of the rest of the men resisted, although all were armed. Each time they found a weapon, Pete and Bruce simply cast it over their shoulders into the trees. Within a few seconds, the five Filipinos were lying on the ground trussed with white electrical cable ties. Mary Ann belatedly realized none of the food servers had appeared in some time.

Bruce's internal clock was on the same pace as hers. "Past time to be out of here, boss."

"Take Mary Ann and half the marines. I'll follow. How much longer?"

"Ninety seconds, maybe a bit more."

Bruce inclined his head toward the senior marine. Six of his men promptly headed for the side of the clearing. Mary Ann followed. As they approached the side of the clearing, she saw there was a different path there than the one by which they had entered. The senior marine handed her a set of night goggles. "Put these on, Captain. There are lots of downed tree branches on this trail, so you'll need to take care, but we have less than a mile to travel to the LZ."

"Captain O'Brien?"

"And two of my men are covering our rear. Captain Parks and the Gunny ordered us to move, Ma'am. We need to chop-chop."

They set off at a run. Less than a minute later, she heard a series of very loud explosions behind her. Some light flashes penetrated down the path behind them. The marines didn't alter their pace. As the sound of the flash-bangs died away she could hear the soft 'whup-whup' of the incoming rescue helos.

CHAPTER TWENTY-ONE

"Pete, you have two treats ahead of you. The first is simply this relaxing weekend in the mountains, and" – Rachel gestured with the tortoiseshell temples of her dark glasses at the passing greenery – "the other is the magnificent scenery once we're out of town."

She was wearing a pale blue blouse, the top three buttons undone to reveal an old-fashioned double strand of pearls that lay along the swell of her breasts. Her blouse was tucked into a fitted white skirt, the hem of which slid up a good half-a-dozen inches above her knees. She had kicked off her champagne-colored shoes as soon as she entered the limousine and was now unconsciously flexing her bare toes in the soft nap of the car's deep-brushed carpet. "Baguio has been the Philippine summer capitol for nearly as long as the Philippines have existed."

Pete absentmindedly responded, "Hmm…mmmm," as he admired her legs. "If it's a summer resort, why is Emilio having a party there in December?"

"You'll have to ask him. It's a lovely resort. Maybe he was looking for a certain ambiance." She slightly arched her back while her hem slipped north another inch. "All I know is it gives us poor Embassy wretches a chance to get away from the insane Manila pressure for a few days."

Settling herself, she tugged her skirt back down the inch modesty had lost and looked meaningfully at the mini-bar. "If my morning ablution has passed muster, how about a tonic with perhaps a half inch of gin? Lots of ice." Pete smiled and fixed her a drink, tipping what remained from the bottle of tonic into a glass of ice that he placed in his own drink holder. He removed his coat, folded it once and placed his jacket in the seat between them before settling back into the deeply cushioned seat. He was carrying a special telephone so the Seventh Fleet Staff could contact him at any time, but, for the moment, calamities appeared to be few and far between. It looked like a good weekend to do some personal research on the Philippines government and perhaps throttle back for a few days.

Nobody on the staff was making much progress in getting to the bottom of any of the important issues in the Philippines. There had been no intelligence progress with the Chinese, the Muslims or the *Pula Alcorán*, and he suspected he might be pressing too hard. If the helos hadn't been Johnny-on-the-spot last week, they might have been forced to kill some Filipinos, which would have been damn stupid and completely his fault!

This weekend might also be an opportunity to relax with Rachel… certainly his best adult option in the Philippines…

Señora Toseña had made it abundantly clear last week he was not welcome anywhere near Miss Kristina Baclayon. As the sedan eased off the blacktop to a hard clay road that led up to the resort and the forest deepened in color, Pete considered whether or not he was prepared to simply move on. A faint scent of jasmine had surprised him several times during the past few days. But the afternoon in the graveyard had been nasty. Madame Toseña's shrill sentiments were unambiguous. No matter the unfamiliar Spanish phrases – if he ever saw Kristina again, it was clear it would only be over her aunt's prostate form.

Pete let his head wearily fall back into the limousine's soft black leather upholstery. He would love to grab twenty winks. The daily staff routine aboard *Blue Ridge* normally ran from six in the morning to after midnight seven days a week. Nevertheless, it wouldn't do to fall asleep just yet. Rachel was still verbally unwinding from events in the Embassy of the last week and she might inadvertently drop a nugget. Interestingly enough, she hadn't mentioned the Chinese. Even after the Shoal incident two weeks ago, the powers-that-be in the Embassy still firmly believed the *Pula Alcorán* was the major threat to Philippines stability. Rachel had somewhat shifted her position. She was now terming this ghostly threat as terrorist rather than communist. Sounded merely like a labeling change to Pete's ear.

He listened, silently sipping his tonic. Embassy thinking appeared to be done through one constant prism, regardless of the different countries or varying circumstances. This was not the first time he had noticed this flaw. Probably, if he knew more about the right social science, he would recognize this as a very human failing. If State didn't understand what was going on, then the cause was terrorism. The boogeyman was always the same.

During the Cold War, that swirling menace was communism. Anything occurring not in the best interests of America was blindly attributed to it. Today, the same slap-dash approach was uncovering terrorism under every rock. He supposed it was easier than trying to understand the different nationalistic dynamics in play in each country.

As their car finally eased off the freeway onto the clay dirt road that led up the mountain, the tropical forest immediately engulfed them. Pete rolled down his window and the driver turned off the air-conditioning. Monkeys and colorful macaws were loudly declaring they were the true rulers of an understory of majestic trees that often rose a hundred feet high. Down at eye level, banana trees grew like ragweed along a country road with rusting sheet-metal signposts nailed to the trunks. Many of the signs had originally promoted tobacco products, but were now over-painted with promotions for the next roadside shop. They were tacked on trees that leaned out perilously close to the road. Currently, they were passing advertisements for 'Fresh P-apple! Only 100 pesos!'

The highway also served as the front yard for a number of lean-tos thrown together from larger sheets of flimsy rusting metal. It didn't look like they did much more than keep the afternoon and evening rains from soaking the families' hammocks and dousing the cooking fires.

As the shacks were clumped along wide spots in the road,

vehicles shared the tarmac with darting children. Like two-year-olds everywhere, the latter were completely unaware of traffic dangers. The driver slowed at every turn and several times came to a stop while a mother hustled into the road and gathered up an oblivious naked child clutching a dusty truck.

In the steady process of slowly winding up the mountains into the cool, shady trees, the crowded, hot, trash-strewn streets of Manila soon seemed far away. Within an hour of leaving the freeway, the temperature had dropped ten degrees. Rachel had finished her therapeutic verbal disgorgement and promptly tucked her chin into her shoulder and closed her eyes. When she did, Pete could see blue shadows of fatigue on her eyelids. He watched the driver slowly navigate the twisting, two-lane dusty road for a while before he also dropped into sleep. He only awoke as they began the climb on the last hill before the resort town.

"Welcome! Pete, I am so happy you could come!" Ambassador Coyle was standing in front of an ornate four-story hotel, The Manor. The three wings, each nearly a hundred yards long, spread halfway around the large drive circle that fronted the hotel. Rachel had told him the Embassy was taking both the third and fourth floors of one wing for the entire weekend in Baguio and Pete had reserved a room on the second floor of the same wing.

He quickly opened his door and moved around the sedan to meet the Ambassador on the first step. He made small talk and commented on the beauty of the locale in order to give Rachel time to collect herself. She had been softly snoring when they pulled into the driveway that led to The Manor.

The Ambassador beamed. "This is a great place! Rachel's going to be busy each morning, but there should be sufficient time in the afternoon for the two of you to enjoy the amenities." He grandly gestured around the grounds. "I understand the stables are excellent and, of course, the golf course is world famous, although a bit difficult, I am afraid. And there is also the pool, the saunas and the spa." He frowned as he paused for a breath and to reignite his smile, "I have planned a cocktail party tonight in the Piano Bar that I hope you can attend. It will run from six to eight and will segue into dinner. Emilio is flying up here from the capitol and I know he wanted to talk to you about when Seventh Fleet is going to support his request for the trucks."

"I would love to attend, sir, thank you…" Pete lost the Ambassador's attention to the pair of shapely legs that were swinging out of the backseat of the automobile. "Rachel, dear, you look as lovely as ever!" Rachel's hair was brushed, lipstick freshly applied and Pete could smell peppermint in the air. She gave Pete a thank-you wink before she was enveloped in the Ambassador's firm hug. The bellboys retrieved their luggage from the vehicle and Pete left her talking with her boss. He needed to accompany his luggage to ensure he, not an overly helpful bellboy, performed the unpacking. There was an M2 Beretta pistol in his bag, as well as two seventeen-bullet magazines, all three of which were in need of a secure, but accessible, storage location for the weekend. He also wanted to conduct a reconnaissance walk in the forest around the hotel before darkness settled in.

Pete rapped on her fourth-floor door promptly at six. Rachel, as expected, was lovely in a simple sleeveless black sheath, which dipped in the back enough to expose her shoulder blades, but only enough in the front to highlight the same pearls she had worn for the drive. Pete had shifted to his blue dinner dress cut-away jacket with miniature medals and the bright gold stripes that circled each sleeve halfway from his cuff to his elbow. They entered the piano bar to find Legaspi in earnest conversation with Don in one corner of the large room. Since there were very few early attendees, it seemed natural for Pete and Rachel to pick up drinks from the bartender's tray and join her boss and the President, both of whom openly appreciated Rachel's swaying walk across the room. The four had exchanged pleasantries for a few seconds when two beautiful young Filipinas also arrived. The President and Don introduced both, and their attentiveness indicated the two young women were their companions for evening.

When the room began to include a substantial number of other stunning young ladies, Pete began to suspect that one reason this conference was conveniently held in Baguio was that it was five hours from Manila – and Mrs Legaspi and Mrs Collingsworth.

Sometime later, Pete was standing alongside one of the indoor miniature palms, amusing himself by attempting to differentiate between wives and mistresses, when President Legaspi joined him, "Captain, I hope you are enjoying our summer capitol?"

"It's very pleasant. I'm surprised how much cooler it is than Manila."

Legaspi caught a waiter's eye and motioned for another drink for both of them. "I trust the *Blue Ridge* sailors are enjoying Olongapo?"

"I hear nothing but praise for the traditional Philippine friendliness."

The President seemed pleased, raised his drink and tapped Pete's glass before taking two deep swallows of his own. "The Philippines are again a good base for America. You will have no problems here. If you do, you must contact me directly. I also want to personally thank you for ensuring I was not embarrassed by the Chinese. That was a great start to our relationship. You note I appreciate what you Americans have done for the Philippines instead of criticizing, as Madame Toseña so frequently does."

"I am afraid I do not follow Philippine politics, sir. I find it best to leave such matters to you professionals."

President Legaspi smiled approval and slightly rattled his ice cubes as his face took on a pensive look.

Pete silently sipped at his own glass of tonic water and waited on the President. Legaspi downed the dregs of his drink with a flourish and shifted topics. "Don tells me the Embassy has already sent a message of support."

Pete raised a querying eyebrow.

The President lowered his voice and leaned closer to Pete's chest. "For the fucking trucks!"

So much for saving the President's ass from the Chinese. How long had that goodwill lasted? Eight seconds? Twelve?

The much shorter man leaned away so he wasn't forced to look directly up at Pete. "Where is the Seventh Fleet's accompanying message of support, Captain? Is your staff trying to remember how to spell 'trucks'?" His voice was low, but nasty and getting meaner with every syllable uttered. "Do they also want help in spelling 'Muslim terrorist' or '*Pula Alcorán*'?"

Pete sipped again on his tonic water as he gazed coolly at the President. This had become a very interesting conversation. Since trucks were ostensibly military equipment, the White House would not reply to the Ambassador's recommendation without at least hearing from the Pentagon and Seventh Fleet. Although the President could do anything he wanted, he probably wouldn't make a final determination without Defense agreement. But before getting to the issue, how the hell did the Filipinos know about the deliberations going on within the Fleet Staff? The knowledge of exactly what they were considering was restricted to a very few people. Who was the leak?

Or was President Legaspi merely fishing with a very imaginative hook?

CHAPTER TWENTY-TWO

Pete stood to the right of the women's tee box. He was holding both of their bags erect while Rachel steadied her pink ball atop a long white tee. She straightened up for a moment to look up the long hill to the green, re-bent her knees, flexed her shoulders and set her feet. She positioned the large head of the driver an inch short of the ball and, without further ado, began her swing, pivoting her hips and powerfully sweeping the club through the ball. When the second bounce took the pink spot beyond the white one already lying in the fairway, the corners of her mouth turned up.

Pete laughed. "Proud of yourself?"

"Yes. Were you paying attention so you can see how it's done?"

"I always watch you carefully. I think your hips waggled a bit more this time."

She playfully arced her tee end-over-end at him before accepting the head cover he handed her and shouldered her bag. There was only time for nine holes before dinner, but both had wanted to stretch their legs. No one was ahead of them and there was an open fairway behind, so the round had been particularly pleasant so far. Pete had taken the precaution of including a nine-millimeter and an extra clip in the most accessible pocket of his golf bag.

His second shot was right of the green, but stopped short of the trees and the chittering monkeys that dwelt there. Rachel spun her ball down on the right edge, but it didn't hold the green, so they walked together along the right of the narrow fairway. As they walked, they kept a watch out for snakes, each retaining in their hands the iron they had just used.

"Rachel, I never asked where you grew up or what you did before you joined the State Department."

"Montpelier, Idaho, population two thousand and one. My sister and I shared the secret knowledge that our departure for college dropped it down one cartographic level, but no one ever repainted the sign that sits on the main highway coming into town."

"What's in Montpelier?"

"Level ground, which is hard to find near the Rockies, along with water. So, it was a great place for farming. Since I left, they've also developed tourism. There's fishing in the lake and lots of winter snow in the surrounding mountains for skiing and snowboarding."

A coconut unexpectedly landed four feet in front of them, rolled past their feet a few yards further out into the fairway. The grassy plunk was accompanied by high-pitched screeches from the nearby trees.

Rachel giggled at Pete's startled expression. "Whoops, we walked too near the monkeys." She detoured back towards the center of the fairway. "Another one of the natural hazards of playing golf in the Philippines. If you get too close to those particular hazards, it's best to just drop a new ball."

Pete chipped up on the green while Rachel was still examining the surroundings. "I should have seen the coconuts lying on the fringe of the fairway. We aren't the only golfers who have been bombarded today. In addition to the snakes and occasional alligator, nearly every golf course here has a pack of monkeys who delight in scaring the golfers. We were just lucky they had coconuts to throw."

"Why?"

"Because if they don't have anything else to heave, you may find yourself covered with monkey poo. They seem to have an unlimited supply of that."

They reached the green and Pete grasped the flag, wrapping it around the stick. "Let's return to Montpelier – how did your family get there?"

She circled behind her ball and took one look at the line before quickly stroking a ten-foot putt. During the last two feet, it curled at least six inches before dropping noisily into the middle of the plastic cup. "My great-great-grandparents were Mormons who emigrated from Wales. They landed in New York and immediately joined a wagon train westbound for the holy land of Salt Lake City.

"They were homesteaders scratching out a living when gold was found in California. My maternal grandfather left his wife with his brother's family and joined the gold rush. He was one of the lucky ones – he wasn't tempted into staying too long, because he had a family waiting. After three years, he sold his strike, returned to Montpelier and expanded the ranch."

They had reached the next hole, a downhill short par three. Here, men and women used the same tee box. The green below them was nearly surrounded by five different sand traps, two with deep lips on the green side. There was water to the left as well as behind the green.

Pete dropped a ball and got a solid seven iron to bite, leaving the ball within six feet of the pin. "So, you grew up with lots of cousins?"

"I think, even today, everyone in that town but the bartender is a relative by blood or marriage, and even the barkeep may be a bastard relation." She wasn't looking at him, hesitating between a four and five iron as she tried to judge how far the green was below their feet.

"I think I've heard of your hometown," he said with mock seriousness. "Isn't it the one with more millionaires than Sun Valley?" As he spoke, he was looking at the woods around them. He could swear he had glimpsed some movement.

She smiled and pulled the four from the bag, choosing to hit the ball off a tee to slightly reduce her length. Both choices proved to be mistakes, as her ball flew the pin and didn't pull up on the back of the green, but luckily, buried itself in the sand trap there, rather than skipping into the pond.

"You're a lucky woman. That soft sand saved you a penalty stroke. It's obvious you're a direct descendant of someone who struck gold. In fact, I hope you have some of that family money left, because you are going to owe me big time unless you can get up and down from there."

He hadn't seen any further movement in the evergreens, but while Rachel moaned about her poor luck, he half-undid the zipper on the bag pocket in which he had stored the Beretta. He could swear he had seen the distinctive manner Kristina's brother held his shoulders. If it were Enrique, what the hell was he doing up here?

"Really? Then let's make this interesting. It seems, Captain, you've forgotten I'm the one who's two up with only three holes to go. How about if we increase our wager?"

"Sure. Your game is completely falling apart. You won't find the next two greens without a seeing-eye dog. What do you propose?"

"In addition to the twenty dollars, loser buys the cold beer after the round and pays for a massage at the spa afterward."

Pete appeared to be thinking. He pulled out his money clip, carefully counted his folded bills and then shoved the clip back in his pocket before replying, "You apparently have delusions about your ability." He shook his head sadly. "I would think that would be a real handicap in the intelligence field."

Rachel gave his shoulder a hard shove and picked up her bag. "You've been ruining my game all day with your talking. No more conversation for you. No more distractions. I was number two on the U-Dub golf team and we were third in the NCAAs. I am going to kick your tight butt."

"Sexual harassment on the golf course is a two-stroke penalty."

Her only answer was to accentuate the sway of her hips as she walked off the tee.

Rachel swallowed a full quarter of the icy mug of beer. "I cannot believe you chipped in from the sand. I thought I had you by the short hairs."

Pete tipped his mug against hers with a clink and a smile. "If you have it, you have it, and I obviously do." He took a deep drink. They were sitting under an umbrella out on the veranda, watching the evening shadows deepen the neatly mowed green. Pete had not seen Enrique again. Maybe it had been someone else. Who? A kid retrieving balls?

Rachel took another drink. "So, in answer to the question you asked before you started making those extraordinarily lucky shots, like everyone else in Montpelier, we farmed the flatland and ran cattle on the open range up in the hills."

"I've always wondered how you knew whose calves belonged to whom."

"Simple, you brand them before they leave their mother's side." She sketched in the frost on the outside of her beer mug. "This center stroke was intended to stand for the gold chute Granddad used on the Eel River in California, and these curlicues on either side represent the elk herd that winters on the far side of Montpelier. We were told again and again that sometimes those elk were the only thing standing between my grandparents and starvation."

She raised her mug to finish the beer. "We had one of the best-known brands in the state."

Pete was looking at the frosty sketch as it quickly evaporated into the warm air. He could have sworn he had seen it...

Rachel snapped her fingers. "World to Captain O'Brien! Since you lucked out and tied, how are we going to settle our bet?"

"Well, I already paid for the beer..."

She stood up. "Which is the cheapest thing at this resort! You're not getting away with that! I want a shower and you can buy me dinner. Then we'll find a pool table. They must have one somewhere. We'll play eight ball. The one who loses three out of five has to spring for a sauna and our massages."

CHAPTER TWENTY-THREE

An older Filipino woman shuffled barefoot into the cedar sauna, wooden bucket in one hand, a white enameled long-handled tin dipper in the other. Her skin was plump, moist and remarkably unwrinkled. She was wearing a worn green bikini. The lining was visible over the bra catch in the back and there were fade marks where the fabric stretched over her right hip. Her long black hair was shot with individual white strands. It was swept up into an elaborate bun and anchored by a yellowed ivory pin with a squared end imprinted with black enameled hanzi characters.

Ignoring the room occupants, the woman leaned over the glowing cast-iron pot and slowly poured a dipper of water over the red-hot rocks in the kettle. Sniffing the light smoke in the air, she reversed the dipper handle and poked the cedar ashes to ensure the fire was well out. She hesitated a moment and then dripped another half dipper of water on the rocks. Steam boiled around the kettle and climbed up into the cabin. Pete momentarily lost sight of Rachel on the bench across from him. When the mist cleared, they were alone.

Pete took a deep breath and held it, letting the hot moist air seep down into the crevices of his lungs. He was uncomfortably warm. He readjusted the white towel on his thighs so it covered only his groin. Actually he was hot. He was damned if he were going to cover anything more. He was not interested in anything that constricted him. Somehow Rachel was managing to keep a long towel wrapped tightly around her from breast to hip, periodically partially undraping to rub some part of her with the loofah that hung above her bench – without even threatening to expose herself! Of course, he had also doubted her ability to squeeze that eight ball into the faded green side pocket. Twice! He was consequently already down a hundred dollars for the evening and had yet to tip the masseuse.

He leaned back against the wooden bench and closed his eyes, relaxing in the wet heat.

He awoke with a start when the old woman touched his arm.

He was alone.

The woman motioned toward a louvered door. She handed him a new towel along with her first words: "Cold closes pores. Red door next."

The water was certainly cold. It reminded Pete of the years he had spent aboard ships, where electricity had been too valuable to waste on non-essential amenities such as hot-water heaters. He shivered, dried, slicked the droplets from his short hair and wrapped a new towel about his waist before stooping and retrieving the folded towel into which he had tucked his Biretta. He pushed the red door back against its long, coiled spring. He stepped into another space twelve to fifteen feet square.

There were two benches in the darkened room, each almost waist high. They were arranged side-by-side in the center of the room, several feet apart from each other. An iPod was softly played Puccini's *La Bohème*. The iPod shared space on a small corner table with a small Tiffany lamp whose diffused and undersized rose bulb lost the shadow battle with nearly half the room. A portable two-panel room divider on large rubber wheels was pushed against the wall alongside the table. Inset into the walls, a dozen fat, flickering candles rested on the sills of glass block windows set high in the concrete walls. The flames provided even more shadows and their jasmine scent permeated the room. Rachel was lying face-down on one of the low tables, her eyes closed, a beige sheet under her on the bench. She was naked above the waist, the visible portion of her left white breast a color dissonance from her tanned smooth back. She had haphazardly draped a dark hand towel across her bottom.

In the candlelight, she looked like an Edward Hopper nude –

haunting, distant. As the spring on the red door creaked reluctantly closed, she smiled without opening her eyes and spoke, "Come in, Captain, and get comfortable. Your pool-table inadequacies have paid for this pleasure."

Pete carefully slipped his gun onto the cement underneath the bench and sat down. He elected to lie on his back, carefully draped the dark cloth that had been lying on the bench over his groin.

Immediately, a soft rap on the door sounded, followed a few seconds later by the entry of two long-haired young women. They were both barefoot and chattering in Tagalog. The first carried a sponge, the other a brass bucket. Below the waist, they were wrapped tightly in flowered sarongs, each elaborately decorated – one in lines of red, the other in images of blue. The delicateness of the designs drew attention to the small size of each woman's waist – waists he felt sure his hands would fit completely around. And – he took a deep breath – oh, God – above those tiny waists they were wearing absolutely nothing! Pete decided to immediately roll over onto his stomach before he embarrassed himself.

He heard the handle of the bucket clink as the latter was set down on the floor between the two massage tables. A few seconds later, he involuntarily flinched as two cool hands positioned themselves on his hips just above his towel. A voice whispered: "Relax. Enjoy" and fingers slowly began kneading up his spine. As they traveled toward his shoulders, Pete found himself estimating just how many inches of thin air separated his masseuses' breasts from his own bare back. He was guessing less than one. Maybe it would be better to think in centimeters – there were almost three of them in an inch. That mentally put the breasts much further away. Off to his right, he heard Rachel sigh in satisfaction.

Two small, strong hands dug into the corded muscles in the back of his neck. He took a deep breath and thought about gun-bore diameters. A short exhale escaped his lungs and hung in the room. A bare nipple touched, momentarily caught and subsequently slid across his right shoulder blade. His body went rigid. All his stress charged into one small room!

The two masseuses were conversing softly in Tagalog. After a minute, the one assigned to Rachel shifted to English: "We blindfold you to build your senses. Then warm oil add more."

"Fine by me," Rachel immediately responded. Pete lifted his head and saw her masseuse fit a black mask over Rachel's eyes, lifting the elastic in the back to ensure it did not catch in her customer's hair. The masseuse ran her fingers around the silk, patting it securely into place and stood up to sweep her own long black hair up into a bun. While she held her hair up, she turned to smile at Pete and held her pose for a few seconds, so he could fully appreciate her breasts and tiny, tiny waist.

She then looked meaningfully over his shoulder at his own masseuse, dipped the sponge in the pail and began to slowly oil Rachel's back. When the lubricant ran down around the sides of Rachel's breasts onto the beige sheet, she pulled the modesty towel away, dipped her sponge and slowly painted Rachel's buttocks and the back of her thighs.

She sat for a second, as if admiring her handiwork, as was Pete, before reaching between Rachel's legs. As Rachel eased her legs apart, the masseuse stroked her butt approvingly and then slowly ran the sponge completely down her cleft. Rachel's gluteal muscles tensed, but then visibly relaxed. The masseuse again turned to look at Pete as she slowly unwrapped her sarong until she stood completely nude. She carefully folded the cloth and handed it across his back to Pete's masseuse. Continuing to hold his eyes with hers, a flat hand on Rachel's bare back, the attractive young woman dipped the sponge in the bucket and began deliberately stroking herself, beginning at her knees and stopping to completely soak her groin triangle of black hair before carefully saturating every single inch of her small breasts. Behind Pete, his own masseuse had both hands around his jaw, her thumbs massaging his vertebrae as she firmly held his head so he looked directly at her naked and dripping partner.

Rachel's masseuse finished preparing herself, momentarily closed her eyes while she used her forefinger and a thumb to pinch each of her nipples fully erect, before reaching over Pete's back and handed away the sponge and bucket. She then removed her hand from Rachel and raised Pete's right arm until it was positioned just so in the air, using him to steady herself as she mounted Rachel's pad, kneeling in the space between Rachel's spread legs, her knees pushing up and denting Rachel's inner thighs and her hands tight around her waist. She took one last look at Pete's masseuse before she transferred her attention to Rachel, lowering her firm breasts to her customer's back and slowly beginning an upward slide.

"Pete, are you blindfolded?" Rachel's voice quivered.

"Yes, Rachel." He lied as he leaned back on his elbows. There was no way anyone was putting a blindfold on him. "Jesus!"

Rachel partially arched off her pad, "Is there a problem, Pete?"

"The oil is cold."

He heard her resettle and the soft, slick, soothing sound of flesh on flesh as her masseuse started sliding downward. Rachel's voice rose and fell during her reply,

"Mine was heated. I think you should try this, Pete. I try to have a massage each time I come up here. I find it relaxes me." Her voice did not sound a bit tranquil to Pete.

Actually, he had no idea about the oil temperature. It was just the first excuse he could think of to keep Rachel's blindfold on. His own masseuse was silently positioning the room divider between the two tables. As she cut off his view of Rachel, Pete abruptly sat up! It couldn't be! He hadn't even looked at the masseuse before! He had been so focused on Rachel. He grabbed at the woman's shoulder. She slipped his grasp and stepped away, moving all the way across the room before she stopped. There she unwound her sarong and carefully folded it, placing it alongside her partner's on the small table before she stood for a few seconds naked in the faint rose light. Oh, hell! He was a dead man. It was Kristina!

She walked slowly toward him, smiled and pressed her small hand against his chest. He let her push him soundlessly back down on the table. She took another small step closer until she stood with her bare legs firmly against his right arm, soundlessly staring into his eyes as she bound up her long hair, securing it with several long pins. With her arms thus raised, it was impossible not to admire her flat belly, brown breasts and the two very long and very pink nipples. The only jewelry she wore was the gold bracelet he had never seen her without. Standing with her lower body firm against his arm, he could feel the heat from her delta reach out and warm the hairs on his arm. His head was spinning. He couldn't believe Kristina had arranged this.

He started to say her name and she anticipated him, placing a forefinger across his lips and shaking her head. Finishing her hair, she bent down and picked up the bucket and sponge, nudging his legs apart in order to place the pail on his pad. She dipped the sponge and began to bathe his chest.

Rachel had been right. The oil was warm.

She used the sponge to circle his pectorals and slowly follow the blond train of hair down his stomach to the top of the towel. Pete watched her breasts sway and the tip of her tongue peek from the corner of her mouth as she focused on her work. She dipped the sponge and ran it down the inside of each of his legs.

Pete reached for her, but she quickly stepped back, once again silently shaking her head. She remained a pace away until Pete lowered his arms to his sides and his head back to his pad. On the other side of the divider, he could hear the other masseuse rhythmically speaking in a low voice.

Kristina stepped back from the table a pace, leaned over, and began sponging herself, beginning with the tops of her own feet In the wake of her stokes, her skin glowed. Pete's hands flexed into fists, she frowned and the sponge halted just below her hips. He forced his fingers to unwind, she smiled and stepped forward until her wet thighs were once again brushing his arm. She dipped the sponge and ran it under each breast, carefully moving the sponge in a circular motion to ensure no square inch of flesh was missed. When the oil threatened to drip from each nipple, she dropped the sponge into the bucket, quietly placed the bucket on the floor and looked meaningfully first into his eyes, and then at the towel still covering his groin.

Pete flipped the towel away. A small smile tipped up the corners of Kristina's mouth before she dipped her sponge and slowly caressed almost all of his previously hidden skin. Just as her colleague must have done with Rachel, Kristina's warm fingers pushed insistently outward against the inside of his thighs. Pete spread his legs until his insteps tucked into either side of the pad. Kristina cradled his testicles with one hand while the soft sponge drenched the area. She placed it back into the bucket and picked up his towel, letting the excess oil on her fingers flow into the cloth.

Holding his eyes with hers, Kristina reached up into her hair and removed a condom package that she silently handed to him. He quickly tore it open and hesitated. When he did, Kristina frowned and took it from him, using both of her hands to roll the sheath in place. She then held her left hand out to his for assistance.

Pete steadied her as she mounted the table. Throwing her left leg over, straddled and sat on his stomach. As Pete held her breath, Kristina remained there for nearly a minute, the heat from her center ticking his metabolism higher, as she slowly removed the pins from her hair, dropping each over the side to sink silently into the bucket. Her wet breasts were soon framed by shiny loops of long black hair.

Finally, she laced her fingers with his, leaned forward upon his body and slowly slid upward, the lubricant from her upper body coating him, until her lips met his. She held their hands off the pad and away from their bodies, tucked her feet inside his calves and wiggled her hips until every square inch of his body had been prepared. Finally she spoke, whispering into his ear, "You have been ignoring me, Captain."

Her voice was accusing. He did not dare reply. He could only put his arms around her and grip her cheeks. He was a prisoner of her murmur.

"You have left me lonely." Her voice dipped lower. "You have made me wanton." She put her arms around his neck, her elbows underneath his arms, and using her leverage, began a deliberate slow slide up and down his body.

Beyond the divider, he heard the slap of wet flesh, but it was becoming less audible the longer Kristina slid.

Again, a sigh tickled his ear: "I have decided the personnel at the American Embassy are not right for you. I have given it some thought and determined I am your woman." Kristina stopped moving and leaned back, looked directly into Pete's eyes and whispered, "Of course, my aunt remains a…" – he could feel her body trembling – "…problem, but I decided life is too…" – she rearranged her grip to seize his biceps and suddenly dipped her head and bit his earlobe.

CHAPTER TWENTY-FOUR

The Manor at Baguio was originally constructed for very senior VIPs Thus, unusual for the tropics, each of the suites was made from sound-proofed thick masonry walls and solid-wood doors. Consequently, when Pete found himself standing at the side of his entryway, Beretta in hand, he was not sure what slight noise had awakened him. He did realize Kristina was no longer in the room. Damn!

Another soft tap on the door. He thumbed the safety off. "Yes?"

"Tom Cooper."

Pete took a couple of seconds to quickly check the bathroom and make sure he was alone. As he suspected, empty. Not good, but for the moment there was no downside to opening the door.

Tom was wearing a white barong shirt over his slacks, the basic uniform of a hundred thousand other Americans in the Philippines. However there was absolutely no sign that he had just completed two weeks in the jungle. Instead of a wrinkled expat look, Tom was freshly shaven, his barong was starched white and his cream-colored slacks had a knife-edge crease.

Tom slung a heavy rucksack into the room and dropped it along-side the door, "Got any San Miguels in here, Chief of Staff?"

The light gray light beyond the window's screen confirmed it wasn't yet dawn, but to give Jimmy Buffett his just due, it was always five o'clock somewhere. Pete moved to the refrigerator, twisted the caps from two Red Horses, handed one to Tom and clicked the bottlenecks before he dropped his body into one of the two soft chairs in the living room.

Tom took a long swallow, sat in the other chair and cupped the bottle in his hands. "Chief of Staff, you look like you were ridden hard and put away wet. I assume some Embassy blond has blood underneath her fingernails this morning?"

Now that he was more awake, Pete could feel the long scratches up and down his back. He had forgotten about them or he would have put on a shirt before he opened the door. Pete took a short sip. "The blackberry bushes behind the 15th hole are murder," he murmured, and shifted to the offense, indicating Tom's barong with the neck of his bottle of beer: "So, from your sartorial appearance, I guess you decided to just spend a week in a cool luxury hotel with your other candy-ass marine buddies rather than getting all hot and dirty out in the field where there might be a little risk to life and limb?"

"I am deeply offended by your typically squid approach to my entire marine brethren, as well as to our personal sense of duty, both of which I represent." Tom took an answering swallow.

The de rigueur rules for military foreplay on the staff required a series of insults, derogatory toward both the individual and his or her branch of military service, each exchange more intense, until a particular volley was fired which was, judgmentally speaking, just short of the point that would instigate a wrestling match in the dirt.

Most times, Pete enjoyed the repartee, but, today, he would just as soon skip to the bottom line. "It was a long night and I have to get back to Subic this morning, Tom. What have you learnt?"

"We spent two weeks sitting around campfires eating monkey brains and sucking down baluts, and guess what?"

"What?"

"We didn't find a single *Pula Alcorán* terrorist. Do you know what's worse than a balut?"

Pete had not shared with Mary Ann that last week's balut was not his first time in that particular barrel. Both he and Bruce had known it was coming. Most Americans found the sulfur smell when the shell was cracked similar to a rotten egg and, even if you suppressed the knowledge of what you were eating, the texture of the balut sliding down your throat was revolting. As a consequence, Filipinos often used aged duck eggs or, alternatively, warm monkey brains spooned directly from the skulls, as the 'rite of passage' portion of a visitor's meal.

"There's nothing worse than a balut."

"Yes, there is." Tom took another swallow of beer. "Knowing you are also going to eat one the next night is worse. I swear I could smell them on my own breath all week. In fact, when I went back to *Blue Ridge* to check on the communication intercepts – and, by the way, all those Agency guys monitoring the Philippine airwaves have not had one single damn indication of *Pula Alcorán* activity – the quarterdeck watch nearly didn't let me on because he said I smelled like I was dying. He thought I must have the infectious malaria there are rumors about."

Pete smiled and went to get another beer for his guest. There was some reason Tom had knocked on his door at 5am, but the marine was determined to deliver that message at his own pace. Pete was now sufficiently awake to know better than to rush him. Playing his game was one of the gestures of mutual respect that kept Tom happy about doing dangerous tasks for his country.

"And the Chinese?"

"No. None of them either." Tom's story would have to be good, because he was not going to make Pete drag it out of him. "There's no room for the Chinese to screw things up at the moment, because the Philippines government is too dishonest for even the Chinese to work with!"

"I guess that makes sense." Pete handed him the next beer and Tom continued.

"Everyone we met in the jungle was pissed off about their own army ripping them off. I'm sure that at least some of the hotter heads in the villages have fired on their own at least a couple of times."

"Why?"

"Because as several of the guys are hearing, the army doesn't really have a retirement system for anyone but the generals, and doesn't pay the enlisted troops enough for them to save for retirement."

"So, why does anyone stay in the army?"

"Aha, Chief of Staff, the hundred-dollar question." Tom took a long swallow, letting the suspense build, "And the answer has been ferreted out by your crack marine staff!"

"And what did my crack marine staff determine?"

"Your crack, brave, loyal, indefatigable marine staff."

"Yes, that same one."

Tom waited expectantly and Pete could not resist yawning deliberately before caving, "What did my crack, brave, loyal and..." He paused, searching his memory while Tom impatiently waited, "indefatigable marine staff determine?"

"They actually have the best retirement system in the Philippines!"

"But you just said..."

"They don't get any money."

"Right."

"They don't, but they do get a monopoly on the one product that coins nearly as much money as the San Miguel breweries."

Pete waved his beer bottle encouragingly for him to go on.

"Yes?"

"I took a quick helo down to Cebu, where everyone hates Legaspi, and talked to a little mustached shit who's the mayor there. He had the story. The army has a giant scam going on. We talked to ten different villages in the area of interest and the story was roughly the same. Remember that all the big teak forests are supposedly designated as National reserves. Each army retiree is invited to move to the area of the forest his old army regiment's control. Once he's there, he works cutting, milling and exporting the most valuable trees – generally teak and some mahogany. The former army personnel thus push out the local villagers who used to make their own living poaching these trees, and, rather than see their families starve, the young men who are losing their livelihood sometimes take up sniping at the old soldiers."

"So, when the soldiers kill the villagers, the army reports they are simply resisting a *Pula Alcorán* attack."

"Recently, they have started calling some of them terrorist attacks, but the pattern's the same. Who knows, if the US loses interest in terrorism, there may be Chinese infiltrator strikes."

"And the trucks Emilio is requesting?"

"The word around the campfires is that, when they arrive, they're going to be turned over to the retired regiments before they even roll off the piers in Manila. The trucks will make it easier for the regiments to patrol their immense forestry areas."

"Essentially, we are going to help one group of poachers kill another."

Tom laconically raised an eyebrow, "More precisely, murder other Filipinos using US Army trucks."

Pete took a small swallow of beer and rolled it around his mouth as he thought. Somehow, beer before dawn didn't taste quite the same as it had only a few hours earlier. "Anyone in the villages believe President Legaspi knows about this?"

Tom shook his head angrily. "Get real, Chief of Staff!" Despite the marine's previous calm reporting, Pete knew his true feelings. From his many trips into the bush, Tom believed most Filipinos outside the big cities were on the verge of starvation and the government couldn't have cared less.

"Everyone we met told us this was Legaspi's personal brainchild. And we didn't hear of any government savings from less military spending going into bridges and roads. In fact, there are lots of rumors linking Swiss bank accounts with Legaspi."

"I think it's interesting that Teak World was most often mentioned as the most likely conduit, but that part may have been speculation." Tom crossed to the refrigerator and put the empty on top. Pete shook his head at the silent enquiry as Tom uncapped another beer, savoring the first sip for a few seconds. "You can't believe the piss they drink for beer around some jungle campfires. My beer consumption is down as much as my s'mores intake."

Pete was idly lightly tapping his forehead with the cold neck of his own bottle. "And you checked with the flagship and neither of our intelligence ships has heard anything?"

"Nothing about the *Pula Alcorán*. Lots of traffic about how pissed the President and Ambassador are about us holding up his request for trucks." Tom looked around at Pete. "Some comments about you and Madame Toseña. Did you kill her fatted calf or something?"

Pete ignored his last comment, "Anything on terrorism?"

"*Nada*, except for the shift in attribution for recent forestry-area attacks."

Pete frowned. "So, the ships are intercepting nothing useful?"

Tom walked over to the door and unzipped the rucksack. "They're hearing lots of chatter about the rising danger to tourist travelers, which I find interesting, and you happen to be the only pseudo-tourist in the Philippines today that I care about, so I brought you some extra toys for your trip back." He held back the green flap so Pete could see the M27 automatic rifle, the multiple-grenade launcher, and an assortment of grenades and magazines. "I also took the liberty of cancelling your limousine and using one of my contacts with the Philippine Army to obtain two Humvees for you – one to serve as an escort and the other to carry you and the lovely Miss Townsend. You leave at 10am sharp." He smirked. "Make sure she cleans under her nails so she doesn't get your DNA all over the upholstery."

Tom reached for the door, turning at the last minute to shake Pete's hand, "I would take the trip with you, but our teams out in the woods are going to join together tonight to visit one of the larger camps. We're taking a lot of care to make sure this particular visit won't go south. In the meantime, I don't like the fact that we aren't hearing any of the normal chatter. The Filipinos normally suspect we're monitoring, but don't particularly care. I suspect someone has told them to go low-tech so we can't track them. There's violence building – nothing I can place my finger on – but it's out there, and you're the only one of us currently without any backup. So, I thought I would provide you with an early report and some extra firepower."

"Tom, I appreciate it. Take care of yourself."

Tom gripped Pete's hand hard before turning and starting down the hall. "I have the easy job. I'm going to be with people I know not to trust. Thanks for the beer."

Pete closed the door and thought for a second, running his fingers through his hair. It promised to be a long day and he needed to prioritize. First, he needed to get the stale taste of the beer out of his mouth. He opened the bathroom door, reaching for his toothbrush and began mentally constructing a list. It was good that he and Rachel were leaving in a couple of hours. He should get back to *Blue Ridge* as soon as possible to personally read the intelligence intercepts. Speaking of priorities, just where the hell was Kristina? She certainly had been here when he fell asleep at 3am. He rinsed his mouth and spat. He was going to have to be more on his toes, but the first thing he needed was a shower.

He reached for the soap and noticed it was acting as a paperweight for a single sheet of hotel paper. The paper bore the faint odor of jasmine.

Captain O'Brien,
Do not again forget you belong to me.
K
310 825 6544

A Los Angeles area code. Had she kept her graduate student cell-phone number?

CHAPTER TWENTY-FIVE

By the time Pete was prepared to leave The Manor, a Philippine Army Humvee, modified for VIP travel, was idling at the entrance. A uniformed sergeant was at the wheel. Rachel was dozing in the backseat, blond hair spread out over the leather upholstery, dark glasses covering her eyes. Her right arm was carelessly flung atop the opened window frame.

Pete stood in the shade of the veranda looking down at the woman who was to be his traveling companion today. He frowned and slowly shook his head. Kristina was absolutely right: life was too short. That thought had been running around in his subconscious ever since Tom had knocked on his door this morning. And yet he still hadn't moved on what his mind was trying to tell him. And he was supposed to be an action guy!

How much had the Ambassador appreciated their work at the Shoal?

Fifteen minutes later, Pete swung Tom's weapons bag into the back seat of the Humvee. The heavy green fabric mostly muffled the distinctive clunk of steel on steel as it landed.

Rachel was already standing alongside the vehicle, just now replacing her phone in the side pocket of her purse. "Pete, I apologize, but I can't go with you. I know we made plans, but the Ambassador needs a briefing ASAP on the terrorism threat in the southern provinces. I'll need to remain in Camp John Hay for at least another day."

As she pointed to which suitcases the driver was to pull from the Humvee, she lowered her voice and looked at Pete over her sunglasses,

"Where in the world did you go last night? And what in the world do you have in that bag – free weights?"

"I got a panic call last night from the ship. There was a snafu and I had to find a place with secure communications capability to sort it out. You were asleep on the table and looked so peaceful – sorry I didn't make it back." Maybe lame, but the best he and Kristina could come up with after they had slipped from the massage parlour. Kristina had cautioned against gratuitously making Rachel an enemy – that an excuse would be necessary – and in the next breath instructed him he was not ever to be again alone with this particular Embassy intelligence officer. Life with Kristina was not going to be easy.

"Some extra firepower…" he stopped. Rachel wasn't listening to his reply. She was already climbing the steps of the hotel, with the driver following her, carrying her luggage. Pete checked his cell phone again and slipped it back into the brand-new multi-pocketed fishing vest he had bought this morning in the Manor gift shop. It had been a great deal. One flapped pocket was just right for his Beretta, another velcroed pouch held the satellite telephone linking him to Flagship. Extra ammunition clips for the Beretta and grenades were fitted in the others.

The driver had returned. This exchange had gone better than he could ever have hoped. Pete slipped inside the car and caught the driver's eye in the mirror. "*Vamanos!*"

They rolled out of the Manor, passing between two brick pillars – an iron gate had hung there when Camp John Hay had been a US Air Force Camp – and began the winding descent through the Baguio streets. A second Humvee, carrying four Philippine soldiers, started up as they reached the first cross street, leading their short procession down toward the heat and humidity of Manila. Everything was moving like clockwork. He checked his phone again. They had left the Manor only five minutes ago. Time to display Tom's goodies.

He assembled the M27 automatic rifle and duct-taped an extra magazine to the metal frame. The tape had been another unexpected find at the gift shop! How was it even possible to consider living a civilized life without duct tape? If excitement knocked, he did not want to have to be feeling around on the floor for a reload. He checked his phone again. No messages yet. It had been eight minutes since they had left the Manor.

Loading the multiple-grenade launcher – or MGL, as marines affectionately termed this particular piece of junk –was a different kettle of fish. He wondered why Tom had included it rather than another M27. He had never heard anyone say anything good about the MGL's spring action. You would have to encounter tons of bad guys to make it worthwhile carrying, and the actuating mechanism was about as elegant as a hog at a feeding trough. Nevertheless, one does not look a gift horse in the mouth and Tom had himself carried it from somewhere. Pete loaded high-explosive cartridges into each of the chambers and held it between his knees for a few seconds in order to check his phone again. Sixteen minutes. Nothing.

He pushed in the last grenade cartridge and tore four more eighteen-inch strips from the roll of duct tape. He used the strips to affix both weapons to the back of the driver's seat, butts resting firmly on the backseat floor. The Beretta he left in his vest – he didn't have a holster and if his adrenaline level peaked, he wanted the weight to remind him where his hand should hover. He was careful to double over the last two inches on the roll of tape, and replaced it in the bag, zipping it closed. He checked his phone again. *Nada*. This was getting old.

The two-car caravan was about halfway through Baguio.

The forecast today was for rain and temperature in the low nineties in Subic and in the high eighties in Manila. The weather would be quite a contrast from the coolness of Baguio during the last three days.

While the break had been quite pleasant, Pete mused, it was surprising that many of the people who had lived in the Philippines all their lives seemed to be unusually sensitive to the heat. For example, the back of his driver's neck was already beaded with sweat, while Pete was quite comfortable. Possibly it was somehow related to all that time he had spent in the engine rooms of various ships. It was seldom less than a hundred and ten or twenty degrees Fahrenheit in any of those spaces. He checked his phone again. Damn. Where the hell was she?

There! Standing alongside the road in a blouse and white shorts, a small denim bag at her feet and her thumb in the air like the smart-ass she was. Pete grabbed the driver's shoulder, "*Para!*" Kristina jumped in, kissed his cheek, incuriously glanced at the weapons and curled up with her bag to immediately fell asleep, like she did this sort of thing every day.

By the time Pete decided he could relax, acknowledging that she was really here, he belatedly recognized another problem had developed. A hundred-yard gap had developed between the two military vehicles and two cars – each of which had seen years of better days – as well as a yellow and black jeepney, were now between the two Humvees. That should have never happened. This was rapidly degrading into a half-assed evolution, and Pete was unhappy with both himself and the sergeant. He should have warned the escort they would be stopping, and their driver was being unprofessionally slow in re-closing the armed guards.

Pete took a deep breath. He had been overstressed in trying to figure out how to get with the right woman. He was harassing himself for nothing. It was getting uncomfortably cool in the car. Pete leaned forward and touched the driver's shoulder. "Air conditioning – *mas calor, por favor*. Also try to keep a little closer to the other vehicle."

The sergeant jerked, his right hand moving toward his gun holster, before his mind processed what was being asked, and he sheepishly leaned forward to lower the speed of the air-conditioning fan. He used his handkerchief to swipe the sweat off the back of his neck before returning both hands to the wheel.

Pete relaxed back in his seat while he watched the perspiration beads re-form on the driver's neck. If anything, the lead Humvee had increased its gap, and their driver had not regained any distance. Pete began toying with a loose end of the tape holding the grenade launcher to the back of the seat. A beat-up Honda turned right into the main street and inserted itself in their traffic flow, pushing the two vehicles apart even further.

Stressed, harassed, that's the way it was – Pete had made a career of acting on impulse. He leaned over and whispered in Kristina's ear, at the same time, placing his hand on her bare leg – by God, she had soft smooth skin – "Wake up. We're about to do something stupid. Remind me to tell you about my morning after you abandoned me."

He felt her jerk awake and wordlessly unwind herself from her dreams. He gave her ten seconds before again whispering in her ear, "I need you to pretend to be sick and ask the driver to stop the car."

She pushed his hand off her leg and slowly sat up, before speaking to the driver, "*Estoy enferma! Quiero salirme del coche. Pare el coche inmediatamente o voy vomitar.*"

The driver quickly looked in the mirror at her and steered to the side of the road. Ahead, where the road began to bend before it dropped down into the town's outskirts, the lead Humvee disappeared.

Kristina had begun to cough, and was now holding her hand over her mouth as she blindly reached for the door handle. The driver hurriedly threw the vehicle into park and came around to assist her from the car. Pete followed, slipping his hunting knife from the sheath on his left shin as he did so. As the driver reached out for Kristina's arm, he slipped his right hand around the driver's waist to hold the gun holster flap down and, with his left hand, held the knife flat against the soldier's chest, blade tip up, an inch or two below his Adam's apple. The driver went very still, and Pete lifted his Beretta from the holster. Kristina took a moment to rub the sleep from her eyes. "What in the world are you doing?"

"After you left, I got a warning that we might be targeted. I've noticed our chauffeur is doing a piss-poor job of keeping up with our armed guard. So, I'm going to take over driving duties from him. Get my rucksack and throw it in the front on the floor and tape the rifle and grenade launchers to the dash between the seats." He checked the safety on the soldier's Beretta and tossed it to her. "Here, now you have a weapon."

Pete removed his knife from the soldier's neck and shoved him back up the road in the direction of the Manor. The soldier shrugged, turned and started slowly walking. Pete watched to ensure he did not suddenly decide to become a hero. As the man moved away, Pete did notice one oddity. Even though he had just had a knife held at his throat, been disarmed and had his vehicle taken, the soldier was no longer sweating.

Pete slipped his knife back in his sheath and unzipped the pocket that held the Beretta before he got behind the wheel. As he started to pull out into the street, Kristina put her hand on the wheel to immobilize it. "Should I do anything?"

"While I try to catch up with our escort, call your aunt and tell her where you are and my suspicions. I'm not sure there is any danger, but I certainly don't trust Legaspi and Bautista." Pete suddenly frowned and pulled the Humvee off the road, braking to a dusty stop.

He wasn't thinking clearly. Why in the world was he even endangering Kristina? "This is a terrible idea. I have to get back, you don't. I fight for a living..." He began backing up to start a U-turn. "I will drop you back at the Manor."

She caught his arm. "Pete, I really shouldn't have taken time off from the campaign. I promised Aunt Toseña I would at least be back today, and this Humvee is the best way to accomplish that. Besides" – her eyes momentarily flashed a look of irritation – "I talked to Uncle Manuel early this morning and he didn't mention any trouble in this province. We Filipinos certainly understand our country better than any Americanos. So" – she raised her hand palm-down above the windshield, and flippantly pivoted her fingers together so as to push the air down the road – "drive on, my lover, drive on."

Tom hadn't been definite about any threat and, goodness knows, they had as many arms in the car as many fire squads. Kristina would certainly make the afternoon pass more pleasantly. After a second, Pete left his better judgment at the side of the road and pulled out into the sparse traffic. They would either quickly catch up with their escort or not. He wouldn't bet his pay check either way.

CHAPTER TWENTY-SIX

Within a few minutes, Pete had brought Kristina up to speed on Tom's warning and they had reached the outer city limits of Baguio with no sign of the other military vehicle.

Kristina undid her seatbelt, got up on her knees, and began relocating and taping the automatic rifles and grenade launcher to the front dash between the seats. "When you get to a convenient point, Pete, I think it's time for you to discuss my 'shotgun' duties for today."

She was right. There was also no sense in having the weapons bag in the back seat. Pete pulled over into a wide space near what appeared to be an abandoned house. The closest person was a small boy, about five years old, sitting by a mud puddle petting a brown dog. "Do you know how to fire any of these weapons?" Pete asked.

"I've watched people shoot automatic rifles that look like these," Kristina replied. "I have no idea about the one with the big magazine, but it sure looks nasty."

The boy was walking toward their vehicle, his dog's frayed and graying rope collar firmly in hand. He reached with wonder as high up on the front tire as he could. On tiptoes, he could not quite reach the treaded area on the very top of the tire.

"It fires hand grenades. It's simple to operate: just aim and pull the trigger. It has a range of about a quarter of a mile. I've already loaded it. It holds six grenades. Some of these weapons have weak magazine springs. If it doesn't immediately rotate in a new cartridge, don't panic, just trigger it again." He grimaced, "Even if we encounter a problem, we will probably never have a need for the grenades. It's overkill for us, but Tom is a worrier and since we're riding instead of walking, it's not an extra weight to carry. You know how to operate that pistol I handed you, don't you?"

"Of course."

Pete pulled the rifle loose and showed her the fire selector. "If you select 'auto', that magazine is going to be empty in less than six seconds, so be ready to throw in another magazine. Also, if you go to 'auto', remember to tuck it firmly into your shoulder and aim down and a bit left, because a burst tends to walk up and to the right."

Pete reached back and lifted the weapons bag from the back, plunking it down between their two seats. "Rummage around in that bag and locate a couple more spare magazines for the rifle and tape them to the dash, and find another couple of clips for your Beretta. Then we will get back on the road. Since our escort has decided to go walkabout, we're going to be our own eyes and ears."

Out of the corner of his eye, he saw Kristina locate two clips and then realize the pockets in her shorts were too tight to facilitate ready access. She grinned at him before slipping a clip into each bra cup, flinching in spite of herself at the cool metal, "Philippine girls are resourceful, my dear Captain."

He swallowed any retort and gently motioned the boy and his dog away from the tire before swinging back out into the road. Kristina was enjoying herself, but Pete was beginning to have a bad feeling about this. He cast an eye at the sky. The rain was holding back. That was something. A minute later, they were out of town and on the blacktop down the slope that ran to the rainforest.

There was no still no sign of their escort, and Pete began summarizing his thinking for Kristina's benefit: "A real military escort would have waited for us, and the Philippine Army is plenty professional."

He was speaking calmly, but loud enough for Kristina to hear over the wind through the car. He had rolled down both front windows so they were more aware of their surroundings and to reduce the overpressure impact of a weapon fired into the vehicle – a lesson driven home by the army experiences in Iraq and Afghanistan.

"Of course, this may simply be a very unprofessional group. But if Tom's information is correct and we are headed to a problem…" His voice trailed away while he thought, then picked back up "And if I were going to plan an ambush, I would select a location where the road had to be cut into the side of a hill in order to get a full two lanes. To escape in that situation, we would have to go over the cliff or attempt to work our way up the mountain. Trying to climb up the side of a mountain in one of these Humvees is theoretically possible, but slows you down so much you become a juicy target."

Kristina was listening attentively, her eyes sweeping the undergrowth and trees ahead. Pete braked for a curve and eased his way around. Although the road was currently deserted, they were not the only people in this area of the forest. Somewhere they could hear several chainsaws start up.

Pete cocked his head at the sound, "Not so good, but it does tell us what's going to happen. Get four of those personal hand grenades out of that bag and put them in my larger vest pockets, will you please?" They were on a half-mile straight stretch and Pete had slowed to thirty miles an hour.

"What do you mean, 'not so good'?"

"The chainsaws."

"Pete, this area's too hilly to farm. Nearly everyone makes their living from some dairy animals and cutting wood."

Pete didn't turn to look at her. "On a Sunday morning, where you are the only Filipino in the country not at Mass?"

He braked the Humvee to a stop in the middle of the road. He was very carefully looking around while keeping his voice casual and conversational. "I anticipate seeing a log across the road when we make one of the next curves and then hearing one dropping behind us." He put the Humvee in reverse. "I think we'll make the run back to Baguio."

"No, Pete. You are only doing this for me, and my aunt should know if there really is something going on. If we go back, we'll never know for sure what's around that next curve."

Pete pulled his satellite phone from his vest and pressed the call button that connected him with the Seventh Fleet staff duty officer. "Bob, I'm returning from Baguio with Señora Kristina Baclayon and it appears possible we may get into a little firefight. What do you have available in the category of armed-helos?"

He listened for a moment. "That's not terribly helpful." He was quiet for another few seconds. "I don't particularly give a damn about anyone's over-flight permission. I want some contingency air cover ASAP. How about doing whatever you have to do to get somebody in the air over me. Make sure they can communicate on this frequency. We're currently about six miles out of the city limits, on the road to Manila."

Pete terminated the call without waiting for a reply and turned to Kristina. "They won't be able to get here for an hour, which is not so good. However, you're right, if we go back, we may never know what was planned. Maybe I'm wrong about Sunday-morning wood harvesting."

Kristina used a black band to pull her long hair into a ponytail and then removed the rifle from its duct-tape straps and set the selector on 'single shot.'

Pete shifted into drive and quickly sped up to thirty miles an hour. He was going to make this as difficult as possible for potential snipers. Ahead of them, Pete could see where the road closed in to the edge of a mountain before dipping into the forest. It looked like the drop-off on the right was at least several hundred feet. He suddenly realized they had passed no opposite-direction traffic since leaving Baguio – again, not good.

They bumped off the blacktop onto dusty Philippine red clay marked here and there by substantial ruts, as well as low spots that showed cupped carabao-hoof marks that were baked into the surface. Pete slowed and braked again to make the curve before gunning it on the next short section. To the right, several hundred feet below the road, a mountain stream had gorged a path into the rocks. The chainsaw activity sounded nearer now, but maybe it was the way the canyon channeled sound.

Around the next curve, Pete's fears were confirmed – a thousand yards ahead, a thick tree trunk lay across the road. Beside him, he heard Kristina gasp as he braked to a stop. Somewhere back beyond the curve they had just passed two chainsaws came alive and began their powerful chewing.

Many people didn't realize how steep an incline a Humvee could climb. Pete shifted the vehicle to neutral and slowly revved the engine as he surveyed the road ahead. The trap-makers had been careless. Pete had driven Humvees over higher walls while practicing on the American General range in Mishawaka. He was certain he could coax the vehicle over the tree. With a couple of grenades to soften up the defenders and Kristina providing covering fire, they could sail right over. The only danger would be from random fire. Pete gripped and regripped the steering wheel while he considered the best approach angle.

As he did, his subconscious mind began tapping against his temple – something was not adding up. Many soldiers in the Philippine Army drove a Humvee and must be as familiar as he with its capabilities. A noise drove the thought from his mind. He heard the creaks and crash of a tree or two coming down behind them. There was no sense in going back to look. They were now trapped!

Pete let the vehicle inch a few yards forward to put some distance between them and the curve behind. "Kristina, shift to the grenade launcher and watch behind us. There will be some people back there coming on foot."

As he examined the situation ahead of them, he finally realized what was bothering him. On the side of the road from where the tree had been felled, axes had been used to clear the trunk of its branches. It was an invitation. An engraved one.

Beside him, there was an oomph, as Kristina pumped out a grenade.

"Too damn high!" A second oomph followed, "There, that's better. Three of those mothers down." Someone behind them let loose a couple of rifle bursts.

Pete didn't look around. He was rolling forward at ten miles an hour, thinking carefully about the line of approach they would have to take and what might be on the other side. A bullet shattered his driver's side mirror. They were going to have to do something definite soon. Pete pulled out his phone and thumbed the key for the *Blue Ridge*. "Under attack, twelve miles out of Baguio."

That transmission would give someone a clue if they disappeared. He replaced the phone and picked up speed. Then he saw it.

"Miss Baclayon, turn around."

"I can't! There are twenty of those bastards behind us!"

"Yes, but we are about to drive into a mine field."

"Mines?!"

CHAPTER TWENTY-SEVEN

Once he had noticed them, the further forward Pete rolled the Humvee, the more obvious were the five disturbed areas in the otherwise hard-packed clay short of the log. Each dark spot was directly in line with the logical place for the Humvee to climb the felled tree. Pete was positive he knew what lay below those spots of untamped clay. The ambushers were trying to have everything on their side. They wouldn't even have to expose themselves to shoot. A half-second after the Humvee rolled over that area, steel shards, as well as little bitty parts of Kristina and him, would be scattered halfway up the mountain.

Pete wondered whether the mines had pressure plates or were wired to simultaneously detonate by electronic command. He would bet on the simpler pressure plates. "Kristina, I'm going to stand up. I want you to reach under my seat, pull the velcro straps off my seat cushion and remove it."

He crouched up and leaned forward over the steering wheel while she reached behind him and found the straps. He sat back down on the latticed metal frame. "OK, now remove your own seat cushion the same way." Kristina let out an involuntary "damn" as the mirror on her side shattered, and he reflexively rolled the vehicle forward a few more yards toward the downed tree.

They were five hundred yards away and Pete edged over to the right to line up with the optimum climb point. "Looks to me as if those mines are about fifty feet from the tree. Most of the shrapnel will go up. I am going to slow a bit a hundred feet away and we're going to roll ourselves out of the car, each with one of these cushions and a rifle." He thought for a second. "Actually, you take the grenade launcher. I'm going to send the car into the minefield. Those cushions are Kevlar. As soon as you stop rolling, put your cushion between you and our car. Keep your head and butt down until you hear the first mine explode. The metal will whizz past us. By the time you hear the bang, it should be safe to come up shooting. Understand?"

Pete glanced over and saw her nod. "OK, jump when I tell you."

Out of the corner of his eye, he saw Kristina look at her Beretta, the grenade launcher and her cushion, and then rip one of the strips of duct tape from the dash and wind it over the Beretta and around her right thigh. She pushed at the Beretta and pulled another of the duct tape strips off the dash and crossed it over the first on the gun and again around her thigh.

"Five seconds."

He counted, braked hard and then tapped her on the shoulder. She rolled out of the door and he immediately depressed the accelerator and selected forty miles an hour on the cruise control. The disturbed area was now only fifty feet away. Pete grabbed the M27 and his own cushion, flipped the door release and hit the door with his shoulder. Tuck and roll, baby – which is easier said than done with an M27 in your arms – then stop and get that cushion between your head… The explosion drove his chin into the ground. His ears were ringing, his arms hurt and a triangular strip of something sharp and jagged had been driven partially though the cushion an inch from his hand.

Pete pulled two grenades from his vest, removed the pins and lobbed them over the tree trunk – one in the area where the tree had been cut and the other at the side of the road nearest the mountain where the broken branches formed a nest. While the grenades were still in the air, he picked up the M27 and started to run forward, scanning for pop-up heads from behind the tree.

He had five seconds until the grenades went off. He needed to be as close as possible to the tree when they did. Their lives depended on what he found on the other side of the log. He resisted the impulse to look back to check on Kristina.

He buried his face in the dirt on the count of three and rolled, diving headfirst over the log as the grenades went off, and coming only to his knees before he checked the branch end of the tree. There were three soldiers flung into rag-doll positions. Two others were struggling to their feet. One had blood on his face and was focused on loosening his holster pouch, the other was bringing his own M27 to bear. Pete stitched them both with three-round bursts and dropped to his stomach and rolled to face the other way. There was one man alive on this side and Pete put a short burst in his chest, subconsciously noting the Lieutenant Colonel insignia an inch below one of his brand-new entry holes. He then rolled over on his back and came up to a crouch to scan the area. There was no movement. He didn't see anything in the woods above the roadblock. Had their attackers been that over-confident? That foolish? He moved to the cliff side of the road and looked down toward the river. No one.

How was Kristina? He looked over the log. Her white shorts were much the worse for wear, but she was moving toward the barrier.

Pete went to the body of the Colonel and opened his tunic, grasping and breaking the dog tags from their chains and placing them in his pocket. He quickly scanned some partially bloodstained papers from the Colonel's inside tunic pocket. Spanish. He also tucked those away in his vest. The other eight soldiers were all definitely dead. At random, he added three more dog tags to his collection.

Where the hell was Kristina? She was still a good ten yards short of the log. Face white with pain, using the grenade launcher as a crutch, she took another halting step.

"What the hell?"

"I twisted my ankle. It really hurts."

Pete placed his rifle on the top of the log and leaped over, running to her. "Next time, call for help, God damn it!"

"I thought you might be busy."

Pete picked her up. "Hold on to the grenade launcher."

He carried her to the log. He saw her face twist and turn even more pale as he inadvertently jostled her right leg. He swung over the log and reached back to pick her up when a volley of shots rang out. She screamed.

Pete pulled her over and down behind the log. "Where?"

"My leg." The flatness of her voice told him the bullet wound on top of the ankle injury was rapidly pushing her into shock.

"Fuck." He took the launcher from her hands and looked down the road. Those sons-of-bitches were coming fast. There must be at least a platoon. He sighted the launcher and pushed out three HE slugs, walking the muzzle from left to right, aiming slightly short so the grenades would skip on the road.

He laid down the launcher, shifted to 'auto' and emptied the M27 magazine, shoving the spare magazine home.

There were now another two-dozen men lying in the road who should have spent the morning at Mass. The rest had taken cover, many of them diving off the side of the road toward the creek.

He knelt down and slit the side of her shorts. The bullet had torn a gouge in her right thigh. It appeared to have missed the bone, but had taken away an inch or more of flesh and muscle. The ragged flesh was bleeding profusely. A quick snick of his knife and her shorts were no more. Pete stripped off his shirt and wound it around the wound, making the clean half of his undershirt a compress pad and using her Beretta's duct tape to hold it in place. Over it all, he placed the belt from her shorts. It was the best field compress he could do at the moment. Her Beretta went into his vest.

"What...doing?" She was barely awake.

"Making it more comfortable for you to be carried." He turned back toward the log, aimed and arced the last grenade back down the road before tossing the launcher over the cliff. Then he bent down and hefted her over his right shoulder, the M27 in his large left hand. He hated to let the grenade launcher go, but he only had so many hands. "Time to boogie."

Kristina's speech was jerky as she gritted her teeth and her stomach bounced on his shoulder, "Ho...w are...we...we...we going...to get ho...ho...home?"

"Those lazy bastards didn't walk here." Pete had about reached the next turn in the road. "Let's see what's around this curve."

Surprise, surprise. Two Humvees were parked neatly in the mountainside lane of the road. Pete put Kristina in the front seat of the first one, buckling her in place and checking the compress hadn't slipped. It not only hadn't, it looked like the bleeding was stopped. He'd check in ten minutes to make sure he hadn't gotten it too tight. He started the engine and checked the gas gauge. Half a tank.

He moved to the other vehicle, started and threw it into gear, aimed it at the cliffside, goosed the gas pedal and slid out, turning the wheel as he did to steer a more direct shot over the edge.

He slipped as he landed and fell flat in the dirt, but at least he didn't catch his pants or vest on anything. The Humvee careened on down the canyon and came to rest against two trees nearly two hundred feet below. Unfortunately, it didn't burn, but good luck getting that one out, he thought, as he spat out a mouthful of dirt, ran back and swung up into their new transportation. They were facing an hour race. The bad guys had chainsaws that would make short work of the road barriers. He was sure they also had vehicles on the backside of the second downed tree. As he accelerated, Pete was wishing he had been more awake during the ride up. He didn't remember a damn thing about the road.

A minute later, he had stuck a roadmap of Benguet between his legs and was thumbing a button on the satellite phone. When the Duty Officer answered, he took a deep breath and tried to keep his enquiry calm: "Have you managed to get anything in the air yet?"

He nodded to himself at the answer and glanced at Kristina. She was asleep. He reached over to check her pulse. Strong but fast. "Nice. Does it have a medic aboard? Good thinking. Radio the bird that he hasn't made the trip in vain. A bullet nailed Miss Baclayon and she needs immediate emergency help. Listen up. If by some chance the bad guys get to us before the helo does, have someone check our driver's side door. I am going to slit the upholstery and tuck dog tags inside of some of the men who attacked us."

Pete now had both hands on the wheel and was using his shoulder to keep the phone pressed tight to his ear. "I killed their rightful owners, Mr Roberts – what did you think?" He shifted his voice into command mode: "Call the Ambassador and have him make a formal complaint about this attack immediately. Then do everything you can to get that helo here! Also, give Madame Toseña a call and tell her what I just told you about who shot her niece." Pete disconnected to focus on his driving. He figured he had a ten-minute lead as long as his pursuers didn't have someone along the route.

With luck, the Ambassador complaining might keep away obvious reinforcements; however, the helo was still almost an hour away and he was woefully lacking in firepower if they encountered another roadblock. He glanced over at his silent passenger. Kristina's face was still white, but when he put a couple of fingers on her neck, her pulse remained strong. She was either asleep or passed out. Unconscious was not bad for the moment. There wouldn't be any painkillers until the helo arrived.

All four tires squealed on the hard clay as they rounded a wide turn and plunged down beneath another stretch of triple canopy.

CHAPTER TWENTY-EIGHT

Pete's key staff advisors gathered round the long table in his *Blue Ridge* office, cradling steaming cups of coffee. Coffee is integral to thinking in a navy unit.

Mary Ann moved around the table, slipping packets in front of each of her fellow staff members. Each folder contained two different intelligence summations as well as copies of the papers Pete had taken from the body of the ambush leader.

On the very top of the file was a blow-up of a grainy photo he had found in the dead Colonel's pocket. It was a long-range shot of Rachel and Pete. It had been taken while the two relaxed on the terrace after their golf game and then blown up 24x. In the photo, Rachel was saying something and Pete was staring past her. There was nothing particularly interesting about the photo except for the large black X drawn across Pete's chest.

Bruce Parks, the senior SEAL, disdainfully used his forefinger to push the photo off the top of the pile, "So, Mary Ann, what is the Embassy's take on the photo?"

"No comment' is all we've heard."

She paused for a second. "The elephant in the room is the lack of the X on Ms Townsend. I know Rachel is embarrassed. Especially since the Ambassador pulled her from Pete's Humvee at the last minute."

Pete interjected, "Actually, I requested…" but the group was focused on Mary Ann, and Pete decided perhaps the time was not yet appropriate.

"Everyone protects their own," Tom Cooper muttered. "How has the army explained the dog tags?"

"To quote the army liaison office, 'The Philippine Army has done an exhaustive record search and determined that the Colonel, as well as the others Pete deposed, were recent deserters.' Their official line is that the men were in an Absent Without Leave status prior to the incident in question."

Bill Rogers disbelievingly looked up from a sheet in the first stapled intelligence report. "Even though this same Colonel is still listed on the army's website as being in command of an infantry battalion – not just any battalion – but the one responsible for the Presidential security group?"

"That was a screen shot we grabbed yesterday, Doc," Mary Ann said. "My staff checked that site right before I walked up here to this meeting and his name has now become ancient history. I assume the others have been scrubbed as well. If you're interested in further suspicious data, go five pages back further in the file. That is a copy of a June *Times* article. In it, Jamie Bautista presents the same Colonel with a medal for 'courage in extraordinary circumstances'."

"Was he in command of the same unit that assassinated Cory Aquino's husband when he was debarking from a plane?" Pete asked.

Mary Ann shook her head. "No, you're thinking of the Aviation Security Command. That unit gunned down Ninoy Aquino when he stepped off an airplane at the Manila Airport. But that was a long time ago."

Pete was still trying to recall what he had read about Philippines history. "What was the *cause célèbre*? Didn't that killing eventually precipitate a civil war?"

She nodded. "It was essentially about politics. Aquino had returned to the Philippines to run against President Ferdinand Marcos – and, yes, eventually events spiraled into a war when Aquino's wife ran in his stead. But it was a unique revolution. No battles were fought."

Tom Cooper had unfolded his knife and was trimming one of his nails. "You know the Philippine Chief of Staff is a West Point graduate.

He attended WooPoo during the same years I was at the Naval Academy. We actually met and became friendly during one of the Annapolis/West Point exchange visits. My sources tell me he was very unhappy when he heard about the ambush on you and launched a review…"

"And?" Pete asked.

"And," Tom folded his knife blade into the hasp and examined his newly shaped nail, "the Palace ordered him to shut down his investigation."

Silence hung in the air for a moment. Then Pete rapped the table with the knuckles of his right hand. "OK. Enough speculation. Mary Ann? Your briefing, please."

She picked up the papers before her, shuffling the photo to the back. "You've all seen the photo and it speaks, or does not speak, for itself. As a related matter, you should know the Chief of Staff believes Rachel and the Ambassador were as surprised by the attack as him. In addition, for everyone's information, Ms Baclayon received first-rate emergency treatment aboard the *Blue Ridge*, including twenty-seven stitches by our own Fleet Surgeon Captain Bill Rogers, and is now at home recovering under the care of her aunt."

The Logistic Officer's voice slipped slyly across the table: "Show Bill a pair of female legs and he'll always be Johnny-on-the-spot." Several in the room chuckled.

Pete needed to keep the meeting on track, "Let's permit Mary Ann to continue."

She got up and picked up a pointer. "Thank you." The picture of Rachel and Pete was on the projection screen and she clicked to the next: a memo on State Department stationery. "State issued a travel warning for the Philippines yesterday. The warning is a direct result of Ms Baclayon's and Pete's adventure and even indirectly refers to their ambush. President Legaspi formally complained to the Embassy today about the memo. Apparently, Ms Baclayon's Aunt is a potential candidate in their next Presidential election. The Palace termed the State warning an interference in their internal election process."

She looked at Pete. "I think you're going to have to take more care about who you have with you when you're attacked." At his withering glare, she rolled her eyes and hurried on. "His staff maintains they have already seen a precipitous drop in scheduled tourist travel. That's a major problem, as tourism employs about four million Filipinos. The Palace contends this one incident is an anomaly by a group of rogue army deserters."

Bruce had separated the report on the ambush leader from the file, folded it into an airplane and was gently tapping the paper nose against his teeth. "I am told by a low-level person in the Embassy that Legaspi himself called Ambassador Coyle to demand the warning letter be immediately lifted. If not, he supposedly threatened that, beginning on Sunday, American ships will be denied mooring places anywhere in the Philippines."

Mary Ann clicked to the next picture, of a waterfront bar that looked like a bomb had just hit it. "This is a bar in Subic owned by a retired Navy Chief. About 4am this morning, someone threw a hand grenade through the front window. Fortunately, the bar was closed."

Bruce opined, "He shut up shop early. Must be a religious holiday."

Mary Ann ignored him. "We overlaid this map of Luzon with police reports of violence from this last week in red. In yellow, we have included any reports referring to either terrorism or the *Pula Alcorán*." She cocked her head and looked at the chart. "Neither my staff nor I have seen anything to correlate with the attack on Pete."

Pete tried to keep his voice casual, "What does Rachel think?"

Mary Ann looked at him thoughtfully. "It's funny, but if it weren't for the trashed Humvees and the dead ex-soldiers, I think the Embassy would have chalked up your incident completely to your overactive imagination. Goodness knows, I couldn't get Don or Rachel to comment one way or another." She reflectively ran the short fingernail on her right index finger under her lower lip and bisected the dimple on her chin. "If I didn't know better, I would say our Embassy was not interested in writing anything down that might reflect badly on Legaspi's government."

Mary Ann flashed up a couple more slides. As she spoke, Pete's mind returned to his most recent telephone call with the Admiral. At the end of the week, the flagship – and, of course, the Seventh Fleet Staff who lived and worked aboard – was scheduled to depart for a short voyage across the South China Sea and a weekend diplomatic visit to Hong Kong.

Pete had suggested, given the recent overt anti-American activity in the Philippines, that he remain in Subic with a small detachment. The Admiral had countered, given his recent adventures, that Pete staying behind would be among the very worst of ideas. Since the Admiral's 'suggestions' were not really suggestions, Pete would be aboard the flagship when she got underway on Friday. For a month, he would be able to monitor Philippine events only through the Press and the intelligence reports the Embassy submitted.

While he had turned down Pete's request to remain in Subic, the Admiral had agreed to add another intelligence ship to the task of monitoring the Philippines' electronic environment.

Sometimes the crust of the loaf was the best you were going to get.

CHAPTER TWENTY-NINE

The welcoming reception in Hong Kong was over. The final VIP had been ceremoniously gonged ashore at 11:15 pm. Four hundred and thirty-four more international guests had received white-glove treatment aboard America's most visible warship in the Pacific. Another memorable goodwill event demonstrating graciousness, awareness of local sensitivities and American military power had been successfully concluded.

Every guest's photo would be hand-delivered to their home before 2pm tomorrow. The pictures would show them standing at the head of the USS *Blue Ridge* gangway alongside a naval officer in full-dress blues. Behind them would be an American flag, as well as four enlisted marines holding polished M1 rifles.

The red receiving carpet they had stood on had now been carefully brushed, spot-cleaned, rolled up and stored. It would remain in its designated locker until Friday, when *Blue Ridge* would steam into Bangkok and the whole process would begin anew. For the moment, Pete finally had time to himself.

He called for the messenger to bring his traffic and meet him at the flag bridge. Pete picked up a bottle of water, and climbed the four flights of ladders to where he could finally be by himself on the flag bridge. It had been a long day. He took a deep breath. It was gorgeous here, high above the harbor. A good place to enjoy the twinkling city lights while he reviewed the weather reports describing pressures, lows and fronts between Australia and Kamchatka.

This was not a task he felt comfortable leaving to anyone else. It was typhoon season in the Pacific. Hong Kong was a great port but she was seductive. Her hills circled and shielded a large bay in which deep waters provided anchorages for any size vessel. The tidal action flushed so much water that the live fish market among the rocks at Wenchai was as world-renowned as the Aberdeen boat city. But no big ship – and *Blue Ridge* was definitely one of those – could ride out a typhoon in Hong Kong Harbor. The flagship's high sides provided too much 'sail area' for the winds to work on. A typhoon would part the thickest lines, pull loose the biggest anchors and drive ships before it like skittering newspapers across a vacant lot. When typhoons threatened, major ships needed to steam for the open seas like frightened chickens fleeing the farmer's axe.

A fast-moving typhoon could travel hundreds of miles overnight – and its gale-force winds would reach out several hundred miles ahead. A good seaman had to anticipate, which could become very easy to forget while drinking champagne and meeting heads of state. Thus, in Hong Kong, Pete drank only club soda and, every evening, took the time to sit down and personally review the reports from the weather aircraft that flew daily out of Guam. But there was no good reason he couldn't enjoy the beauty of Hong Kong while he did so. At the moment, there was only a worrisome low-pressure area west southwest of New Zealand.

The well-greased hatch dogs on the nearby hatch to the stairwell rotated and the gray steel door swung open. "Chief of Staff, what are you doing up here all by yourself?"

"Finding someplace to relax where I'm not bothered all the time by bloody marines."

Tom Cooper artificially deepened his normal Texas drawl: "Now that is the very same attitude that always brings a deep pain to my heart, Chief of Staff." He sat down in the chair opposite, kicking at Pete's heels until Pete groaned and shifted to provide space on the polished brass pipe running along the bulkhead so Tom could elevate his own legs.

"Damn, boss. I get tired of standing on that ship's hard steel deck just to look pretty during those receptions! So, I've come all the way up those long steel steps to continue our conversation about the best times of your life – that are undoubtedly those that have been spent with your own Fleet Marine Officer in discussing the extraordinary capabilities of America's finest fighting corps!"

Pete continued looking at the Hong Kong skyline. "My fondest times are when my Fleet Marine Officer doesn't know where I am or what I'm doing."

Tom placed his hand over his heart. "I sincerely believe I am in danger of suffering a myocardial infarction from the sacrilege I have just heard."

"If you do have a heart attack, you will receive triage care from a navy corpsman and a navy doctor. You will then be flown by a navy airplane to a navy hospital where you will be cared for in a naval hospital. All of this will be performed free of charge to the Marine Corps, and yet you and every marine will still bitch every second about not being properly appreciated."

Pete could see Tom hide a smile and take a deep breath while shaking his head. "This is the thanks I get for walking important news all the way up from the intelligence office? An office, that, when the wonderful Mary Ann is not present, is manned by men and women who do not understand your needs?"

"At least one or two of whom are marines."

"Those exceptional warriors are probably not currently on duty."

"You should volunteer to serve with our Ambassador to the Philippines. You both have the same casual relationship with reality."

Tom chose not to reply. Instead, he took his time to unwrap a cigar and put it unlit in his mouth, the cellophane in his pocket. Pete's curiosity got the best of him. "OK, I give up. What did the best marine in the fabulous Marine Corps ferret out and bring me?

"Just fabulous?" The cigar shifted to the side of Tom's mouth.

"Will you buy extraordinary?"

"Always, Pete. Here you are." Tom retrieved a piece of folded paper from his uniform-shirt pocket and extended it between two fingers.

Pete unfolded the single sheet and scanned the three paragraphs. "The President of the Philippines is calling for a snap election? Is this really true?"

"It is, and since you swabbies don't appreciate or probably even read history, you should know the last time this happened in the Philippines was when President Ferdinand Marcos called for such an election. That was just after the scurrilous rumor swept through the islands that he had assassinated Aquino. A rumor that was much later subsequently proven to be true."

Pete waved the paper, "It doesn't give a reason."

"In a couple of hours, the intelligence people will have a briefing pulled together."

"What do you think it will tell us?"

Tow scowled and kicked at the polished pipe under their heels while he thought for a few seconds. "Probably that they believe President Legaspi wants public support for a full-out war against the *Pula Alcorán*."

"Of whom, to date, we have found absolutely no sign."

Tom kicked the pipe again. "Like Bigfoot, there may be a few somewhere."

"Granted. Will it even mention the Shoal or the Chinese?"

"Mary Ann is already writing the briefing. She says *nada*."

"That stupid bastard! We can't keep saving his ass." Pete reread the message and creased it into an airplane, which he accurately flew into a trashcan, "And who is going to pay for this war?"

"Well, we know Legaspi has already asked for free trucks. I can't believe he won't now pad that request to his good friends from America – the same ones who have returned to the Philippines after such an ungratefully long absence."

There was a loud knock on the same door by which Tom had entered and the intelligence messenger entered with the aluminum box containing the file by which top-secret messages were routed about the ship. The man stood at attention in front of Pete and extended the file. "The Intelligence Officer sends her respects, sir." Pete lifted the spring-loaded metal cover and read the ten single pages contained within, initialing the lower-right corner of each as he did so. He then passed the file to Tom.

Neither said anything until the messenger left the bridge with the box, then Tom threw his thoroughly gummed cigar in the trash. "Well, put a bonnet on me and call me Granny. The intel ship's finally come through. I never expected that!"

"Me neither. I wonder how long Jamie's been talking directly with the Chinese?" Pete folded the weather reports, swiveled his chair and looked out again at the harbor as he thought.

Tom let the silence build for several seconds before he pulled out a new cigar and began carefully examining it. "You know the Chinese-Philippine interaction is interesting, Chief of Staff, but seriously, we expected it, and in the meantime, we've been chasing our tails around this truck issue ever since the day we first moored at Subic. But neither one is the most interesting thing that happened today."

Pete swiveled back to the Fleet Marine. "No, what is?"

Tom ran the new cigar appreciatively under his nose. "You already knew that Feliciaño Segura Toseña had announced her candidacy. But there are two new political developments. Yesterday, Archbishop Antonio Luis Ver pledged his personal support to her rather than Legaspi."

Tom nodded at Pete's upraised eyebrows. "It was apparently a surprise to a lot of people. Because of the Archbishop's endorsement, Mary Ann says that some of the news shows in Manila are predicting that Toseña starts out within single digits of Legaspi." Tom grinned, "In fact, one of the minor TV stations is stirring the pot by referencing your little Humvee escapade with Toseña's niece as indicative of America's support for the challenger. Of course, our Embassy immediately issued a statement."

Tom looked longingly at the cigar. "I am so sorry we gave this up, Chief of Staff. You and I used to look damn impressive smoking those Madras."

"Life moves on. Now we get to live to be a hundred and fifty."

Tom stuck the unlit cigar in his mouth and spoke around it. "I left the intel spaces because Mary Ann is so pissed she wasn't even speaking to me. She was trying to call Hollingsworth in Manila."

"What over?"

"The Embassy decided not to ask us for any comment, but to go out on their own and use the words 'sailor relationships' in the press release to explain Kristina Baclayon being in that Humvee. Mary Ann took some offense. Since I was coming up here to talk to you, I asked her if I should pass on that our Embassy had thrown you under the Aniceto bus line in Manila or maybe it was the Candon one. I personally thought that you might enjoy the joke, but, as I said, she was in a real snit, so I didn't get a reply I think I should repeat."

It was probably a good time for Pete to be in Hong Kong. But was it the right thing for Kristina?

"In fact, the airwaves in the Philippines are bouncing with all sorts of disparate messages right now, which is why your intelligence briefing may be a moment or two late tomorrow morning."

Pete was gazing at the twinkling lights. If they weren't careful, America could well find itself in the middle of a Philippine civil war. That was definitely not what the President of the United States had in mind when he had directed *Blue Ridge* back to Subic Bay. On the other hand, this was shaping up as exactly the type of situation the Seventh Fleet was designed to influence…and if the Americans did not choose to do so, the Chinese…

Tom interrupted his thoughts, "Chief of Staff, I haven't told you the very best part."

Pete swiveled in this chair to look at his friend. "Which is?"

"The word on the street is that a Miss Kristina Baclayon Toseña is going to be announced as her aunt's campaign manager!"

CHAPTER THIRTY

The USS *Blue Ridge* (LCC-19) was four hours out of Hong Kong, headed south-southwest toward Bangkok, and was bucking both a twenty-knot headwind and a freshening sea. Pete had completed his morning five-mile run (forty times around the *Blue Ridge*'s rolling steel deck), showered off both the sweat and the salt spray and was now ready for the morning staff meeting.

As usual, Mary Ann led off with the intelligence portion. "There are rumors that Rodel Luzario has been appointed the new acting head of the Aviation Security Command."

Charlie Harper, the Operations Officer, frowned and shook his head. "That can't be accurate, Mary Ann. Isn't he still a director of Teak World? It's a complete conflict of interest! That company does at least a billion dollars' worth of business in the Philippines alone."

"Two point seven billion last year. And Luzario is actually more involved than just being a director," she evenly replied. "Our information is that he is one of only three executive vice presidents of the company, although we're not sure of his precise duties." She shrugged. "There's been no official announcement, but we're monitoring a great deal of internal Philippine Army chatter discussing his assignment to the Aviation Command. We also don't know whether he's resigned from Teak World."

Bruce whistled under his breath. "This is akin to setting the fox to guard the hen house."

Mary Ann raised her hand. "We don't know Philippine law. This sort of arrangement may not be illegal here."

Tom Cooper reflexively reached for his pocketknife and then shifted to pull out a cigar to chew. "Actually, I think it's a worse problem than old-fashioned graft. Wasn't the Aviation Security Command the unit the Palace has historically used for assassinations?"

Charlie doggedly replied in shorthand. "Years ago – nothing ever proven."

Bill Rogers snorted, "Give me a break!"

Tom shifted the cigar between cheeks, "Only because Marcos and his shoe-lady controlled the courts."

Tom looked around his little group, "We all know that the most difficult thing to ever change is the culture of a military unit, and once they get dirty…"

Bruce finished for him, "…the only cure is to shoot the leaders, disband the group and pour salt on the foundation."

Tom and Bruce gave each other the thumbs-up across the room. While military units were built to deliver force, the very atmosphere of violence was often corrosive to ethics. Everyone knew stories of units that had lost their moral compass. The results were inevitably ugly. Recovery, while possible, was never easy.

Mary Ann was losing control of the time allotted to her intelligence briefing. Pete knew he was at least partially to blame and drew a tight circle in the air, the universal signal to wind up all conversations and listen. Mary Ann projected a communications summary on the bulkhead. "Our two communication-monitoring ships report nothing on any channels historically used by the Chinese. They also have no *Pula Alcorán* intercepts, but they note Rodel is making an unusual number of encrypted calls. The National Security Agency doesn't have immediate access to Philippine keypads, so it is taking four or five days for the NSA computers to brute-force decode these personal conversations."

Pete frowned. There had to be a way to eliminate that delay.

Mary Ann took a deep breath. She knew bad news did not get better with age, but the Chief of Staff was really not going to like the next bulletin, "NSA called me this morning. They have priority needs elsewhere in the world – my best guess is Afghanistan. Our monitoring was taking up too much of their capacity and I'm afraid the requirement for it wasn't supported by State." She ignored a loud raspberry from Bill. "At the beginning of the next radio day, NSA is going to go to a sampling technique."

The tip of Tom's unlit cigar pitched up. "Which will very probably start at one in a hundred and go downhill from there – those worthless Embassy bastards."

"Possibly," she admitted.

Bruce was obviously still thinking about her earlier comment. "Lots of intercepted phone calls from Rodel, but none from any Chinese or *Pula Alcorán* sympathizers?"

"Yes, that's correct."

"No," Bruce corrected her, "it may be right but it's definitely not correct." He held out his empty coffee cup and Mark reached over and refilled it. "There can't be a *Pula Alcorán* fire without at least some smoke. We all know what those intelligence ships can do. Hell, they're currently sniffing everything but Rodel's underwear." He paused. "So, if there are no footprints, is there a body? How can anybody still believe there even *is* a *Pula Alcorán* organization?"

Mary Ann shrugged to indicate she had no answer and, when no one else commented, proceeded with her briefing, "While we were in Hong Kong, Mr Carpenter and Ms Townsend flew over and we all compared notes. I have a copy of the various analyses the Embassy has done, along with the police reports of reported interactions with the *Pula Alcorán*…"

Bruce enquired, "How many of the dissidents did the Embassy Staff interview? Tom and his team must have talked to more than a hundred."

"I asked that question. Don and Rachel said their people speak only to official sources."

Bruce snorted with disgust. "Did the Legaspi government also write their study for them?"

Pete was thinking along the same lines. "Did you actually see Rachel's analysis?"

Mary Ann's mouth made a moue at his implication, and shook her head, no.

Pete was struck by a thought. "Did the Pentagon agree to share the Hong Kong intercepts yet?"

From Mary Ann's quick shake of her head and the warning look in her eyes, he realized Defense had decided not to inform State or the Manila Embassy that Legaspi was negotiating directly with the Chinese.

After a long second, she shifted the briefing papers in her hands as well as the subject, "As everyone knows, a few days after we sailed from Olongapo, Legaspi unexpectedly called for a snap election. The short campaign season is already well underway. There are only two announced candidates for President this time: Legaspi and a woman who was formerly in his cabinet, a Señora Toseña. This looks like it will be a rough election." She paused for a second and looked directly at Pete, "For their own safety, the Admiral has decided to place election areas 'off limits' for our sailors and marines."

Pete kept his face as expressionless as if he were pushing five hundred dollars across the table betting on a pair of fours. *Mary Ann! You went around me to the Admiral to save me from myself and keep me away from Kristina!* He stared at her.

"There's been violence either during or after nearly every one of her public appearances and there were press reports of shots fired into her headquarters late last night." Mary Ann continued to look directly at Pete as she spoke. "No casualties were reported."

Bruce pursed his lips. "They won't be lucky forever." He shook his head as his fountain pen drew graceful curlicues on the paper in front of him and cut each curl with a sketched Bowie knife blade. "Somebody is going to get killed and then the violence in every province will quickly ratchet up. I wish we were back there."

"I quite agree." Everyone looked up at the familiar voice in the doorway and all scrambled to attention.

"At ease." The Admiral took one of the empty chairs and lowered himself into it. A cup of coffee magically appeared on the table at his elbow even before his butt compressed the gold cushion. "I think the situation in the Philippines has the potential to cause us a great deal of angst, and I fear my friend, Ambassador Coyle, may need some solid military advice on scene.

"At the same time, we have been too long without a senior American military presence in Bangkok and Malaysia, and we've already announced both visits, so I do not want to divert *Blue Ridge* from her formal schedule. I will stay here and travel with her. However, I will feel better if we have more fighting power in the Philippines. Pete, I think you need to pick a dozen or so staff and helo over to the USS *Chancellorsville*. Select a couple of escort ships out of the Battle Group to take with you and make the best time possible back to Olongapo."

CHAPTER THIRTY-ONE

Bruce, Tom, Bill and Mary Ann remained behind after the meeting, Mary Ann shuffling her papers, Tom with his hands patiently folded together, Bill casually leaning back against the bulkhead and Bruce impatiently drumming a staccato rhythm on the edge of the table with two fingers.

Bruce spoke up first: "We've been sitting and observing for long enough. We need more than a plan – we need to do something! We've all seen the same things. This country is about to go over the edge! Every time I make the trip into Manila, there are fewer working lights and deeper potholes in the streets."

Tom nodded his agreement. "Before we left for Hong Kong, I was talking to some of my Philippine Army friends. They see the same things we do. I believe most of them are hoping Legaspi loses this election. As conservative as a military mind normally is, that's saying something!"

"We can't be part of anything like this!" Mary Ann exclaimed. "We are guests in their country. If anyone is to do something, it needs to be led by the Embassy!"

Tom looked up at her from where he was sitting. "Even if the boys and girls from State can't find their asses with both hands?"

"Even so!"

Pete tipped his chair back on two legs. "Mary Ann, you need to think carefully. Would you be more comfortable for the next thirty days not knowing everything?"

An incredulous tone crept into her voice. "Do you mean you intend to violate regulations?"

Pete kept his voice calm, "I'm simply asking, if I might decide sometime to bend what you might consider a 'rule', would you be more comfortable not knowing?"

Mary Ann abruptly sat down in a chair at the table, her right hand raised to her cheek.

Pete continued inexorably onward. This needed to be resolved. He could not have her going behind his back to the Admiral again. "I value your advice and counsel, Mary Ann, and I would prefer you continue to tell me when you disagree with me, but situations are often very complex and, when the Admiral isn't here, I'll be the one responsible for making decisions." Pete slowly took a sip of his coffee, still holding her eyes with his, "I need for you to decide now if you're going to be able to live with me not taking your advice."

"But you're thinking about doing something which is against regulations…"

"There's a possibility that I may decide circumstances require flexibility that may not have been previously wholly envisaged, yes."

Her cheeks were flushed. "And that would be wrong."

"Success will have a thousand fathers, and no one will ever desire to be briefed on the details. However, if we fail, then I would fully expect for you"– he made a gesture to also include the men – "as well as everyone else in this room, to testify against me at my court-martial."

"In the meantime…" her voice was slightly faltering and Pete realized she was working to control any tremor.

He finished her sentence: "You either act as part of our team or I will no longer include you in all my thinking."

"I am your Intelligence Officer."

"Mary Ann" – there was a touch of asperity in his voice – "there are five hundred officers on our staff. Look around. Do you see the General Counsel in this room? Do you see Charlie, your boss?"

She shook her head slightly.

"That is because I have already found both of them too inflexible, and their advice, while sometimes of value, not nearly worth the hours they waste with their pompous explanations." He paused, "I appreciate your judgment. I like the way you think. On the other hand, I suspect we may be about to venture outside your comfort zone. It may be time 'to fish, cut bait or go ashore' and I am giving you a free pass to walk away and not hurt your career. If you want it, take it."

Mary Ann dipped her head so Pete couldn't see her eyes and tapped her papers on the table, bringing them all squarely into alignment. Pete watched her steadily as she considered. After a few seconds, she raised her head.

"You realize I will testify against you if you do something contrary to the Uniform Code of Military Regulations?"

"I wouldn't expect anything less."

She looked at him and then at her teammates around the table. "Put me down as a fisherman."

Pete nodded and leaned back, including them all in his view. "From today onwards, I want this group to informally consider itself as the 'Manila Cell.' Share everything with each other, but think twice and then once again before speaking with anyone else. I will keep the Admiral informed by special compartmented correspondence." Pete spread his hands out on the table. "Now then, let's brainstorm. Tom, I could tell from your earlier comment that you have a proposal."

The marine nodded. "Everyone I talk to – even my Philippine Army friends – is a bit skittish about what's going on here. Many Filipinos feel their country is spiraling toward an out-of-control state. At the same time, they also know the President and his friends have survived many challenges, including two known assassination attempts in the past few years. It is a given he is going to jimmy the constitution to run again. No one wants to be on Legaspi's enemies list when the music stops."

Pete nodded. "The situation is very fluid. I am sure many of them feel much like Mary Ann. The additional wild card this time is the Chinese. I can't believe that Legaspi or Bautista doesn't already have some sort of an arrangement with them."

Tom nodded. "Several in the Army have told me they're worried that Legaspi and Bautista are planning something with their friends across the South China Sea if he somehow doesn't win the next election outright."

Bruce suddenly quit drumming his fingers and flipped out his knife, leaving it closed, but spinning it in a black circular blur on the table, "Tom, your contacts. Would they look the other way?"

Pete saw Mary Ann involuntarily swallow.

Tom was carefully watching her while he answered Bruce. "Look the other way when?"

"While you and I tap the Palace phones."

The room was silent while Tom balanced the pros and cons. Finally, a smile crept over his face. "Tapped the phones using American technology, with an ultra-high frequency feed of the conversations to an antenna on one of our ships in Olongapo? I think my Filipino friends might consider that gave them sufficient deniability."

Mary Ann cleared her throat and Pete spoke before she could: "The National Security Agency doesn't have time to relocate an appropriate satellite to focus on the Philippines. If any violence starts, the situation here is likely to quickly go south and endanger the hundreds of thousands of American citizens who live here. I am going to approve this effort." He turned to Bruce.

"This will be difficult. It certainly won't work if anyone even suspects. You can't be caught. You certainly can't kill anyone."

Bruce and Tom nodded. Pete held their gazes for a second and then looked up at the overhead while he reconsidered the more difficult task. "The Palace uses a highly centralized phone system so they can ensure all their calls are encrypted. We've all seen their setup. It makes Bruce and Tom's job at least possible. But what if someone is outside the Palace when they decide to do something? How do we track that? There are a million cell phones in the Philippines. We are already experiencing four-day delays getting into Rodel's cell and you know he will be involved if anything dirty goes down."

Mary Ann coughed and Pete again avoided looking at her. It was disappointing she was not going to work out.

She cleared her throat and addressed him directly, "Chief of Staff?"

Pete kept his eyes on the overhead. "What now, Mary Ann?"

"Sir, Rodel's SIM card is what provides the encryption for his telephone calls. I have someone in intel who knows how to reprogram subscriber-identification module cards…"

The corners of Pete's mouth curled up. Mary Ann was actually going fishing. He kept staring at the overhead. "But we need physical access. According to everyone I talk to, he carries that phone with him everywhere."

"Not when he's sleeping," offered the Fleet Surgeon.

Tom added, "And not when he's screwing."

"Which," Bruce added, "we know he does more than he sleeps."

The Fleet Surgeon was looking directly at Pete. "I have some pills that will encourage a person to sleep very soundly."

Mary Ann tucked a stray curl back in her bun, "Perhaps one of us could buy him a drink?"

Pete shook his head. "I can't imagine him being careless around any of us. We'll need help to bell this particular cat."

CHAPTER THIRTY-TWO

"Detengan ese!"

The jeep eased to a halt immediately behind the white bar that was dropped across the road. Balancing their M27s on their hips, Efran and Ruben raised picture IDs for the guard to read. From the shadows in the backseat, uniform caps pulled down a bit over their carefully stained brown skins, Bruce and Tom pushed their borrowed IDs forward through the forest of steel barrels, sling webbing and lanyards.

"Adelante!" The guard stepped back and the bar swung up. The jeep moved forward, zigzagging between the concrete barriers, and pulled around to the service entrance. Their target was the communications center on the second floor and its 'red switch' – data-processing terminology for the specialized electronics in the Palace that served as the physical and electronic dividing line between raw conversations and encrypted ones. Efran and Ruben needed to electronically check in their normal teammates (Antonio and Rafael) and proceed about their regular duties. Tom and Bruce had to remain undiscovered by anyone in the Palace security team for the entire shift and also compromise the switch. It would be a tense night.

A physical relay station for their sabotage was already established. Immediately after Pete's meeting, as Tom was mining his Philippine Army sources, Bruce had coordinated with Guam. Last night, a team of SEALS had planted a new sea buoy five hundred yards out from the Palace. The buoy was packed with long-term batteries and had a direct line of sight to the correct second-floor window. From there it was 64,000 miles straight up into a MUOS-4 satellite-communication horn in synchronous orbit around the earth, and an instantaneous slight redirection right back down to the *USS Chancellorsville* antenna sixty miles away alongside the Olongapo pier.

Bruce opened the door to the second-floor spare-equipment room with the key Efran had provided and stepped inside. They were next door to the communications center. Tom followed him and Bruce locked the door, while Tom used his penlight to search the room. They were going to spend several hours in here. The immediate problem was to quickly locate hidey-holes that would fool a random security-team inspection.

Their brute-force problem wasn't that difficult. If one could physically access it, the red switch was susceptible to simply being bypassed. Tom was carrying an electronic package, that, when properly placed, would capture five per cent of each unencrypted communications and divert it out of the window directly to the bobbing buoy the SEALS has planted. That would eliminate any elaborate and lengthy codebreaking problems! For his part, Bruce was carrying an elaborately carved and configured matching teak cover for their electronic package. From the photos Efran and Ruben had provided, they expected the cover, especially after it had been liberally covered with dust, would simply fade into the background of the room and the hundreds of dreamcatchers, monkey-pod carvings and other knick-knacks the Palace operators had accumulated and hung over the years. The task was to get into the manned room and secretly place the package.

The door was suddenly flung open and the lights went on. Two heavily armed Palace security-team members stepped into the room, noisily pushing the folder-filled waist-high filing cabinet aside so they could fully open the door. The smaller man moved completely into the room, audibly sniffing the air, rattling several dangling locks to check they were closed, including one on the locker in which Bruce was standing. Bruce held his breath, a lead-weighted sap in his left hand, his favorite throwing knife in his right. If the door popped open, what the hell would they do with the bodies? What if the guard noticed the loose string on the floor he had jerked to alert Tom the second he heard the key inserted in the door?

The soldier turned, took two steps and drove the butt of his M27 against a curtain alongside the room's window. Some plaster exploded and the guard kicked the debris aside before leaving and locking the door behind him. Bruce felt the dial on his watch: 12:20.

An hour later Bruce soundlessly pushed the door open and felt around in the dark for a scrap of paper. He balled it up and lobbed it in an arc across the room. There was a snort and the ball of paper winged back hitting the wall beside him. Bruce silently laughed. Despite the earlier scare, he had known Tom could never stay awake in the dark. The man was a stud, could go for days, but let him sit down and within minutes he was fast asleep. It was shocking he had been awake when the soldiers had checked. It was now two am, the lowest part of the human circadian rhythm. They had time to make something happen, check for success and still join Efran and Ruben in the jeep going home. He reached up for Tom's hand and let the marine pull him to his feet.

First Bill pulled aside the cover and checked the fisheye that had been installed in the wall yesterday while a flight of helicopters was overflying the embassy. No one could hear themselves think while Ch-53's were in the air, and President Legaspi had gratefully accepted the offer to see a close-up demonstration of the American power he now had at his disposal. Pete had even thoughtfully furnished ear protection for everyone in the Embassy during the demonstration. Inside the room, the two watchstanders were both reading. One was engrossed in the Star and the other was apparently updating her Facebook account. Bill leaned back and let Tom look before both donned their headsets and shifted to covert throat mikes. Tom moved to the door with the electronic package and it's surreptitious cover.

Bill looked back through the eye and put his hand on the regulator from the canister of methyl propyl ether (painted green and labeled OXYGEN). The hole through the wall had also been predrilled yesterday. It came out behind one of the rack fans. The ether would work quickly. The trick was not to be impatient. No regulator squeal and no sudden pressure change. He eased the valve open. After a minute, he opened it another quarter-turn before slowly easing it two full turns in the same direction. A minute later and the newspaper slipped out of the man's hand and fell to the floor. The woman didn't at first react that much. A few seconds later and her head fell forward onto her keyboard. "OK, Tom. They're out. Ensure you're good and tight."

In the corner of his eye, he saw the door to the comm center swing open and a lean figure step inside, his head completely covered by a plastic hood. Inside that mask, Tom had ten minutes of air to complete his task. Bill began throttling down on the ether. He would wait to completely disassemble the setup until after they had checked for success. He watched as Tom positioned the diverter and slipped on the wooded cover. He stepped back and pointed. "How's it look?"

"Good. Try the call."

Tom picked up the newspaper, folded it neatly and put it on the table and arranged the man so his body sat more comfortably in the chair. Then he picked up the supervisor's telephone and, pulling the plastic tight over his right eye, dialed a number from memory. Bill had two phones in front of him. One was the encrypted phone borrowed from Efran for this call. It was ringing. "Hello, marine."

"Extraordinary marine to you."

"We will see. So far, no one from the ship has called. You probably screwed up and put the diverter on a water pipe. It's hard to get electrons out of water and we have to return this phone to Efran in fifteen minutes. In the meantime, you will use up all your air vainly seeking the praise of the Marine Corps and, in a very short time, I will have to cart your unconscious body out of there and save your ass again."

"Ye of litt…"

"Hold on, my phone is ringing."

"Bill, this is Mary Ann. Tell Tom he is coming through loud and clear!"

"It worked, Tom! You are a bona fide hero. Now get the hell out and let's wake these people back up."

CHAPTER THIRTY-THREE

"How's your girlfriend? All recovered? I understand she'll have a nasty scar." Rachel and Pete were sitting in the Champagne room of the Manila Hotel. They had met in the lobby for a working lunch. After an air kiss, she hadn't looked him directly in the eyes. She was currently fully occupied in picking at the hotel's Caesar salad.

"I haven't seen her for several weeks. She's busy with her aunt's campaign. I understand she's made a full recovery."

Rachel abandoned her salad and turned her attention to her tea, crushing the mint and lemon into a spoon and focusing on coaxing two drops of the mixture into her glass. "It was a terrible, terrible incident you two went through," she murmured, taking a ragged breath, "but I should share with you that the Ambassador has directed us to be restrained in our approach to our hosts. He believes you had sufficient warning about the dangers of the *Pula Alcorán*. I know everyone here at the Embassy certainly sent up the right smoke signals."

Pete felt the blood vessel in his throat begin to pulse. He wondered if it were visible. Mary Ann had cautioned him before he left the ship that Rachel would probably take this approach. Pete hadn't believed her. Now he swallowed and lowered his voice to a whisper. "Are you insane, Rachel? The men who attacked Kristina and me were in uniform. They were decorated members of the uniformed Philippine Army!"

Her eyes flicked up to his and then quickly back down to the tea she was stirring. Her voice was flat. "No...we've been assured they were all recent deserters."

"Men don't desert by platoons!"

"Rodel Luzario told me there were some isolated morale problems, He says those issues are being addressed."

"Isolated morale problems leading to wholesale desertions by Palace guards?" Pete let the sarcasm well up in his voice. "What a quaint idea. What flavor Cool-Aid does the Embassy have in its water coolers today?"

Rachel ignored him, completely focused as she was on tasting her tea.

Pete put an elbow on the table and leaned toward her, resting his chin on his fist. "If there is such a serious morale problem among the guards, don't you think you should at least warn the Ambassador to avoid the Palace until President Legaspi addresses his problem? In the interim would you like us to augment the marine guard at the Embassy?"

She put her glass down and directly met his eyes for the first time since they had sat down. "I do know you're personally not welcome in the Palace." Her voice gathered heat. "I've relayed that information to the Ambassador."

Pete thoughtfully sipped his own tea. Well, he had obviously succeeded in pushing Rachel out of her comfort zone and gotten a look at her true feelings. He shouldn't count on her to volunteer to assist in sabotaging Rodel's cell phone.

The waiter arrived with their main courses and Pete let the man's interruption provide an opportunity to redirect the discussion. A secondary issue he knew she and Charlie had been discussing was how to share the Subic Air Field between commercial and military airplanes. The FAA had several issues with what Seventh Fleet had proposed. After a few minutes discussing the bureaucratic complexities of this issue, he could see Rachel's shoulders begin to visibly relax. As long as he was willing not to press her on anything relative to the Philippines government, she was her old charming self. Interesting.

"I will inform the Señorita you are calling."

The porch swing was suspended on either end by worn jute cords. Pete sat and, after the lines held, he used one toe to push back to start the bench swaying. Here on the wide veranda, protected from the sun, it was almost cool. It was also relaxing. The yard was green and shaded and the faint scent of jasmine filled the air every time a breeze stirred the bushes. Fifty feet away in the partial shade of a spiky-leafed traveler palm, the usual guard squatted, his shotgun lying across his lap. Behind Pete, from inside the screen door, came a familiar voice: "Please come in, my Captain."

Without looking back, Pete touched his right toe to the ground and pumped the swing. "I'm not sure your aunt would like me in your house. An American uniform might cost her some Philippine votes." He patted the patterned seat cushion beside him. "I thought we could sit out here."

He heard the screen door behind him open. "And precisely because I am now her campaign manager, I would rather we sat inside where it was not so easy for anyone passing by on the road to take pictures. Come inside, my Captain."

"I take it your aunt is not at home?"

"She's not, but your girlfriend is."

Pete stepped into the dim living room. As soon as the screen door closed, Kristina stepped into his arms and pushed up on her toes to kiss him under his chin. "You are a very stubborn man."

He circled her waist with his hands. When his thumbs rested on the shell belt buckle on the front of her dress, his forefingers almost met in the small of her back. She leaned back mischievously as he pulled their hips together. "Is this the proper manner that the United States Navy should address the campaign manager of the next leader of an important ally?"

"It is the only acceptable approach when they are as beautiful as you," he replied as he leaned forward to kiss her.

She swayed her upper body further away, batting her long black eyelashes, while at the same time thrusting her pelvis hard against his. "And talented?"

"Don't start that with me! I get that at work from the marines!"

Behind him, he heard a swirl of soft clicks from the wood-bead-curtain that led to the kitchen. Kristina, looking over his shoulder, put both hands in the middle of his chest and pushed the two of them apart, twirling away from him. "Maria, please put the tea on the table where the Captain and I can sit. Could we also have some of your delicious butter cookies? *Gracias.*"

She winked at Pete and continued to speak to the closed kitchen door. "I want to tell him about the results of our recent polls in the Northern Mindanao and Davao provinces."

She moved to the bamboo love seats, primly seating herself on one of the blue suede cushions and motioning opposite to a similarly cushioned rattan chair, "Sit down, Captain. I would like your advice and I would like to explain Philippine politics to you."

She pursed her lips in a thoughtful manner and brought a forefinger to the tip of her chin, "With respect to the race for President, we believe we are currently only slightly behind and closing rapidly. Archbishop Ver's public support has been invaluable – for while there are fifteen archbishops in our country, he is not only the most respected, but everyone believes he will be our next Cardinal. He is also the only senior cleric publicly supporting a candidate."

Pete assumed the role of an American newspaper reporter: "Do you think you will win?"

"Aunt Feliciaño does, which is what is important, because her energy is driving our campaign." She twirled a tendril of her hair thoughtfully for a second. "I sometimes worry more what Legaspi might do if he began to believe he were losing."

"Have you heard that Rodel Luzario has been appointed the acting head of the Aviation Security Command?"

She immediately lost all her former artifice, "No! They are the President's goon squad." Her voice was unambiguous with concern. "Even he would never take that job."

Pete was confident her reaction was not faked. "My intelligence people think he's already secretly in place."

Kristina grimaced, "That's not funny. It's almost the very issue on which I wanted to seek your advice." She paused, a frown wrinkling the skin between her eyes. "I'm worried about my brother. He has not been actively supporting our aunt's campaign and I think he is avoiding me. Even though he and I have always been close" – she put her fingers on her gold bracelet, half-raising her left arm – "I know this must have cost him a month's wages..." – her voice trailed off and then restarted – "He has come to think the sun rises and sets in Rodel Luzario, even though..." Her voice trailed away.

"Even though what?"

Kristina replaced her tea on the silver serving tray. "I have several times tried to tell Enrique that Rodel is not the person he seems."

"But...?" Pete encouraged.

"But brothers are not terribly fond of listening to older sisters and Enrique feels the same as my aunt does about Americans."

"I thought you and your family were friends with Luzario."

She wrinkled her nose. "Rodel is part of the Manila social scene, but he has never been invited into this home." She grimaced. "And he never will be."

Pete looked at her questioningly.

"I will never forgive him for Analyn."

"Analyn?"

"My best friend in senior high school." Her voice became lifeless. "When she was home from college between our junior and senior years, she accused Rodel Luzario of rape."

Her face looked controlled, but she had brought her hands together in her lap and was twisting her fingers together. "He was taken in by the PNP for questioning. He swore the relationship was consensual."

She released her fingers and balled her fists, "I never had the chance to privately talk to her. Analyn died two evenings later in her mother's car."

Pete raised his eyebrows.

"Her car went off the road and caught fire. Her body was terribly burned. Her *padre*'s business also mysteriously burned the same evening."

"And Luzario?"

"Without an accuser, the police dismissed the rape investigation. She was an only child. Her parents subsequently disposed of all their Philippine property and moved to Los Angeles. When I was in graduate school, during university holidays, I sometimes stayed at her parents' house." She leaned back in the sofa, "Do you think I would ever associate with that man?"

She rotated her bracket once around her arm, "Rachel Townsend tells me Luzario has changed, but I don't believe it for a second. I... I suspect the Americans have established intelligence inroads into Philippine politics." The wrinkles above her nose returned, "Will you promise to tell me if you hear anything about Luzario that I can use to help make Enrique see reason?"

Pete pulled a small plastic bag from his breast pocket and laid it on the silver tray between them. "Let's go for a walk in the garden while you think about the girlfriends you trust."

There was one unencrypted telephone line in the USS *Blue Ridge* Intelligence Suite and it was both clearly marked, attached to an clunky old black telephone and kept in an unlocked wooden box on the corner of Mary Ann's desk. It was never used except sometimes for ordering pizza when they were in port. When it buzzed, it took a few seconds for Mary Ann to correlate the sound with the phone. Finally, she answered it: "Captain Saunders."

"This is the quarterdeck, ma'am. There is a Miss Kristina Baclayon calling for you on an insecure line. Do you want us to take a message?"

Kristina Baclayon? Was that Pete's Kristina? She opened her safe, paged through a file on him he would flip if he knew she had, looked at a photo there, and checked the name, her eye running down the bio. "Please put her through."

"Captain Saunders, this is Kristina Baclayon, I am a Filipino friend of your Captain O'Brien. He came to see me this afternoon."

"Yes, I know who you are." She pushed her glasses back on her nose. Pete hadn't shared any of his plans with her. Had he approached Kristina?

"Are you alone?" Kristina's voice was hurried. "I mean, may we talk for a minute?"

Mary Ann looked around. There was no one near and normally everyone kept their distance from her desk. "Kristina, I work for Pete and also like him, but not in the way I imagine you do. I have all the time you need." She paused. "And call me Mary Ann."

"Mary Ann, Pete asked me to – oh, this line might be bugged…"

Smart girl. Her aunt's niece. "Right."

"OK. He asked me to find another girl to do something that might be dangerous. Do you know what I'm talking about?"

"I believe I do. If it involves a SIM card, I'm sure I do."

She heard Kristina draw a deep breath.

"Mary Ann, I need to honestly know. Is this really important to Pete?"

Mary Ann took the pencil out of her bun and tapped it on the table. There was a difference between talking about intelligence and actually going out and getting your hands dirty. She looked down at the photo again. Kristina was truly lovely.

Mary Ann knew she was about to push over the first domino. "I'm the person who provided what I believe you have in your hand."

"Oh."

There was a long pause.

"Thank you."

The phone went dead.

CHAPTER THIRTY-FOUR

Rodel tucked his silver-tipped cane under this arm, bowed and kissed Kristina's hand. He stood up and moved closer to her so the crowd of campaign supporters in the Hotel Manila ballroom could not overhear him, "so *las esposas'* tales are true?"

She kept her weight on her toes and held her ground. "Dare I ask?"

He smiled. "That politics makes whores of everybody."

She didn't even blush. "You always have said the nicest things. Does Rachel find that part of your charm?"

"Many gringas do, but you never did."

"Maybe because I knew Analyn so well."

Rodel's eyes flashed and his goatee quivered. He moved even closer. The handle of his cane nudged under her arm and against the side of her breast. "And even although I publicly support our President, you invited me to your Aunt's campaign event – you even messaged a second invitation to me with a handwritten note."

He reached out a hand to stop a tuxedo-clad waiter, handing her a glass of champagne and securing a second for himself. "Why were you so anxious for me to attend?"

"Aunt Feliciano wants to ensure that each of the key Filipino decision-makers has the opportunity to personally hear her message and ask her questions." She made her voice as coquettish as she could manage. "You know you are one of those individuals." Kristina turned her head to the side to sip the champagne. If he leaned another centimeter closer, she might throw up. She even found the smell of his skin repugnant.

She hoped Rodel didn't sense this. She managed to give a tight smile to the Adivongs as they walked by. She hadn't spotted her brother since shortly after the event started – Enrique had followed Rodel around like a dog for the past few years, but blood had to be thicker than water!

She could feel Rodel's eyes boring into her. She avoided returning his gaze, mouthing 'Michael. Katrina' in the direction of the Vice Major of Cebu and his wife as they passed, and inclining her head towards another couple from Pilar she knew she was supposed to recognize, before turning back to the man still standing uncomfortably close. Enough of this. She brought up her arm between their bodies and took his. "Shall we see what my aunt would like to say to you?"

He resisted her moving him. "Only if I may buy you a drink afterward somewhere away from this circus."

"This circus is my life right now."

"And I am a 'key Filipino'."

"We have a hospitality suite upstairs."

"A private hospitality suite?"

She pasted what she hoped was a tremulous smile on her face. So far, God help her, this was all in accordance with the plan she had laid out with Enrique. "As private as I get for you. My Aunt is over by the palms."

Kristina's anxiety rose until her throat actually threatened to close when they entered the large suite and found it completely empty. Where the hell was her brother?

She reached out and caught herself on the wingback of a chair to keep her knees steady. She checked the room again. Rodel was surreptitiously easing the bolt on the door closed. She closed her eyes for a second. *Madre de dios!* What was Pete always saying, in for a dime... At least Rodel was distracted. She crossed to the bar she had prepared earlier, "Do you want a drink?"

"Absolut and Seven."

One thing Enrique had right. She poured the vodka over ice, added lime juice, an ounce of Seven-up and stirred slowly until Rodel crossed the room. She handed the drink to him with a Manila Hotel bar doily. He took a sip. "What are you having?"

"Ginger ale. My stomach is reeling from all the salted fish and adobo I've eaten on the campaign trail the last few weeks."

"Try this." He extended his drink. "It's the best solution for our hot afternoons."

A toilet flushed and Enrique came out of the bathroom. Thank God!

"I would rather not. Enrique, would you like a drink?"

Rodel looked at her. "Is there something wrong with my drink?"

Which had always been the soft spot in her plan. "Of course not!" Did her words ring true?

He was still holding the glass out to her. She reached up and took a small sip for taste. "It's good."

She needed to sell the story. She took a larger swallow before returning his drink to him and held up the Absolut bottle. When he nodded, Kristina refreshed his glass, passed Rodel a dish of salted nuts and began to fix her own ginger ale.

She looked out of the side of her eye at her reflection in the bar mirror and forced her jaw to relax. She had done what needed to be done to make the sale. Rodel had already drunk half of his cocktail. His tongue licked along the bottom of her right ear and she moved away from him, walking toward several overstuffed chairs. Her brother was still standing by the bathroom. "Enrique? A drink?"

"I just came up to take a leak. I think I'll return to the reception."

Oh no you don't! This is not what we discussed! She moved over and put her arm around his waist, "Brother, stay with us. We need to convince Señor Luzario that our aunt will be great for the Philippines."

Rodel had downed his drink, moved to the door and thrown the bolt back. "And he needs to do his job by mingling while you convince me. I want to better understand the Americans, and you're the one who went to school there."

Enrique slipped from her grasp, was out of the door and quickly gone down the hallway. Tomorrow she would kill him!

"You are the one that invited me here to talk." Rodel refreshed his drink at the bar and then crossed to the conversational area. "Come over and sit." Kristina looked at the door, made sure it was unlocked and then took comfort in the fact that Rodel was on his second spiked drink.

Was it only in her imagination that she could already feel the cloudy tendrils from the date-rape drug Rohypnol reaching for her own brain? This was going to be payback for him! She was relying on the stick of butter she had swallowed before the reception to slow the absorption for her. Now she had only to outlast him until the drug took effect. Then she could get to his phone. Of course, she was smaller than Rodel and normally only drank wine. She dug her fingernails into her palms. What the hell had Enrique been thinking when he left the room? She moved away from the door and sat down in a chair just as Rodel stood.

His two arms came over her shoulders and pinned her down into the chair, while his head burrowed between her head and shoulder, his wet lips finding her neck. "Get off me!" Her body somersaulted onto the floor and she scrambled immediately to her feet. "What the hell are you doing?"

"You know you want it." His cane was on the floor, partially rolled under a chair. His pupils were so large they were taking over his eyes. Was he moving more slowly? Was she? He was so much bigger! She looked around frantically for a weapon. He was between her and the bar. She backed toward the door. He followed. The door opened inward and she was essentially trapped in the small hallway. He put down his glass. She backed until the doorknob was square against her spine. He reached out with one hand and grabbed her jaw, immobilizing her face as his other hand began to slowly pull her dress down her body. "Analyn was not nearly so well developed."

"You bastard." She spat as hard as she could toward his face.

His forceful fingers squeezed her jaw, "You're going to learn this afternoon not to be so high and mighty." Her dress was hanging from her waist. He reached for her right nipple, "And your lessons start…"

The doorknob shoved painfully into her back as someone else pushed into the room.

CHAPTER THIRTY-FIVE

Pete dismounted the jeepney in front of Kristina's house. He had a jump in his step as befitted the bearer of particularly good tidings. She had made a perfect selection! Rodel's cell phone had been transmitting a strong unencrypted signal all morning. The wavering tone was interrupted by five or six seconds of static every couple of minutes, but except for that minor random technical hitch, one that IT specialists aboard *Chancellorsville* were currently looking for a way to correct, Mary Ann was ecstatic.

The guard recognized him and swung the gate open. Pete was whistling. The afternoon rain was not yet here. It had been a close call. The first drops were beginning to fall as he walked up the brick walk. Kristina opened the screen as he reached it and, since he sensed no one behind her in the unlighted living room, Pete leaned forward to kiss her. "Success, love."

Her slap rocked him back on his heels. As he stepped back in surprise, she closed and locked the screen against him. A stroke of lightning momentarily illuminated the dark living room. Abruptly, Pete realized her left cheek was contused. The skin around her left eye was swollen and purple. She spat her next words at him, "Eat a stick of butter so the alcohol doesn't reach the bloodstream and then slip Rohypnol in his drink!"

A tear began to run down her right cheek. "What if he is much more used to drinking than I am? What happens if he forces me to share his drink?" She flipped open the top buttons of her blouse and

216

shrugged it from her left shoulder so he could see the scratches across her breast and the bruised nipple.

Her voice was low but intense: "I thought you loved me! Why didn't you ask your precious Rachel?"

"You said you would get a friend!"

"You think I would ask a friend to do something I was afraid to do? To do something so important to you." She was now weeping. "I told you what kind of man he was. You knew he frightened me. Why weren't you there?"

"Kristina, what the hell did he do? Unlock the screen!"

"Why did you let him hurt me?"

Pete hipped the wood frame of the screen until he felt the iron yield and the hook latch straighten. He stepped inside and wrapped both his arms around her. She looked up at him for a second before tucking her head between his right arm and his chest.

As he looked down from this vantage point, he could see scratches raked across on her back.

Pete lowered his head and pressed his lips against her hair. Her shoulders moved up and down as she sobbed.

He whispered, "I'm so sorry, Kristina. This was a terrible idea." Pete held her closer and felt her wince. He tried to pull back, but her arms were wrapped tightly around his waist.

They stood in the darkening room as the lightning intermittently streaked through the windows. As the storm swept over the house, her tears soaked his shirt and burned his skin.

"Chief of Staff," Mary Ann's voice was unusually tense. "You don't need to read each and every word of the Rodel intercepts. That is why you have me and my staff. You will be the first to know if we get anything important."

Pete ignored her. He knew he was meddling in his Intelligence Officer's business, but he was in no mood for banter. This particular information had already cost too much. His guilt demanded an immediate and extraordinary return. What if Uncle Manuel had not gone to that suite to check on Kristina! As yet, the transcripts only reflected Rodel using his government contacts to manipulate teak prices, plus an occasional call to flirt with two married women. Since Pete was not interested in extortion or adultery, nothing of significance thus far. One good thing was that Rodel's numerous discussions did not include any mention of the 'event' with Kristina. It was unclear what he remembered. There may well have been some value to the Rohypnol after all. It was obvious he didn't recall or suspect losing control of his cell phone.

He finished reading the afternoon's spy-ship intercepts and dropped the sheets back into Mary Ann's wire basket. While there was a continued conversation between the Philippine Government and the Chinese Embassy, and several million dollars in bribes had been arranged, the intelligence ships had noted little else. So far Kristina had paid a high price for squat.

Feliciaño was campaigning in Isabela Province today, where polls had her six to eight points behind. Kristina was accompanying her aunt, the healing bruises disguised with makeup. They would be back in the national capitol region in three days. Then it was only a week until the election. Toseña's schedule has made it impossible for Pete to see Kristina since the day she had cried in his arms. The Philippines were already well into the election-season crazy period in which the most minor detail could quickly assume King Kong proportions.

He didn't believe her aunt knew what had gone down with Rodel, but she was certainly doing everything to keep Kristina close to her side. Pete was left with only work. In the past week, he and the staff had put the finishing touches on a proposal for the Ambassador which would mean jobs for several thousand Filipinos at Subic's Cavite shipyard, building ships with the surface-to-surface and anti-air capability to defend Philippine territory in the South China Sea. The Ambassador reportedly floating the plan with President Legaspi, who didn't appear particularly interested – which was unusual for any politician Pete had ever met.

Pete inadvertently knocked all six volumes of the master Cavite

Shipyard proposal to the deck and, from the look Mary Ann gave him, he sensed she could do well without him and his foul mood in her intelligence spaces. It was time for a long solitary run before his emotions affected the entire staff. But first a quick phone call.

Pete checked the directory, picked up Mary Ann's phone and dialed a number. "I know you're busy, Rachel, but I just have a quick question that I didn't want to bother Mary Ann with relaying to you. Do the campaigns provide the Ambassador with a copy of their itinerary?"

Mary Ann looked at him and then returned to reading an intercepted-traffic file.

He had prepared an answer for Rachel's expected response and it rolled off his tongue, "Simply so I can keep our sailors away from those areas. Since we don't want the US Navy presence to become an issue in the election, I thought I would make election events 'off-limits' in order to minimize the number of potential incidents the Embassy might need to deal with."

He held his breath. Rachel had become increasingly uncooperative as the election date approached – actually ever since the weekend at Camp John Hay, if he were to be honest. After a few seconds of silence, he pushed before she could say no, "Aren't you reading the papers? Toseña has been advocating a US Navy ship withdrawal in nearly every speech. On the other hand, Legaspi and his surrogates are correctly pointing out she is ignoring the military dangers which threaten the Philippines. They are using every opportunity to emphasize that her position on American assistance simply proves she has her head in the clouds and is unfit to be President of the Philippines."

He continued with the cover story he had chosen, "Well, I certainly don't want to be in the middle of this one and that means we should do everything possible to ensure no one wearing a navy ice-cream-suit inadvertently shows up at the wrong place."

Pete waited, hearing Rachel's fingers tapping keys as she searched her electronic folders.

"Will you just forward it to me, or do you want to read it and I will copy it down?"

"OK. Read it to me." Pete watched Mary Ann slowly turning the message-file pages. He knew her curiosity was piqued, but her eyes remained fixed on her printed intercepts.

"Tomorrow morning, Toseña in Bimundo. Is that with an 'i' or an 'e'? An 'i'? Thanks. Legaspi in Santa Mesa."

"I should have asked earlier – is the election running you ragged?"

"Tomorrow afternoon, Legaspi in Intramuros, Toseña in Gagalangin. Right. Can you spell the 'gag' one for me?

"No? That's good. Need a good sleep every night. Tomorrow evening, Toseña in Ermita and Quiapo. Right. Does Ermita begin with an 'i'?" Pete smiled to himself and tapped his pen against the pad. He had not yet written down anything. He was waiting for Rachel to lose her patience and that moment had finally arrived, "Yeah, I agree a text would be simpler. I understand the message has other information on it like the hotels they are staying at, hosts and stuff. We won't let that information out."

"I will personally see to it. In the meantime, I know you're all very busy monitoring the election, so I won't waste any more of your time. We'll get guidance out today to make the campaign areas taboo. Just send it to Mary Ann."

He waited until the cloud delivered her email, then reached over Mary Ann's right shoulder and ran his finger across the columns until he was sure it contained what he wanted. He asked her to print a copy and after he tucked one of the pages in his hip pocket, Pete went to see if Bruce and Doc were interested in investing some nervous energy in a long jungle run before it was dark.

"Ummph!" Kristina struggled against the hand over her mouth and kicked back with her right heel as the arm around her waist lifted her high in the air. She was never going to step into a dark hotel room again! But it was the Manila Hotel! God damn it! She might be able to drive one of her three-inch spikes into his groin if she twisted…

"Kristina, stop! If you succeed, you will regret it nearly as much as I."

She relaxed, her heart still racing, and her dead weight tumbled them both into a soft bed, "You bastard," she whispered, twisting in his arms while searching for his mouth with her lips. She settled on straddling him and teasing the pulse in his neck with the tip of her wet tongue.

Pete kissed her temple and whispered, "Are you OK? Your wounds?"

She scooted up higher, whispering as she did, "All better." She kissed where his shirt was open over his throat and gathered herself to slither higher. He stopped that attempt by holding her tight so his mouth was near the lobe of her ear, "Are you lying to me?"

She nuzzled into his shoulder and bit the flesh there, marking him, while her soft, sultry voice proceeded directly to his heart. "My Navy Captain, as your marine would say, I am deeply offended at your lack of trust in your girlfriend. As a direct representative of the next President of the Philippines as well as the Malolos Republic, I will not be satisfied until you make your own personal inspection."

They lay on the bed, their breaths slowing, her leg over his flat belly, her head resting on his chest. The large ceiling fan over them slowly rotated, rhythmically creaking each time one particular blade passed over the tall ornate mahogany bedpost nearest the door.

Kristina broke the silence., "Thank you for bringing the lavender oil. I not only feel special, I smell loved."

"You are. Thank you for not yelling."

"I would have if I could have gotten your fingers out from between my teeth."

"You are a strong woman."

She shifted her leg and struck him in the stomach with her fist. "And aren't you lucky I am!"

She undid two buttons on his shirt that somehow had stayed closed. Wetting her index finger, she began drawing racetracks between his nipples, "Why don't you accompany the campaign for the next couple of days?"

"Is the campaign manager at work or the girlfriend speaking?"

Her forefinger circled his right nipple. "What do you think?"

"I think it's the campaign manager, who wants her aunt to have it both ways on the American issue. She can give speeches in Spanish about how the Americans must leave the Philippines, while photographers are taking pictures of her favorite niece with an American captain." He paused for a second, trying to search for just the right words. "I can't do that. It would be like showing up in uniform at a politician's rally back home. Actually, it'd be worse, because publicly appearing with you could be interpreted as interfering in the internal politics of an ally."

She pinched his right nipple. "And what if I just want to be able to have sex with my boyfriend every possible night?"

"That would be an added benefit for me, but it still wouldn't be right."

Her cool right hand stroked his nipple and she leveraged her hold on his chest to snuggle her wet warmth even closer to his side. "It would be very OK for the nefarious campaign manager, but I am still glad you said no." She kissed his chest, the tip of her tongue drawing a wet circle around his other nipple. Suddenly, she raised her head. "The day after the election, I want to tell my aunt you're my boyfriend. *Are* you?"

"No."

She shoved him, trying to push away, but his left arm held her clamped tightly to his side. "I am your 'man-friend'. We will *both* announce it to the world after the election next week."

He rolled her up so she sat astride him, and interlaced their fingers. "Let's talk about what is truly important. How many hours of sleep do you absolutely need before tomorrow?"

CHAPTER THIRTY-SIX

It was early morning in the Philippines. Minutes before, the first sun rays had clawed their ways over the eastern horizon. The mist was already beginning to abandon the thin strip of tarmac running along the head of the piers where USS *Chancellorsville* was moored. The road was the common gathering place for the morning run. Aft of the forward gangway, the Seventh Fleet Staff were stretching tendons shortened by sleep. They were unbothered there. In practice, the other crews gave them a private zone. Most of the staff had already been up for at least an hour reading last night's message traffic. A great deal of business tended to be informally consummated while everyone warmed up for the day.

As was his habit, Pete was wandering through the group, quietly speaking to each member. He approached Mary Ann last, putting his right leg up against a piling to stretch. She was standing with her arms crossed across her chest, her right hand nervously curling a tendril that had come loose from her bun, and she spoke as soon as he stopped next to her. "The last twenty-four hours in the Philippines has been ugly, Chief of Staff. I don't like the way the Philippine election is shaping up. Demonstrators at Toseña's events are becoming violent."

Pete shifted legs, massaging his right ankle, as Mary Ann took a shallow breath before continuing, "We have no idea if this is due to outside agitators or if she is just drawing out-of-control supporters. At the same time, we are also noting a general rise in violence across the Philippines. There is no obvious connection or smoking gun, but someone could draw the conclusion that her candidacy is fueling the anti-law-and-order element."

Pete raised his right arm and made a circular motion, and the group was off in a jog. Mary Ann stayed at Pete's side. "I think we need to worry about the quarter-million American citizens, many retired former military, who now live in the Philippines." She glanced around at the closest runners, one of whom was her boss, Charlie Harper. "I haven't yet seen an adequate plan for protection of the expats – and I expect it's only a matter of hours before Pearl Harbor and Washington are going to be asking questions."

"You know it's impossible..." Charlie Harper started to speak, stopping only when Pete looked at him. This senior group knew it was Charlie's clear responsibility to have such contingency plans prepared and in hand, and that Mary Ann's comment was career suicide.

She plunged on, ignoring her boss, swinging her arms in rhythm with her shorter stride. "In fact, given how high emotions are running, I don't see how Señora Toseña can be at all comfortable with the protection the police forces are providing her. I think she may be in physical danger whether she wins or loses..." The intelligence officer's voice lowered. "...possibly more, if she wins."

Pete kept his own voice level, "What exactly are you hearing, Intelligence Officer supremo?"

She looked around. Charlie was still at her side and Bill Rogers was on the far side of Pete. Mark was running alongside Bill. "Probably nothing different from what Tom or Bruce is picking up in the jungle."

"But neither has recently reported in, so...?"

"The election is next Friday, four days from today..."

"That part we know."

"And the crowds at Ms Toseña's rallies are becoming increasingly unruly. Her staff is claiming that President Legaspi supporters are attending to try to shout her down and instigate incidents. They also maintain the police are not arresting the agitators, but only Ms Toseña's supporters."

Bill Rogers interjected, "Isn't this pretty standard fare for Philippine elections?"

The group turned off the tarmac and on to the dirt road that paralleled the jungle. Mary Ann ran another ten yards while she caught her breath, "That was my first reaction. But Ms Townsend sent a dispatch to Washington yesterday in which she provided data showing the current violence is at least an order of magnitude worse than for any previous election."

She looked off into the distance, as if recalling something, "I can show you a particularly descriptive set of graphs when we get back. I asked the staff to break down reported violent crimes – murders, rapes, armed robberies, and assaults – by election districts. When you cut the data in that manner, when compared with the last two elections, there is a significant rise in incident rates in every district. The capital district of Luzon shows a quadruple rise!"

Mark took a couple of quick strides ahead so he had visual contact with Mary Ann. "What does it tell us to do?"

"I'm not sure." She shrugged her shoulders. "But I believe the data is significant."

Charlie Harper volunteered. "I know we need to plan for a large number of potential refugees." No one in the group looked at him. It was obvious to everyone that Charlie was still reluctant to accept responsibility for something squarely in his bailiwick – but even if he were a late arrival, it was good news that he was finally beginning to realize something was going on.

Pete nodded. "I agree. In addition, we need more assets. I would like you to contact the Marine Aviation Combat Element in Okinawa and get a dozen helos flown down here." They passed a dog that was worrying what looked like a dead chicken. Another couple of hundred yards and they would begin to circle back, "On second thoughts, have him provide a dozen Ch-53s and another dozen armed 46s."

Charlie's response was immediate, "They're going to be reluctant to give up their CH-53s."

Pete just looked at him. The Marine Aviation Combat Element

worked for and reported to Seventh Fleet, just like all other naval forces west of Hawaii.

Charlie stumbled for a second and added, "The marines are reluctant to release the Ch-53s because they are so capable and flexible."

"Exactly why I want them here. I know your marine counterpart is going to object. Explain the situation and tell them you have no option. If he wants to push his luck, have his General call me. Also contact the afloat Marine Expeditionary Brigade and turn them around. I want them here at best speed."

The group wheeled around and began the run back to the ship. The group ran for several hundred yards before Charlie broke the silence again. "The marines are planning on pulling in at White Beach for liberty tomorrow."

"And?" Pete had been thinking about the weather reports he had read this morning.

"They undoubtedly have some spouses meeting them there who will be very unhappy."

Pete wondered if Charlie could read the expression of disinterest on his face.

"OK, I will order them to immediately change course…but they've already been at sea for two months…and if we turn them around they may well still not arrive in the Philippines until after the election."

"Charlie, can you guarantee that any violence will be contained to before the election?"

"I guess not."

Pete wondered if he was going to be able to contain his impulse to fire his Operations Officer until after they got back to the ship. They were running alongside the Bay. Maybe he would simply bang Charlie over the head and roll his body into the water. No, that would probably not set the best example. "Charlie, I realize I should have turned them around sooner. My failure to act earlier doesn't mean we shouldn't do something when we do become smarter. Have them head south now and tell the Commander I want him here as soon as possible – definitely by Friday afternoon. Who's in charge, by the way?"

"Jack Griffin commands the amphibious assault ship and I think the senior marine is Brigadier General Bill Heard. The three ships that carry the marines and their equipment also carry another thirty helicopters."

"Good. Jack and Bill are both good people. We're going to need every helo we can lay our hands on. Get all the ships headed in the right direction first and then set a time tomorrow morning to thrash out your refugee plan. I want to link Jack and Bill into that discussion, so provide them with your tentative plan before the telcon." He was through with this conversation. "Last person back to the gangway is an Air Force Officer!" Pete sprinted away.

Two days later, as Mary Ann had predicted, election violence had become endemic throughout the Philippines. The *Manila Times* front-page 'above the fold' article this morning dealt with two men, armed with assault weapons, who had been arrested the previous evening at the last checkpoint before a Toseña rally. The story noted that machete wounds at her rallies were becoming almost commonplace.

Pete had a copy of the paper in front of him as Mary Ann kicked off the morning briefing aboard USS *Chancellorsville*. "This morning, President Legaspi called on Feliciaño to abandon her campaign, citing the lawlessness of her followers. He stated that Filipino law-enforcement personnel could not remain responsible for her personal safety if she continued campaigning."

"And?" Pete queried.

"Our source within her campaign says that Ms Toseña does not intend to pause. He reports that she believes Legaspi allies are staging the violence because the polls indicate people are swinging her way. He thinks her followers will probably form their own para-military group in order to provide protection for the candidate."

Charlie shook his head. "That never works. Civilians don't have the discipline."

Mary Ann's eyes flicked over to her boss and then returned to Pete. "I believe they intend to man the military protection unit with retired Philippine police officers and retired army officers."

Charlie shrugged. "Then they will be too ancient to be effective."

Pete kept his own counsel. "Their problem, not ours. When do you expect our Marine Expeditionary Brigade to arrive?"

"This afternoon, about 1400. They had good weather en route."

"Good. How about the preparations to use Corregidor Island for refugees?"

Charlie scratched his head. "That's possible. Since the weather is mild, we can use tents for shelter. The constraints are the usual ones: potable water, food and sanitary facilities. However, I recommend we go instead with Grande Island. It doesn't have the World War II connotations. It's also physically closer to Manila and, believe it or not, there are still some facilities left from when it was Fort Wint a decade ago."

"I'm OK with the island change, but you still need answers to all the logistics questions. Do you have better solutions than you did yesterday?"

"Yes. We just need time to brief you on specifics."

"Right after this meeting. How do you intend to provide more protection for the Embassy if things go south?"

"As we discussed yesterday, as soon as they got within helo range, the marines began flying in ammunition and reinforcements to the Embassy. Starting at noon, every four hours a platoon of marines visibly fast-ropes into the Embassy compound, familiarizes themselves with the area, and then departs with the next wave of helicopters. That way we don't overwhelm the Embassy and no one outside the gates knows exactly how many defenders are present."

"And the Ambassador agrees with his approach and understands the number of marines inside the Embassy is to be kept a secret from all Filipinos, including his friend, the current President?"

Charlie nodded. "No one is paying attention to the 'copter after that demonstration you arranged for the President last week, I think you can fly helos nearly anywhere in the Philippines you please for a while. President Legaspi packed the Palace with his political supporters for that demo."

Mary Ann's eyes flickered to Pete. Charlie hadn't quite answered

Pete's question. And little did he know that the fruit of Bruce and Tom's night trip to the Palace was currently being monitored (and simultaneously recorded on tape) by two marine analysts in the locked stateroom four doors down the passageway from Pete's office.

Charlie chose this moment to interrupt Pete's meeting to explain again to the group about why he personally favored Legaspi. "What do you think would happen with a woman president in a society such as this? It would certainly make our job more difficult. I also hear she doesn't like Americans."

Pete kept his voice even. "Are you asking how the Philippines could have a woman president? How this would work in a matriarchal society where women traditionally control the family money? Where would you get executives to run the Philippines government in a country where women currently fill half of the executive positions in private companies?"

Charlie shook his head. "In the Filipino families I know, and I believe I have some excellent personal contacts in this country, the men definitely wear the pants. No real Filipino man will ever listen to a woman."

Pete decided this was not the best disagreement to have in public. "You may well be correct, Charlie. But while the Filipinos are settling their own succession, we need to focus on worrying about the American citizens who live here. I'm not yet comfortable with your plans for food and water for possible refugees. If things get dicey, we could even have some beginning to show up tonight."

Charlie had a pained expression on his face. "Let my staff work this some more and we'll brief you before the amphibious ships anchor this afternoon."

The clock above the desk where Pete was typing his nightly report began tolling. Eight bells – midnight already. The Admiral was at that moment winging his way from Vietnam to Tokyo for a meeting with the Japanese Defense Forces. Pete stretched and took a sip of water. He was trying to find the right words to ensure the Admiral had an accurate picture of what was currently happening in the Philippines.

With all that was going on, it was becoming more difficult to keep his messages concise. There was a knock on his door.

"Come in!"

Mary Ann stuck her head around the door jamb, her arms, as usual, holding nearly a ream of reports. "Captain O'Brien, I thought you might like to know, Charlie was right. The Manila TV stations have all called the election for Emilio Legaspi. Apparently, it wasn't even close."

Pete sat back in his chair and nodded. "Very well, Mary Ann. Thank you for thinking to inform me."

He looked at her, assessing the dark circles under her eyes. "The violence in the streets has almost completely ceased. You ought to get a good night's sleep."

She started to close the door. Pete had another thought and called out to her: "Let's continue monitoring the Palace phones for another couple of days. Also pass to Charlie that the end of the election doesn't affect our concern about the Chinese, so I want a plan to keep at least one of the intelligence ships on station off the Philippines for the next twelve months."

"Aye aye, sir." Pete turned back to his message, struck a paragraph and added a new one discussing the election results before pressing 'transmit.' *Blue Ridge* would arrive back in Subic tomorrow and the Admiral was anxious to fly to Tokyo. These election results would make it possible. When the green dot on his computer flickered, Pete turned off his light and fell into bed.

CHAPTER THIRTY-SEVEN

A bright sunny new day and an early-morning jungle run had been completed with no new broken bones and only a few whines about aching shin splints. By the time the ship's bosun had finished trilling 'officers' call' and the staff had drawn new cups of coffee, Mary Ann was ready to begin the morning intelligence briefing. Her kick off was delayed for a few minutes when Tom Cooper and Bruce Parks stuck their heads in the door. It was useless for anyone to try to impede the animalistic process males use when welcoming strays back to the herd – involving punching biceps, slapping backs and the old standby from boot camps everywhere, tapping breastbones with a knuckle extended from a fist.

Pete let it go on long enough so Tom and Bruce could be comfortable that they were again part of the tribe and then terminated it by tapping the table twice with the heel of his hand. "OK, I guess congratulations are in order for a SEAL and a marine who managed to successfully find their way to Olongapo, but *Chancellorsville* is moored to the pier, so your feet get wet if you don't stop, which even a marine might notice." He saw Tom's lip was curling up. "And the direction signs are in English, so a SEAL, even with his very limited cognitive abilities, might still be able to discern, so let's get this meeting on the road."

Bruce protested. "It was harder than that, Chief of Staff. It was still very dark outside this morning and we only had one flashlight." Everyone hooted their approval.

Pete held his hand in the air. "Enough. We're all happy you both made it back. Don't push it any further. Mary Ann, hit it."

Despite the entertaining horseplay, and the fact she looked slightly better rested than she had yesterday, Mary Ann's expression was grim, "The *Manila Times* has a story buried on page six today that says some districts are reporting widespread fraud in yesterday's election."

She took a deep breath and put up a picture of the Philippine voting districts, with nearly a quarter of them checked. "Apparently, more than one polling area recorded no votes for Toseña."

Charlie shrugged his shoulders. "I personally didn't think she was very popular. I think this vote proves it."

Mary Ann closed her eyes for a second, obviously controlling an impulse to interrupt her boss. When she was sure he had finished speaking, she continued, "I had the staff check results from the last two elections. President Legaspi never received more than 70 per cent of the vote, even in the polling areas where he was the strongest. The check marks show precincts that didn't cast even one vote for Señora Toseña!" She drew a breath. "A couple of those 'no-shows' were precincts in the very province in which she grew up. These are not small voting areas. One of them contains more than five thousand active voters!"

Not even Charlie had a comment to offer.

She wrinkled her nose and pushed her glasses back on her forehead. "None of the television stations are carrying it yet, but there are some radio stations, including a very popular one in Cebu, that are already publicly alleging fraud and advocating a recall."

Charlie drew an X on the paper in front of him. "President Legaspi won by five per cent, which is decisive in any country, and he already has his hands on the levers of government. Even if isolated fraud did happen, what difference does it make? Legaspi is in office and controls the army. Toseña has no options."

Tom interjected, "Doesn't any hiccup in government transition just play into the hands of the Chinese?"

No one answered.

Mary Ann's eyes suddenly looked even more fatigued. "Rachel

Townsend called me right before the briefing. She wanted to know if we had heard anything about the rumor making the rounds in the capital that Archbishop Ver was going to personally celebrate Mass tomorrow at Manila's largest church."

Pete was curious. "Doesn't he celebrate Mass every week?"

"No. It's usually performed by a more junior priest. Ms Townsend also heard reports the Archbishop plans to deliver a homily on election fraud." Mary Ann had good reason to have tired eyes, Pete thought, and they might get darker if that last item proved true. He asked, "Did she share the source of that rumor?"

"She said it comes from the Palace. Her sources there are reporting Legaspi is considering declaring a state of emergency and cancelling all police and army leave."

Pete nodded. "I know this is primarily a Catholic country, but do you have any estimate for how many Catholics there are?"

"Eighty-three per cent of the almost hundred million Filipinos are Catholic, which computes to the high seventy millions. The Philippines has one of the largest concentrations of Catholics in the world. They are behind Brazil and Mexico, but a few million believers ahead of the United States."

Pete asked, "How many would you say are devout Catholics?"

"Eighty-two point nine per cent of everyone over the age of five."

Bruce gave out a low whistle. "Well, it may well be an interesting Sunday."

Tom Cooper's drawl slid across the table, "More than the Palace anticipates. While Bruce and I were making our way back to the ship last night, we overheard someone speculating that one of the two Philippine Cardinals may assist Ver at Mass."

As everyone stood to leave Charlie said, "On an administrative note, *Blue Ridge* moors in an hour, so everyone shift back aboard the flagship this afternoon and the evening meeting will be held there."

CHAPTER THIRTY-EIGHT

The sudden glow of Rodel's cigar was a harsh red against the dark of his bamboo garden. He slowly blew the gray smoke out into the black night and spoke into his cellphone, "And what may I do for my most esteemed friend, the Honorable Jamie Bautista?"

"Did you hear what that bastard Ver is planning?"

When Jamie had called, Rodel had immediately left the house to return the call. He thought Judith was asleep, but there was always the first time for a woman to make a fool of him. The Lord took care of those who also took care. He had long suspected someone might be tapping his landline. It could be the Chinese or perhaps Jamie. Maybe both. "I did. I also hear that Cardinal Baccay will assist."

"Jesus!"

"No, I think he's busy somewhere else tomorrow."

"Don't be such an asshole, Luzario."

Rodel took a sip on his cigar and let the silence build for a few seconds. "Jamie, let me give you some free advice. You won the last election. You won this election. Now all you have to do is to control the fallout. Third time may not be a charm. Next time, you put someone in charge of election results, call him into your office, sit him down, look him straight in the eyes and tell him, for God's sake, leave some numbers where the candidate herself votes! Three thousand, seven hundred and eighty-four to zero in her home province?! Of course, that is going to get press attention!"

"It was my cousin," Jamie murmured.

Rodel broke the tension by laughing. "We are Filipinos. It is always a cousin." He was rolling the cigar in his fingers so it would burn evenly. "Fortunately, most of mine died of smallpox. Now, how can I help get Legaspi and you to the next election?"

"The President thinks that Ver talking about the election will tear the Philippines apart. If what you hear about the Cardinal is true, that makes the situation infinitely worse."

"So you have the *Inquirer* and Star print some articles hinting he may be suffering from early Alzheimer's. You pay all those people to control t…"

Jamie interrupted, "The President had an emergency cabinet meeting this evening that has just broken up. He was very disappointed with the attitudes of both the Secretary of Defense and the Chief of Staff of the Army, who will be key figures in protecting our people from any violence." From the tone of his voice, Rodel knew Jamie was well past the listening stage.

"The elections reflected the will of the people. President Legaspi does not intend to permit a situation to develop in which innocent people will be hurt while conducting unlawful protests. It is the President of the Philippines' clear responsibility to protect all the Philippine people, even those who may not agree with him."

Jamie paused and Rodel took a pull on his cigar. He checked the doorway behind him to ensure Judith had not followed him down to the garden and let the cigar smoke swirl into his lungs. Here it comes.

CHAPTER THIRTY-NINE

"Chief of Staff, wake up!"

Pete immediately rolled over in bed and turned on a light. Mary Ann was at his stateroom door, holding it partially open, in uniform but obviously hurriedly dressed, her blouse misaligned by one button, her hair not up in her usual bun, a piece of paper in her hands.

He was instantly awake, a learned response after thousands of middle-of-the-night calls. "What is it?"

She waved the single sheet. "You need to read this."

As he flung back the single blanket, she closed the door, saying, "I'll be out here while you dress."

Pete pulled on some pants, slipped into some shoes, not bothering with socks, and followed her out of his door.

She was already sitting at his meeting table, the paper spread out in front of her. He put his hands on her shoulders to keep her from getting up and leaned over her head as she ran her index finger down the sheet while she explained what the Tagalog said: "This is an intercept from Rodel's phone and is the record of a conversation ten minutes ago. A little after midnight, he made a call to his deputy at the Aviation Squadron. Look here." Her finger stopped halfway down the page. "This is Rodel telling him to assemble three squads: one to kill Señora Toseña and the other two to assassinate the Philippine Secretary of Defense and the Army Chief of Staff." She moved her finger down another inch. "This implies Rodel will then be appointed as the new Secretary of National Defense."

Pete thought for a second. "Do we know the locations of the targets? Do they?"

She was apologetic. "We're not yet sure. I don't know what they think – they didn't say. I thought I should wake you as soon as they woke me."

"You did exactly right. Now, go back and see if your team can find any location information. If not, we will assume that the Defense Minister and the Army Chief of Staff are at home, and the same for Feliciaño. I need their house locations, or wherever you think the individuals are currently, in latitude and longitude. Come back here in fifteen minutes for a meeting."

"Feliciaño?"

He impatiently motioned her to leave. "Señora Toseña's first name. And Mary Ann" – she stopped in the doorway – "as you leave, smash the glass in the fire alarm next to my door and pull the lever down."

He replied to her quizzical look. "I want everyone aboard this ship awake right now." The alarm would ring in every space, immediately stirring everyone to action.

Pete buzzed the *Blue Ridge* Officer-of-the-Deck on the special circuit from flag quarters and waited until the fire alarm stopped ringing to speak: "This is the Seventh Fleet Chief of Staff. Pass the word that there is no fire but I need everyone up and about. Use the 1MC to have my staff officers report to my stateroom immediately. Then ask your Commanding Officer to also be present in ten minutes. After that, locate the other Commanding Officers who are in port, as well as the Brigade Commanding General and request each of them to report in my stateroom in half an hour."

He made the next call on his private cell phone and listened to the buzzing of the Philippine exchange for a full ten seconds before her sleepy voice answered, "*Hola?*"

"Love, wake up. I need you to be alert. Are you with me?"

He heard her soft intake of breath and then, "Yes, my Captain."

"Legaspi has sent out death squads tasked to kill your aunt, along with his Secretary of Defense and his Army Chief of Staff. I know she doesn't like Americans very much, but we can damn sure protect her. I favour us as the best choice for safety – both hers and yours. I'm sending a car to pick the two of you up. It'll be at your house in half an hour to forty-five minutes. I need you to persuade her to come here to *Blue Ridge*. Bring Maria and your uncle if you like. I intend to send you all out to sea, so you are all safe from prying eyes and assassins."

He stopped to take a breath. "We will keep it a secret as to where she is, but she needs to stay safe for the sake of the Philippines. OK, love?"

Nothing on the other end. She couldn't have fallen back asleep, but there was no dial tone. "Sweetheart?"

"OK, Pete. You are my captain."

He had brushed his teeth and was fully dressed by the time Tom and Bruce simultaneously arrived at his door. Pete inclined his head toward the lone piece of paper Mary Ann had left on the table, while he poured each of them some coffee. He knew Bruce spoke and read Tagalog.

He gave them two minutes to read and assimilate while he tucked in his shirt.

"Tom, aren't you friends with the Army Chief of Staff?"

"Yes, sir."

"I assume you have his personal cell-phone number." Tom nodded. "Good. Call him. Tell him the situation. Get him out of his house and moving, so he'll be harder to locate and target. If he wants, promise to pick him and his family up at an agreed location by helo."

Pete took a deep breath. "I know he and the Defense Secretary are close. See if he can reach the Secretary. If you can't raise either of them by the time the staff assembles here, grab a couple of helos and riflemen and see if you can find the Chief of Staff before the Aviation Squadron does. I will send someone else for the Secretary."

"Bruce, you lead the team to get Ms Toseña. There is no helo pad near her house, so you're going to have to drive there and pick them up."

"I thought she didn't like Americans."

Pete ignored his implied question "If you hustle, her home is only about a half-hour drive from here. By the time you get there, her campaign manager should have convinced her that she needs us. Pick up everyone who lives there and bring them back here ASAP."

"Her campaign manager?"

"Her niece. Goes by the name of Kristina Baclayon. I called her while you two were combing your hair. Make sure you at least pick up Kristina as well as her aunt. Probably ought to get everyone that lives in the house in case someone torches it."

"OK if I leave before the meeting?"

"Please do. Mary Ann should have both the address and the lat/long of the house. Take a couple of marines with you."

Bruce laughed and slugged Tom, who was leaning against a bulkhead dialing a number. "I never go anywhere without some marines to protect me." He disappeared out the door. Tom followed him, now talking on his cell. It was another minute before the other staff members began to straggle in.

CHAPTER FORTY

After a frantic evening spent reacting to President Legaspi's attempted assassination orders, the flag spaces aboard USS *Blue Ridge* were relatively quiet on Sunday morning. It had been a long night. Most officers were still groggy or catching up on their sleep.

The Army Chief of Staff, when informed of Legaspi's intentions, angrily declared he controlled more of the army than the President. He had noted, perhaps not so cryptically, "The President has placed himself at terrible risk."

For himself, the Philippine Secretary of Defense had declined any offer of sanctuary, opting instead for the familiarity of his home province, where he, along with two bodyguards, were reportedly headed. Neither appeared interested in keeping Seventh Fleet informed as to their whereabouts.

However, whatever their personal opinions about America, each Filipino principal had been more than pleased to have their immediate family protected by the thick steel of a US Navy ship steaming on the wide blue sea. Thus, hours earlier, shortly before the first light began seeping around the Subic Bay breakwater, USS *Cowpens* had slipped her mooring and steamed out to sea. Along with the Secretary of Defense and Army Chief of Staff dependents, Señora Toseña and Señorita Kristina had been safely aboard and below decks out of sight of any camera.

While Pete had been unable to intuit any intentions, he had noticed both men had held long private discussions with Señora Toseña and

Kristina before *Cowpens* departed. Pete had subsequently taken a few minutes with each of the men to discuss possible options in the event that a potential hostile power should choose this period of unrest to mount Philippine territorial challenges.

Señora Toseña had been a different and difficult kettle of fish. She didn't have an armed force at her beck and call. She was also not willing to kiss and make up with Pete or anyone else who sailed under the stars and stripes. It had taken several hours last night for her to accept that Legaspi was personally involved in her death decree. Finally, Kristina had taken the direct approach of donning headphones and listening to the tapes of the intercepts. She then forced her aunt to listen to the key forty-second segment. Subsequently, Toseña and Kristina had then spent an hour privately sequestered in a stateroom before Kristina had emerged and extracted a pledge from Pete to control and limit the number of people who knew her aunt was aboard a US ship, as well as to immediately land her on her homeland if and when she so requested. Only then did Señora Toseña reluctantly board USS *Cowpens*.

The caution was fine with Pete. He had his own reasons for the utmost of discretion about his guests. He did not want information on last night's Seventh Fleet involvement in Philippine events to reach anyone in the Palace or the Embassy before the Admiral had the opportunity to personally sit down with the Ambassador.

Toward this end, Pete had spent thirty minutes on a secure line with the Admiral early Tokyo-time bringing his boss up to speed. The Admiral and Pete tended to think the same, and Pete was a succinct briefer, so less than half the call had been spent on reviewing the evening's events. The rest had been on the pros and cons of the Admiral traveling personally to the Philippines to brief the Ambassador.

The delay a face-to-face meeting would entail would also give them a reason to have another 24 hours to gather information. In his gut, Pete knew the tap would be compromised shortly after the Ambassador knew about it. Rodel's phone had already prevented one bloodbath. But all Embassies were leaky, with a large number of trusted foreign nationals. Some would inevitably be double agents. Pete had already cautioned everyone in 'the Manila Cell' to resist the temptation to discuss any of last evening's events.

In the meantime, using the ostensible rationale that possible widespread violence might follow this morning's Mass, he had gained the Ambassador's agreement to a five-fold increase in the guards within the Embassy. Marine helicopters were now flying every four hours over the Embassy. Their racketing sent a visible (and very loud) message of American strength throughout Manila.

After Mary Ann reported that none of the Philippine news agencies appeared to yet realize Toseña – much less their Army Chief of Staff and National Defense Secretary – were missing, Pete had ordered her to get some rest. There would be a lull until the Archbishop spoke.

Pete got a fresh cup of coffee, accessed his own little black book of numbers, and dialed one in DC. "This is Captain O'Brien from Seventh Fleet. May I speak to Colonel Winters?"

"Stan, have you been able to win that tournament since I left?"

Pete listened to the reply and then genially responded, "I'm surprised you even made it to the semi-finals. You are slow and old, just like that F-15 you used to fly." Pete chuckled, "You need to abandon the handball court to the younger officers."

Pete smiled at his Air Force friend's retort. "Do you kiss your wife with that same mouth? Speaking of Karen, is she still enjoying teaching those sixth-grade hellions?"

He listened patiently to Stan for nearly another minute. "I know, once someone lets them get out of control, that age is hell-on-wheels, which is funny for that is exactly why I called you. We have our own unruly group and I find myself needing a really good classroom monitor."

Pete looked out his porthole at the breeze through the palm fronds. "I'm curious as to whether you could break loose one of your Global Hawks for a couple of days. Over the Philippines – primarily Luzon and Manila."

Pete listened to Stan call to someone in his office and an indistinct background conversation that lasted more than a minute. He took a sip of his coffee. He liked it hotter.

A half-hour later and three decks below Pete's office in her own intelligence lair, Captain Mary Ann Saunders was in the process of keeping her opposite number at the Embassy routinely informed: "Rachel, Mary Ann here, hasn't it been crazy these past couple of days?"

"Us too. I don't know anyone that's gotten a good night's sleep. Pete wanted me to let you know that the Pentagon has agreed to loan us a Global Hawk for a few days so we can better keep an eye on the developing situation. It should show up in the Philippines air space some time tomorrow.

"Yes, I am aware Congress doesn't provide State with that kind of money, but we will have the picture on all of our ships and if you wish, you can send someone to *Blue Ridge* to observe and report back to Don and the Ambassador. Certainly we would welcome the Ambassador! Just let us know so we can prepare for his visit."

The clock tolled three bells over Pete's head. Ding-ding. Ding. The Global Hawk had launched out of Nevada an hour ago. It should be overhead sometime early tomorrow. Then he would have complete large-scale visual and radar information on the Philippines.

The next few days would be an endurance slog. As much as they might prefer, neither he nor the Admiral could drive events. Only the Filipinos controlled what would happen in the Philippines. The Americans had helped even up the odds for the Army Chief of Staff, the Defense Secretary and Señora Toseña, but the next steps were up to the locals. The United States Navy could not do much more without being viewed as interfering.

History had unkindly proven several times that once the US became involved, it either had to be very committed for the very long haul or it would turn ugly, ugly, ugly. At the moment, Pete would be surprised if the average American could find the South China Sea on a map if you gave him three clues and a compass.

The critical question would be whether the Philippine people were sufficiently fed up with Legaspi to risk their personal safety. If so, the election ballots might be recounted – this time in the streets.

Pete yawned. He had gotten less than an hour's sleep last night and the afternoon's staff briefing would come much too soon. He turned out his bedroom light, pulled the green curtains across the sunny porthole, and was instantly fast asleep.

In the intelligence spaces, another routine communication inquiry from the Embassy had just rung in on the telephone and Mary Ann was in the midst of answering:

"Rachel, I will need to bring that up to Pete for approval."

Damn. Mary Ann gritted her teeth and held the receiver to her breast. She had just screwed up. She scrambled to recover.

"I know Rodel Luzario has been a guest aboard *Blue Ridge* before and is now a member of the Philippine – never mind, I plead momentary insanity from lack of sleep. Of course, we will be looking forward to having you and the Ambassador, Don and Rodel aboard tomorrow to see a demonstration of the Global Hawk technology. Anything else we need to discuss today?"

"*Ciao.*"

Mary Ann took off her glasses, lowered her head to her desk and banged her forehead softly against her ink blotter. What the hell was she doing even momentarily objecting to Luzario accompanying the Ambassador on a visit? In the white world, they were all still the very best of friends. She hoped her reaction to Luzario's name hadn't spooked Rachel, but it very well might have and if Rachel said anything to Rodel…

She was going to have to give Pete a heads-up.

"First," Pete sipped from his mug of coffee, "I think we should all congradulate Tom and Bruce. Not only did they each lead successful missions last night that saved the bacon of some VIPs…" – he paused for dramatic effect – "but neither one got lost!"

"A definite first," Bill Rogers quickly opined.

"Unexpected," was Mark's contribution.

"With the added benefit" – Pete raised his eyebrows – "that we discovered the grid map the Embassy provided us for Manila actually shows the city two-tenths of a mile south of the real latitude of the streets and buildings."

"Which," Tom drawled, "scared the hell out of me when the designated landing zone was empty. But we'd flown over two automobiles stopped with their lights on a couple of blocks away and my pilot, being a bright young lad – as are all marines, as you well know, Chief of Staff..."

Bill snorted, "What you mean is some nineteen-year-old kid saved your ass again!"

Tom adopted a pious attitude: "We are all part of America's Team, which the Marine Corps is honored to lead."

Pete smiled raising his mug in a toast. "Enough. Good and brave work by all concerned." He swiveled slightly in his chair. "Mary Ann, what do you have for us this morning?"

She began the briefing from her chair. "As had been heavily rumored, Archbishop Ver gave his homily on fraud this morning and, to the apparent surprise of the news media, he was assisted at the Mass by Cardinal Reyes."

The room was silent.

"In a nutshell, it is being reported that Ver preached about the responsibilities of good Catholics. According to the Archbishop, true believers have a sacred duty to not acquiesce to those who would perpetuate fraud and violence."

Pete looked at her quizzically.

Mary Ann slowly stood, shaking her head. "He didn't say anything specifically about the election, and the one radio station that immediately drew that parallel was off the air thirty minutes later and hasn't come back up."

Bruce looked up from examining his knife. "Anything about last evening's guests?"

"No. Not a whisper. Those in the Philippine government who know they were supposed to be assassinated are certainly keeping quiet. If there was anyone we don't know who was also targeted, they are either still running for a safe location or are dead and the bodies hidden." She shook her head. "I have no way of knowing."

She pushed her glasses back on her nose. "Rachel is sending a transcript of the homily back to Washington as soon the Embassy completes the translation. I asked her to include us on the distribution list. Of course, I already pushed a copy of our intercept of the death order back to the Joint Staff via CincPacFlt on a black circuit.

"Rachel reports that the Ambassador is sending a dispatch to Washington saying he is surprised Archbishop Ver intervened in a political affair. Apparently, Ambassador Coyle talked with him late the previous afternoon and was led to believe that he had defused the situation."

Bruce laughed, "If he were surprised by the homily, then I bet he was shocked by the Cardinal's participation in the Mass."

"He was."

Pete impatiently interrupted: "The Ambassador should go back to waste management if he thinks we can micromanage a country's politics." He caught himself before he commented further. "Let's get back to business. Charlie, has the *Cowpens* reported any problems? What do you hear on the time of the Global Hawk's arrival and does anyone think we should pre-position troops on Grande Island?"

Mary Ann did not immediately relinquish her mechanical pointer as Charlie reached for it, but, instead, handed him a laser one. "One more thing, Chief of Staff, we are beginning to get reports of crowds of people starting to gather at Señora Toseña's house."

"Any estimates as to how many people are gathered? Is it a mob?"

"A few thousand, sir, and reports are that they are being very orderly. One person told a TV reporter that they were all Toseña supporters. Another source reportedly promised more are on the way."

"Our mooring is only a half-hour away from her house. Do they appear to be a threat to our ships and sailors?"

A frown crossed her brow, "I don't know how to judge that."

"Very well, that's an Operations question anyway, so this is a good opportunity for us to shift to thinking about what else we should be doing if violence breaks out. Captain Harper, please proceed. Include how you're doing on plans for using Grande Island."

For the second straight night, seemingly right after Pete had gone to sleep, Mary Ann knocked at his stateroom door and stuck her head in, "Chief of Staff, it has been four hours since Rodel has used his telephone."

Pete woke from a dreamless slumber. He didn't bother to turn on a light. He could see her backlit from the light from the other room. "Maybe he is asleep."

Mary Ann was so upset she didn't recognize his weak attempt at sarcasm. "I don't think so, and this is usually the time of the day when we see the most activity on the phone. He was talking and texting every few minutes until about eight tonight."

Pete rolled over in bed so he could see her silhouette against the light from the passageway. "What do you think?"

"I think" – her voice was so low Pete almost couldn't hear her – "I think I must have let something slip today to Rachel. You know she and Rodel Luzario are close. For several hours, I've been becoming more convinced she was spooked over our conversation about the visit they scheduled and then cancelled." Her voice was resigned. "What if Mr Luzario put two and two together from me being reluctant to have him attend?" There was a lengthy silence. "I'm really sorry, Captain. I'll let you know if it starts up again." She eased the door shut and, a moment later, the outside light completely disappeared.

Pete rolled over on his back, put his hands behind his head and stared at the metal ceiling. There was no use crying over spilt milk, but if Rodel and Legaspi suspected Rodel's communications had been compromised, how did that change the chessboard? What should they now anticipate?

After a few minutes, he got up, dressed and went looking for fresh coffee. His sixth sense was telling him something needed to be done. Maybe he would first go for a run.

CHAPTER FORTY-ONE

"This is the best picture we can provide until the Global Hawk gets here, Chief of Staff." Charlie Harper put the laptop in front of him, pushed a key and the scene began to roll. "*Eisenhower* launched a photo recon mission at first light. This is from a couple of F/A-18 aircraft equipped with Hughes electro-optical PODs. This film is from a pass they made near Señora Toseña's residence."

Pete increased the screen contrast and then let the gray-green picture unfold. Mary Ann reached across him with the eraser end of her ubiquitous yellow pencil to tap what appeared to be a Tinker toy arrangement and keyed a magnification increase. "Those are barriers thrown up across a paved road to stop wheeled army vehicles from passing through at speeds faster than walking. I've seen scenes in Libya and Iraq like that. Normally, those barricades are thrown together from furniture and old cars. Here they are adding felled logs." As the picture moved, her pencil tapped several other road junctions. "Looks to me like the citizens have turned out to establish a protected sector of the countryside for Toseña. She isn't inside her complex, but they don't know that."

Charlie interjected. "Chief of Staff, essentially, all the roads to Señora Toseña's house are presently closed to vehicular traffic. Some radio and television stations are reporting there are more than a hundred thousand people camping out in the immediate vicinity of her residence."

Pete looked up from the laptop presentation, "Peaceful?"

"No reports of violence that we or the Embassy have received." Mary

Ann noticeably flinched at the word 'Embassy' but Pete didn't even glance her way. He didn't intend to rehash last night. If Mary Ann changed her pattern of co-ordination, the Embassy might suspect Seventh Fleet was hiding even more. Although Rodel's phone was dark, the taps in the Palace were still providing useful information. Pete and Mary Ann had together reviewed the latest intercepts less than an hour ago.

She was tapping her eraser on a different picture when Pete refocused his attention: "…flatbed trucks filled with cargo are being led around the barricades. They are reportedly from several of the nearby provinces. The trucks appear to be loaded with porta-potties, food and tents."

"I appreciate the F-18 infra-red pictures, but they're always time late. When will we have the Global Hawk real-time feed?"

Mary Ann wrinkled her nose, grimaced and pushed her glasses back' "There is some sort of technical difficulty. The Global Hawk is already overhead at 25,000 feet, but we aren't yet receiving images."

She added, "The *Cowpens* somehow knows it is there. They've been calling hourly, asking when the link is going to be up."

Charlie Harper, who had been standing at her shoulder, broke in: "I have put our Air Force liaison officer and two computer techs on this problem full time."

Pete smiled to himself. He wasn't happy about the glitch, but he was surely glad he wasn't the current object of Feliciaño's frustration. He could only imagine the situation aboard *Cowpens*. He would have to recommend the Commanding Officer for some sort of award – perhaps for bravery under wrath, if there were such a category. "In the meantime, see if you can tell from the morning F-18 pictures whether or not there are any armored movements. If there are it would be useful to know if we think they are from troops loyal to Legaspi or alternatively to the Army Chief of Staff." Pete thought for a second before he returned to his typing, "Let me know as soon as you have a rough conclusion of what's going on, and Mary Ann" – she looked up from her notepad – "I want to see the very first Global Hawk picture that wends its way earthward."

*

Twelve hours later, a montage of pictures of Luzon from several sources, including several taken by the Global Hawk, were laid out on the flag space plotting table.

Mary Ann was using the eraser of her pencil to touch different blurs on the mosaic. "These gray things are people. From this altitude, they look like dots, but" – she handed Pete a magnifying glass – "if you use this, you can sometimes discern individuals. If you look carefully, it appears some couples have brought their children." She paused and tapped an area of the Global Hawk picture that looked more like a starry sky than anything else. "We think these pinpoints of light are campfires."

"We don't see that many Global Hawk images, so Charlie called back to the States and asked for specialists to analyze this particular one. The specialists estimate the crowd near her house to be on the order of at least two hundred thousand."

Pete nodded and changed the subject. "What about Philippine Army units?"

"With the exception of the Aviation Squadron, we haven't seen anybody moving. The Aviation Squadron has relocated to the Palace grounds."

She answered the unspoken question conveyed by the lift of Pete's heavy eyebrows. "They have ten tanks with them. According to the Philippine battle-element breakdown, the Squadron is composed of five hundred infantry and includes thirty-two Humvees. I would stipulate each of the vehicles has at least one heavy machine gun mounted on it. Some may also have mortars welded or bolted onto the flatbed."

Pete nodded. These would be powerful against unarmed citizenry. On the other hand, armed power was always relative. If a squadron of navy or marine aircraft struck, after one pass, there would be nothing left but smoldering heaps of rubble.

Mary Ann took a breath. "Everybody else in the army is officially confined to their barracks." She pushed back her glasses. "On the 'special circuit' from the Palace, we heard Bautista ordering various army commanders to gather their forces and move to the capitol region, but his orders appear to be largely ignored. None of the pictures of the main roads shows armored vehicles rolling." She wrinkled her nose and temporized: "We could obviously miss individual units of infantry if they are not operating as a cohesive force."

She left unsaid that if units were not organized, they would be easily rolled back and eliminated by even the limited number of US marines already in Subic.

She worried her pencil, absentmindedly pushing the yellow #2 back and forth in her bun. "Filipino soldiers may be traveling secretly, but all our sources indicate those armed forces who might be expected to be loyal to the President are currently camped out in their own headquarters. They appear to be intent on staying there. We see nothing to the contrary. None of Bruce or Tom's sources is talking, and Ms Townsend says the Embassy is also puzzled."

Mary Ann gave Pete a look she clearly intended as meaningful, "She mentioned she hadn't seen or heard from Rodel since a Saturday-night reception at the Palace."

Pete suspected Mary Ann hadn't shared with Charlie or the other staff members her concern that one of her conversations with Rachel had ultimately been the cause of Rodel's phone shutdown, so he simply said, "Do the times correlate?"

She nodded unhappily.

"Ah well," Pete said dismissively, "that's life in the big leagues." He ran his hands over the photo mosaic as if expecting insight to flow up from the black and gray pictures. "Make sure the other ships and the Marine Expeditionary Brigade are receiving these."

CHAPTER FORTY-TWO

Kristina was sitting in her room's single chair, reading her iPad, pretending she had not heard the ten minutes of dry-heaving from their shared bathroom. Feliciaño Toseña finally knocked on the interconnecting door and stepped into Kristina's stateroom, dressed as if for a day at the office, complete with inappropriate four-inch heels, her face drawn in pain. "They have poisoned me."

"We've eaten the same food for both days we've been here, Auntie. You get seasick if you so much as look at a boat. Remember when you made that trip to Hong Kong with Uncle and insisted on flying back? And that was a much larger ship."

As if to underline her words, *Cowpens* took a slight roll and Feliciaño lost her balance. Kristina immediately stood up and steadied her aunt. She held her affectionately. "We need something else for you to think about. Let's go talk to the Captain and see if Pete's Global Hawk is here."

In the excitement of the campaign, it had been more than a week since Kristina had done her nails. She had been completely oblivious in the adrenaline of the final days. She probably wouldn't have noticed now if she hadn't been so attentive to the gray drip of overrun paint she was picking at on the gyrocompass repeater in the *Cowpens* Command Center. Of course, it was either focus on this particular imperfection or reconsider her wisdom in taking a seasick woman with considerable anti-American sentiment out of their private staterooms and into the public of a United States' warship's nerve center. It might not have been her best idea of the decade… Her aunt was currently about to drill herself into the overhead over a non-issue,. "I was elected to represent my province, so why can't I see it?"

The *Cowpens* Captain was shaking his head. "None of us have access. The Global Hawk is up there, but there's something wrong with the video link. When we do get it, we will project it on to the large screen in the overhead. At the moment, we're not receiving any…"

Feliciaño whirled on Kristina, "I bet your precious Captain O'Brien is looking at all of Luzon right now."

The pointer fingernail on her Kristina's left hand was on the verge of chipping.

Toseña hissed at the *Cowpen's* Captain. "I demand that you let me speak with Captain O'Brien."

The Captain reluctantly turned to one of his men just as a blue and gray picture fortuitously began unfolding over their heads.

It was time for the Tuesday-morning staff meeting. The normal key advisors, less Bruce and Tom, but including Marine General Bill Heard, were gathered around the largest table in the flag spaces.

Pete waited until everyone had coffee. He added cream to his own before rapping his spoon twice against his heavy mug. At the distinctive clinking sound, everyone found a seat and Mary Ann turned on the projector and rose to take her usual position beside the wall screen. She started to speak, but Pete held up his hand. "Before we start, everyone should know that Señora Toseña has decided she wants to be put ashore."

"We will make one last-ditch effort to convince her that is not the best option. Mary Ann will be going out to *Cowpens* this morning to ensure the Señora has our best interpretation of all the latest intelligence. If that mission fails, and I suspect it will, *Cowpens* will come alongside pier number three on Grande Island this evening shortly after dark. At that time, Toseña and her party will be disembarked. The Secretary's wife and the General's family have decided to accept our afloat hospitality a bit longer."

Pete looked around the room. "Obviously if anyone disembarks into these several hundreds of thousands of protestors, this will change the country's dynamics. At the very least, I expect significantly elevated tensions. I want everyone thinking about the Philippine situation in light of these expected events. At the same time..." – Pete looked individually at each of the eleven attendees for a split second – "I don't want information about any of our guests known by anyone other than those currently in this room."

He leaned back in his chair and cradled the hot coffee in his hands. "OK, Mary Ann, start us rolling today."

"The image analysts at Pearl Harbor estimate the crowd currently camping near Señora Toseña's home to be in excess of four hundred thousand, which is a hundred thousand more than yesterday, and the number is swelling every hour. Ms Townsend tells me they have reports that place the Army Chief of Staff in the crowd..."

"It just isn't right!" Charlie Harper interrupted the briefing.

Somehow Pete wasn't surprised. "What isn't, Charlie?"

"The Embassy is keeping us abreast of the situation. But we are withholding vital information from them!"

"What vital information?"

Charlie was red in the face and his voice was indignant. "The fact that Toseña is returning. That we have been protecting her for the last several days. That someone on this staff illegally tapped the Palace phone network! The fact you are spying on the entire Philippines with electronic-intercept ships and Global Hawks!"

Pete interrupted, "Only one Global Hawk, Charlie." Pete was giving Charlie one last opportunity to control himself.

Charlie ignored this invitation to let the issue slide and plunged ahead: "I feel dirty every time I talk to Don Collingsworth!"

Pete ran his hand over his face and rubbed his eyes. He had avoided the 'Charlie issue' for too long. The situation was not going to get any better and it was not going to fix itself. And now Charlie had raised a trust issue in public. It was past time to fix this. Pete lowered his coffee cup to the table. "Did we save some lives last Saturday night?"

Charlie didn't respond.

"You were there. On Sunday, you and I personally called on the Ambassador. Did he believe us when you and I told him what Legaspi had done?" From the corner of his eye, Pete could see Mary Ann's startled glance. Until now, she had no idea that Pete and her boss had even spoken to the Ambassador about the top-secret information.

Charlie again didn't respond and Pete gently prodded, "Did he?"

"No."

"What did he do?"

"He said you were attempting to destroy Legaspi's reputation."

Pete took a sip of his coffee. Charlie's face was turning pale. Perhaps he finally realized he had gone too far. Too late. Blood was in the water. The room was quiet. Pete said, "What reputation?"

"The Ambassador…said Legaspi is…is the greatest President in Philippine history and the book the Ambassador is writing will document that fact."

"Yes." Pete paused and waited, taking another sip of his cooling coffee. What else did the Ambassador say?" It became very quiet. Sounds from Blue Ridge activities began to seep in the room. Far down the passageway someone was practicing soft trills on a bosun's pipe. On the weather deck directly overhead could be heard the soft thumps of a sailor flaking out a five-inch line.

Charlie's voice was low: "He said he would personally destroy both you and the Admiral." His face had gone through white and was now turning pink. His eyes were focused directly on Pete like a rat does on a cobra that has him cornered.

Pete let the stillness build for a few more seconds before inquiring quietly, "And then?" Thank God for whistle-blowers everywhere and their trust in men in uniform.

Charlie literally gushed with disapproval. He had been just as offended on Sunday. "You asked what his specific partnership percentage was in the teak export company he and Rodel had secretly established!"

Pete rubbed his chin, as if checking the completeness of his morning shave, purposefully ignoring the surprised faces around the table. "And?"

"He threw us out of his office."

"Did he deny it?"

"He didn't say anything." He muttered, "He shouldn't have to. He's an Ambassador!" He lowered his voice to a whisper, "You were insulting."

Pete ignored the *sotto voce* comment. "And what did you find out about those papers I gave you?"

"Don Collingsworth says they look like forgeries to him."

Pete finally let his voice rise. "I am not interested in what Collingsworth says, any more than I am about any lies Rodel tells." From the look on Charlie's face, it was immediately obvious he had also showed the papers to the latter. "I want to know the results of *your* investigation!"

"Rodel denied it."

"This is all you have accomplished in two days?"

Charlie gave a slight nod.

Pete kept his voice as level as he could manage. "Captain Harper, stand at attention."

When he had done so, Pete also stood. "Captain Charles Harper, I have lost faith in your performance. You are hereby relieved of all duties. You will turn over all of your responsibilities to your Deputy, Commander John Stevens. You will proceed directly to your room and remain there for the remainder of the deployment or until the Admiral gives you other orders. You will not communicate with anyone in any way."

"Do you understand?"

"Yes, sir."

Charlie left the room. Pete looked at Tom. The latter got up and followed Charlie.

Pete sat and made a circular motion with his right index finger to Mary Ann. She turned back to the Global Hawk picture.

The staff meeting was done and Pete had spent two hours signing some of the routine paperwork he had been avoiding when there was a sharp knock at the door. Tom Cooper and Bob Bruce entered, carefully closing the door behind them. Pete stacked the signed documents in a pile and looked over at Tom. "Did you locate him?"

Cooper nodded affirmatively. "He knows when *Cowpens* moors." Tom paused. "He asked what you suggested they do."

"And you replied?"

"That we believed Philippine events were up to the Filipinos."

"Good answer. Welcome back." Pete shifted his questioning gaze to Bruce.

"Ditto with the Archbishop. Roughly the same question asked – a little less direct since he is a civilian – and I provided the same answer."

"Thank you. I believe that's all we can do. Get a good night's sleep. I expect the next couple of days will be long ones."

Pete put aside papers that needed to be signed and turned his attention to the draft of his daily report. The Admiral had directed that Charlie Harper be sent directly to Pearl Harbor. Bad apples and barrels, etc. Now Pete was drafting a message for the Admiral to forward to Honolulu and Washington on the existing situation. These reports were becoming longer each day.

CHAPTER FORTY-THREE

Even without the nasty chop, it was not Mary Ann's favorite way to spend a morning. Scuttling back and forth from a small boat to a warship in any kind of weather involved some degree of danger.

Looking at the whitecaps, she was estimating it was a wind of at least thirty-five knots. Maybe gusts to fifty. It probably presaged rain this afternoon, a sideshow of the low-pressure area the meteorology briefer had predicted was bearing down on Hong Kong. But sailors need to be able to ignore the whip of sea spray. It's part of the job description.

Thus, Mary Ann watched the coxswain gun their small boat into the leeward side of USS *Cowpens*. The deck seamen reached up to hook the lowered sea painter to steady the bow. All the rubber fenders were lowered on the port side of their small motorboat. She was impressed how the coxswain ignored the drenching as he evaluated the incoming waves. He was in slickers, but was still taking a lot of water at his station in the very stern of the boat.

Old wives' tales were right: the biggest waves were about five to seven apart, and selecting the right one was crucial. *Cowpens* had lowered a transfer platform and two strong seamen were standing at its lowest extension. The coxswain needed a wave that lifted them high enough for Mary Ann and John to be able to leap to safety, but not so high that the passengers might be crushed between the motorboat and the receiving platform.

A wave passed that had been perfect – peaking four or five feet under the heavy planks, steel I-beams and canvas covering that made up the platform. She saw the coxswain glance at her through eyelashes that dripped with seawater. She understood his challenge. She wasn't a bit interested in being squashed against the platform or falling short, being dropped in the water and being churned into fish chum by the *Cowpens* screws before she could be rescued. Would that event even rate a *Star* headline back home? 'Bridgeport Navy Girl Lost at Sea!' Probably not. She gave him a casual salute. She would stick with her career in intelligence and leave him to the giant waves.

A few waves later, the coxswain revved the engine, threw the rudder over, and the motorboat fenders banged hard against the gray side of the *Cowpens*. A slop of seawater geysered up dramatically between the motorboat and the hull, wetting everyone. Mary Ann stepped on the gunwale and leaped for the suspended metal platform. Two sailors caught her arms beneath her elbows and heaved her up the ladder that led to the weather deck twenty feet above. John Stevens was right at her heels. As she climbed, she looked down. The deckhand had cast off the knotted line and the motorboat was circling away to starboard none the worse for wear. She could reverse the process when the meeting was over. Maybe she would be dry by then. Oh, right, it was going to be raining.

"Señora Toseña" – Mary Ann stepped to one side – "if you and your campaign manager stand in front of me, you will have a better perspective and it will be easier for me to show you what the Global Hawk is seeing." The drone's sensors were now focused on the western suburbs of Manila. They were programmed to shift to the airport area in fifteen minutes. She keyed in an increase in the gray contrast to enhance the morning shadows. From these acute overhead angles, most people had great difficulties identifying the most common of objects, but while Kristina quietly observed, Toseña had quickly begun working with the operator to manipulate the pictures herself.

Mary Ann stepped back from the display and watched the two women looking at their country from five miles in the sky. She probably shouldn't be surprised by how beautiful Kristina was – she had sensed how much Pete was hung up on her. And she should not have been surprised at Toseña. She had heard that, in the past forty-eight hours, the woman had been quite difficult to some of the senior officers of the *Cowpens*! Several of the latter had attempted to complain to Mary Ann, but she had ignored them. She had watched Pete destroy Charlie Harper in public just yesterday, and Toseña seemed nothing less than his female equivalent. Mary Ann had no desire to step between the two. In fact, the thought of both in the same room gave her chills. As her Grandpappy used to say, she would pay cash money to be a fly on a wall to watch that. It would almost be worth that goddamn boat ride out and back to the *Cowpens* – but not quite.

"Niece, I must be there." Feliciaño was speaking rapidly as she leaned closer to the bathroom mirror. "This is our best chance to get rid of Luzario." She was using an eyebrow pencil to darken the portion of her left eyebrow where some gray first tended to show. "You saw the America pictures – this was your uncle's dream! There are hundreds of thousands of people already in the streets. We have come so far. Ligaya died to give Filipinos this opportunity." She finished, grimaced at her reflection, turned and handed her small purse to Kristina, who dropped it inside her own much larger one, "Without me, there is no one for the people to follow."

And, Kristina thought, boats make you very seasick. But she only said, "I will ask the Captain to land us on Grande Island and see if we can find a transportation from there to the airport."

I know my aunt is probably correct, she thought, but I do so wish Pete were here.

Mary Ann and John Stevens had changed into dry clothes and John was making the report. Pete was obviously bothered by indications of friction between Toseña's and the *Cowpens* wardroom and he questioned John closely: "Perhaps she was uncomfortable aboard the ship. Was she pleasant to Mary Ann and you?"

"She was very formal. That young woman who is her campaign

manager seemed really nice, but her brother is as prickly as his aunt. That is one strange family."

As a messenger brought John some papers to read and sign, Mary Ann stepped to Pete's side and lowered her voice to a whisper: "That campaign manager asked me about you, Chief of Staff. She is much prettier than her file photos. She and I had only previously talked on the phone."

"Previously? I didn't realize you'd met."

"She introduced herself the night she called the ship and asked if getting the SIM card in Luzario's phone was important to you."

"She called you?" From the look on Pete's face, Mary Ann knew this was new information. Thankfully, the Deputy Operations Officer choose that moment to thrust the sheaf of papers back at the runner and break into their conversation, "Excuse me, Chief of Staff, but I don't think Toseña wants to be seen disembarking from a navy ship. That's the reason she asked to be landed on Grande Island tonight. In accordance with your general instructions I approved *Cowpens* putting Ms Toseña and her immediate family on the island after nautical sunset tonight and loaning them a motorboat. The motorboat will then make landfall somewhere on the perimeter of the Subic Bay International Airport."

Pete looked at Mary Ann. "She didn't change her mind?"

Mary Ann shook her head. "I don't think she was even listening. She was not about to stay aboard that ship another day."

John was also not listening. He was focused on his papers and the plan for landing the Toseña party. "Once she is ashore, since she could have arrived in that location from nearly anywhere in the Philippines, no Filipino will have the slightest idea where she's been."

Pete nodded "How about protection for them in the interim? Does she need guards?"

John shook his head "She was almost unbalanced on the subject of Filipinos killing Filipinos. She was adamant about no American guards, and she didn't want the loan of any guns. She has asked for Archbishop Ver to meet her in the terminal."

Pete asked, "Did she say anything about the mantle of the Church protecting her?"

John lifted an eyebrow. "Not to me" He shrugged his shoulders. "She wouldn't listen to anything I said out there on *Cowpens*." His tone was getting snarky and Mary Ann wondered how much longer Pete was going to let it go. "I know the Church" – his voice added emphasis to those two words – "is a big deal here, but I think she's making a huge mistake. There are a lot of guns in the Philippines, legal and illegal – and since the election is over, the prohibition against publicly carrying one is over."

Pete visibly controlled himself. He stepped in front of John and used his hands to carefully adjust the latter's uniform shirt, making sure the pocket flaps were level and the lapels even, while looking down into his eyes. "John, we need to help the Filipinos through this period. We all believe they are on the verge of extended violence that will endanger them and the two hundred and fifty thousand Americans who live here and are immersed in the populace. We don't have the manpower to protect all those US citizens, so we'd better keep it non-violent. I didn't think Charlie was appropriately attuned to the need to keep the peace. Therefore, I removed him." Pete stopped to make sure John understood the threat. "Make sure you remain properly sensitized."

"Yes, sir."

"Good." He simultaneously clapped John on each bicep and turned away, sat down at the table and picked up his coffee cup. "I approve your plan. Make it happen while remembering this is their country and their culture. They thus get an input on the decisions. Now, I don't want any of our people to be at the air terminal when the Señora makes her grand entrance; however, if there is any chance you could get your people to install a couple of Mary Ann's special little cameras at the airport before this afternoon, do it."

"That bitch is at the airport! Rodel, you *puki*, do you hear me!"

"I hear you, Mr President."

"If she leaves there alive, you and your *binbutingting* company will both be worm meat!"

*

Ten minutes later, Mary Ann burst into Pete's office with a single strip of thin yellow communications tape in her hand. "Chief of Staff, there was action on the special Palace circuit again." She grabbed a blank piece of paper from his desk and, stripping the protective coating from the back of the tape, began tearing the intercept into sections and pressing the sticky side of the tape onto the paper.

"When I saw it, I tore it directly from the printer without waiting for the translation." She sat down at the table, yanking the yellow pencil from her bun. Pete stationed himself behind her.

"It's Legaspi himself. We've never heard him personally use the Palace telephones before. He always has someone else make his calls. We've suspected he had an overdeveloped fear of the National Security Agency. He called Luzario. It's a very short call."

Her pencil hesitated at the very first section of pasted tape. "This is Legaspi telling Rodel that intelligence places Toseña at the airport."

Pete stood up. "I suppose if there are several hundred thousand of her supporters there and live TV coverage, it's not too much of a surprise the President knows."

"That's not the reason I bothered you."

Pete looked down again. Mary Ann's pencil was, again and again, silently underlining the last section of torn tape. She had written the translation underneath.

CHAPTER FORTY-FOUR

Tom passed Mary Ann's information to the Army Chief of Staff, who assured him that soldiers loyal to the Chief had yesterday taken action to account for and confine all members of the Aviation Security Command to their Manila barracks. In addition, other soldiers under his command had already occupied the airport terminal. While the General was concerned at the report of the President's latest attempt at mischief, he assured Tom that there were sufficient soldiers at the airport to prevent any problem from escalating. Nevertheless, Pete and Mary Ann both tried to reach Kristina. Neither was successful. They kept receiving 'all circuits busy' messages.

The latter was understandable, since the televisions aboard the *Blue Ridge* showed Filipinos arriving at the airport by car, truck, foot and Jeepney at the rate of several thousand an hour. It could be safely assumed that each one carried at least one portable electronic device to document their own participation in Philippine history. Consequently, the available bandwidth all around the airport was being clobbered!

If that weren't enough, the major Manila TV stations were in the process of transitioning from Toseña's house to the airport. Five had arrived and were already on the air. Three had positioned cameras at Gate 2, looking past some barriers and a squad of soldiers down an empty concourse. The other two were doing roving crowd interviews. The *Blue Ridge* internal communications team had run split feeds from one of the topside antennae to seven screens that had been relocated from the Command Center to the larger dining room. The Seventh

Fleet Staff was gathered there to watch and listen to the talking head rapid-paced speculation. At the moment, all channels were muted to reduce the staff's sensory overload, since Pete and Mary Ann were still trying to dial Kristina every five minutes.

Mary Ann had downloaded the latest Global Hawk picture. It was centered at 14.80 N and 120.27 E, the GPS coordinates of the control tower for what had been the navy Cubi Point airport during Vietnam. Since Toseña's home was only ten miles distant, her residence was included just inside the left-hand side of the image. Mary Ann centered the image on her personal computer screen and used the overhead interface projector to cast the picture on the light green steel bulkhead area below the flat panel displays.

Conversations in the room died as Bruce reached up to adjust the lens slightly to focus the image and Mary Ann began using her pointer to advantage.

"As you can see, nearly everyone who was camped near her house is either already at Cubi or well on their way. Some estimates are that we are talking about five or six hundred thousand already around the airfield or crowding the roads!"

Bruce moved over closer to the image, "I don't believe it. There are only three or four Philippine cities that large!"

As usual, Mary Ann was queen of the factoids: "Ten, actually."

Tom Cooper positioned several straight-backed chairs facing the screens and sat down in one, leaving the center seat free for Pete. "What time does she arrive?"

Mary Ann grimaced, "We don't know for sure. *Cowpens* debarked her two hours ago at Grande Island. They reported that Toseña's launch motored away almost immediately. Their radar tracked it for an hour in the direction of the airport until the launch's return merged with the land clutter."

Tom filled a glass of water from the beaded silver pitcher on the table, "Do we have someone who knows Tagalog well enough that we can turn up one of the channels and understand what is being said?"

"I can translate." Mary Ann pushed the control to unmute the set tuned to GMA-7. "This is the station most people in Manila watch." She gestured to the right, "I think the one on the end, ABS-CBN-2, is slightly more popular in the provinces."

Bruce moved his chair so he was sitting beneath and alongside the end screen. He adjusted that TV volume so he could just hear it. "I can usually understand most things that are said. We can do this together."

Mary Ann leaned closer to her set and listened for a second. "Currently, it's all filler. They are talking about the size of the crowd – the commentator just estimated it at more than a million – and wondered where Señora Toseña will appear."

As she fell silent to listen, Bruce jumped in. "They just interviewed a General reportedly close to the Army Chief of Staff. He was quoted as saying that elements of the army have been mingling with the crowd in order to protect Señora Toseña. That correlates with what we know. He also estimates the crowd size as more than half a million."

When he paused to listen, Mary Ann inserted, "GMA is broadcasting a retrospective of Toseña's life. I believe this is the fourth or fifth time they have run this same footage in the past couple of hours. It's obvious all the channels are desperate for new pictures or a new angle." She looked over to Bruce.

"What you are seeing on ABS is a previously recorded clip in which various citizens postulate the whereabouts of Señora Toseña. About forty per cent of those interviewed believe she has been murdered and that the rumor about her presence at the airport is simply a means for President Legaspi to target his enemies."

Tom Cooper voiced what most in the room were thinking, "If five or six hundred thousand Filipinos are willing to journey to the airport to see someone who is probably dead – I think I smell a toasted President!"

Bill Rogers sat down next to Pete, saying softly, "If Legaspi didn't have problems before, he certainly…"

Mary Ann held up her hand and the staff immediately became quiet. Every television was showing different images of the crowd surging toward the metal barriers surrounding Gate Two.

*

The sailor on the bow of the *Cowpens'* motorboat cast a nylon line over to the Filipino soldier standing on the bank near the end of runway thirty-one and Kristina awkwardly threw over an accompanying line from the stern. A Colonel on the bank called his men to attention and saluted as the Toseña party scrambled ashore.

"I am Colonel Bayani Rafa, señora. The Secretary of Defense and Chief of Staff both send their sincere respects. If you accompany me to Terminal Three, I will brief you on the additional assets I can place at your disposal."

They proceeded across the runway complex into the newest terminal. Once there, Archbishop Ver joined them and the Colonel quickly briefed everyone on the general airport layout and where the airport had established checkpoints. As soon as that was completed, Feliciano immediately pulled the Archbishop off to the side for a few minutes of whispered discussion. Kristina used the time to try to reach Pete, but, although she had four bars, all the lines were busy. Then Ver disappeared and her aunt motioned her niece and nephew to accompany her by her side. The three were now in a concrete hallway proceeding toward the black curtain that led out to the lobby. Bayani had reported there were literally thousands of people packed in the terminal and tens of thousands more outside. Kristina couldn't imagine what a crowd like that would look like, but she could feel the energy pulsing from the lobby. That intensity was seemingly causing the black curtain to billow back and forth.

Feliciano suddenly turned and threw her arms around her niece and nephew, pulling down Kristina's head and murmuring quietly into the taller woman's hair, "Kristina, I so appreciate what you have done over the recent months. I could never have done this without you. I have a good feeling about all this. I know your uncle would be so proud."

Kristina put out her right arm and pulled her brother into the group. She felt tears forming in the corner of her eyes. "I have enjoyed being with you, Auntie. I love you." She patted her aunt's shoulder. "Go do your thing. Enrique and I have your back."

The Colonel pulled back a side of the plastic. The appreciative roar and the crowd surging against the barriers in front of a podium stopped the trio in their tracks. They could hear the echo of television and radio commentators saying, "She's coming out!"

Kristina reassuringly rested the palm of her left hand against the back of her aunt's waist.

CHAPTER FORTY-FIVE

The sudden roar from the crowd was so loud that both Bruce and Mary Ann rushed to lower the volume on their respective sets. Five screens showed an identical picture as Feliciaño Toseña appeared and walked toward a speaking area just behind a set of yellow plastic crowd-control barriers. A step behind her, arm in arm, were Kristina and Enrique. Feliciaño stopped just short of a podium surrounded by so many microphones it looked like an irregular steel fence. All the TV cameras were focused on the face of the former Presidential candidate. Señora Toseña smiled and waved to close friends as she patiently waited for the applause to die. It was as if she had not been missing for nearly a week.

Pete shifted uncomfortably in his chair. WTF! This situation was all screwed up. Kristina was out there on the pointy end of a television camera, in the middle of an unstable situation. He was miles away sitting on his butt. He was the man in uniform. She was the beautiful woman. This was not the way a relationship was supposed to work! He got up from his chair and made his way to the back of the room. He stood there, his arms folded hard across his chest.

In the airport, the applause showed no signs of abating. As the wave of approval seemed to rise, Feliciaño visibly squared her shoulders, stepped forward and put a hand on the podium. Immediately the crowd quieted.

"My fellow Filipinos, my deepest apologies to you who have worried about me. I needed to go away, think and spend time with my niece and nephew." Toseña leaned back and drew Kristina and Enrique forward so they framed her, her arms around each of their waists.

"But then my good friend Archbishop Ver" – Toseña loosened her arm from around Kristina and motioned at the Archbishop, who was standing a bit off to the side near the front of the crowd – "the man who has heard my confession since I was a small girl, convinced me there was no question about the will of the Filipino people." Kristina moved back and the Archbishop made his way to Feliciaño's side.

Kristina shifted her purse to her left arm and began scanning the audience as she listened. Her aunt planned to ride her current popularity as far as it would go. It probably meant that the three of them would either be in jail or the Palace by the end of next week. She was personally hoping on the Palace, but...was that Rodel? What was he doing here in the terminal? He had never supported her aunt. He was the President's butt boy.

Toseña was waiting for the Archbishop to arrive at her side and the crowd's roar from her last words to die. When he did her voice lifted, projecting itself over the residual murmurs. "He convinced me that your election had been stolen." Another bellow rose from the audience, which she smiled into for a few seconds until she choked it off with a deliberate frown.

"He convinced me that I needed to fight President Legaspi." Thousands of feet stamped approval on the terminal floor. An equal number of hands loudly clapped. But Toseña held up her hand and stilled the clamor. "However, I still required time to pray."

The crowd became deathly quiet.

Aboard *Blue Ridge*, Pete was watching for glimpses of Kristina on the various channels. Both women looked weary. Their body language told of their interdependence. The aunt would need Kristina at her side for significant parts of the next several years. But it was really no different from having a family in San Diego and being assigned to a ship that was making fifteen-month deployments to the Far East. Just the mirror reverse. They could make a long-distance relationship work...

Kristina Anne Baclayon was also daydreaming. She was tired. Aboard ship, she hadn't gotten as sick as her aunt, but she had never quite been comfortable. She had only gotten a few hours' sleep each night. No matter what her family thought, she was going to raise the wages of each and every person in their shipping company that had to go out in one of those smelly, rolling, nasty things. Ugh! She shook her head.

"We have had too many Filipinos killing other Filipinos." Feliciaño paused and deliberately lowered her voice, deepening it with emotion, "I decided I would not be your President if I had to be a part of killing Filipinos." She stopped.

The crowd cheered, but when her silence continued, some began moaning in disappointment. Was she stepping down? A few individual unintelligible shouts rang out, and the group nearest the podium surged against the flimsy barrier.

Kristina involuntarily stepped back. Her aunt had polished this pose during the last week on the campaign trail. Kristina knew her aunt's eyes were closed and suspected the cameras were rolled in on the deep creases in Feliciaño's cheeks. When you were part and parcel of the speech planning process – when you had watched as the Archbishop directed Toseña how to suck in her cheeks and silently count *un mil uno, un mil dos, un mil tres…perfecto*!– it made for a different kind of magic. Not the fairy kind, but rather the "'Damn, I can't believe that illusion can be created on demand.' "

Even when you knew how it was done, it was still impressive. Maybe it was more magical when you knew it was deliberately staged.

She saw Feliciano Segura Toseña's shoulders rise as her Aunt took a deep breath. Her voice literally leaped out into the terminal as she threw the challenge into the microphones. "But this time Legaspi has gone too far!" The crowd noise grew so loud Kristina couldn't even hear her aunt's next few words, and she was standing immediately behind her. "…stolen Philippine riches and murdered loyal Filipinos!"

Toseña unwrapped her arms from her nephew and the Archbishop so she could gesture with her entire body, extending her hands out in front of her, imploring the crowd: "If you will all go with me…" the thousands of people were obviously putty in her hands. Pete had told her about seeing a bullfight in Seville in which the matador had been awarded both ears. Kristina suspected Feliciaño was now going after the tail.

"If you are with me, we will walk together to Legaspi's Palace and demand he resign!" The crowd's roar shook the terminal. Several very small pieces of insulation broke free from the ceiling at the very top and began drifting down. The thin white mites sparkled in the shards of sunlight. Was it an indication of a structural problem? Even though it was the newest terminal, Kristina had never heard of any questions about the construction. But there certainly was a much larger crowd here today than had ever seen. She looked around for other problems. No! It couldn't be!

Kristina pushed her aunt to the left and leaped forward. She sprung at the assassin. That bastard. "Rodel!"

Her nails touched his cheek as the bullet entered her chest and shoved her back. The devil was smiling. *Dios!* The pain! Help me, dear Analyn!

The explosive sound of a shot brought all the Seventh Fleet staff out of their chairs. On the screen, two of the microphones in the steel fence fell. The center camera rotated to Kristina, as she caught herself with her left hand on the top of the barrier and then, in slow motion, took a half step backward, fought to remain erect and crumpled to the airport terminal's tile floor.

"Kristina!" Pete found himself standing in front of the center screen. On the displays, there was a melee as men beat the assailant down to the ground. Three of the cameras were tipped over. One went blank. One showed only a mass of bodies.

On the remaining screens, he glimpsed Señora Toseña, Archbishop Ver, a white-shirted man and three young women bent over Kristina. The picture was immediately lost in a swirl of frantic people rushing to her side. Pete realized he was holding his breath. A gray mist gathered around the edges of his vision as he moved around the table until he was standing within a few inches of the screen, near Mary Ann. He closed his eyes.

Mary Ann touched the back of his hand. "Captain. You can see again."

The camera panned down to Kristina and zoomed in. There was blood on her face. Ver's fingers were moving on her forehead.

Within a few seconds, the white-shirted man stood and said something to Ver and Feliciano. Señora Toseña was unmoving, staring down at Kristina. Slowly, as if fighting gravity, she sunk to her knees and brushed her lips against both of Kristina's cheeks.

Ver handed her a white handkerchief from his sleeve. Toseña carefully unfolded it and draped the cloth over her niece's face. As she did, her back collapsed and Feliciano fell prone over her niece's body. The television showed the tears flowing down her cheeks. The crowd was so quiet the television mics picked up her ragged breaths and sobs.

Finally, with the aid of the Archbishop's arm, Toseña pulled herself erect, ignorant of the blood that dripped from her fingers and stained his vestment. She focused her gaze on her niece's killer. Four men held him erect, his face battered and his clothes torn. Toseña looked at him for a long moment. She motioned the men to cross the press barrier and bring their prisoner to her in the space in front of the microphones.

When they arrived, she had them turn him. She put her hand under the killer's chin to raise his face to the cameras.

Holding the man's bruised face up, she put her other bloodstained hand heavily on the Archbishop's arm and leaned into the microphones. The crowd hushed. Each camera framed her and the assailant. "This is the tragedy that comes from Filipinos killing Filipinos. Rodel Luzario has destroyed my niece, and for that I swear he will rot in prison." The crowd was still in shock and there were only scattered yells of approval. "But before he goes to his cell, we will walk him to the Palace to see his boss, President Legaspi!"

The crowd found its voice and gave out a thundering cheer.

She waved them to silence. "We will also carry the body of the woman who saved my life. She will march with us! Her sweet face will always remind us of the terrible results of Filipino violence upon Filipino!"

Pete turned away from the bank of televisions, his face unreadable. This was a major event. No matter how much this affected him personally, it needed to be dealt with professionally. And action was always the best antidote for grief. "Staff meeting in an hour."

He left the room, stumbling once, right before he reached his stateroom.

An hour later, Pete had sent a quick message to the Admiral, a shorter one to Honolulu and was waiting impatiently for the staff to finish gathering. Nothing would help Kristina anymore. It was time to work to ensure she received the legacy she had earned.

He motioned Mary Ann to commence, but John Stevens hesitantly raised his hand.

"Don Collingsworth called. I didn't bother you because I knew we were having this meeting. Legaspi has contacted the Ambassador and asked for asylum in the United States."

Mary Ann inserted, "Bruce's taps confirmed that conversation. Legaspi said he had watched the return of Ms Toseña and it is obvious the country has gone crazy. He informed the Ambassador he did not intend to be crucified by some ignorant crowd."

"And?" Pete kept his voice calm.

John continued, "The Ambassador thinks the United States will agree." John glanced at his watch. "He is scheduled to speak to the Secretary of State right now and expects a decision within eight hours. Several channels of Philippine television are carried worldwide on the internet. State will be able to see the situation in the Philippines at first hand. It is clear Legaspi can't stay here. No matter how much Ms Toseña thinks she can control it, there are going to be widespread riots and firefights. Ambassador Coyle has requested that Seventh Fleet plan for the President's safe extradition."

Mary Ann added, "Jamie Bautista, who apparently also thinks it is a good time to emigrate, has also contacted London, Riyadh and Brasília. None of them has immediately said yes. I suspect they are talking behind the scenes with their American counterparts."

Pete asked Mary Ann to project the latest Global Hawk picture on the bulkhead. Then he turned to John. "How long until the crowd reaches the Palace?"

"Probably three days for those walking, but I expect a lot of people will be there before nightfall. I bet there weren't a dozen Filipinos not glued to their televisions, so I wouldn't be surprised to see the Palace literally surrounded by hundreds of thousands of people before morning."

Pete nodded. Time waited for no man. Events were already in motion. Decisions were needed.

"OK, to avoid a firefight, we need to have the bad guys gone by first light tomorrow. Let us assume there are a dozen evacuees. I would rather not use a helo, because that screams 'USA involvement' and it gives something noisy for everyone to shoot at. What else is available?"

Tom Cooper drawled, "Trucks of course, or armored vehicles if you think somebody may be shooting. There are many both in and around the Palace that we could borrow from the army."

John shook his head, "The Embassy says that people are already building barricades in the streets that lead from the Palace. There is even talk about closing Manila International Airport until Legaspi is brought to justice. They are estimating thousands to tens of thousands of casualties and tens of millions of dollars in destruction downtown. We can't let that happen!"

Pete folded his hands and let the team work.

Finally, the Fleet Surgeon looked down the table at Bruce Parks first and then at Tom Cooper. "From your earlier reconnaissance, didn't one of you mention you had noticed an old canal that crossed the Palace grounds?"

Both nodded and each began to smile.

"And didn't you say that a couple of guys could take one of our swift boats up the coast and then paddle into the Palace grounds as quietly as a jewel thief?"

Bruce objected: "I don't think I used the word 'thief'."

Bill continued, "How many passengers could you squeeze into one of those swift boats if you had to?"

"About a dozen."

"And if you started within the hour, when would you be at the Palace?"

Bruce consulted the large diving watch he habitually wore, "Between 3 and 4am." He addressed the unasked question, "Yesterday was a new moon. It should still be fairly dark when we arrive."

John was using his fingers to roughly measure on one of his charts. "Which gets you back in the vicinity of Cubi by early morning. If you landed on that beach near the end of the runway, and one of those FedEx planes happened to lower its ladder and some people scrambled aboard, that plane would be in the air and out of Philippines airspace in less than five minutes."

He paused. "Most of those FedEx pilots are reserve officers in either the Air Force or the Navy. I bet if we called around we could find a pilot one of us knows that we could press into service."

Pete swirled his coffee and noted John was working much better with the team than Charlie ever had. For a second, he regretted not firing Charlie earlier. Then he returned to the immediate issue. The problem was there was no time to get all the proper permissions. If they had a couple more days, State would probably approve asylum. If they didn't, some other country would and inevitably the result would be the same – Legaspi gone and Toseña President. But action tonight would ensure Legaspi got out with minimum Filipino bloodshed, and if the sun rose with Legaspi still in the Philippines, itchy trigger fingers would prevail. What did he owe Kristina? Pete carefully placed his coffee cup down on the table in front of him.

He looked up at the SEAL and marine. "Let's do it. Leave your radio on for any further guidance." Bruce and Tom immediately rose from the table and left the room.

Pete stood. "I'll explain to the Ambassador that he has two hours to obtain approval as well as get Legaspi and no more than eight other people packed. I want that son-of-a-bitch on a plane for somewhere else before noon!"

"John, arrange for an airplane and a pilot, and get some marines over to Cubi to assist those fellows with security." He paused for a second and looked around the table. "Everyone understand, we are going to put Legaspi and his family in the air. Where they go is not our concern. But they are not relanding on Philippine soil. Plan accordingly."

A knock on his doorjamb accompanied by the words, "Chief of Staff?" brought Pete back to the present. He was constructing a status memo to the Admiral. The writing was going slowly. He was mentally and physically exhausted. He had deleted almost as much as he had written.

"Sir?" It was Mary Ann with the inevitable piece of paper in her hand. She had borne up really well over the strain of the last two weeks. Pete was sure she had gotten even less sleep than him.

"Sir, I think you should know that Señora Toseña's supporters have discovered that Legaspi has left the country. Apparently, her nephew – I think his name is Enrique Baclayon – heard the rumor, and he and some others grabbed an army truck and raced ahead to the Palace."

"Does anyone have any idea we were involved?"

"No. So far, so good, sir."

Pete leaned back in his chair and ran his hand through his hair. Probably the Philippine Supreme Court would have to declare the Presidency abandoned. Would there be a new election? Would Toseña run again? He suddenly realized he didn't care. Those were questions for the Ambassador. It was time for him and the other staff members to turn to the problems in the rest of the Seventh Fleet's area of responsibility. Next week, *Blue Ridge* would be en route to Australia. Who knew what had happened during the past week in Thailand. Pete certainly didn't. He hadn't been paying the attention he should…

"Chief of Staff?"

Mary Ann was still standing in the doorway, a single sheet of paper in her hand.

"Yes."

"I thought you might like to know that GMA-7 has begun carrying a story that Rodel Luzario is dead. They are saying there was a mystery assailant. Also, ABS-CGN-2 apparently has an eyewitness source inside

Señora Toseña's immediate staff that report her nephew returned from the Palace wild-eyed, rushed into the marchers and slashed Rodel's throat with his machete. There are unconfirmed reports that Señor Enrique has escaped to Cebu."

Pete closed his eyes.

CHAPTER FORTY-SIX

Leaving Manila's International Terminal, Pete stepped out of the stream of arriving travellers and took a deep breath. All Souls' Day morning in the Philippines. The familiar musky tropical smells slipped back into his soul, bringing with them memories of the year past.

He was already checked in for Narita. He would be in Japan before sunset. He had asked for three days. but the Embassy had been very specific that his visa was good for only twenty-four hours. It wouldn't be extended. Apparently, some people had long memories.

Beyond the steel barricades, dozens of men jostled to offer wooden carvings, cadiz trinkets or a ride. In the crowd of tourists, Pete stood out both because of his height and his starched white navy uniform with the four gold stripes on each shoulder board. His distinctiveness caused most vendors and beggars to weave around him in search of easier marks. Pete had changed clothes in the terminal restroom, leaving his rolled civvies in a locker. He had only retained a small white two inch by three inch bag that now hung under his shirt from the long drawstring around his neck.

Pete pushed through the crowd until he reached a black Crown Victoria that appeared to be in better shape than most of the others. Opening the passenger's door himself, he moved the driver's morning newspaper aside in order to sit down in the front seat, "Cementerio del Norte, *por favor.*"

When they arrived, he gave the driver half of a thousand peso note, tearing the blue currency down the black dotted line to avoid defacing the portraits. The man seemed satisfied and had returned to reading his paper before Pete closed the door.

After eighteen hours of travel from halfway around the world, he was an hour early.

He stood under the shade of a tree near the entrance portal, unconsciously assuming the parade rest position, weight evenly balanced, knees slightly bent, feet as wide apart as his shoulders, large hands clasped in the small of his back. Over the years, he had learned it was a comfortable way to stand. The military actually knew one or two things.

Exactly at the prearranged time, a black BMW, sandwiched by two shiny black boxy SUVs, pulled up to the curb near him. Pete came to attention and saluted as the back door of the BMW swung open and President Feliciaño Toseña emerged. She was immediately encased in a protective square by four men in black suits. Two were from each of the escorting vehicles, professionally marked by the small curling wires leading into their left ears.

She pretended not to see him, so Pete walked up to her and extended his left arm. She ignored his arm and did not meet his eyes, only saying, "I wish you had not come," but nevertheless gestured to the guards to permit him to accompany her into the cemetery. A small entourage of three women fell into their wake. Enrique was conspicuously absent.

They walked a hundred yards in silence before she stumbled, reflexively catching Pete's arm to balance herself. He could feel her hesitate for a moment before she left her hand there. The tips of her nails dug into his arm. He felt them through the starched long sleeve of his formal uniform. He heard her whisper, "You were as much to blame for her death as me."

She continued looking straight ahead as they walked, keeping her voice quiet so her guards and retinue could not hear. He leaned his head down toward her to better hear. Her tone was bitter. "She constantly told me she wanted you to be as proud of her as she was of you. Her death was all on you."

After another few steps, Pete felt her fingers clench his arm. He could swear he felt a tear on his hand. He didn't dare look down to check. They walked another fifty feet before Señora Toseña again broke the silence, "When my sister and her husband died and she came to live with me – she became my greatest pride and joy." The path turned and the President returned greetings from a family gathered at a crypt, waving, and forced a smile. Another murmur. "She was the light of my life!"

Toseña stumbled again and Pete laid his hand over hers to hold her erect. "She was going to be such a wonderful Filipina woman! If I had not let you talk me into hiding on that ship, she would never have been killed!"

Pete remained silent. He had spent time alone making similar accusations of himself.

Over the next hundred yards, Feliciaño spoke to a number of people, many of whom she called by name. She did not introduce Pete, nor did anyone address him, but her hand remained firmly on his arm.

They came to a gap between tombs and Feliciaño stopped. She turned to Pete, pulling down on his arm so he looked down. He could clearly see her eyes for the first time. They were damp, but her voice was steady, "I had them approve this one-day visa for you, because she spoke of you with love, but I wish never to see you again." Her voice was emotionless as she drew herself up to her full height in her heels, the top of her bun nearly reaching his shoulder.

"Please don't ask to come back." Her voice was now pleading, rather than demanding, "Go somewhere else in the world. The Philippines are dead to you." Her voice trailed off as she turned away by herself and resumed walking uphill. "Just as they are to me – but I must remain."

Pete caught up to her in a few strides. Several yards later, Feliciaño again placed her hand on his forearm.

When they reached Kristina's grave, one of the President's female retainers quickly spread a blanket on one side and Feliciaño immediately knelt and wordlessly began brushing away twigs and pulling tufts of grass that were encroaching on the stone.

Pete spread his own handkerchief to protect his uniform from stains and knelt on the other side of the stone. He unbuttoned the top two buttons of his blouse and removed the traveler's bag. From it, he removed a candle, placed it immediately below the words Kristina Anne Baclayon and lit the wick. He cupped his hands around the small flame until he was sure it had caught. As the wax began to vaporize, a faint scent of jasmine rose.

Pete removed his cap and removed the single white fresh rose curled inside. He carefully placed the bloom a few inches above Kristina's name and then proceeded to groom his side of the stone.

When he finished, he placed the last item: a cell phone. The actual SIM card from Rodel's old phone he wore around his neck with his dog tags. If only he hadn't come up with that plan, if only Kristina hadn't been so brave...

Pete felt a cold hand upon his. "I ask you to go," Feliciaňo said softly. "I am sorry. I know you also loved her, but I will not be able to make it through the day if you are here." Her head was down and he heard a sob. "She was too precious to lose."

Pete rose and folded his handkerchief, keeping the grass stains on the inside to avoid marking his whites. He drew himself to attention, his heels together; his thumbs on the seams of his trousers. For the first time he realized everyone in the vicinity was covertly watching the two of them.

Pete bowed once to the still-kneeling Feliciaňo before planting a kiss on the top of the headstone. He closed his eyes for a second, then put on his cap and saluted. "Ms President, I wish you and your country the very best."

He kept his head up on the way back to his car, nodding pleasantly to many of the Filipinos on their way up the hill to visit their own loved ones. Some ignored or looked though him, others recognized his uniform as representing a friend. As he stepped off the path to let a large family by, Pete thought he heard, "Don't ever forget, you were once mine" in the wind. When he turned to locate the voice, there were only three older men walking slowly, one with a cane – and the faint scent of jasmine.

Pete walked even faster down the hill. As the cab driver pushed open the door, he looked once back up the path. He knew he could never return.

AFTERWORD

The Seventh Fleet is the Navy's largest operational command. In military parlance, for the wide ocean expanse between Africa and China and the countries that touch those waters, the Seventh Fleet is the point of America's spear. For the men and women entrusted with directing these forces, every day dawns with fresh challenges, and dusk often brings new surprises.

I wish to express my admiration of a particular set of individuals who, during a critical moment on the Far East rim, helped define what our world would be in the twenty-first century. They memorably included Vice Admiral Paul McCarthy (air warfare) and Colonel Tom Campbell, USMC (both now deceased), Captain Bill McDaniel (later to become a Rear Admiral in the US Navy Medical Corps), Captain Bruce Dyer (Navy Special Forces), Captain Ray Addicott (a surface warrior) and the staff logistics ace, Captain Don Hunter.

I honor the Seventh Fleet in general and their accomplishments during the Cold War, as well as in the decades since. Nevertheless, the particular events and characters in this book were drawn purely from the imagination of the author.

A THANK YOU

This is the first book I have written not dedicated to my spouse. Linda was too involved this time. She is not only the only person with whom I have ever enjoyed an oil massage, it was she who noted during one Filipino political regime that each time we flew into Manila we were seeing a city with more potholes and fewer streetlights.

The reader may have discerned a peculiar rhythm to several of the 7thFleet staff's exchanges. If so, that is due to the invasive influence of the Texas drawl and wry humor of the late Tom Campbell, Colonel, USMC (retired). He should be held accountable. He was also just the sort of person who might have tapped a Palace's phone system.

Several individuals were particularly invaluable in the writing of Intent to Betray. Marlene Adelstein was one. She is a go-to book doctor. Bruce Dyer (Captain, USN, retired) was my small arms expert. Unfortunately, in my pursuit of the lovely Kristina, I changed software twice, hardware once and revised my manuscript once too often, resulting in the inadvertent loss of my list of those who assisted me. The following scroll is thus far too short; but I truly appreciated the help the following people provided:

Bill McDaniel
Fred Rainbow
Ginger Oliver
Jay Davis
Michael Zimring
Mike Hough

Nancy Merrick
Nancy Spruill
Steve Spruill
Sunjin Choi
Tim Oliver
Vago Muradian

www.ingramcontent.com/pod-product-compliance
Lightning Source LLC
Chambersburg PA
CBHW050354260626
47156CB00003B/727